W9-ATJ-459

PRAISE FOR *THE LAST KINGDOM*

"High-octane…A fun page-turner with historical elements." —*Publishers Weekly*

"When readers crack open a new Malone adventure, it's like reuniting with an old friend. Another strong entry in a consistently fine series." —*Booklist*

"What you'd expect if James Bond were an American who consulted with the CIA. Bring it on." —*Kirkus*

"Berry once again proves that history matters, skillfully crafting a fictional story around historical truths."
—*Library Journal*

"What continues to amaze me about the Cotton Malone books is how Steve Berry can consistently find global stories about legendary loopholes or unwritten history that I am completely unaware of….Berry is in very limited company when it comes to thrillers of this magnitude, which includes those written by the likes of Brad Meltzer, Brad Thor, and James Rollins. This series never disappoints!" —*BookReporter.com*

PRAISE FOR *THE OMEGA FACTOR*

"Not since *The Da Vinci Code* has a thriller so deftly combined religious conspiracy, a message hidden within a world-famous work of art, and pulse-pounding suspense. *The Omega Factor* is one of the best thrillers of the year." —Douglas Preston,
#1 *New York Times* bestselling author

"Berry once again smoothly blends action and history. Dan Brown fans will want to check [*The Omega Factor*] out." —*Publishers Weekly*

"Nick is a good character, with plenty of room to grow. Here's one vote for Berry making a series out of Nick's adventures."

—*Booklist*

PRAISE FOR STEVE BERRY

"[Berry] proves once again that he has a genuine feel for the factual gaps that give history its tantalizing air of the unknown."

—*New York Times*

"Berry is the master scientist with a perfect formula for the bestseller lists."

—Associated Press

"Dive into bestselling author Berry's latest that mixes history with some serious action."

—CNN

"[A] crackerjack plot and terrific new hero...Berry is in firm command of the material and maintains his equally firm hold on the subgenre that Dan Brown created with *The Da Vinci Code* and its sequels. *The Omega Factor* is every bit the equal of those, a textbook perfect thriller."

—*Providence Sunday Journal*

"Berry pumps the veins of history with action-packed adrenaline."

—*Chicago Tribune*

"Bestseller Berry once again shows there's no working author more skilled at combining thrilling adventure with engrossing historical detail."

—*Publishers Weekly*

"Prolific writer Steve Berry has been creating intelligent, top-shelf fiction for decades."

—BookReporter.com

ALSO BY STEVE BERRY

NOVELS

WITH GRANT BLACKWOOD

WITH M. J. ROSE

THE
LAST
KINGDOM

STEVE BERRY

GRAND
CENTRAL

NEW YORK BOSTON

This book is a work of fiction. Names, characters, places, and incidents are the product of the author's imagination or are used fictitiously. Any resemblance to actual events, locales, or persons, living or dead, is coincidental.

Copyright © 2023 by Steve Berry
Excerpt from *The Atlas Maneuver* copyright © 2024 by Steve Berry

Cover design by Eric Fuentecilla
Cover copyright © 2024 by Hachette Book Group, Inc.

Hachette Book Group supports the right to free expression and the value of copyright. The purpose of copyright is to encourage writers and artists to produce the creative works that enrich our culture.

The scanning, uploading, and distribution of this book without permission is a theft of the author's intellectual property. If you would like permission to use material from the book (other than for review purposes), please contact permissions@hbgusa.com. Thank you for your support of the author's rights.

Grand Central Publishing
Hachette Book Group
1290 Avenue of the Americas, New York, NY 10104
grandcentralpublishing.com
@grandcentralpub

Originally published in hardcover and ebook by Grand Central Publishing in February 2023
First oversize mass market edition: May 2024

Grand Central Publishing is a division of Hachette Book Group, Inc. The Grand Central Publishing name and logo is a registered trademark of Hachette Book Group, Inc.

The publisher is not responsible for websites (or their content) that are not owned by the publisher.

The Hachette Speakers Bureau provides a wide range of authors for speaking events. To find out more, go to hachettespeakersbureau.com or email HachetteSpeakers@hbgusa.com.

Grand Central Publishing books may be purchased in bulk for business, educational, or promotional use. For information, please contact your local bookseller or the Hachette Book Group Special Markets Department at special.markets@hbgusa.com.

ISBNs: 9781538721001 (oversize mass market), 9781538721018 (ebook)

Printed in the United States of America

BVGM

10 9 8 7 6 5 4 3 2 1

ACKNOWLEDGMENTS

My sincere thanks to Ben Sevier, senior vice president and publisher of Grand Central. To Wes Miller, my editor, whom I've greatly enjoyed getting to know and working with. He's a man of remarkable insight. This book became much better thanks to him. Then to Tiffany Porcelli for her marketing expertise; Staci Burt, who handled publicity; all those who worked hard to create the cover and make the interior of the book shine; and to Sales and Production, who made sure both that there was a book and that it was widely available. Thank you, one and all.

A deep bow goes to Simon Lipskar, my agent and friend.

A few extra mentions. Jessica Johns and Esther Garver, who continue to keep Steve Berry Enterprises running smoothly; Peter Rohde, who escorted us around Bavaria; Slobodan Gudalovic, our guide for Herrenchiemsee; and Augela Finley, who was most generous with her time at Linderhof.

And, as always, to my wife, Elizabeth, who remains the most special of all.

Novels have a long lead time. For me that's two years. This book was written in 2020 but not published until 2023. During the course of its creation, Elizabeth and I decided to move. Building a home is never easy.

It could rank as one of the most difficult things a marriage can endure. But building a house from 150 miles away, and during a worldwide pandemic, now that's a challenge.

But we did it.

Countless talented trades and craftsmen worked on our house. Too many to even attempt to list here. But five stand out. Collectively, they expended thousands of hours of time and stretched their imaginations to the limit. Without them, nothing would have ever been created.

First, our builder, Derrick Koger, and his son Nick, who oversaw the entire construction at Derrick Builders. Then there is Toni Sims Design Studio. Run, of course, by Toni Sims. But there's also her daughter, Trinity Dorner (a.k.a. TOO), and Kelsey Deal. You'll note later that Derrick, Trinity, and Toni have characters named for them. Please know that the real-to-the-fictional bear little resemblance, save for a shared name. And Kelsey and Nick? Their names were front and center in the 2022 novel, *The Omega Factor*.

Elizabeth and I want to thank them all.

So this book, the first to be finished in our new home, is theirs.

For Derrick Koger, Nick Koger, Toni Sims,
Trinity Dorner, and Kelsey Deal,
Imagineers Extraordinaire

At least permit me this final joy. I adore the mysterious and wish to remain an eternal enigma.

—King Ludwig II

PROLOGUE

LUDWIG FRIEDRICH WILHELM VON WITTELSBACH LOVED the night. He'd long ago stopped living in the sun, finding the serenity of a velvet sky dotted with sparkling stars far more preferable to the warmth of a summer day. For an ordinary person such a preference would not have mattered.

But he was far from ordinary.

He was King Ludwig II. Duke of Franconia and Swabia. Count Palatine of the Rhine. The latest in a long line of Wittelsbachs who'd ruled Bavaria for over seven hundred years. He'd occupied the throne for the past seventeen of those years, governing a principality that stretched from the jagged Alps in the south to the forests of Prussia in the north. In between flowed the Danube, Inn, and Isar Rivers. It was a diverse and rural land of hamlets and villages, home to four and a half million subjects who lived under both his rule and the fading influence of the Catholic Church. One of thirty-nine independent states that made up the Bund, the German confederation formed seventy years ago from the last remnants of the Holy Roman Empire.

Bavaria was *his* kingdom.

He owned it all.

But he hated it.

A strange attitude for a monarch.

And one he'd come this night to change.

His carriage stopped.

The bumpy trip east from his palace at Linderhof had taken several hours. He'd sat well back, out of sight, muffled in a cloak, the curtains on the windows drawn, lanterns on the carriage lighting the way. He loved his nocturnal journeys. He took one nearly every night. Some only a short ways through the dark Alpine forests. Others deep into the mountains to places that few ventured. Those were his favorite since solitude had become his refuge. He hated politics, people concerned with politics, or anything even remotely associated with politics. His crown had become nothing more than a burden. Government more a nuisance, not an end to any means. Instead, he preferred to dream, to build, to be enveloped in a peculiarity all his own, a law unto himself, a ruler from some ancient mystical legend subject to no one.

How marvelous.

He'd found that safety existed in fantasy.

Relief too.

Plus enjoyment.

The Bavarian constitution mandated that the monarch must reside within Munich at least twenty-one days each year. What a ludicrous requirement. But he obeyed. Then, on the twenty-second day, he always fled the capital for the mountains in the south. To a glorious place. One he truly loved. He'd heard the talk. Some had begun to call him Mad King Ludwig.

Nothing could be further from the truth.

Instead, like everyone, he was simply searching for peace.

The carriage door opened and he shifted his bulky weight off the silk-lined bench and maneuvered himself out the small door into the night. One of the footmen offered a hand as he stepped down onto stairs that had been positioned on the ground for his convenience.

He was thirty-six but looked far older, his body a disgrace. Once he'd been tall, slim, with long curly hair and piercing blue eyes. Handsome. Desired. A brilliant horseman and fine swimmer, like a heroic character from one of his beloved operettas. But that lean figure had been replaced by a girth that grew ever larger each day. The fire in his eyes, so bright in the beginning of his reign, had been dulled by the many disappointments he'd been forced to endure. His walk, formerly a slow and dignified gait with his head held high, was now more a waddle. His passion for sweets and a fear of the dentist had rotted away his teeth. His mouth constantly hurt, his head pounding from headaches. Narcotics and alcohol had become his closest friends. He knew both of those were wrong. But they were far more faithful companions than the quivering acolytes who liked to surround him. He'd grown to detest both them and all of the pomp and ceremony that came from being king. Instead, he preferred the simple quiet life of the peasants, many of whom he'd met during his nightly forays into the milieu of hill farmers and woodsmen. Tonight, though, he'd come to meet a special visitor from far away who was bringing what he'd dreamed about for a long time.

A man approached. Short, bespectacled, with a whiskered face, wearing a dark suit. He looked the part of a Herr Professor but he was actually the director of the Bavarian archives, trained as a lawyer and historian, and one of the few people Ludwig trusted.

"Welcome, Majesty," Franz von Löher said to him, bowing.

He nodded an acknowledgment of the greeting, but said nothing. He'd chosen an Austrian uniform to wear for the occasion with a grand cordon sash—red with white stripes bordering the edge—aslant across his broad breast. Upon it was pinned an octagonal silver star, with a companion cross, suspended by a red ribbon trimmed in white. He'd been awarded the medal in 1865, one year into his reign. A somewhat insignificant platitude at the time from a foreign monarch that had now become all important. Normally he shunned military dress, preferring simple trousers, a shirt, waistcoat, and jacket. Armies and war had never interested him. But this was an occasion that demanded the highest of protocol.

He'd selected the location for the meeting with care. Altach. Beside the cold waters of the Walchensee. Which, ironically, meant *strangers* in High German. His geologists had told him it might be the oldest lake in Europe. But on this night the fact that it lay not far from Salzburg loomed most important, since that was where the nearest train station was located.

"Is he on the way?" he finally asked.

Von Löher nodded. "A messenger rode in a short time ago. His train arrived and he is now headed here by carriage, less than thirty minutes away."

His gaze drifted out to the small meadow and the solitary mountain scenery, all filtered by the grandeur of a summer's Alpine night. He loved nature, with its solemnity and magnificence, along with an eternal everlasting youth that had to be admired.

Four torches illuminated an oak table with a red woolen cloth draped over it. An enormous bouquet of fresh wildflowers decorated the center. He also loved flowers, particularly those that grew in abundance along the mountain slopes. A Turkish carpet covered the grass beneath and two high-backed chairs waited at either side. Beyond the torches' glow stood two attendants, stiff as ramrods, dressed in blue-and-white liveries, three-cornered hats perched atop powdered wigs, ready to pull back the chairs for both himself and his visitor.

"How is he to be addressed?" he asked von Löher.

"I am told the same as you. Majesty."

He liked that. The single word. No *Your* added to it. Much more suitable for an absolute monarch.

"What is he like?"

"Six years ago, when I met him, he was a man of fine presence. An educated gentleman of good abilities. He's now forty-five, but he makes little display and does not talk much of politics. There, you are similar."

He liked that as well.

"From my previous visit I found him to be a quiet, dignified, sensible man, who would do no discredit to his kingly office. He loves to sing and play an instrument called a ukulele. Quite well, too, I might add."

"I wonder if he brought it with him."

"I doubt it. It seems something he only does at home."

A shame, but he liked everything he'd just heard. Definitely a kindred spirit. "Are the papers properly prepared?"

"The lawyer assured me they are."

"Can Lehmann be trusted?"

No one could know what he was about to do.

"He is bound by secrecy and absolutely loyal to you. Rest assured, nothing will be revealed."

Good.

In the distance he caught the flickering light of an outrider, bearing a torch, signaling that the carriage was not far behind. He'd provided the coach for his visitor. All gilded, lined with velvet, drawn by six dapple-gray horses harnessed with Moroccan leather.

Definitely fit for a king.

He was weary—always weary—and restless. But the unbroken silence around him comforted his frayed nerves. He gazed up at the moon and stars. Hopefully, they'd smile upon him tonight.

"My goal is in sight," he whispered to von Löher. "Finally. I shall have it."

"That you will, Majesty."

His dream.

Come true.

Das letzte königreich.

The last kingdom.

PRESENT DAY

CHAPTER 1

Cotton Malone kept his entire attention on the man and the woman. He and they were part of a tour group at Herrenchiemsee, a seventy-room nineteenth-century palace tucked away in southern Germany. Ludwig II had wanted his own Versailles, a Temple of Fame in honor of his hero, the Sun King, Louis XIV. So he'd bought a heavily wooded island washed by the cold waters of the Chiemsee and erected not a copy, but his own paraphrase to Versailles. As with the original practicality had not been part of its design. Instead, both palaces had been built as monuments to absolutism. Ludwig's version came with an added memorial to his Wittelsbach ancestors, a way to align himself, if only in his own mind, with that storied past.

But the palace was never finished.

When Ludwig died in 1886 only the central axis had been erected and twenty rooms completed. None of the immense side wings, pavilions, or the famed dome were built. Still, what he'd managed to create was definitely impressive. A nearly overpowering mixture of baroque and rococo, each room more gilded and grander than the one before. Which all seemed to send a clear message of power and wealth to any visitor.

Cotton's attention, though, remained on the man and the woman.

He'd noticed them immediately once the group had formed on the ground floor. They'd arrived at the last minute, coming in out of the cold with the final two tickets of the day. The palace closed at a quarter past four, so this was the last tour. He'd noticed earlier that a few had made the journey across the lake on the ferryboat, then either hiked or taken a horse-drawn carriage from the dock. He'd opted to walk the half mile through groves of pine and birch, enjoying a brisk winter's afternoon in Bavaria. Before heading out he'd purchased his admission ticket and a pamphlet in a gift shop near the dock, one that not only told him all about Herrenchiemsee but provided a schematic of the second floor. He was particularly interested in one room in the north wing, between the king's bedchamber and the dining room, and was pleased that the booklet contained some useful information.

He loved this corner of the world.

Bavaria seemed to float in a haze of myth, with the towering Alps, deep valleys, caves, fortresses, and quaint villages ready-made haunts for mimes, gnomes, fairies, and goblins. The adventures of legendary Germans like Tannhäuser, Lohengrin, and Parsifal had given rise to endless tales that poets, composers, and writers had mined for centuries. And he'd long been a fan of Ludwig II, reading several books about the storied monarch who dreamed backward, then dared to bring those dreams into reality. But, sadly, that vision had not connected with his contemporaries.

Many dubbed him mad.

He'd visited Herrenchiemsee before, along with Ludwig's other two fairy-tale residences at Linderhof and Neuschwanstein. All lovely fantasies. But reality was the theme of this day, and that involved the man and the woman.

They were young, maybe early thirties. She was blond, curly-haired, slender with high cheekbones. He was clean-shaven and sinewy, with dark hair trimmed close to his scalp. They both wore lightweight wool coats, which, like his own and unlike those of the rest of the tour's participants, had not been left at the coat check downstairs.

Cotton followed the group as they climbed an ornate stone staircase in the south wing. The guide droned on about the multi-colored marble floors and stucco-clad walls, all modeled after the former ambassador's staircase at Versailles. He noticed the friezes. Full of allegory. Power. Strength. Truth. Justice. Along with the four corners of the earth. A bull for Europa. Tiger for Asia. Buffalo for America. Lion for Africa. More images represented the elements and seasons. Through the glass-paneled roof, which the guide said had pushed nineteenth-century technology to the max, he saw the sky beyond darkening to a fading afternoon. Being so far north, night came early to Germany in late autumn.

The guide pointed out that Ludwig visited the palace only a few days each year, from September 29 to October 8, for an annual inspection of the work progress. So the grand staircase had rarely echoed to the tread of feet, the rooms barely knowing the sound of human voices. When Ludwig had been there, the staircase had always been littered with lilies and roses. One of the visitors asked why and the guide shrugged, explaining it was just more of the fantastical that the so-called Mad King of Bavaria had loved to be surrounded with.

He had to admire Ludwig. A true individual. A visionary. The story was that he bought the island to save it from loggers intent on stripping its timber. But the grand silence among the solitude of its woods had captivated him. Supposedly he'd said, *Here shall I build me a home, wherein no man, nor woman either, can disturb my peace.*

The tour continued through a series of ornate spaces adorned with massive oil paintings. Mainly Louis XIV. Lots of lilies too—the emblem of the Bourbons—in the friezes and the parquet floor. Unlike Versailles, the rooms were not empty. Furniture abounded. *Sacrosanct* was the word Ludwig had liked to use to describe his French idols, their likes, habits, and customs too important to be interfered with. He'd loved that the French form of his name was Louis. So, as the tour guide stated, he'd felt a relationship to them had been sealed by baptism, a bond superior to any physical lineage, one that, to him, bestowed upon him his fantasies of purity and grandeur.

They entered a state bedroom paneled in white, all aglitter in gilding, the rounded bed alcove fenced off by a golden balustrade. Gilded stucco mythological figures adorned the ceiling. The windows were framed by red velvet draperies lined with gold embroidery, which, according to the pamphlet Cotton perused, had taken seven years to make. The bed was large enough to accommodate a dozen people. When finished it had been the most ornate room in all of Germany, the first to be completed at the palace in the early 1880s. But no one ever slept here. Instead, it had been created only for show.

Slender and Sinewy tried to act interested.

But they weren't.

Their interest would be piqued shortly.

In his brain he visualized the schematic of the second floor that he'd studied on the walk over. The ability came from an eidetic memory inherited from his mother's side of the family. Not photographic, as many called it. Just a remarkable ability to recall details. He knew the spectacular Hall of Mirrors loomed just ahead with the tour continuing through another smaller, more practical bedroom that had actually been used, then into the king's study, or writing room as the pamphlet had labeled it.

That's when the party started.

Right now was just foreplay with Slender and Sinewy trying to act like tourists. The rest of the group included four Chinese and two other ladies speaking French. Usually Herrenchiemsee would be packed. Hundreds of people visited each day. But that was in spring and summer when the hedges were high, the fountains spewed sheets of water, and people filled the gardens and grounds. This time of year was not tourist season, which more than anything else explained why Slender and Sinewy were here.

The last thing they needed were crowds.

Twelve years he'd worked as an intelligence officer for the Magellan Billet, a special unit within the United States Justice Department, before retiring out early and moving from Georgia to Denmark. Now he was an entrepreneur, the owner of his own shop dealing with rare books in Højbro Plads, an olden cobbled square in the heart of Copenhagen. He lived in a small apartment above the store and loved his new life but, occasionally, like today, he slipped off his shopkeeper's hat and redonned the one he'd worn for so long as a spy.

He'd never particularly liked that label.

It connoted something devious and sordid.

He'd never been a spy. Instead, he'd been the eyes and ears of the United States government, charged with a mission and trusted to carry it out. His job had not been to simply look, listen, record, and report. He'd been required to act. Make decisions. Deal with consequences.

He'd been an intelligence officer.

And a damn good one.

The group moved to the next room and he watched as Slender and Sinewy admired the grand Hall of Mirrors. The guide was saying how Ludwig had built his version larger than the one at Versailles, stretching it to ninety-eight meters. Three hundred and twenty-one feet. Its walls were a swirl of light gray and green stucco marble. Seventeen arched windows lined each side. The ones on the right opened to the front of the palace, the ones on the left were faux and gave the room its name, containing only mirrors. A barrel-vaulted ceiling with murals spanned its entire length and supported thirty-three cut crystal chandeliers. Another forty-four candelabra stood at attention down each side.

"There are twenty-five hundred candles," the guide said, "All thirty three chandeliers could be lowered simultaneously, where they were lit at once. When they were raised, the hall filled with a sudden, almost intolerable glare and heat, which was multiplied into many more thousands by the mirrors. It was a sight just for the king. Ludwig saw his palaces only through candlelight. He loved to roam this hall and dream."

Easy to see how that was possible.

Even the incandescent light being tossed off seemed

a pyrotechnic display of flashing white and prismatic color.

Almost hypnotizing.

He was always amused at how Ludwig was described as either a tyrant, a lunatic, or an incompetent. But none of those labels were correct. Today he might have been characterized as bipolar, or a manic-depressive, and treated with medication, living a long and productive life. But no such assistance had been available in the nineteenth century. His father, Maximilian II, had been stiff and pedantic, keeping his distance, dying far too soon. His mother had been someone who never understood him. One observer at the time noted that his *dark eyes swirled with dreams and enthusiasm, his fine forehead, elegant address, and dignified presence winning him instant admiration.* But his faults came from a bit of megalomania, a debilitating indecision, and a love of change that seemed common to his age. Eventually, the world fell upon him, with political infighting and his own insatiable desires compounding his troubles. Ever so slowly he lost a grip on reality, withdrawing into himself, his castles, and the night where he became a king from a fairy tale, a mythical figure of poets, this grand hall proof positive of that obsession.

Photography was not allowed inside the palace, though two of the four Chinese toted cameras around their necks. Expensive looking, too, with high-intensity flash attachments. Cotton made a mental assessment of the possibilities ahead and decided one of those cameras might come in handy.

The tour group left the Hall of Mirrors and headed toward the north wing, inching ever closer to the king's study. When they finally entered that space he noted the time.

4:05 P.M.

The room was a perfect square with a doorway in on one side and another out, opposite, on the other, consistent with the French style of rooms-to-rooms with no hallways. The walls were white-paneled with more gilt carvings. A large portrait of Louis XIV dominated the wall behind an ornate writing desk. Two astronomical clocks sat on console tables to each side. He knew about the large rolltop desk from the pamphlet. Made in Paris, 1884. Inspired by the one in the Louvre that had belonged to Louis XV. It had been delivered after Ludwig II died in 1886 and had remained here, inside the palace, since around 1920. The guide told the group about the room and the desk, repeating some of what he already knew.

Time was short. He needed a plan.

And one came to him.

He was good at improvising. Which, more than anything else, accounted for the fact that he was still alive, considering the risks he'd once taken on a daily basis and still liked to take on occasion.

Everyone headed for the next room, led by the guide. He drifted toward the rear of the pack. Slender and Sinewy lingered even more. The next space was oval-shaped and had served as Ludwig's dining room. The guide began pointing out the fireplace, the Meissen porcelain, and the Wishing Table that could be lowered down below, set with food, then winched back up so the king could always dine alone without attendants.

"The whole thing was impractical, as the table was so laden with supports that the king's legs could not fit beneath and his knees were cut by lots of sharp edges. Still, he dined here. But not entirely alone. Three other places were always set for his imaginary guests.

Usually Louis XIV and some of his court. Ludwig would talk to them and drink toasts in their honor."

The guide seemed focused on her spiel and did not notice that she was missing two members. Slender and Sinewy had remained in the study and he needed to give them a few moments of privacy. He stood just beyond the doorway that allowed access between the two rooms, far enough inside the dining room that the guide was happy and the two behind him were not disturbed.

He figured the couple of minutes he'd allowed them were more than enough, so he stepped over to one of the Chinese and smiled as he pointed to his camera and said, "Excuse me, might I borrow this?"

Without waiting for an answer, he slipped the strap from around the man's neck. Shock filled the older man's face but the suddenness of the unexpected violation and his smile bought enough time for the theft to be completed. He hoped the camera was on standby, ready to be used, and he immediately retreated to the doorway.

As predicted, Slender and Sinewy were busy with the rolltop desk.

He aimed the lens at them and said, "Smile."

The two looked his way and he snapped off three flashes, the camera clicking away. Pictures weren't the point. But the bright lights were. Both Slender and Sinewy raised an arm to shield their eyes. Behind him he heard the guide saying in a loud voice that photographs were not allowed.

He snapped two more.

Across the study, in the doorway leading out, a third man appeared, his blond hair more mowed than cut, the bright face clean-shaven and glowing with good health and outdoor life. He wore a dark pullover shirt and jeans, matted to a muscular frame, his waist-length, fleece-collared bomber jacket open in the front, a black scarf around his neck.

He knew him well.

Luke Daniels.

United States Justice Department.

Who leveled a pistol straight at Cotton.

And fired.

CHAPTER 2

LUKE WAS PLEASED THAT EVERYTHING HAD PLAYED OUT according to plan. He'd called Malone three days ago and asked for a favor.

"I've got three months of work on this," he told Malone. *"Finally, I'm on the inside. But I need a little help."*

"Which I'm sure it pains you to ask."

"Not really. Everybody needs help some time. Isn't that what you like to say?"

"I do. And I'm glad you remembered. Tell me what you need."

"These people are intent on doing some bad things to the US. So far, it's all big talk. But now they are in motion."

Something lay hidden within an old desk that had been sitting inside the Herrenchiemsee Palace for the past one hundred years. The possibility of a discovery had only recently come to light and the information seemed credible enough that some of those he'd been dealing with had been dispatched to investigate. If true, Luke had to obtain whatever was there to be found. But he also could not blow his cover. So he'd asked Malone to cause enough of a disruption so that they could learn the hiding place within the desk without allowing anything to actually be retrieved.

At least not until the bad guys were long gone.

Two of the team had ventured inside and taken the final tour of the day. He'd drifted around to the rear of the enormous palace and found a way inside near an elaborate marble stairway, where glass doors led out to a rear courtyard. Darkness had aided his prowling, as had the lack of outdoor lighting. He'd then made his way up to the second floor and over to the north wing, waiting for Malone to do his thing.

Which happened with flashes from a camera.

Inventive.

But he would have expected nothing less from ol' Pappy.

He'd waited a few moments, then appeared and fired a shot at Malone, high enough not to hit him, but close enough to get everyone's attention.

"We need to leave," he called out to his two compatriots. "Now."

Malone had dropped the camera and disappeared beyond the doorway into the next room, but the gunfire had surely alerted others downstairs. He'd been privy to some of the intel on the island and the palace. There was almost no security, few cameras, and the local police were nowhere near. Still, people would be headed this way.

Which was fine.

That was exactly what he wanted.

"Let's go," he said, motioning at them.

"One second," the woman he knew as Lexi Blake called out.

He darted toward the desk, his gun still aimed at the doorway where Malone lurked. "We don't have a second."

"Thanks to you firing that gun," she spit out.

"That guy is an eyewitness to what you're doing. He snapped pictures. We have to go."

He watched as they continued to fiddle with something beneath the rolltop desk, jiggling, pounding the ornate wood with their fists. Probably trying to release some sort of switch or lever. Finally, the guy whom he knew as Christophe stepped back and slammed the heel of his boot into one of the marquetry side panels. The old wood cracked but did not yield.

A second blow shattered it.

Christophe's assault had revealed a small compartment hidden within the desk. Apparently they'd known where it existed, just not how to open it without being destructive. Inside lay a book, which Lexi retrieved. Okay. Time for plan B. Whatever that might be, which he would worry about later.

"Now we go," Christophe said.

But first Luke ran across the room and grabbed the camera off the floor. "We can't leave this."

They then raced from the study, back toward the staircase they'd first climbed.

Luke had been a Magellan Billet agent now for a few years. Malone liked to call him Frat Boy, surely a reference to youth and inexperience, and an excellent counter to his label of Pappy for the older former-agent. They'd first met in the cold Baltic Sea north of Copenhagen. Ever since, their paths had seemed to periodically cross. Along the way he'd handled some difficult assignments, notching his share of successes. His Army training helped, as the Rangers taught him how to handle himself in tough situations. But being a product of east Tennessee, growing up in the Blue Ridge mountains, wasn't a liability either. You figured out how to take care of yourself fast there and, with three older brothers, he'd learned at an early age how to hold his own. *Talk slow, clear, and smart. If you can't do all three, keep your mouth shut.* Good advice his father had taught him, which, the older he got, the more he tried to practice. He was definitely no longer a rookie and, as much as he hated to admit it, Cotton Malone was a wealth of knowledge and experience. Someone to learn from. The man was good. No question. A bit of a legend within the Magellan Billet.

So who better to help him out.

Ingratiating himself with these crazies had not been all that hard. Industrious bad guys were always on the hunt for good help. Especially reasonably priced help. So he'd made himself available and they'd hired him. But keeping their trust might prove more vexing. Especially since this operation had not gone according to plan. But at least they'd retrieved what they came for.

Which should count for something.

They kept moving through the rooms, each brightly lit, the windowpanes black to the outside. Before entering he'd located a work truck that would make the perfect getaway vehicle, parked conveniently just outside in the courtyard with the keys in the ignition.

They needed to return to the dock. Fast. A boat was waiting for them, the same one they'd taken over from the mainland. No one had been around when they'd arrived, the dock office closed and locked. Sure, the palace could use a cell phone to contact the police in the nearby towns that dotted the Chiemsee's edges. But the lake was huge—about thirty square miles—the locals called it the Bavarian Sea—which meant there was lots of shoreline. And they'd chosen a particularly remote spot to the northwest from which to begin their journey across.

He loved his job. None better in the world. The mix of adrenaline and action seemed to be just what he needed to keep life from being dull. Having the ex-president of the United States, Danny Daniels, as your uncle came with some advantages. But he'd never availed himself of a single one. He wanted to make his own way.

And he had.

Stephanie Nelle, who headed the Magellan Billet, seemed to trust him. And he liked her. But she was currently embroiled with problems of her own, having incurred the wrath of the current president of the United States, Warner Fox. She was suspended, pending a hearing on her termination, which, strangely, had yet to occur. He'd offered her his unconditional assistance, but she'd so far not asked for any help. Magellan Billet operations had been severely limited the past few months, but his presence here in Germany had been personally approved by the attorney general.

And who was he to argue with the big boss.

They came to the stairway and scampered down the low stone risers toward the bottom. Up above, Malone appeared on the second floor. Christophe saw him and immediately reached beneath his coat and found a gun. Luke still gripped his and preempted any assault by aiming above Malone's head and sending a round into the stucco wall.

They kept rushing down the stairs.

Christophe aimed his weapon Malone's way.

CHAPTER 3

COTTON KNEW LUKE WAS FIRING HIGH. BUT THE OTHER guy? He was deadly serious so he dove to the floor, the thick marble balustrade providing some protection from the bullets trying to make it his way.

He counted four rounds.

The firing stopped.

He risked a peek through the stone spindles and saw three forms scamper out of the glass doors into the night. The plan had been to keep them moving, so he hopped to his feet and rushed down the stairs in pursuit. Before leaving upstairs he'd noticed that the camera he'd intentionally dropped was gone. Good. He'd expected Luke to take it. He'd also quickly examined the rolltop desk and saw an empty exposed niche. He'd noticed a few moments ago that while Luke toted the camera, the woman carried a book. Most likely what Luke had been tasked with retrieving. But that had not worked out. At least he could keep up the pursuit, driving them toward the dock and back out on the lake.

Frat Boy would have to take it from there.

He came to the ground floor and bolted out the

glass doors into the cold, seeing the taillights of a pickup truck speeding away.

Really?

He looked around and spied a utility vehicle, no more than a golf cart with a work bed. He ran toward it, slipping on his leather gloves, and turned the ignition key. The gas engine roared to life and he whipped the steering wheel to the left and sped off. The cart came equipped with a weak headlight that illuminated only a few feet ahead. Overhead, the sky was a sea of diamond stars on a velvet mat, the night all around him black as soot. He was following a paved road that ran from the palace, paralleling the island's north shore. The lake beyond, past the reed beds, seemed even darker. Cold air whipped over him, chapping his lips, parching his throat with each breath.

The truck was way ahead, moving faster thanks to more horsepower. But the idea was to maintain pursuit and keep Luke and his cohorts moving away. He gave Luke a hard time but, if the truth be told, he was proud of him. Their first encounter, a few years back, had been a series of errors on both their parts. Ever since, their paths had crossed on occasion and, each time, Luke had delivered. He recalled his own formative years, right after he transferred from the Navy to the Justice Department. He'd been young and green too. Making his share of mistakes. Stephanie Nelle, who'd personally recruited him, had never held back, though. Instead, she'd pushed him hard. Insisting on excellence. And he'd responded.

So had Luke.

He'd been surprised when the call had come a few days ago. A first. Luke specifically asking for help. He'd had his own mentors during his first few years with the Magellan Billet. People he'd asked for help from too. Nothing wrong with that. But there always came a point when you had to do the job, on your own terms, by your own rules. And whether you succeeded or failed was a result of your own choices.

He'd succeeded.

So had Luke.

Funny how life dealt its cards. So random at first. No rhyme nor reason. Then, ever so slowly, patterns always emerged. The trick was to recognize and seize upon those, turning a pair of deuces into not exactly a royal flush, but something that could be made to work like one.

Improvising.

The key to success.

His own life a perfect example.

One day he was an intelligence officer for the United States government with a reputation for getting things done. The next he was retired, divorced, and moving to Denmark to open a bookshop. A complete turnaround, which he'd never regretted. Now he was an entrepreneur, financially well off, deeply involved with a woman who loved him. Cassiopeia Vitt. He'd told her of Luke's request and asked her to come with him, but she'd declined, saying that her castle rebuilding project required her presence.

And he'd understood.

He loved her dearly. They were a couple. A team.

But not tonight.

He was on his own.

Ahead the truck continued racing down the paved road, its headlights cutting a bright swath in the darkness. They were past the trees, now in an open meadow between the old Augustinian monastery, high on a hill to the left, and the lake on the right. Lights burned in a few of the monastery windows. The truck raced straight for the dock that jutted out into the lake.

He sped ahead.

Cold air kept searing his throat and lungs.

The truck came to a stop and its occupants fled. He saw them run down the dock and hop into a small boat tied at its end. He maneuvered the cart up alongside the truck.

An engine cranked, then revved.

He trotted down the concrete dock, watching as the boat disappeared across the black water. He stopped under one of the amber lights that illuminated the dock, offering plenty of brightness for those in the boat to see him.

Mission accomplished.

The lake's large ferryboat, the one he'd ridden over in, floated to his right. Once it had been a true saloon steamer with a wreath of smoke announcing its presence across the lake. Now it was diesel-powered. He spotted a few people inside the enclosed cabin. Its engines revved. The boat was departing on its half-hour run back to the mainland. He should hop aboard and leave too. Maybe he'd stay in Munich a few days and check out the antique bookshops. Similar establishments all across Europe had yielded treasures before. Perhaps some of the local dealers harbored a few first editions he could resell to collectors. Or maybe instead of heading back to Copenhagen, he'd take a flight to France and visit with Cassiopeia for a few days.

That sounded great.

He wished Luke Godspeed.

Any assignment came with risks. A fact he well knew. His last with the Magellan Billet, in Mexico City, a perfect example when a bullet tore through his shoulder. He'd managed to take down the shooters, but the resulting carnage had left seven dead, nine injured. One of them had been a young diplomat assigned to the Danish mission, Cai Thorvaldsen. Ten weeks after that massacre a man with a crooked spine—a grieving father—appeared at his front door in Atlanta. Henrik Thorvaldsen.

And changed his life forever.

The ferry's engines seemed to come to full power.

Lights out on the water caught his gaze. Another boat. Starting to speed toward the boat Luke left in.

Odd.

Then he heard the distant *rat-tat-tat* and spotted the flash of muzzle fire coming from the new boat.

Aimed Luke's way. What the hell?

Things had suddenly escalated.

True, he didn't have a dog in this fight, but it was not his nature to do nothing when a friend might be in trouble.

The ferry eased from the dock, its bow pointed out toward the dark water. Lights illuminated its hull and cabin, a powerful flood lamp pointed ahead off its bow.

Improvise. Use what you have.

He ran toward the ferry.

And leaped aboard.

CHAPTER 4

Luke stood in the boat and allowed the frigid air to chap his face. It felt great. His two compatriots stood with him as they powered across the lake toward their parked vehicle onshore. Christophe piloted the small craft, standing at the wheel, Lexi beside him keeping watch ahead. She was slim and curvy, her body definitely honed by copious amounts of diet and exercise. Her mouth was full but a little wide for her nose, a small imperfection that he'd concluded only added to her allure. She wore jeans tucked into knee-high boots and a loose black sweater beneath her wool coat. No makeup painted her sultry beige complexion, and never had as far as he'd seen. Her long-lashed, barely angled eyes definitely added a mysterious quality he liked. He'd detected a slight accent in her voice. Australian, if he wasn't mistaken. He knew little about her and none of the few overtures he'd made her way had been returned.

Which was a bit annoying.

"Are you that lousy a shot?" Christophe called out. "The only thing you hit was the wall."

"On purpose," he said, not looking over at either

one of them. "Would you have preferred him dead? That would have gone over great. Along with two snapshots of the both of you." He held up the camera. "Luckily, I got the damn thing."

"I would have preferred that we not be interrupted," Christophe noted. "It was your job to make sure that didn't happen."

He wasn't going to take any crap off these two. "Then you shouldn't have taken so long. All I heard was rattling around. I thought you were briefed on where to look."

"Don't you worry about what we were told," Lexi said. "We did our job."

"Yeah. Right. You kicked the damn thing open. Why didn't you just do that to start with?"

He knew the answer. The idea had surely been to retrieve the book without revealing they'd actually been there.

"I tried to tell the prince that this one was trouble," Christophe said. "But he would not listen. Maybe now he will."

Luke shrugged. He'd dealt with idiots like this all of his life. People too arrogant to know how stupid they really were. "Please do. I wasn't planning on reporting anything to the prince. But I will now. Especially the part about the photos in this camera."

"How about I just shoot you," Christophe said.

"You can try."

And he meant it.

He'd always been blessed with a toned body undamaged by alcohol, cigarettes, or drugs. He'd spent seven years in the military, going right from high school to the Army and Ranger training. Sixty-two days of hell. One of the toughest experiences on earth. He'd passed, which was admirable considering the failure rate hovered around sixty percent. The whole idea had been to learn how to push yourself to the max. To do what you never thought possible. Twenty hours of training per day, all while eating two or fewer meals, with an average of three hours of sleep. He'd carried ninety pounds of weapons, equipment, and ammunition and patrolled more than two hundred miles across the training course.

And survived.

With his head held high.

So dealing with a cocky ass bully who thinks he knows a winnable fight when he sees one was a piece of cake.

"What's so important here?" he asked, motioning to the book Lexi held. "Why all the fuss?"

"Not your concern," Christophe said.

It was worth a try. That book was obviously important. They'd taken a lot of chances to get it. Too many really. And now the damn thing was out in the open. In play. How was he going to get hold of it, or even sneak a look?

Good question.

But he'd figure something out.

He looked around at the black water and noticed lights speeding their way. A boat? Then muzzle fire. Rounds whizzed by.

"Get down," he yelled.

He and Lexi hit the deck.

Christophe crouched low, alternating his attention from what was ahead to what was following.

*

COTTON WORKED HIS WAY FROM THE FERRY'S LOWER deck, up through the spacious interior cabin that held a few passengers, to a staircase that led to the bridge. He hopped up the metal risers, burst into the small cabin that accommodated the pilot, and did not bother with an introduction. Instead, a hard-right uppercut sent the uniformed man to the floor, not moving.

"Sorry about that," he said.

He gripped the ship's wheel and pushed the throttle forward, increasing the engine's rev and the ferry's speed. Luke's boat was off the port bow, the other one firing a weapon off the starboard but closing the gap. He figured he had the advantage of size and power so he increased the throttle.

The boat lurched from the added horsepower and the bow planed with the new speed.

LUKE SAW THE BIG FERRY HEADING ON AN INTERCEPT course between where they were located and the boat firing on them.

That could not be happenstance.

God bless Pappy.

Rounds kept zipping by.

One of those stray bullets could eventually find flesh. That was the thing about automatic weapons. Aim meant nothing. Just send enough metal toward a target and some of it almost always hit the mark.

He stayed down, but kept watch on the ferry and on Christophe's progress to get them off this damn water.

COTTON HELD TO HIS COURSE AND WAS RAPIDLY COMING between the two boats. Luke's was nearing the shore, and the pursuer kept firing. He'd served in the Navy for a number of years, mainly as a fighter pilot and a lawyer, but there'd been a couple of tours at sea. Never, though, had he piloted a large craft. But, thankfully, the lake was a wide-open expanse with plenty of room to maneuver without fear of hitting anything.

Except—

He spun the wheel hard left and swung the big ferry's stern around, generating a huge wake that quickly swept toward the boat firing on Luke. In the penumbra of the ferry's floodlights he saw the craft slow to avoid the oncoming wave. Two men stood in the small V-hull, one holding an automatic rifle. Both were trying to maintain their balance as the boat caught the swell that swept past. Cotton closed the gap and brought the ferry's starboard side close to the bobbing craft. He then shifted the throttle to neutral and fled the bridge, scampering down the steps and back through the passenger's compartment.

The five people there looked concerned.

"Nothing to worry about," he told them. "The captain will be awake in a few minutes."

He kept going, exiting out the rear door onto the open deck. He eased back toward the bow along the starboard side down a narrow walk. The ferry bobbed in the water, as did the small craft below that kept banging into the hull.

He hopped atop the gunwale.

Waited for the right moment.

Then leaped down.

CHAPTER 5

Derrick Koger lowered the night vision goggles.

He'd watched with interest as Luke Daniels had made his way back to the dock and fled with his two compatriots. He stood a kilometer away on another island in the Chiemsee. And where Herreninsel Island, with its Augustinian monastery and massive royal palace, signified a male refuge, he'd established a base on the smaller Fraueninsel, the woman's island, named after the convent that had stood there since the eighth century.

Thirty nuns still called the convent home, the abbess an old friend who'd allowed him the privilege of utilizing one of the olden building's towers as an observation point. He'd devoted the better part of his adult life to the Central Intelligence Agency, starting as a junior field officer and working his way up to his current so-called exalted position as chief of special operations, Europe. He'd been around the intelligence business a long time. Taking chances was not something he'd ever shied away from and risk was just part of the job.

Like tonight.

Which had been all about taking chances. But

he loved when things came together. It brought a measure of satisfaction to his anxious soul.

He raised the goggles back to his eyes.

And saw Cotton Malone standing on the lighted dock.

He smiled.

Captain America had done his job.

He would have expected no less.

Then he heard a distant *rat-tat-tat*.

Like firecrackers.

He scanned the lake and spotted a small boat with two occupants in pursuit of Luke. Back to the dock and he saw Malone leap onto the big ferry that was easing away from the dock.

Whoa. None of this was part of the plan.

Which seemed the story of his life. Wonderful highs, miserable lows. The worst coming a decade back when he'd ordered several al-Qaeda senior leaders waterboarded. Torture? Probably. Nothing about it was humane. But his orders were clear. Get information, however necessary. Per procedure the entire "interrogation" had been videotaped. But, as field supervisor, he'd ordered the tape destroyed to protect the identity of the interrogators.

Which drew the attention of Congress.

What had Mark Twain said? *Suppose you were an idiot, and suppose you were a member of Congress. But I repeat myself.*

Yep.

He was subpoenaed to appear before the House Intelligence Committee, which was then investigating the use of so-called "enhanced interrogation techniques." Field intelligence officers were not usually part of that inquiry, but what he'd officially, in writing, told his superiors about why he'd destroyed the tape had become important.

He wasn't going to allow his people to get nailed for something they were ordered to do.

So who ordered him?

And that had been the wrinkle, since the White House itself had authorized both the torture and the video's destruction.

But he'd never given anyone up.

He was a lot of things, but no snitch.

Three years the Justice Department investigated him, finally concluding that no charges would be filed.

But the stain became indelible.

Which, probably, more than anything else, accounted for why he was closing in on sixty years of age and still remained in the field. And not as a division chief, overseeing a huge array of assets. No. He handled only "special operations," which these days came few and far between. The CIA had a deputy director for anything and everything. Analysis, operations, science and technology, support, digital innovation, talent, study. You name it. And there wasn't a place for him? Apparently not. The presidential administration he'd protected was long gone, and never once showed its gratitude. And now here he was, in Bavaria, right in the middle of another mess.

He watched through the goggles as Malone brought the ferry into play, intercepting the boat that was firing on Luke, then leaping down into it. God he loved talented, motivated people. They required so little prompting.

He, too, was motivated.

His mind ticked off the possibilities the situation presented and he settled on one. Should he do it?

Hell, yeah.

He reached for the walkie-talkie and pressed Send.

LUKE WATCHED AS THE FERRY ANGLED BETWEEN THEM and their pursuer, stopping the boat's advance, keeping the gunfire on the far side, out of harm's way.

He stood from his crouched position.

Christophe kept the boat aimed straight for shore, which was drawing ever closer.

"Who was shooting at us?" Lexi said.

A really good question.

That was totally unexpected.

Christophe pulled back on the throttle and the boat slowed, sinking low in the water. The motor went into reverse and the bow gently kissed the shore. Lexi hopped out with the book and Luke followed, still holding the camera. He debated taking both of these morons out now, retrieving the book, and getting out of here. But this party was just getting started. And he was never one to come late or leave early from a good time.

Christophe switched off the motor and jumped out onto dry land.

Still—

Luke stepped up and planted his right fist into Christophe's jaw, sending the idiot to the ground. Lexi reacted and rushed toward him, but his reared-back right arm stopped her advance. "I have no problem pounding you too."

Christophe sprang to his knees and did exactly what he thought would happen, reaching for his gun.

He kicked the weapon from the man's hand. "Let's call all this even. You two rode my case back there. Which I don't like. I just rode yours."

Christophe lunged forward. But Luke was ready, sidestepping the advance and jamming his knee into the other man's gut, doubling him over.

"We can keep this up all night," he said. "Your choice."

He knew only he and Christophe carried guns. So he'd kept one eye on Lexi to make sure she didn't make a beeline toward the weapon lying a few feet away.

Smartly, she'd not moved.

"Look," Luke said. "What happened back there was a tough one. We had to make some quick calls. You decided to smash that desk open. I decided to scare the guy with the camera. We got the book and the camera. So let's call it a win."

He hoped that letting them know they were all on the same team would give them pause.

Christophe slowly stood, struggling for breath. "All...right. Even."

Luke decided to hedge his bets and found the gun on the ground. Which he'd keep. For now. No sense being foolish. Bad enough that the operation had gone haywire, he could not afford to totally alienate the people he needed to be friends with. But he also wasn't going to be pegged a weakling either.

They headed for the car.

He glanced back out across the lake. No sign of any activity. No cops. No more boats. Just the ferry's lights bobbing in the darkness. Pappy was out there, on the lake. Doing something. What? He had no idea. But he appreciated it nonetheless.

They all climbed into the car.

He knew where they were headed.

Munich.

The prince awaited.

CHAPTER 6

Stefan von Bayern loved hookers. What he hated was finding them. Prostitution had been legal in Germany for over a hundred years. But that didn't make the task any easier.

Especially for a man in his position.

Women for sale could be found in apartments all over town, even in areas where brothels were expressly prohibited. But there were also porn theaters, tea clubs, escort services, and, of course, the ever-popular online connection. He particularly avoided any *laufhaus*, where you walked the halls to see who was available, then headed for a room.

Way too much exposure.

The open clubs were not much better. Guests and girls mingled around the bar or the pool or in a sauna, then headed for the private rooms. Street walkers were the riskiest, standing on the sidewalk or displayed in windows for all to see. Most were also unwilling participants, working out of some personal necessity. He had a rule. Never force himself onto anyone, whether directly or indirectly.

The private clubs offered a clear measure of

discretion where a madam rode herd, the main advantage being those women were definitely there by choice, professionals, eager to please, appreciative of the money.

Willing participants.

And he'd frequented more than one club across Munich.

But the independent contractors were the best. All professionals too. Women who advertised for customers on their own. Strictly a one-on-one arrangement that offered a huge measure of privacy. No other people to be seen or be seen by. It was even better when they came to you.

Like now.

This evening's choice had been particularly skilled. A lean, thin blonde from Avignon, now living in Germany. He'd told her what he wanted and she'd delivered. And the best thing was that it all came with no attachments. Pay and play. No questions. No issues. A simple oral contract.

In more ways than one.

"Your money is there, on the dresser," he said, pointing.

She finished zipping her dress and scooped up the euros. Smartly, she said nothing and merely smiled, slipped on her heels, and waved goodbye as she strutted from the hotel suite. Chitchat was not part of their bargain.

He'd definitely hire her again.

He stood from the bed and approached the suite's outer windows, standing naked before them. The eighth floor of the Charles Hotel offered a panoramic view of a darkened park, then, beyond the trees, a jumble of rooftops surmounted by the lit twin copper spires of the Frauenkirche, upthrusting through the mist. A stunning sight. By municipal law, no building in Old Town could be taller than those two towers.

Munich was lovely at night. A bustling metropolis, the most populous city in Bavaria, sitting on an upland plateau straddling the banks of the river Isar. Started by Benedictine monks in the twelfth century, it had grown into a thriving center of politics and culture, still regarded, as in medieval times, as an intellectual place, clothed in the royal habiliments of stately buildings, splendid streets, and beautiful parks.

Once the capital of the sovereign kingdom of Bavaria, its most notorious claim to fame came from Hitler and his supporters, who staged their famed Beer Hall Putsch to overthrow the weak Weimar Republic there. The revolt failed, but ten years later, after the Nazis rose to power, Munich became their *Hauptstadt der Bewegung*, capital of the movement. No coincidence that the first concentration camp sprouted at Dachau, just a few kilometers to the northwest. Nazi Party headquarters and many of the *Führerbauten*, the führer-buildings, still survived as a cancer on a great city's legacy. The White Rose student resistance movement to Hitler also rose here, its core members all arrested and executed. But at least they tried. Seventy-one air raids by Allied bombers had done their share of damage. Three-quarters of the buildings were obliterated. But it all had been rebuilt, hard now to tell the old from the new.

The city survived.

Just like himself.

And his family.

Who harbored nine hundred years of Wittelsbach lineage.

He checked his watch.

6:30 P.M.

Time to start the revolution.

But first he should dress.

Stefan entered the Jesuit Church of St. Michael. A sixteenth-century masterpiece that had nearly not made it past World War II, reduced to little more than a few walls and rubble. Most of the decor around him was a 1948 restoration with some 1980s touch-ups. It was now a prominent fixture on Munich's main pedestrian-only way, a bustling route that led from the Karlsplatz to the Marienplatz, both sides of the cobblestones surrounded by a sea of commerce. And while the nearby Frauenkirche, the Cathedral of Our Lady, belonged to everyone, St. Michael's had always been held privately, created by Wilhelm V, Duke of Bavaria, as an embodiment of his family's ruling position.

Stefan's ancestor.

A Wittelsbach.

Famous too.

Time had even bestowed him a title—the Pious— thanks to a daily routine of prayer, Mass, contemplation, devotional reading, and pilgrimages. Nothing like a noun attached to your name to foster immortality. Which one would history add to his? *The Restorer? The Bold?* Or maybe just the all-purpose *the Great*.

What a time Wilhelm V had lived in. When Catholics and Protestants fought each other in bloody wars, trying to establish the one true Christian faith, whatever that might be. The building of a new church had seemed like a good way for Wilhelm to show his preference for the Catholics. So he created a huge house of worship with the largest overhead vault in the world at the time, save for St. Peter's in Rome.

What a visionary.

But old Wilhelm had also been reckless. He spent so much money on church-related projects that he strained the Bavarian treasury to its breaking point. He'd been forced to abdicate in favor of his son, then retired to a monastery where he spent the remainder of his life in contemplation and prayer. Another Wittelsbach three hundred years later, a similar romanticist who'd lived within an enchanted realm of the past, had not been so fortunate.

Ludwig II died.

Or was murdered.

Just over a day after his crown had been stolen.

Which was exactly why Stefan now found himself standing within this olden church on the brink of revolution.

He acknowledged the prior who'd opened the side door for him, then stood silent for a few moments in the dimly lit nave, both hands stuffed into his coat pockets. Wilhelm's mighty barrel-vaulted ceiling spanned unbroken above him. Galleries and side chapels encircled on all sides. A nave without aisles cast an airy appearance. Even today, centuries later, the faithful still gathered to hear the gospel proclaimed from a freestanding pulpit, the first in Munich to ever be set among a congregation.

Another of his ancestor's many innovations.

He savored the hush, the dance of shadows thrown by the sloping banks of votive candles, and breathed in the warm, dry air. Once the entire building was owned by the Wittelsbachs. Now they controlled only the crypt beneath. All part of the deal after World War I that cost his family their heritage, their kingdom, and most everything they possessed.

A wrong he intended to rectify.

"Is it open?" he asked.

The prior nodded.

He avoided the bronzed angel holy water font and turned right, walking across the hard marble floor to the crypt's entrance. Life-size terra-cotta figures in high niches stared down at him. Many of them were his relatives, now bearing firsthand witness to what was about to happen. Wilhelm the Pious had razed nearly ninety houses, ignoring all public protests, to build his church, acting boldly, decisively, and definitively.

In the days ahead, Stefan intended to emulate all three of those traits.

CHAPTER 7

Cotton dropped through the night air and landed on the small craft. Maybe a ten-footer. Certainly no more. The deck rocked beneath him. But as the boat pivoted away from the ferry the water calmed. The two occupants were gone. Perhaps they'd been swept overboard by the turbulence. Or had they jumped? The water temperature was certainly near freezing. No way anyone could last long without thermal protection.

The ferry kept drifting away.

Hopefully, the pilot had regained consciousness and reassumed control. He should make a sweep for the two men. But before he could take the wheel, a figure appeared on the ferry's rear deck.

Pointing a weapon.

Shots rang out.

Rounds pierced the cold air around him and popped into the water.

Somebody was shooting at him.

To hell with the guys in the water.

He grabbed the automatic rifle lying on the deck and sent a volley toward the ferry, careful to keep his aim away from the passengers' cabin.

The firing stopped.

The shooter disappeared from the stern and he used the opportunity to swing the boat around in a wide arc, eventually angling the bow back toward the ferry, approaching from behind. He heard the big diesel motors fire up and watched as the ferry began to steam away. Apparently the pilot was back in control. From the far side another boat emerged, visible for a moment in the floodlights' range. Small. Like the one he was piloting.

The shooter?

Who else?

He should actually get out of here, head for shore and let Luke handle things. This was not his show. But old instincts told him that was a bad idea. Frat Boy was long gone, doing whatever he had to do to complete his assignment. This was a new threat. Aimed his way. Sure, he'd stuck his nose deeper into this than necessary.

But why fire on him?

He increased speed and planed the bow, following the other craft that burned a single red light in the distance. They were headed away from Herreninsel toward the next largest island in the lake, Fraueninsel. He'd visited there before. The Lady's Isle. Not large. Less than fifty acres. About three hundred permanent residents as well as an active Benedictine convent, famous for its Kloster Liqueur made by the nuns. The lake's ferryboats routinely stopped there, the whole place now a tourist attraction.

And the shooter was headed straight for it.

He powered ahead and arrived at a lighted concrete dock about three minutes behind his target. He recalled as much as he could about the small island. Low-lying. Dotted with broad branching trees.

Shallow banks. Surrounded by moorland and tiny bays. Lots of shops and cottages, many covered with creeping vines. Gardens everywhere, the lake banks crowded with beached boats. A concrete walk led from the pier along the lakeshore. A solitary church tower pierced the night. Hundreds of tiny white lights lit the trees and shrubs. He heard music and singing and caught a waft of sweet-smelling aromas. Cinnamon. Apple. Roasting meat. A Christmas market. Most German towns and villages hosted one this time of year. Lots of art, crafts, cakes, and mulled wine. Any other time he'd love to take a stroll through it. Right now he had to find the guy from the boat.

But the path ahead was empty.

He was about to leave when something caught his eye on the concrete. He bent down and studied the red splotch. Fresh. Still liquid. Blood. Unlike in the movies or on television, he did not dip a finger in and test the sample. What idiot in the real world would actually do that? The amount of possible contaminants would be incalculable. Like when the on-screen cop pierces a bag of white powder with a knife, then tastes it.

Really?

A few feet ahead he spotted another blood splotch.

Had one of his rounds found its mark?

Maybe.

He walked toward the sounds and lights at the end of the dock, which seemed farther away, past darkened buildings, into the village. The blood trail continued, though the spots began to be spaced farther and farther apart.

The ancient convent hugged the shore. A high stone wall, its mortar crumbling in places and lit to the night, encircled it, but an open gate allowed access. The blood trail led straight through the gate, and instead of veering left toward the convent, it went right toward the church, whose lit steeple pierced the darkness.

Cotton approached the double oak-paneled doors that stood between two pillars and opened them. The interior was high-vaulted, supported by more pillars bathed in a solemn amber glow. The walls were artistically chiseled and beneath the choir stood a flower-adorned sarcophagus. A placard noted in German that it held the first abbess who'd ruled the convent over a thousand years ago.

His gaze raked the stone floor searching for more blood.

He spotted a small splotch near where an arched entrance led back behind the main altar. The space beyond was dark with no lights burning. He found his phone and used it as a flashlight, spotting another smudge on the tile floor.

He stopped.

The blood ended.

At a door.

He shook his head.

This just kept getting better and better.

He turned the iron latch and opened the heavy slab. Steps led down. He slowly descended, the wooden risers creaking from his weight. At the bottom he used his phone to reveal a tunnel, maybe four feet wide and not quite six feet high. A few feet away from the bottom of the stairs he spotted another splotch.

Everyone had their kryptonite.

His was enclosed spaces.

Something about being encased with no way to escape just rattled his nerves. A weakness. Definitely.

One he despised acknowledging.

But he sucked it up.

And walked ahead.

CHAPTER 8

COTTON KEPT MOVING DOWN THE DRY FLOOR OF PACKED earth.

The tunnel stretched in a straight line about fifty yards and the farther he ventured the more uncomfortable he became. The air hung clammy and close, with an almost textured feel pressing against him. The darkness ahead extended beyond the reach of the phone's light. But the eventual sight of a metal ladder brought some relief.

He hustled toward it and climbed.

A wooden panel at the top hinged upward. He grabbed a metal ring and pushed. The warped wood groaned and the rusty metal hinges screamed their resistance. He climbed up through the scuttle hole and emerged inside a small, lit room barren of furniture. A door on the opposite wall opened. Two men entered. Middle-aged. Plain-faced. Wearing smiles of contempt. Both were armed.

"Somebody would like to speak with you," one of them said in perfect English, with not a hint of an accent anywhere.

"And you are?" he asked.

"Come with us," the other said, gesturing with the gun he held.

"You do know that I have little to nothing to do with any of this," he said.

"Except you just shot one of ours."

And there was that.

He was led through a series of twisting corridors. From the look and decor he assumed he was inside the convent. On the walk he studied his two minders, trying to decide just who exactly wanted to talk to him. Couldn't be military intelligence. These guys were too old. The military liked the young and lean with thirty-inch waists. FBI? A bit out of their jurisdiction, but a possibility as the bureau maintained several European offices. No. The more likely candidate was the perennial pain in the ass.

CIA.

During Cotton's time at the Magellan Billet there'd been one turf war after another with Langley. Everybody liked to proclaim cooperation against the common enemy, but America possessed far too many intelligence agencies and everybody wanted to be a hero. The whole system ran on mutual mistrust, the military and civilian intelligence services never close, the whole thing designed to keep anyone from becoming either too complacent or too powerful. The problem wasn't who was in charge. It was that *everybody* considered themselves in charge.

Which bred little goodwill.

The CIA especially hated the Magellan Billet since, when Danny Daniels had been president, the Billet was his go-to agency. He routinely relied on both it and Stephanie Nelle to get the job done. Sure, that had generated results. But also animosity. Daniels never cared. He was the boss and everybody who worked for him knew that if you crossed him, there'd be consequences. Two CIA directors had been fired, along with one director of national intelligence. But with the end of the Daniels administration, and the beginning of the Warner Fox presidency, things had changed. The old went out and the new came in. And from what he'd been told, the new was not all that impressive. A few months back he'd witnessed firsthand in Poland the level of that incompetence. Now here he was, on a frozen night in southern Germany, once again caught in the crosshairs of something strange.

They entered a foyer where other corridors began. Its vaulted ceiling showed representations from the life of St. Thomas. Above the entrance to an inner corridor he caught the inscription in stone. *Faciendi lures libros nullus est finis*. From the Bible, describing a library. Of the making of books there is no end.

How true.

A winding staircase led up and they climbed in silence. Wood-paneled walls exuded an oily, satiny glow. Framed art hung in rows, each with its own portrait light. Down a long corridor they entered a brightly lit hall of graceful proportions. Like a church without pews and aisles. A door at the far end opened and a man paraded into the room. Tall, with sparse ash-blond hair and candid brown eyes topped by bushy, almost amused, eyebrows. His midsection toted a bit of a beer gut and he walked with a shifting gait, his shoulders rising and dipping with each step. He flashed a cheeky smile and held out both arms in a mock welcome embrace.

"Harold Earl 'Cotton' Maloney in the flesh."

He heard the *y* added to his last name, something this annoyance had once loved to do.

"Derrick 'No Middle Name' Koger. It's been a while."

He knew the story. Supposedly Koger's parents were so poor they couldn't afford him a middle name.

Koger was career CIA. Last Cotton heard he'd risen to some sort of special operations manager. Every enterprising CIA field officer aspired to a desk at Langley, but that reward was tied to a clock. Don't rise fast enough and the train simply passes you by. Koger was at least twenty years into his career, definitely into overtime on the clock. Their paths had crossed several times back when he was an active agent. Some good. Others not so much. All part of those turf wars that came with the territory in his former profession.

Koger pointed. "When Luke Daniels said he was bringing you in, I couldn't believe my good fortune. Here we'll have a certified legend in our midst. The storied Cotton Maloney. Captain America himself, in the flesh. Damn. Watchin' you on that ferry was like somethin' right out of a Marvel comic."

He heard the sarcasm the false praise carried. But it came with a smile and sufficient amusement to make the insult acceptable. That was Koger's style. Just enough bullshit to keep his listener off guard. Thankfully, he'd worn his lizard skin today so a little ribbing was not a problem. Koger dismissed the other two men with a jerk of his head.

They left the hall.

"Who did I shoot?" he asked Koger.

"The man I had stationed on the lake, who I sent to chase you my way. Thankfully, it was a through-and-through in the shoulder. Clean wound. Bled like hell, though. He's on his way to a military hospital."

"He was shooting at me."

"I told him to miss."

Nothing about what he was hearing sounded good. "You were watching the whole thing?"

"I was watching Luke's progress, along with that other boat shootin' at him. A boat that wasn't supposed to be there. I was just about to order my man to intervene when, lo and behold, here you came with that ferry. Really imaginative. Did you read that in a book? I hear you sell books now. I never figured you for a shop owner."

"I never figured you to still be with the company."

What he left out were the words *and in the field*. A lot of people with Koger's longevity were retired and out writing revelation books about excess and deceit or appearing on cable news as a talking head. Yet this long, tall glass of water was still on the job.

"I'm a boots-on-the-ground kinda guy," Koger said. "Always have been."

He let that bullshit pass. "Luke is working a CIA operation?"

Koger nodded. "Stephanie Nelle is in some deep crap. Which you know all about. Word is she's gone, along with the Billet, but Fox is lettin' her dangle. Now, as I'm sure you realize, I'm not the biggest fan of the Justice Department being involved in international operations, but they're some good folks over there. So we decided to give a few a trial run during this sad time of…indecision. Luke seemed a good fit for us."

A detail Frat Boy had kept to himself. Cotton nearly smiled. The younger man was learning even faster than he'd imagined.

"Luke is on temporary loan to me, through the esteemed attorney general himself," Koger said.

He caught the message. "You don't approve?"

"Any stupider and we'd have to water him twice a week."

Colloquial, as always. "I assume you're not a fan of our new president either?"

"No comment on that one."

He smiled. "You heard about me and Fox?"

"Oh, yeah. We were ordered never to use you on any operation. Period. Persona non grata. No exceptions. Never. Ever."

He held his arms out. "Yet here I am."

"Abso-friggin'-lutely."

"You sure you want to get this stink on you?" he asked.

"If I wasn't, you wouldn't be here."

Fair enough. "That blood trail was for my benefit?"

"Since you'd already shot him, it seemed like a good way to get you here."

"This was a freebie. Just a favor for a friend. Nothing more."

Koger had a reputation as a tough ball of wax, with the instincts of a riverboat gambler. Cunning, shrewd, daring. A quintessential hands-on man of action in an agency loaded with desk jockeys. Cotton knew how things worked. The president issued an order, or expressed a concern, and it reverberated through the government like thunder. Directors summoned division chiefs, who emailed station chiefs, who called case officers, and so on until all of them had mobilized to deal with something the president had long forgotten. Ironically, any intelligence agency's greatest success came from simply being straightforward. Everything depended on one thing. People talking. Or texting. Emailing. Posting on social media. Doing anything where information could be ascertained. But, as with the Magellan Billet, he knew that the reckless, weak-kneed, naive, or plodding rarely survived long in the CIA. To Cotton's knowledge, no one who ever worked with Koger ever doubted his loyalty or ability. But that didn't mean they'd enjoyed the experience.

Despite the good-ol'-boy rhetoric, this guy was a stern taskmaster who demanded your all.

"My favor is done," he said. "I'm finished."

"How'd you like to stick a corn cob up Warner Fox's ass?"

He stared into brown eyes that had suddenly turned to hard points of light. "What do you have on him?"

"Enough to get Stephanie Nelle out of trouble and back on the job."

The last time he spoke with Danny Daniels, the ex-president had told him that Stephanie had frozen him out from helping. She wanted to deal with her problems herself, without the help of her boyfriend. Daniels had not liked the rebuke, but he'd respected her wishes. She was facing a disciplinary board and almost certain termination. All bullshit and horribly unfair. But both Cotton and Stephanie had crossed the new president in Poland. Cotton paid the price by being ostracized. She would be fired and her intelligence agency, the Magellan Billet, the one she'd created and nurtured for so long, would be disbanded. So, yes, he'd love to stick a corn cob where the sun didn't shine.

"What do you have?"

"It comes with a price."

"Which is?"

"What do you know about a man named Prince Stefan von Bayern?"

"Not a damn thing. Why is he important?"

"He wants to cause the United States of America a lot of trouble."

CHAPTER 9

DERRICK STUDIED EVERY DETAIL OF COTTON MALONE. The guy looked great. Tall, broad-shouldered, the sandy-blond hair lacking even a hint of gray. Malone had to be pushing fifty, now retired out of the Justice Department for a number of years. But from what he'd seen on the Chiemsee Maloney had not lost his edge. He'd jumped right in, literally, and protected Luke.

Like a good agent should.

"Bavaria has been around since the twelfth century," he said to Malone. "Ruled by Wittelsbach dukes. Officially, the place became a kingdom in 1806, thanks to Napoleon. But, after Waterloo, it melded into the newly formed German Empire. That wasn't a popular move. Bavaria was Catholic, so its people resented being ruled by mostly Protestant Prussia. There were separatist movements, even a few rebellions, but it stayed part of the empire. Today, landwise, it's one-fifth of Germany. The largest state. Seventy thousand square kilometers. Eleven million inhabitants. A place of few natural resources. A former agricultural and agrarian society that has modernized into an industrialized state. Cars, chemicals, electricity, air and space, high-tech. It's all there."

"You're quite the local historian," Malone said.

"Let's just say this place, at the moment, has my undivided attention."

"Officially?"

He shrugged. "Does it matter?"

Malone shrugged in turn. "Never meant much to me."

"Good to hear. The Wittelsbach monarchy was abolished after World War I. November 12, 1918. That's the magic day. Ludwig III signed the Anif Declaration, which released Bavarian civil and military officers from their oaths of allegiance and the kingdom ended. Most people considered that an abdication. But, and this is important, nobody in the House of Wittelsbach has ever formally renounced the throne."

"I don't recall any of them asserting any claims to it either."

"No, they haven't, and the Bamberg Constitution of 1919 created the Free State of Bavaria within the new Weimar Republic. After World War II, the Free State chose not to sign the founding treaty that formed the Federal Republic of Germany. The Bavarian parliament didn't sign on to the Basic Law of Germany either. So the new German nation was created without Bavaria's approval."

Malone seemed intrigued. "You're saying Bavaria is part of Germany, but not necessarily happy about it."

"It never has been. People here consider themselves Bavarians first and Germans second. A recent opinion poll showed that seventy-four percent of them want to be away from Germany."

"Secession?"

He nodded. "Exactly. The current Duke of Bavaria, Albert, is seventy years old. Of course he has no kingdom, but he's been head of the House of Wittelsbach for the past twenty years. His great-grandfather was King Ludwig III, the one who was deposed in 1918. He currently lives at the Nymphenburg Palace in Munich and is not married."

"No heirs?"

"Only a brother. Prince Stefan von Bayern."

"Who's a problem?"

"You could say that. Luke has infiltrated a group that works directly for Stefan, and he's managed to get close to the prince."

"And the purpose of that?"

"Stefan suffers from second child syndrome. He's twenty years younger than his sibling and is meaningless—unless his brother is dead. But, thankfully for him, nature has taken its course there. Duke Albert is dying from cancer."

Malone seemed puzzled. "That's too bad. But the Wittelsbachs are nothing but a historical curiosity."

"Unless they manage to regain their kingdom."

"How's that possible?"

"That's the whole point. It might actually be possible." And he explained how the German courts had repeatedly held that no state could legally secede from the federal republic. "But the Bundestag could change that. The national parliament can amend the constitution and allow a referendum in Bavaria, for secession, which it would respect. I know it sounds crazy, but we're headed right for that."

It did sound crazy, but Germany was currently in a state of political turmoil thanks to the sudden death of its longtime chancellor, Marie Eisenhuth. She'd died right in the middle of a hotly contested race with an opponent who likewise perished, throwing the national elections into chaos. Derrick knew that Malone had somehow been involved with that. To what extent? That he did not know. But it had been enough to attract the wrath of the president of the United States. Eventually, replacement candidates were selected by their respective parties. But no one achieved a majority vote, so a weak coalition government was formed, and Germany had been in confusion ever since.

"Why would the Bundestag even consider such a thing?" Malone asked. "Like you said, Bavaria is Germany's largest state."

He raised his index finger in protest. "Now that would be classified."

Malone shook his head. "Which is my cue to leave. Good luck with all this."

"I wasn't kidding when I said I can save Stephanie Nelle."

"Then do it."

He shrugged. "It's not my fight. But it could be yours."

He was gambling that Malone owed Stephanie Nelle more than could ever be repaid. She'd changed his life. Taken him from a nobody Navy JAG lawyer to a respected intelligence officer. He knew Malone had been one of her first recruits for the Magellan Billet. He also knew that many of Malone's assignments had changed the world. Along the way Malone had gotten divorced, retired out, and moved to Denmark to own a bookshop. Some sort of midlife crisis? Who knows? Now Malone's former boss was in big trouble and he was banking on this guy wanting to do whatever he could to help. No matter how he might feel about the guy offering that help.

"What's in it for you?" Malone asked.

He decided to be honest. "Opportunity."

"To get out of the field?"

"There is that."

Everything hinged on Malone feeling helpless regarding Stephanie Nelle. He knew that he and Stephanie had poked the bear in Poland, and the bear had scratched back. So offering a second chance to make things right seemed the perfect bait. But he also realized Malone's quandary. Was this empty opportunism? An enticing deception? Or the jackpot?

"All right," Malone said. "I'm in."

Jackpot.

"Now tell me the classified parts."

"We're dealing with a mystery here that dates to the nineteenth century," he said to Malone. "One that partially came back to life during World War II and had been dormant until a few months ago."

"And solving that provides us both with...opportunity?"

He nodded. "The proverbial two birds with one stone. Fox will do anything to have what we find."

"And what is this silver bullet?"

"The Germans had a name for it. *Das letzte königreich.*"

The last kingdom.

CHAPTER 10

It is difficult to adequately describe the scope
and breadth of my mission. It began in March
1873 with a summons to the royal Residenz
in Munich. Ludwig II had requested my
presence. I was acquainted with the king,
having supplied him on more than one occasion with reading material. As director of
the Bavarian archives I was intimately familiar with the royal library. The king was an
avid reader, progressive in thought, mindful
of technology. The two of us had developed
somewhat of a rapport, though I would never
have presumed to consider myself one of his
confidants.

On arrival at the Residenz I was shown to
the Hall of Antiquities. It had been built in
the sixteenth century by another Wittelsbach
and lovingly maintained ever since. I was
ushered inside and told to approach the king,

who waited at the far end, seated in a high-backed throne on a raised dais. No one else was present, which I thought quite odd.

"Come closer, Von Löher," the king called out, motioning. "Hurry, good man."

I stepped up my pace, but it was nearly seventy meters from one end of the magnificent space to the other. The hall carried the distinction of being the largest Renaissance enclosed space north of the Alps, once serving as a banquet hall and housing the ducal library. Ancient paintings adorned the highly decorated walls. I noticed ones by Peter Candid, Antonio Ponzano, and Hans Thonauer the Elder. I kept walking and stopped short of the dais, before a gilded wooded railing.

"Not there," Ludwig said. "Come here."

I bowed and stepped up on the dais.

"I have a mission for you, Ludwig said as I drew close, his voice low. "One that only you and I will know about. Are you agreeable with that condition?"

I nodded. What else would I say?

The king leaned forward, close to me. "First, I have something to tell you," Ludwig said. "It's been on my mind for several years now."

It sounded serious.

The king faced me.

"I cannot bear this place any longer."

"This palace?" I asked.

"No. This land. My government. Politics. All of it." The king paused. "I hate it all. I want a new kingdom."

Had I heard right? But I knew better than to ask questions. Instead, I said, "But your subjects love you. Your very presence on the streets of Munich brings rejoicing."

Ludwig rubbed his forehead. "I can no longer bear to be stared at by people, to smile and to extend greetings a thousand times, to ask questions of persons who mean nothing to me and to listen to answers that do not interest me."

I could not believe what I was hearing.

"Sometimes, when I have read myself to exhaustion and everything is quiet," Ludwig said, "I have an irresistible urge to hear a human voice. So I call one of the servants or postilions and ask him to tell me about his home and family. If I did not, I would completely forget the art of speech."

The admission tore at my heart. The common talk was that this man loved to escape reality and surround himself with the splendor of a fantastical Middle Age. All agreed Ludwig had a wistful manner and was passionate about the arts, especially music. But the whispers noted that he could also display an irrationality, along with a demeanor of unspeakable sadness.

"Nothing here satisfies my needs," the king said. "I feel so forsaken and lonely on this earth. Like a leftover from a better time, blown into the present, which I hate, and where I shall always feel a stranger."

I still did not know what to say.

"It is surely understandable that I am sometimes attacked by an absolute fever of anger and hatred, and that I turn away in disgust from the world around me. Perhaps one day I shall be at peace with this earth, when all the ideals whose sacred flames I cherish are destroyed. But I do not wish this." The king's eyes bored into me. "Before that happens, I wish to remain an eternal enigma to myself and others."

"In what way, Majesty?"

"I want a new land. A world of dreams where everyone is my friend, where I might be an autocratic master, unhampered by the

confines of government. Far away, across the
sea. A *tabula rasa*, a blank slate, where I can
have all my dreams come true. Wagner said
it best in *Lohengrin*. 'In a far country, out of
reach of your footsteps.'"

I was stunned to hear my monarch speak
of abandoning his kingdom. But I was not
ignorant to the rumors that said this man
was morbidly anxious about his health, prone
to long bouts of brooding, and apprehensive
of his own sanity. His grandfather and aunt
both had exhibited traits of eccentricity. His
brother was clearly mentally deficient. Some
said the same of Ludwig. But he was still
the king.

Not to be questioned.

"Majesty, how does your desire concern me?"
I asked.

Ludwig sat back in the chair. "You are to find
me that new kingdom."

The suggestion shocked me, which surely
showed on my face.

"Come now, Von Löher, you are a bit of a
radical. Surely my suggestion cannot be that
upsetting to you."

I had no idea the king was so versed in
my personal history. Twenty-five years ago I

took part in a political uprising and was
imprisoned by the government for agitation.
Ludwig's father, Maximilian, had been king.
Thankfully, after a trial, I was acquitted. So
I settled down and became the assessor of
the court of appeal in Paderborn, afterward a
professor in the universities of Munich and
Göttingen. Eventually, I was chosen to head
the state archives, my revolutionary past, if
not forgotten, apparently forgiven.

"You are Franz von Löher, a Bavarian
public servant of high regard," Ludwig said.
"Learned in the law, history, and natural
sciences. You have also traveled extensively
throughout Europe, Canada, and the United
States. You are a man of the world."

True. I had traveled all over.

"During your visit to America I am told you
lectured on the significance of the German
people in world history," Ludwig said. "How
was that received?"

"Quite well, Majesty."

"Come now. You are being modest. I was
told that you even fostered a legend. I read
your book. *History and Condition of the
Germans in America.*"

I had indeed generated controversy by re-
telling the story of how the single vote of

Frederick Muhlenberg, the first ever Speaker of the American House of Representatives, prevented German from becoming the official language of the United States. Muhlenberg broke a tie vote for English. Many had taken issue with my recounting, saying I was wrong, and that it never happened. But I had always stood by what I wrote.

"I also read much of your other book, *Lands and People of the Old and New Worlds,*" the king said. "Your writings are what convinced me that you are the man for this task."

Derrick took back his phone, from which he'd allowed Malone to read. "That's an English translation. Part of a narrative Franz von Löher wrote in 1889."

"Is that public record?"

He shook his head. "It was removed from the Bavarian archives during World War II and has remained classified, by us, ever since."

"You're saying the king of Bavaria wanted to ditch his crown and go find another kingdom?"

He flashed a broad grin. "Not me. That's what Franz von Löher, then head of the Bavarian archives, is saying. But the rub to this itch is that they actually found one."

Malone seemed amazed. "Is that what the prince, Stefan, is after?"

He nodded. "In a manner of speaking."

"How does that affect the United States?"

He resisted the urge to smile. Malone had taken the bait. Hook, line, sinker, even the whole damn boat.

"Because that new kingdom was located in America."

CHAPTER 11

STEFAN STOOD IN THE FAMILY CRYPT BENEATH ST. Michael's.

Forty-one members of the House of Wittelsbach occupied the tombs and niches around him, including the esteemed Wilhelm the Pious himself, who'd founded the church.

Royalty everywhere.

His dear older brother, the current Duke of Bavaria, would soon become the latest occupant. Within the next six months, was what the doctors had told his brother.

He stared around at the square-vaulted space, its low ceiling supported by stout stone pillars. Access was always guaranteed to the family, no matter the hour or day. But what he planned for tonight was not part of that privilege. He was about to take an irrevocable step. One that would propel him to either a glorious victory or an utter defeat. Which outcome would come his way? That was impossible to know. Yet it had to be done.

And all because of what happened at Lake Starnberg on June 13, 1886.

*   *   *

Ludwig II had withdrawn from the world, harassed by the burden of royalty, a mass of contradiction. He greatly sympathized with republicanism, yet idolized Louis XIV, the prince of autocrats, who clapped anyone into the Bastille who dared to have an opinion of their own. He constantly complained about his cabinet and dismissed them all in 1876. But the replacements were not any better. His restlessness was legendary, weary of everything, staying only a few days in any one place. Like a fever in his blood he desired constant everlasting change, along with constant theatrical effect to enhance anything natural.

According to witnesses he routinely consulted spiritualists to converse with the dead, became irritable and excitable with furious ebullitions of temper, tolerated not the slightest contradiction, or any delay in gratifying his wishes. He even, at times, tore out his hair and beard, and, most strange, lost all sense of seasons or temperature, thinking winter summer and vice versa. All of which was contained within a secret medical report prepared by an eminent group of psychologists led by Dr. Bernhard von Gudden. A report that concluded with a finding of mental insanity. Most of the evidence was solicited testimony from former servants, aides, and stable boys. Some paid for, others coerced. Not a shred of counterevidence or anything exculpatory was offered. A medical assessment made entirely without the benefit of any examination of the patient.

But why?

The best explanation was that the Bavarian government had become paralyzed. Ludwig had stopped receiving ministers and refused to sign official papers. He'd never comprehended the value of money. The tangled debt from his many building projects, a mania that always cried out for more, had skyrocketed into the tens of millions. He'd finished his castle at Linderhof, and partially completed his other two, Neuschwanstein and Herrenchiemsee. But much more work remained to be done. His motto was the same as that of his idol, Louis XIV.

Le roi le veuti. *The king wants it.*

So he shall have it.

Thankfully, no public money had ever been used for construction. Instead, Ludwig had allocated the sums he was given each year by the government, as monarch for his yearly upkeep, to pay the bills. When that source ran out he'd borrowed heavily. Being the king of a long-standing realm had, at first, made him an attractive borrower. But not anymore. Creditors circled like buzzards and wanted their money. The possibility of the crown being sued or having to declare bankruptcy loomed large, both of which would expose the royal family to an unprecedented scandal.

"What is the world coming to when kings cannot spend as much as they want? Is there no loyalty? No David Bernard among them?" Ludwig many times cried out.

But no one seemed to understand the reference.

Bernard had been a rich banker who defrayed the whole expense of one of Louis XIV's wars in gratitude for simply being allowed to walk beside Louis in the garden, to the envy of others. No, there were no David Bernards in Bavaria.

The only answer to the dilemma seemed to be found within the Bavarian constitution, which provided that a monarch could be removed for mental instability—provided the disability would last more than a year. So a commission of four doctors had certified just that.

To facilitate an easy transfer of power, Prince Luitpold, Ludwig's uncle, agreed to assume the regency since both Ludwig and his brother and heir, Otto, would now be declared insane. Neither had any children. The prime minister acquiesced on the assurance he would remain in office under the regency. Further, the government would assume Ludwig's debts and pay them in full. Which would make the creditors happy. The various government ministers reenforced the deal by agreeing that if Ludwig remained king, they would all resign. But, if there be a change at the top, they would stay.

So Ludwig II was removed and a regency proclaimed.

A bloodless coup d'état.

It helped that Ludwig lived in virtual isolation, sleeping through the day, immersing himself at night in a fantasy world of ideas. His lack of political savvy made him even more vulnerable. The aristocracy detested him, since he continuously shunned them. His family was nonsupportive thanks to his reckless spending. The people, though, loved him. And that fact urged caution among the conspirators.

On June 8, 1886, a state commission headed south from Munich to take the king into custody. It was agreed he would be held at Linderhof, which stood deep in the Alps, sufficiently isolated, making for a perfect prison. They arrived during the afternoon at Hohenschwangau, a castle where Ludwig had spent most of his childhood, and where their spies had reported he was in residence. But they discovered that the king had already withdrawn to nearby Neuschwanstein.

So they spent the evening deciding what to do next.

At midnight they enjoyed a seven-course meal originally intended for the king. To fortify themselves, they drank forty quarts of beer and ten bottles of champagne. That loitering, though, allowed Ludwig to order Neuschwanstein sealed, preventing the commission from entering. He then sent a sentry to the nearby town of Füssen to alert officials of the coup. The local police arrived to help protect the castle gates. Around 3:00 A.M. the commission finally headed up *the fir-clad slopes to Neuschwanstein's rocky perch. Soldiers immediately surrounded them. By then the local peasants had arrived armed with axes, rifles, knives, and swords. All of the commission, save for one, was arrested. The one who escaped traveled back to Munich and alerted officials. Ludwig did not help his cause of mental stability when he ordered the detained men flogged, an eye removed, skinned alive, then starved to death and left to decay in their own filth. Of course no one followed that order and the commission was released at around noon on June 10.*

The locals withdrew back to their homes.

Ludwig refused to listen to any advice offered for him to flee south across the Alpine wall to Austria and seek the Hapsburg emperor's protection. He was also advised to release a public statement and one was prepared, but it did not achieve wide distribution. Bismarck telegraphed and told him to return to Munich and appeal to the people. They were comfortable under his rule and adored him. All he had to do was present himself. But he declined. Instead, he spent the afternoon of June 10 destroying papers and burning correspondence.

He seemed to sense that the end was near.

He told his most trusted servant, a man named Alfons Weber, "I do believe in the immortality of the soul and in God's justice. To be catapulted down from the highest level of life into nothingness. That is a life lost. I cannot bear it. That they take away my crown I could bear, but that they have declared me mentally ill, I will not survive. I could not tolerate the same fate as my poor brother, Otto, whom any guard can order around, whom they threaten to beat if he does not obey. May my blood be upon all those who have betrayed me."

Ludwig's refusal to flee allowed the government the opportunity to send soldiers to seal off Neuschwanstein. Telephone lines and power to the castle were cut. This time there would be no theatrics from the locals. Ludwig telegraphed his equerry to come at once, ordered an immediate march of a rifle battalion to the castle, and finally wired the German and Austrian emperors and Bismarck for help. But all those communiqués were intercepted. None made it to their recipients. The king began to drink, the alcohol making him aggressive and nervous. He toyed with suicide. Perhaps taking poison or tossing himself off the castle's highest tower, he mused to servants.

"Half past twelve I was born and half past twelve I shall die," he declared.

In the early morning hours of June 11, a second commission arrived at Neuschwanstein and appeared before the king.

"This is the saddest obligation I have ever fulfilled," von Gudden said. "Your Majesty has been evaluated by four experts and, based on their recommendation, Prince Luitpold has taken over the political responsibilities on your behalf. I have the order to accompany Your Majesty to Berg Castle tonight."

"Evaluated? How can you declare me mentally ill when you have neither examined nor spoken to me?" Ludwig shouted.

"I took this step," von Gudden said, "on the strength of the servants' evidence."

"On the strength of the evidence of paid lackeys that I have raised from nothing and they betray me in return? And how long, assuming I am really sick, do you think my cure will take?"

"That will depend upon Your Majesty. It will be necessary for you to submit to my instructions."

"We are not living in an age of might before right. My subjects shall judge whether I am crazy or not."

Though of weak mind and body he could, on occasion, display extraordinary resolve.

"You have come to tell an insane man that he is insane? Does that not imply that I be sane, so as to understand?"

No one offered him a reply.

A great horror began to steal over him. Only a few servants remained in the castle, and no one seemed to want to fight for him.

So he fought for himself.

"No Wittelsbach—let me tell you once and for all—need ever submit to anything."

"That may be so," von Gudden said, "but I have been ordered to take you away."

A little after midday on June 12 three coaches arrived on the shores of Lake Starnberg at Berg Castle. This new location had been chosen for the king's confinement after all of the drama that had occurred at Neuschwanstein. The government could not afford any more local uprisings that might grant Ludwig freedom. So he would be confined closer to Munich in a locale that could be readily defended.

The ride north had taken eight hours.

Berg Castle was a special place for Ludwig. He'd spent much time there during his twenty-one-year reign, enjoying its peaceful tranquility. But now the door handles to every room had been removed, the windows crisscrossed with heavy iron bars, the doors themselves drilled with peepholes for observation. Clearly a lot of preparation had occurred prior to his arrival.

The king took lunch, then lay down to rest. He rose at midnight and asked for his clothes, but the guards refused. He fell asleep again around dawn, on Pentecost Sunday, June 13. His request to attend Mass was refused. During the day he stayed by himself, then ate around 4:30 in the afternoon. After the meal, Ludwig reminded von Gudden that he'd promised a walk. The doctor reluctantly agreed, *telling someone, "I wish the king would spare me. The man is so tiresome with his many questions."*

Before the walk, von Gudden telegraphed Munich to say that "everything is working out wonderfully."

Near 6:45 P.M. von Gudden left with the king, with two guards in tow. But the doctor dismissed them, saying they would walk alone and be back before eight for supper.

The rain started around seven.

By eight, when the king and von Gudden had not returned, the police were informed and all available men headed out with lanterns and torches.

More rain and wind made the search difficult.

The king's rolled umbrella was found laid across a park bench. His overcoat and suit jacket were also located. Both seemed to have been removed quickly, turned inside out, the arms of the suit jacket still stuffed into the overcoat. Nearby, onshore, several branches were broken, as if someone had pushed their way through the underbrush to the lake. The king's bowler and von Gudden's silk hat were spotted in the water.

Ludwig was found floating facedown, his eyes open, his skin cold to the touch. Von Gudden bobbed nearby in a half-kneeling, half-sitting position. Rigor mortis had set in on both, but attempts were made at resuscitation. Von Gudden's face had scratches along with a large bruise over the right eye, a deep cut on the forehead, and a gash in one cheek. The nail of the middle finger of the right hand was gone. The king showed no visible injuries. Ludwig's watch had stopped at 6:54. Von Gudden's at 8:00 P.M.

The corpses were returned to Berg Castle.

The next day Ludwig's body was washed and laid out for the many peasants, who'd gathered beyond the castle gates, to view. They made a death mask, sculpted his hands, and cut a few locks of hair.

Then the body was returned to Munich.

*An autopsy was performed and its findings released
to the public. To bolster a claim of mental insanity, the
report noted an inflammation of the skull, a thin scalp,
and a small growth near the front of the brain. All
supposedly pointing to degenerative brain disease.*

*For the next three days the king lay in state at the
Residenz, under a rich blue silk pall, smothered in fresh
flowers, allowing the public to file past the open casket.
He wore the black robe of the Order of the Knights of
St. Hubertus and held a sword in his left hand, a small
bouquet of jasmine in his right. He seemed to be merely
sleeping, a slight smile on his ashen lips. The bells of every
church in Munich rang for an hour on Saturday, June 19,
as cannons boomed in the distance.*

Stefan stood before Ludwig II's bronze tomb.

Which had been here since 1886.

A waist-high, wrought-iron railing encircled it on
all sides, there to keep the curious at bay. It disgusted
him that the crypt had turned into nothing more
than a tourist attraction. Two euros gained admittance
six days a week, photos included. And people paid
that fee by the thousands, generating revenue for the
church. Disgraceful. But it seemed the ways of the
modern world.

He would change that too.

Above, in the nave, he heard voices.

His people. Finally. Arriving.

He was anxious to know what happened at Herrenchiemsee. He'd ordered the intrusion knowing it
also to be an irrevocable act. But the time for planning
had ended. Time for wishing and hoping over. If he
was going to change Bavaria, change his own life,
change Germany, then risks would have to be taken.

Big ones.

He'd always been the most ambitious of the current stock of Wittelsbachs. His brother, Albert, was a helpless, dying soul, who'd lived a quiet life among the few remaining estates the family had retained, surviving off ancestral money, wisely invested and prudently spent.

But that austerity came with limits.

Ones he'd long come to resent.

Sure, he could keep enjoying a life of privilege. Traveling from one warm spot to another, enjoying women and his status as supposed royalty. But, thankfully, fate had offered a reprieve. A new option.

All he had to do was take it.

The voices from above drew closer.

Footsteps descended to the crypt.

CHAPTER 12

LUKE BOUNDED DOWN THE STAIRS INTO THE CRYPT beneath the Jesuit Church of St. Michael. The ride west from the Chiemsee to Munich had been all autobahn and uneventful. The theatrics that occurred onshore had served their purpose. Everyone seemed satisfied that they'd made their points. He doubted either Christophe or Lexi would mention any of the problems that had happened inside the palace. Instead, they'd revel in the success of their mission.

"We got it," Christophe said, holding up the book.

Prince Stefan looked pleased as he accepted the offering. "Well done. To you all. Any problems?"

"Not a one," Lexi quickly answered.

And neither he nor Christophe contradicted her, which was fine by him. They'd destroyed the camera and ditched the pieces in a dumpster on the walk over from where they'd parked the car. He needed things calm, not more turmoil. The only problem was the book. He had to get a look at it. Snap some images. And, most vital, learn why it was so important.

"That's good to hear," the prince said.

Luke glanced around at the array of sarcophagi

resting atop a tile floor. All shapes and sizes. Young and old apparently. Crowns adorned a few, signaling a king or emperor. Plaques on the wall identified occupants. Wilhelm V, Duke of Bavaria. Maximilian I, Elector of Bavaria. Charles II, Duke of Zweibrücken. King Otto, Ludwig's younger brother.

And, of course, Ludwig II.

That grave seemed the most elaborate, protected by a low iron railing and adorned with fresh flowers and candles. A framed black-and-white photograph of the king as a handsome young man hung on the wall just behind.

He watched as Prince Stefan thumbed through the stolen book and managed to catch a couple of glimpses that showed it was indeed an ordinary printed volume. He caught a few words on the title page. *Tannhäuser* and *Wartburg*. The rest of the lettering on the spine and cover had all faded. He was careful not to show any excess interest, returning his attention to the solemn surroundings. The prince's instructions had been clear. Retrieve the book, then come to the church.

Luke had assumed the two were related.

All this started three months ago when Prince Stefan von Bayern sprang onto the US radar. How that happened was above his pay grade. But he'd been dispatched to Munich, charged with working his way into the prince's good graces. That effort had started with the hired help and Christophe, who headed the two men and one woman currently on the payroll. Here he was known as Jonathan Smith, ex-military, dishonorably discharged, mercenary for hire. The CIA had even created an entire personnel jacket and inserted it into the military record system, just in case anyone went looking.

He knew that Stefan wanted both a kingdom and

the throne. As best he could determine, the prince was looking for something that related to Ludwig II, lost when the king died in 1886. To this day no one knew what happened that rainy June evening along Lake Starnberg. Two men went for a walk and never returned. In the aftermath Bavaria was governed for thirty years, first by a regency, then for a short time by Ludwig III, until it was absorbed into post–World War I Germany, its monarchy abolished, most of the Wittelsbach assets confiscated. He'd been told that Stefan wanted to reverse all that. Exactly how and why that concerned the United States remained murky. But his orders were clear. Ascertain what the prince was after and report. Not neutralize. Or interfere. Just report.

Stefan stepped close to Ludwig's sarcophagus.

The prince stood medium in height, narrow-shouldered, his firm cheeks darkened by a beard beginning to show only hints of gray. He had an angled face with sharp corners and a chilling smile. He spoke with the accrued authority that success brought to intelligent people. His coal-black hair was most likely colored and coiffured to perfection, his bronzed skin and crinkly-brown eyes those of someone much younger than the fifty Luke knew him to be.

"I want you to open this tomb," the prince said.

Really? That's why we're here?

Christophe hopped over the iron railing with no hesitation. Lexi assumed a position on the opposite side of the sarcophagus, jumping the railing too. Luke decided he had no choice and joined the party over the rail, at the head. The sarcophagus was about eight feet long and half that wide, fashioned of green marble and resting on four carved lion's paws. At its corners were finials topped with gilded representations of more lions. The lid's center was raised to form a platform upon which rested a gilded crown atop a velvet pillow. Christophe removed both and handed them to the prince, who reverently laid them on the floor.

"Please slide the lid away so I can see inside," the prince said.

Seemed like an ordinary request for this guy, though it was a first for Luke. He'd never opened a grave before. But nothing ventured, nothing gained. So they all grabbed hold of the top. It was heavy and awkward, but they were able to maneuver it enough to create a wedge of darkness. Stefan approached and shined a light from his cell phone into the opening.

"This can't be," the prince said.

Luke saw the incredulous look on Stefan's face.

The first break in the controlled mien he'd ever seen.

He glanced down.

The tomb was empty.

CHAPTER 13

STEFAN DREW BACK FROM LUDWIG'S SARCOPHAGUS. HE'D expected many things to happen tonight, but the one contingency he'd not planned for was the tomb to be empty.

That was not what he'd been told.

In 1886 Ludwig II had been buried with great fanfare. Eight white horses draped in black palls had drawn the hearse through Munich. On either side walked adjutants, chamberlains in gold-braided costumes, and the knights of the Order of St. George. The king's favorite horse, also draped in black, followed. The mourners included the prince regent, the crown princes of Austria and Prussia, all the princes of the Wittelsbach house, Bavarian noblemen, foreign ambassadors, high officials, and the ministry and deputations from nearly every Bavarian town. The cavalry and infantry assumed the rear, their regimental bands playing funeral marches. It took two and a half hours for the procession to go the short distance from the Residenz to St. Michael's. Mourning banners had draped the church's entrance. The coffin was laid on an inclined bier before the altar, surrounded by white candles and a sea of flowers. The archbishop blessed the remains, then Capuchin monks carried it down to the crypt. Where it stayed four months until the tomb was ready.

Was that when the corpse vanished?

Or had it been later?

During one of the world wars?

His initial shock had been hard to conceal but now, after a few moments of contemplation, he realized that he could not show any concern in front of his subordinates.

"Close it up," he ordered.

He stepped back and watched as his people slid the heavy marble lid back into place. He loved how acolytes viewed him with unquestioned respect.

Like a king.

He handed the book back to Christophe.

"Deliver this to Ertl for me. The rest of you are done for the night."

And he left the crypt.

The trip from downtown to Nymphenburg took a half hour by car. Stefan had driven fast with a bold confidence that made the best of both the wet pavement and the potholes. A light rain and snow started along the way, the city lights tossing a mirrored dazzle from the glistening streets. He'd stayed chilled despite the warmth seeping up from the car's heater, huddling deeper into his coat, resisting the sleepiness induced by the car's metronomic sound.

Once the Nymphenburg Palace lay in the woods west of town. Now it was just part of the sprawling suburbs, a tranquility of silence in the midst of a metropolitan clamor. Another of the many attractions that brought millions to Munich every year. He'd never cared for it. Too big. Too disjointed. The complex had been created by a succession of five Wittelsbachs over a two-hundred-year period, mainly used as a summer residence. One pavilion after another was connected by long wings, all surrounded by five hundred acres of grass and trees. Today the graceful rococo edifice accommodated multiple uses for tourism, cultural events, even the headquarters of the government department that oversaw all of the national palaces and parks. Stefan's favorite part was the Schönheitsgallerie, where thirty-six portraits of women who'd caught the eye of Ludwig I, between 1827 and 1850, were displayed.

Talk about vanity.

One small chancery building toward the north end of the property served as home to the House of Wittelsbach. Where his brother, Albert, resided, as had their father before them. It had once been a hunting lodge, but a twentieth-century remodel had converted it into a residence and added most of the modern conveniences.

He parked out front in a small paved lot.

Stark trees, like gallows to the cold, rose all around, visible in the floodlights. The family had a private entrance onto the grounds through an electronic gate. No fence or security, though. None at all. Why? Nobody cared about a former royal family that barely existed outside of the history books.

He stormed into the chancery through the front door and found his brother in the ground-floor study, a spacious room with heavy furniture and even heavier drapes and upholstery. Hunting trophies dotted the walls, a couple from animals he'd killed himself. A sparkling, unlit Venetian glass chandelier hung from the stucco ceiling. Half a century ago the place had probably been an agreeable location to live. Not anymore. Now it reeked of age and failure.

A fire burned in a stone hearth. On the mantelpiece an ornate clock chimed 9:00 P.M. His brother sat before a table with his stamps spread out before him. Glass cases lined the walls, each filled with hundreds more postage stamps. Some yellowed with age, others bright with flowers, fierce warriors, or long-dead personalities. Each represented, as his brother liked to say, *a gummed serrated testament to the rare*. Stefan had always thought collecting them a waste of time. Just something done by a beleaguered class of hoarders doomed to frustration because their work was never done, since new stamps were created every day.

"By a typewriter's error," his brother said, staring down through a magnifying glass, "this stamp was given the wrong value. So the presses were stopped and the run destroyed. Except for a few, always a few, of which this was one of the survivors." Albert looked up. "It's the errors that draw the big money. Ironic, isn't it, stamps that cannot even be used to mail a letter escalate in value to the thousands of euros."

"Where is Ludwig II?"

"He's dead, and has been for a long time."

His brother was a fleshy man, built like an egg, with sloping shoulders, a wide girth, and stout legs. Like all Wittelsbachs, he had a dense crop of dark hair now frosted gray that matched his skin, which had lost all shades of pigment. Long ago Albert had abandoned any semblance of personal pride, content to gorge on rich food, drink expensive liquor, and collect stamps. He reminded Stefan of the gnomes the locals loved to carve out of pine and sell to tourists. Eight months ago the doctors had told Albert that he had an inoperable brain tumor. They gave him a year, maybe fourteen months at most to live. Not much remained of that time.

He needed to calm down so he walked over, splashed some amber-colored liquid into a tumbler from a decanter, and enjoyed a few sips of whiskey. Finally, he calmly asked, "Where is the body?"

His brother laid the magnifying glass down. "I received a call from the rector a few minutes ago. He told me of your visit to the family crypt. One I did not authorize."

"I do not need your permission."

"Actually, you do. I am still the head of this family. What were you doing violating our ancestor's grave?"

He had no intention of explaining himself, and the rector reporting his visit was not unexpected. Of course, if he'd found what he'd believed was there, none of this would matter.

"Where is Ludwig?" he asked again.

"Not to worry, dear brother. Apparently, our beloved king is safe."

"You knew the tomb was empty?"

Albert said nothing.

"Answer me."

His brother nodded. "I had an idea. But I wanted you to find out."

Stefan had learned that something may have been buried with Ludwig from Albert during one of their rare civil conversations. It happened about the time he learned of his brother's illness.

"You wanted me to go look?" he asked.

"I was curious. I have been all my life. So I tickled your curiosity and, sure enough, you went. But it took you a while. Father always said you were difficult to prod along."

Their father had been from another generation. The grandson of the last official monarch of Bavaria, Ludwig III. A duke without a kingdom his entire life. Bavaria had always been a patriarchal society with succession coming only from the male side of the family, the oldest son first in line. Albert had never married. Why? Who knows? His brother's personal life was of no concern. Truth be told, bachelorhood worked favorably into his plans. What bothered him was that Albert might know something he did not. Something their father may have confided only to the eldest son.

"What were you told?"

His brother stayed seated at the table. "That was something between the duke and his heir."

He hated those hereditary distinctions, which, by definition, totally excluded him. "Where is Ludwig's body?" he asked again, the anger growing.

"Adolf Hitler and Dwight Eisenhower asked the same question. They all received the same answer."

"Why would they be asking?"

His brother pointed an index finger. "For the same reason as you. *Das letzte königreich*. The question is, though, why do you want it?"

"Finding the last kingdom is good for both of us."

Albert shrugged. "Not for me. I'll be dead soon."

He decided to try being conciliatory. "Would you not like to die a king?"

"I became satisfied with being a duke long ago."

"I'm not."

His brother's indifference and complacency irked him. It always had. And he'd always found it difficult to fathom much past that inscrutable reserve.

"Now that you know the tomb is empty, do you care?" he asked Albert.

"My curiosity is satisfied."

Albert crouched back over the desk, seemingly lost in the nostalgia of another time, admiring his stamps.

Enough.

Stefan stormed across the room and upended the table, sending the stamps, magnifying glass, and lamp to the floor. The bulb exploded and the glass shade shattered into pieces. His brother never moved from the chair, head down at the carnage.

"Your temper will be your ruin," Albert said. "Father believed the same thing."

"Like I care what that beleaguered old fool thought of me. Like you, he, too, was content to be a duke."

An atmosphere of hate seeped into the room. Like a record stuck in a groove they were going around all of the old sounds. As brothers they'd never been close. Differences in age, lifestyle, and beliefs had long kept them estranged. He'd married young and fathered three children, all daughters, his wife the kind of woman who asked few questions and cared little, so long as everyone was discreet. He and his brother had different friends. Different interests. Different ambitions.

"Leave this be," Albert quietly said. "It has remained hidden for a long time and it should stay hidden. We owe that to Ludwig II and Ludwig III. You, my dear brother, will soon be Duke of Bavaria. Be happy with that title."

His natural dignity shook with agitation. "It means nothing without the title *King*."

"It means everything."

For the first time, Albert's voice went brittle.

Someone once said that *how a person mastered their fate was more important than what that fate was.*

He believed that. With all his heart.

"Let it go, Stefan," Albert said again. "Let the past stay in the past."

His resolve only solidified.

"Never."

CHAPTER 14

LUKE LOVED MUNICH'S BEER HALLS. SURELY THE MOST famous was the Hofbräuhaus, which definitely catered to tourists. But he favored the ones farther away from Old Town, where the locals hung out.

He'd visited several. This one tonight was full of Bavarian charm, complete with a spacious traditional interior, amber ceilings, and a stylish bar adorned with shiny copper and dark wood. Folk music shook the room. People bounced, jiggled, and whirled to the beat of an oompah band, the warm air bustling with loud conversations. A sweet waft of hops filled his nostrils and reminded him he was thirsty.

He'd walked over from the church with Lexi.

Christophe met them there.

A young maître d', wearing a green frock coat and sporting a winged collar, showed them to a long table near a stage adorned with rows of hunting trophies. A buxom, dark-haired woman in traditional German garb left menus that featured baked pretzels, roasted ribs, and local Augustiner brews. Everybody seemed at ease, relaxed, their job complete. The fact that Ludwig's tomb had been empty was not their problem.

The prince had seemed concerned, but he quickly fled the church and told them they were done for the day. So they'd retreated to the beer hall. He'd acted disinterested when the prince handed the book over to Christophe and told him to *deliver this to Ertl.*

Christine Ertl.

Who'd appeared a few times, in person, meeting with the prince.

Luke had managed to follow her back to her Munich apartment and learned that she was an academic at Ludwig Maximilian University. A professor of European studies and author of six books on German history. So when Christophe appeared at the beer hall without the book, he assumed the delivery had been made.

He was here to gather intelligence. Most times that meant just keeping your eyes and ears open. But sometimes you had to track it down. So after ninety minutes of letting off steam, gulping beer, and eating ribs, they all decided to call it a night. Christophe and Lexi headed off in one direction—he'd come to the conclusion that they were an item—and he in another.

A cold, snowy drizzle drifted across the city in a gray wash. He stuffed his gloved hands into the pockets of his leather jacket and started walking. Knots of people clung together under umbrellas made shiny by the moisture. Soles rang loud off the cobbles. Streetlights glowed with halos in the misty air. A series of shops lined the way, increasing in price and prestige the farther he walked. He passed the former royal Residenz, closed for the night, its elegant facade heavy with the crestfallen look stone took on in the rain. He assumed it was Ertl who'd aimed the prince toward Herrenchiemsee. Some of the conversations he'd managed to overhear had been on that subject.

Sure, he was playing a hunch.

But that seemed to be the story of his life.

He kept walking, following curving streets that zigzagged and turned, never coming to an end. He found the apartment in the exact location he remembered. He'd always been blessed with a perfect sense of direction. They'd called him Bird Dog in the Rangers, a nickname he'd come to embrace. Hell of a lot better than Frat Boy. He wondered what Malone was doing. Probably by now snug in a warm hotel suite enjoying room service before flying back to Denmark tomorrow. He'd need to call and thank Pappy for helping him out, though things had not gone according to plan.

Close enough, though.

And like in horseshoes and hand grenades, close definitely counted here too.

He entered the apartment building, greeted by a miasma of aromas that an eternity of German cooking had left behind. One wall of the dingy vestibule held an array of brass-fronted mailboxes, each bearing a name card barely legible in the weak light of a ceiling bulb. He found the one for Christine Ertl and climbed the stairs to the third floor.

Listening from outside he heard nothing through the door. If this woman was home, and recognized him, that would be the end of things. So he quickly descended back to ground level and stepped out into the weather. No lights burned anywhere on the third floor. Looked like he had no choice now. He hustled back up to the apartment and knocked on the door. He waited a few seconds and lightly rapped again.

No answer.

He fished the picks he always carried from his wallet and quickly opened the lock in under thirty seconds.

Only ambient light leaked in through the windows of the apartment. Small. Four rooms. Sparsely furnished. Books everywhere. Stacked on the floor. Lining shelves. Piled on the sofa. He examined a few and noticed a commonality. Ludwig II, Bavaria, Germany. Most were older volumes from the early to mid-twentieth century. Their frayed covers evidenced much use. All bore the stamp of the Bayerische Staatsbibliothek. Foreign languages were not his thing, but he knew *bibliothek* meant "library" and *Bayer* "Bavaria." Since the person who lived in the apartment also worked at the Bavarian State Library, it was a safe assumption as to where the books came from.

He glanced around the room and noticed a laptop on a small desk. That needed to be studied, but there was no time. Christophe had delivered the book, but it was nowhere to be seen.

Had Ertl taken it with her?

He stepped over to the desk and tested the drawers. Locked. He sat in the chair, found the picks, and easily opened the center drawer.

Inside sat the book.

Perfect. Lady Luck was with him tonight. That previous fumble might now result in a touchdown.

The printed text was all in German, 278 pages, each yellowed from time. On what appeared to be the title page in front was a printed date. 1875. He quickly thumbed through the pages. Nothing written on them anywhere. He returned to the title page. "Tannhäuser und der Sängerkrieg auf Wartburg." Two of the words he recalled from his quick peek into the crypt, whatever they meant. The author was noted as Richard Wagner. On his phone he located Google Translate and learned the words meant "Tannhäuser and the Minnesingers' Contest at Wartburg."

He typed in a search, further learning that *Tannhäuser* was an 1845 opera in three acts, music and text by Wagner, a nineteenth-century German opera composer. It was based on two German legends, Tannhäuser, the mythologized medieval German *Minnesänger* and poet; and the tale of the Wartburg Song Contest. The story centered on the struggle between the sacred and the profane, and redemption through love. Further scanning revealed something much more relevant. Ludwig II was intensely interested in the operas of Richard Wagner. This interest began when Ludwig first saw *Lohengrin* at the impressionable age of fifteen, followed by *Tannhäuser* ten months later. Wagner's operas appealed to the king's fantasy-filled imagination.

Talk about connecting the dots.

He read from the screen a little more.

On May 4, 1864, the 51-year-old Wagner was given an unprecedented audience with Ludwig. Wagner later wrote, "Alas, he is so handsome and wise, soulful and lovely, that I fear that his life must melt away in this vulgar world like a fleeting dream of the gods." Shortly after, Ludwig became Wagner's patron, providing him financial support for over a decade. When Wagner died in 1883 he ordered no music to ever be played in the palaces again and all of the pianos draped in black.

What was so important about this old book?

An awful lot of effort had been expended to obtain it. Surely there were other copies out there somewhere. Why was it necessary to obtain this exact one? He laid the volume out flat and snapped an image of the title page. Thoughts of spies in the movies and on television using a mini camera, clicking off clandestine photographs on some sort of microfilm, came to mind. He smiled at how times had certainly changed.

Now everyone could be a spy.

He rifled through the entire volume and saw no markings anywhere inside except for an embossing on the title page.

A swan.

The bird's form was pressed into the old paper, its neck bisected by two lines. He made several images of that and other random pages, along with the cover. Then he reviewed the photos, satisfied they were clear and readable, and replaced the book in the drawer. Okay. No harm, no foul from the mistakes made earlier at the palace. Sure, having the book itself would be great, but at least they now possessed enough information to move forward. He'd turn it all over to Koger and let the brains at Langley work away.

He rose from the chair and turned for the door.

The front doorknob jiggled.

He froze.

Somebody was testing the lock.

That ain't good.

CHAPTER 15

COTTON DROVE THE CART BACK TO THE PALACE THROUGH the cold. He'd left Derrick Koger at the convent and used the boat he'd commandeered earlier to head across the lake to Herreninsel Island. The night had turned even more biting with a new wave of moisture in the frigid air.

Koger's comment about some sort of last kingdom being in America had intrigued him. What in the world? But Koger had declined to elaborate further, saying all would be made clear in the morning. Since it was late, and he was tired, he'd decided to give that stall a pass.

He followed the same road back to Herrenchiemsee and parked in the rear courtyard. Inside, he climbed the stairs to the second floor and returned to the king's study. Koger had wanted him to take another look at the desk and make sure nothing, in all of the haste, had been left behind. Luckily, no one was around, though he heard voices from somewhere far off inside the building. He took a moment to examine the desk, which contained a gaping hole in its marquetry on the front right side. Definitely some sort of secret compartment. He knew nineteenth-century desks like this often contained hiding places. A trend of their time. Stephanie told him about one in the Smithsonian that had figured into a previous assignment that had taken him to Croatia.

He bent down and stared into the open cavity and spotted metal workings. He reached in and jiggled the rods, which apparently would have released the compartment's door. He saw that when he pulled, one of the drawers also moved.

He stepped to the other side of the desk and noticed the symmetry in design and decoration. The same bulge in the woodwork existed and he wondered if its makers had included a second hiding place. He approached the drawer that had moved on the other side and tested it. Locked. An antique letter opener lay on the desk. Surely some sort of Ludwig II artifact. He had no choice, so he jammed the metal edge of the opener into the tight-fitting crease and heaved.

Nothing.

Two more attempts finally forced the drawer open. But something prevented it from sliding all the way out. He reached in and felt a metal stud protruding down, which seemed spring-loaded. He pressed and the stud pivoted upward, allowing the drawer to be freed from its slot. Farther inside he felt a lever that, when pulled, rattled the metal exposed in the already open cavity. Apparently the intruders, in their rush, had failed to find the concealed release.

Quickly, he pried open the drawer on the other side and discovered a similar stud. He freed that drawer from its slot and yanked on a metal rod. A panel released on the left side of the desk in exactly the same place as the cavity on the other. He stepped close and saw that the compartment contained a small envelope, once white, now faded to yellow. No time to read it at the moment. He was already pushing his luck, so he stole the envelope and slipped it into his back pocket. He then snapped the compartment's panel back down and replaced the drawer.

He then walked downstairs and found the tour group from earlier just inside the Ludwig museum, which filled a portion of the ground floor. He walked over to the camera's owner and offered an apology, which the man seemed to accept. Three hundred euros also eased any hard feelings. The tour guide was there, along with an older man who was introduced as the site administrator.

"What did you do up there?" the man asked in English.

"I tried to prevent a theft."

"I was told you snapped pictures. Did you photograph the thieves?"

He shrugged. "I have no idea. When the guy shot at me, I dropped the camera."

"It wasn't found upstairs."

"Its owner just told me that. The thieves must have taken it."

"Why did *you* take it?"

"I saw what they were doing and decided to get some photos. I thought you might want those."

"Why didn't you tell the guide what was happening?"

He feigned confusion and shrugged. "Heat of the moment. But I didn't think they'd shoot at me."

The edgy little man did not like that explanation.

"The desk that was vandalized," he asked the administrator, "is it valuable?"

"I should say so. It was made for Ludwig II and was

used for many years by his uncle, the prince regent Luitpold, during his time in power and, for a while, by his son King Ludwig III. Eventually, it made its way here in 1920. Where it has stayed. Inviolate. Until tonight."

The man sounded quite agitated.

"What was inside it?" he asked.

"Who are you?" the stodgy little German asked.

"Just a guy who tried to help out."

"Your help made things worse. I need you to stay here, along with everyone else, until the police arrive. They have been called and will have questions."

Like that was going to happen. "Sure. No problem. But why would anyone want to break into that desk?"

"I have no idea. Nothing like this has ever happened before."

Except that it contained both a book and an envelope, two things someone else knew all about. He checked his watch.

Time to go.

"Where is the restroom?" he asked.

And he was directed to a set of doors beyond the museum, out in the palace's main entry foyer. He thanked the man and drifted away from the knot of people, toward the doors. Thankfully, the administrator, tour guide, and the other few palace employees were occupied with the situation.

Which made it easy to leave.

Unnoticed.

Cotton walked back to the dock.

The half-mile trek from the palace through the dark had taken nearly thirty minutes. Across the water he caught the flashing blue lights of a police boat headed toward the island. Thankfully, he'd be long gone by the time it arrived, and cleverly, he'd managed not to mention his name to anyone. He'd also left the desk just as he found it so no one would know there was anything else to find.

Which begged a question.

Were the two with Luke after one, or both, compartments? Their entire attention had been on the right side of the desk. But had he just not allowed them enough time to explore both sides? If so, then Luke would need the envelope.

Which reminded him to read what was in it.

He stood on the dock under one of the pole lights and felt in his pocket for the old envelope, removing a single sheet of brittle paper.

Upon it was writing. In German.

Wo Matthias Die Saiten Streichelt
Edelwei Über Schwarzwald
Kein Wasser Kalt
Predigtstuhl Kruz u. Kranz
Nordost Die Krone
Enden der Tanz
HLNESRNTANME

He silently translated, as he was fluent in German.

Where Matthias Strokes the Strings
Edelweiss Over Black Forest
No Water Cold
Pulpit, Cross, and Garland
Northeast the Crown
Ends of the Dance
HLNESRNTANME

A puzzle.

Great.

And what did the scramble of twelve letters mean at the bottom?

He shook his head and replaced the sheet in the envelope, then slipped it back into his pocket. The words and letters were now ingrained into his mind. He should report the find to Koger. After all, he'd been sent back to make sure there was nothing left behind. But right now he wanted to get back to Munich and a warm hotel room. Some food would be good too. This favor had turned into something much, much larger.

"I have some additional people I want you to talk with tomorrow," Koger had told him right before he left. "I'll set up a meeting in the morning and be in touch with details."

Fine. He'd hand over the envelope then.

He hopped into the boat he'd used earlier and powered off across the lake, away from the approaching police craft. Onshore, he walked past the closed buildings that accommodated tourists who flooded to the Chiemsee in warmer times during the day. More bright pole lights illuminated the concrete path back to the parking lot where the fixtures became fewer and far between. The lot had been about a quarter full when he arrived a few hours ago. Now only a few cars sat scattered across the asphalt. Most likely they belonged to the tour group still waiting at the palace and the few employees.

He approached his rental vehicle and opened the door with the fob. He was just about to climb inside when he felt a sharp blow to the back of his head. Its suddenness caught him off guard, but he quickly recovered and was about to spin around and deal with the attack when another blow brought bright spots before his eyes, dazing him.

A cloth sheathed his face and he smelled a sharp, acrid odor.

Then the world went black.

CHAPTER 16

Luke stood within a small closet.

He'd fled inside as someone knocked a third time on the apartment's door. In the next instant the door was forced upon, splintering the jamb with such force that the lock was wrenched from its mounting. Two men entered. Neither one of whom appeared to be an academic. More the "guys you hire to handle the dirty job" type.

He'd left the closet door cracked open enough to see what was happening. The two newbies began searching, examining the books on the sofa, checking the cushions, stripping the shelves. Crap. The closet would surely be on their agenda. One of the men approached the desk and forced open the drawers, finding the book.

"Is that it?" one of them asked.

The other checked something on his phone, then nodded. "It matches the photo perfectly."

Photo? Matching perfectly? These guys were seriously informed.

One man held a phone with its flashlight activated, while the other opened to the first few pages.

"This is definitely it."

The other guy switched off the light and made a call.

"We got it," the man said into the phone. A pause as the guy listened. "We'll be there."

The call ended.

Luke debated whether to abort the mission, deal with these two, and just take the book. That would also allow him to get his hands on that cell phone, as he'd love to know who was just called.

But stupid moves led to stupid problems.

Like the guy who went fishing and saw a snake with a frog in its mouth swimming in the water. Feeling sorry for the frog, he reached down and gently freed it. Then he felt sorry for the snake, having taken away a tasty meal. So he looked around the boat for some food. Seeing none, he noticed his bottle of bourbon, which he opened and gave the snake a few shots. The reptile accepted the offer, then slithered off. He thought everything was over until ten minutes passed and he heard something knock against the side of the boat. The fisherman looked down in the water and saw the snake was back.

With two frogs this time.

That's what this little venture had turned into.

He watched through the crack in the doorway as the intruders left with the book. The apartment door still hung open, dangling from two of its three hinges; the desk drawer lay open and empty, the place a wreck. Clearly nothing subtle was occurring here. They wanted Christine Ertl, and surely the prince, to know they'd taken the book.

His mind swirled with possibilities.

At times like this he thought of his father. A saint of a man who'd been his idol. He had three older brothers, prophetically named Matthew, Mark, and

John. When he came along Luke completed the four
evangelists. His mother was devoutly religious, his
father not so much. But he still went to church
with her every Sunday, since *that's what husbands do*.
The older he got the more he understood his father's
comment. His mother tolerated hunting and fishing,
which were a year-round obsession in the Daniels
home. So his dad indulged her with religion. Com-
promise and giving.

Both helped with relationships.

His father had never been a man of many words.
But when he did speak, people listened. He recalled
one summer day when he and his father had gone
fishing. They were out on the boat, alone, when he
asked his dad, *"How does this boat float?"*

"Don't rightly know, son."

A little later, he asked, *"How do fish breathe under-
water?"*

"Don't rightly know that either."

A few minutes later. "Why is the sky blue?"

Again, his father said, "Don't know, son."

*Finally, a little frustrated, Luke had said, "Do you
mind me asking all these questions?"*

*His father smiled. "Of course not. If you don't ask
questions, you never learn nothin'."*

He never knew if his father was being funny, serious,
or just trying to tell a noisy kid to hush. He learned a
lot from his father. The most important lesson?

Get the job done.

So he fled the apartment back to ground level and
out into the cold, misty rain. The two intruders were
fifty yards down the street, headed away, walking side
by side with their hands stuffed into coat pockets. He
kept pace as they walked back toward the Altstadt and
its pedestrian-only area. Countless streets from every

angle broke the normal spoke-and-grid pattern seen in most cities. His two targets bypassed the shopping areas and headed toward the entertainment district. Music echoed from the bars and brasseries.

What was happening here?

These were new players. Out of the grandstands and onto the field.

Somebody else was definitely interested in what Prince Stefan was doing. And whoever that was possessed a solid information network since, after all, the book had been stolen from Herrenchiemsee only a few hours ago. How did they know? Easy. A spy lurked within the prince's ranks.

And a close one too.

He glanced at his watch. 9:40 P.M.

The two guys ducked into one of the beer halls.

He followed them inside and his nostrils caught the familiar waft of heady beer. A tall one would hit the spot right now. The two men wove their way through the noisy crowd to a table toward the rear where another man waited for them. Older, with a drawn, tense face, a receding hairline, and a spade of a white beard sharpening otherwise bland features. His gaunt figure looked even thinner in ill-fitting clothes. Everything about the guy reminded Luke of the stereotypical pilgrim.

The two newcomers sat at the table and handed over the book.

Luke angled over closer and motioned to one of the servers for a beer, keeping an occasional eye on his targets. There was so much commotion that it would be impossible to know if anyone was paying attention. The two delivery boys did not linger, rising from the table and leaving.

Pilgrim remained.

The server returned with his beer. He savored a long gulp. Amazing how often the realization that things had gone wrong coincided exactly with their getting worse.

But his father's words rang in his head.

If you don't ask questions, you never learn nothin'.

Damn right.

CHAPTER 17

Stefan was back at Starnberger See.

He'd meant what he'd told his brother. Never would he stop. Half of what he'd attempted had paid off. He had the book.

Now he had to build on that start.

Where Albert occupied part of the Nymphenburg Palace, he preferred the smaller, more intimate family residence that bordered the shores of Starnberg. The lake stretched twenty-five kilometers north to south, its southern shores rising to the distant Alps. The old Berg Castle, where Ludwig II spent his last day alive, was gone, replaced by a simple, unadorned house with a garden and park. It was one of the few properties the Wittelsbachs were allowed to retain after 1918. Now it stood among a cluster of other expensive weekend villas, though the Wittelsbach acreage came fenced, with restricted access. A gate led to a path that paralleled the shore, eventually ending at a votive chapel that had been erected long ago at the spot where Ludwig and von Gudden died. Tourists flooded there every day to photograph the wooden cross standing out in the lake. Thankfully, none of those visitors ever bothered him. Apparently, a modern-day Wittelsbach was of little to no interest.

At least for now.

He motored through the electronic gate and parked. The swishing of the snow under the tires, the throatiness of the engine, even the modest speed at which he'd been forced to drive all conspired to frustrate him. The time was approaching 10:00 P.M. and his day was not done. His appetite for detail, his prodigious memory, his divinations—had all carried him to this point. The moment had come to make things happen and he intended to seize that opportunity despite what had happened at St. Michael's.

He entered the house and headed straight for his study. Brocades, fringes, tassels, and thick rugs smothered the elegance of white wood paneling that still managed to retain its delicacy through peeling paint. The whole place was an abomination, one he intended to raze and rebuild once he became king. Sherry, brandy, and champagne waited on a sideboard in the study beside a tray of Baccarat crystal laden with foie gras and truffles.

He was pleased.

All seemed ready for his guests.

The plan had been to secure the book from Herrenchiemsee, then examine Ludwig's crypt, hopefully finding what had been left there long ago.

"They buried the dead king with such pomp and circumstance," his father said. *"How considerate of them considering that they killed him."*

"Who are they?" Stefan asked with the wonder of a teenager. *"Who killed Ludwig?"*

"The government. His uncle, Luitpold. Bismarck. The people of Bavaria. All of them conspired to end him."

"But only Ludwig and von Gudden went on that

walk," Albert said. "No one else was there. No one knows how they died."

His father smiled. "It's no mystery, son. We like to make it so. But it is no mystery."

Now he was curious. All of his young life he'd heard the tales of how Ludwig had died so conveniently only one day after being deposed. Two men went for a walk and never returned. It had to be murder, right? What else could it have been? How could such a difficult political situation simply eliminate itself at precisely the right moment? It had to have been foul play.

Still—

"How did the king die?" Stefan truly wanted to know.

"It is quite simple," his father said.

And he listened.

The king and von Gudden were walking in the rain. Ludwig was anxious and angry, having been betrayed by his uncle, declared insane by doctors who'd never examined him, and imprisoned by his own government. He'd been helpless when they seized him at Neuschwanstein but now, free along the shores of Starnberger See, he became empowered. So he seized the moment, turned to the older man walking with him, and swung his rolled umbrella, striking von Gudden on the forehead. He then tossed the umbrella onto a nearby bench and began to flee. Von Gudden recovered and tried to stop the escape, grabbing hold of the king's overcoat and jacket, stripping them off as Ludwig rushed toward the lake, turning them inside out. The doctor pursued and grabbed the king again. They both tumbled into the underbrush, but Ludwig was able to break free and plunged into the lake. Von Gudden kept pace and entered the water too. The king struck the doctor in the face, bruising the right eye and scratching him. Von Gudden kept fighting, tearing the nail from his right middle finger in the process. The doctor, dazed from the struggle, *lapsed into unconsciousness and drowned in the cold water. As a young man Ludwig had been a strong swimmer. But being older, overweight, and exhausted from the fight, the cold water overcame him, too, and he drowned.*

It all made sense.

"No murders?" Albert asked. "No plot?"

"I'm afraid not, son. They were both just overcome by their struggle and died."

"So there's no mystery?" he asked.

"Did I say that? Quite the contrary. The mystery is not in Ludwig's death. It's in what happened after."

That it was, Stefan thought.

And quite a mystery it was.

Unfortunately, his father had told him only bits and pieces. Not nearly enough. Apparently, the rest had been *for the duke and his heir*.

A soft tap on the study door brought him back to reality.

One of the house staff entered and told him that his guests had arrived.

"Show them in."

CotTon RESTED IN THE DEPTHS OF BLACKNESS, A whirlpool of lights swirling ever larger, ignoring his subconscious pleas to go away. A voice could be heard, soft at first, growing in volume as the glow grew in brightness. A familiar voice. One that never grew old. Never lost its strength.

Cassiopeia's.

Telling him to wake up.

He opened his eyes to a throbbing ache in his head and the acridity of a strong disinfectant in his nostrils.

Chloroform.

He hated the stuff.

It caused depression of the central nervous system, producing a deep coma and respiratory failure. The mean lethal oral dose for an adult was only 1.6 ounces. Medicine quit using it as an anesthetic because it killed too many people. Even worse, it induced tumors in rats and mice. And the person who'd accosted him felt compelled to use that crap?

He stood from a chilly tile floor, blew the fog out of his mind, and surveyed his surroundings. He was alone inside some sort of cellar, illuminated by several overhead incandescent lights. The space was a large rectangle with a center aisle dividing racked wine bottles on one side from casks and jugs on the other. Most of the bottles were crusted with dust. At the far end a litter of discarded casks, rotted out, perfumed the air with a heavy vinous smell.

Where was he?

He checked his watch. 10:20 P.M.

He'd been out about ninety minutes. Plenty of time to take him to God knows where.

He stood and settled his wobbly legs.

An aching knot at the back of his neck reached all the way to his shoulders, tightening with every breath. He'd been chloroformed a couple of times back in his Magellan Billet days. But that had been a lifetime ago. When he was younger and could take it. He shook more cobwebs from his brain and grabbed control of his senses. He checked his pockets. His wallet and passport were still there, but the envelope he'd found in the desk was gone.

No big surprise.

Thankfully, he still wore his coat, gloves, and scarf. This trip to Bavaria had certainly turned interesting.

Nothing was ever simple. Not his career. His marriage. Fatherhood. All of them came riddled with issues. He was concerned about Luke and, considering what was happening to him, he hoped Frat Boy wasn't in over his head. But Luke had to take care of himself. And Stephanie? She was a big girl too. He couldn't save everyone and everything.

But he sure as hell could try.

He stepped down the center aisle to a short set of wooden steps that led to a wooden door. He was about to head up when he heard a sound from the other side of the door.

Clicks.

Like a key in a lock.

Somebody was coming.

He rushed back to where he'd been laid and stretched back out, his right cheek pressed tightly to the chilly tile floor. From that vantage point he was able to squint his left eye open enough to see a man enter the chamber and bound down the steps.

He lay still.

When the legs came within range he lunged with his outstretched right arm and swept the man's feet out from under him. Then he jabbed the heel of his right hand into the face. His glove cushioned the impact, but a snap signaled a broken nose. Blood poured out. The man clamped a free hand across the flow. Cotton rolled to his feet and sent a kick to the head that ended all resistance. He quickly checked the pockets and found nothing other than a key.

He was on full alert.

What was the old saying?

I was young and foolish then. Now I'm old and foolisher.

Not tonight.

He headed for the exit and stepped out into the cold, locking the door with the key. He gazed up into the black dome of a marvelous near-winter sky and caught the scent of mountain pine in the air. Trees surrounded him, as did snow. He'd definitely climbed in altitude. A cleared path led away from the door, winding upward. The wine cellar had apparently been built from some sort of natural cave. Darkness surrounded him, except for a flickering glow off through the trees.

A fire?

He headed for it.

CHAPTER 18

STEFAN GREETED HIS GUESTS.

The two had traveled from Berlin and busied themselves in Munich all day, giving him time to do what he'd planned. Of course, that had not gone well.

"Guten abend. *Bitte,* come in," he said, keeping his voice jovial.

Julia Maas served as the federal minister for Special Affairs, a title bestowed to the chief of staff for the German Chancellery, a position that provided her both a vote and a voice in cabinet meetings. The current chancellor had come to power through a hastily arranged coalition, one Maas had personally orchestrated. She was here on behalf of the chancellor, as his personal envoy. Peter Scholtz was the current president of the Bundestag, charged with overseeing the federal parliament. He, too, had helped pull together the working coalition. Per the German constitution, the chancellor was selected by the Bundestag, so the current holder of the office also owed his post to Scholtz.

Talk about bought and paid for.

"There is food and drink there on the cart," he said, motioning. "Please help yourselves."

Neither accepted his offer and both sat. Apparently, they wanted to get down to business. Fine. So did he. But first he poured himself a drink.

"Has your day been productive?" Maas asked.

"Absolutely," he said. "We continue to move forward."

"What happened?" Scholtz asked.

He could not tell these two the whole truth. "It went as expected, and my expert is currently examining what we found at Herrenchiemsee. Hopefully, it will lead the way."

Scholtz chuckled. "And I thought I was obtuse. What does that mean? What of *das letzte königreich*? Is the last kingdom real? Or just another Wittelsbach myth associated with Mad King Ludwig."

He allowed the insult of his ancestor to pass. "That remains to be seen. But we found the book exactly where I thought it to be hidden. Now we have to study what we acquired today. But, yes, to answer your question, it seems that *das letzte königreich* is real."

He was posturing, buying time.

But his ancestors had not made this easy.

Luitpold Karl Joseph Wilhelm Ludwig served as prince regent of Bavaria, the de facto ruler, from the removal of Ludwig II in 1886 to Luitpold's death in 1912. Initially, many accused him of the murder of his nephew. But, over the course of his twenty-six-year regency, he overcame by modesty and ability all of that initial uneasiness and became quite popular. Ever so slowly he transferred Bavarian interests into those of the German Empire and pointed the country toward parliamentary rule. He'd also transformed Munich into a cultural center. His legacy remained in the many streets, towns, and institutions named after him. Even a pastry, the *prinzregententorte*, a multi-layered cake with chocolate buttercream, had been created in his honor.

"Luitpold may have left us a true gift," he said. "Not so much one at the time of his death in 1912. But one much more important now."

"You still have not fully answered the question," Scholtz said. "Where do we stand?"

He caught the hint of irritation in the man's voice. True, the day had not turned out as planned, and normally, he'd hold things close. But he also had to keep these two powerful politicians satisfied. Without them, nothing would happen. So he told them what he definitely knew.

"Luitpold used the desk, on display at Herrenchiemsee, for many years. It has long been known within our family that he may have also used it as a secret repository. My father hinted to that many times. I now know that information to be correct. The book was there."

He paused a moment and sipped his drink.

"Luitpold spent his life protecting both Ludwig and Otto. He felt it his duty as their uncle. Otto was certified insane and institutionalized, though he was officially king for twenty-six years after Ludwig II died. To his credit, Luitpold never allowed the people to forget King Otto. He did the same for Ludwig. He was the one who opened Herrenchiemsee, Neuschwanstein, and Linderhof for public tours, allowing the people to see what Ludwig II had created. That shows respect. So it is logical to assume that he may have preserved what Ludwig had wanted most."

"*Das letzte königreich?*"

He nodded. "And we now have what the regent left behind."

"Which is?" Maas asked.

He waved off the inquiry. "I prefer to hold those details to myself. After all, this is a Bavarian endeavor."

Maas shook her head. "Hardly. We are in this together, as is the chancellor. We all have vested interests here. And they all turn on the success of whatever it is *you* are doing."

"I am solving a mystery that is a hundred and thirty-five years old," he said. "A mystery that has been a part of my family since the death of Ludwig II, which happened right out there"—he motioned to the window—"on the Starnberger See. This is not something easily accomplished. There are obstacles, placed there intentionally. But I shall get by them."

"Do you really think the people here want to be separate from Germany?"

He did. With all his heart.

Between 1862 and 1871, Otto von Bismarck used a combination of persuasion, strategy, skill, and war to create the Second Reich, ruled by a kaiser. Bavaria had been swept up in that German nationalistic fervor and Ludwig II signed off on a document that brought his kingdom into the union, all while preserving much of its eight-hundred-year-old independence. After the German defeat in World War I, all that vanished and the cursed Weimar Republic was declared. Bavaria became a part of that when Ludwig III, Luitpold's son, walked away from his crown. Ever since, Bavaria's identity had been tied to Germany. Sometimes with disastrous results. Nazism had been born here. Hitler called it home. The land was eventually ravaged and bombed to oblivion over its loyalty to a führer. He admired Bismarck, though. Hard not to. One of the geniuses of European history, and mainly because he'd known when to stop. None of the German leaders after him shared that insight. But he would. First, though, he had to make Bavaria a kingdom once again.

"The people will vote overwhelmingly to secede," he said. "Every poll shows that a clear two-thirds favor that move."

Scholtz stood and approached the cart with the drinks and food. The head of the German parliament poured himself a splash of brandy and sampled the foie gras.

"My compliments to your chef," Scholtz said.

He wasn't interested in platitudes. "I will deliver exactly what you want and you will give me what I want. My brother will die of his cancer, and I will become king of Bavaria."

Maas seemed unimpressed. "Just don't take too long, or this deal is off. Time is critical."

Scholtz enjoyed some of the truffles. "That means in the next three days. After that, we will be moving to another route to satisfy our benefactors."

That was news. Three days? "This is the first I have heard of a deadline."

"First we learned of it too," Maas said. "But those benefactors want immediate results. As do we. The politics here are volatile. Our ruling coalition in the Bundestag is shaky, at best. We can hold it together, but that will take some outside assistance. If we can't deliver, those benefactors will make a deal with others. One that does not include us or you. And we will all not get what we want." She paused. "They set the three-day deadline, not us."

He gazed into the drink like a fortune-teller reading tea leaves, looking for insight. Three months he'd been preparing, ever since first learning of Albert's terminal illness. He'd made the best use of the limited information he possessed, hoping to learn more. But he needed more time.

"My path is the fastest and quickest way to achieve all of our goals," he said. "Make that clear to our benefactors."

"Just get it done," Scholtz said. "In the next three days."

CHAPTER 19

Luke harbored a great admiration for Germans. They were a people who loved to have a good time without shame or regret. Each stein of beer they downed seemed a reminder of the bygone glories of royal Bavaria, kaisers remembered, and wars forgotten. Within merriment, Munich, and all of Germany, seemed to forget its troubled past.

He stared around at the revelers, most with a stein clasped in one hand while endlessly gesturing with the other. The hall, colorfully decorated in the old German style, reeked with atmosphere thanks to dark paneling and leaded glass. Two huge, green-tiled stoves in the far corners caught the glow of several immense wrought-iron chandeliers. He sat at one of the long wooden tables and kept watch on the man with the pilgrim beard. He'd also ordered a broiled bratwurst with sauerkraut. A portion of the hall had been cleared of tables for a dance floor and a brass band shook the rafters. Many of the patrons kept time with the music by banging their glasses on the tables.

He joined in.

The gaiety mounted higher and higher, offering plenty of distractions.

He watched Pilgrim as the older man paged through the book. Who was this guy? Who were the other two? Movement caught his eye. Up toward the ceiling.

A bird flying across the vaults, trapped inside.

Huh?

Where he grew up superstitions were a part of life. His grandmother had been a big proponent. She lived in Blount County, Tennessee, as did all of his family on both sides. Once he was visiting her on a warm August evening when a bird flew through an open window into the house and flittered around until they were able to shoo it back outside.

But his grandmother became really upset.

He had no idea why, but she finally told him, *If a bird flies into your house, it's a sign there'll be a death in the family real soon.* He'd been no more than nine or ten and the seriousness on her wizened face, and the danger in her words, had scared him. Later, when he told his mother what happened she'd said, *It's just an old woman's silliness.*

But his great-uncle died a week later.

So he made a point to learn more of the superstitions handed down through the generations. *If you tell a bad dream before breakfast, it'll come true. Petting a calico cat brings good luck. If the bottom of your right foot itches, you're about to take a trip. It's bad luck to kill a ladybug.* And one that always drove him crazy. *A way to tell if the mother or father is the boss is to look at their toes. If the one next to the big toe is longer, that's the boss.* He'd studied both his parents' feet and determined that neither one of them was the boss.

Yes, it was all crap.

But it was the kind of crap that stuck with you.

To this day the hair on the back of his neck always rose when he heard a dog howling mournfully in the night.

He watched the bird and could hear that dog.

Something was up.

Big-time.

Pilgrim seemed comfortable at his table. He decided to follow his father's advice and start asking questions, zeroing in on one of the servers whose majestic natural endowment was something to be admired. Definitely a looker. He'd noticed that when the other two guys left, she'd talked with both for a few moments. Time for some of that country boy charm.

He rose from his bench and headed for her. She was busy taking orders from rowdy patrons. He waited until she headed back toward the kitchen and approached her.

"Excuse me," he said over the revelry.

The woman stopped and turned around.

She was pretty and knew it with golden hair and hazel eyes. Perfect teeth and creamy skin further testified to a healthy life.

"I'm afraid my German is really bad," he said. "I hope your English is better."

She tossed him a smile. "My English is quite good. And who are you?"

He handed her a hundred-euro note. "Someone who needs a little education. I was hopin' you could help me."

She swept the money from his fingers. "What do you want to know?"

"The two guys you talked to earlier. The ones who were sittin' with that older guy, there, with the beard."

"That's Frederick," she said. "He comes here all the time."

"And who might Frederick be?"

"You with the police?"

"How many policemen offer you a hundred euros?"

And he tossed her one of his trademarked million-dollar smiles, which rarely let him down.

"I'd still like to know who you are."

"Jonathan Smith."

She glared at him with suspicious eyes. "All right, Herr Smith. Frederick is one of the black robes. The other two who were there with him are black robers too."

"What are black robers?"

"They're a strange lot. The Guglmänner."

A new word. "Can you translate that for me?"

She seemed to enjoy his ignorance. But a hundred euros had to buy him a full explanation.

"*Gugl* is an old word for 'hood.' They wear black robes with pointy hoods. Men bitter about everything."

She motioned for him to follow her across the hall. He'd not paid much attention to the pictures on the walls that lined the hall. Large black-and-white images of German life. He'd thought them just innocuous prints, there for show, but now he saw them to be enlarged photographs. Blondie led him to one on the far side, near the alcove for the restrooms. An image of black-robed men, in pointed hoods, marching down a street, carrying torches.

Like the damn Ku Klux Klan.

CHAPTER 20

COTTON WORKED HIS WAY THROUGH THE DARK underbrush, weaving a path across patchy snow and around thick tree trunks, careful with his steps as the hard earth was seamed with slabs of slippery rock. He snaked his way clear of the snatching brambles and began a leopard crawl up a slight rise. A near-winter wind whipped through the naked branches with a lonely primordial moan. A shrouded moon offered no useful light. His breath came in puffy blue clouds and he kept his attention ahead on what he now saw was a blazing fire, the flames licking high into the night air.

He approached closer and spotted silhouettes near the flames, off to one side. Shadows? No. Six people wearing black robes with pointed hoods. His mind floated back to images from the early twentieth century and other men gathered around burning crosses. But their robes and hoods had been white.

What was this?

The figures were huddled together in seeming conversation, but he caught only the faintest burble of voices. It seemed a friendly exchange of words, most muted by the wind. He huddled in a copse of birch trees, obscured by the dark foliage. The fire continued to rage, confined to its circular stone hearth, crackling with life. The cold air was clearing his head of the chloroform.

He'd been brought here for a reason.

Time to find out what that might be.

The six figures left the fire and headed off into the darkness. He slipped from the woods and followed, finding a path that wound through the trees and up another short incline. Snow lined its edges. Tree limbs rattled overhead, jiggling in the cold wind and raining bits of snow down on him. He passed an intersection for another route and concluded that it probably led back to the wine cave. Ahead, he spotted lights and realized they were headed for a house.

No. Not a house.

A castle.

Round towers. A portcullis and drawbridge over a dry moat. The crenellated walls battlemented with arrow slits, all visible from floodlights that illuminated towering stone walls. Once, long ago, a retainer's village would have clustered to them like barnacles, dependent on the castle for protection in time of invasion. The six robed figures disappeared through the open main gate. He stayed back and followed, crossing the stone bridge, keeping to the shadows, careful with the crunch of his own footfalls on the snow.

He entered a courtyard.

A battery of spotlights lit the pavement. Cantilevered galleries and wall-walks encircled, all with neat and orderly woodwork. The figures entered the main building through a lighted doorway. Soft lights twinkled in many of the windows. He decided it best not to follow them there. So he scampered off to the right, down a short alley between the outer walls and inner buildings where firewood was piled high in tight rows. Tarnished copper downspouts and gutters fit right in with the ancient slates and dark dormers of the steep roof.

He was unsure as to any of this, but decided that he had no choice but to investigate. Whoever *they* were could have simply taken the envelope and left him in the parking lot back at the Chiemsee. Instead, they'd gone to the trouble of bringing him along. He also had to admit he was curious about those black-robed figures. So he kept moving down the darkened alley, his eyes surveying everything around him, until he spotted a door.

He tested the latch. Open.

He stepped inside to warm air and a lit corridor that led straight into a roomy kitchen. At its middle, below an iron ceiling rack of copper pots and pans, stood a large butcher's block. An array of knives protruded from a chunk of hardwood. He selected the largest, satisfied that its edges were more than amply sharp, and kept moving.

Back toward the front of the castle he noticed the luxury of space, along with the high ceilings, old-world chandeliers, rich floorings. The pale yellow walls were covered in old-style German paintings along with coats of arms and figures from legendary times. If not for the circumstances, he would have been captivated by the ambience. He loved the Middle Ages. Perhaps his favorite time in history. Not a period in which he would have wanted to live, but definitely interesting to study. He wondered where the six robed men had gone. No sign of them anywhere among the many doors, passageways, and niches. Not a sound disturbed the troubling silence. He stopped at

a junction of two dim hallways. One led farther back
into the ground floor, the other to a set of double doors
where shadows played across the light that leaked out
from beneath.

Finally.

People.

He approached the doors, careful with his steps,
but the stone floor did not reveal his presence. Now
what? Nothing ventured, nothing gained. So he readied the knife, turned the lever, and pushed the paneled
door inward.

A sole man occupied the room.

"Please, come in, Herr Malone. I've been waiting.
We need to speak."

LUKE RETURNED TO HIS BEER, BRATWURST, AND
sauerkraut. He also found his phone and searched the
word *Guglmänner*.

Like Blondie had said, it meant "hooded mourners." Famous in the Middle Ages for accompanying
funerals. The latest incarnation seemed nothing more
than a bunch of young men obsessed by the reputation
of Ludwig II, builder of fairy-tale castles, patron of
Richard Wagner, and one of the last kings of an independent Bavaria. The Guglmänner were convinced
that Ludwig had been murdered in 1886, according
to them shot twice in the back by Otto von Bismarck's
secret agents.

He had to admit, it had a Hollywoodesque vibe to it.

As their story went, Ludwig never wanted to be
part of Bismarck's newly formed German Empire.
Instead, in 1871, he was forced into the union because
of the war Bavaria lost against Austria. Supposedly,

at the time of his death, Ludwig was working against the empire, secretly negotiating with France to set Bavaria free again. So Bismarck ordered his death. Of course, no proof was offered to back up any of those claims. But fanatics had never required much in the way of evidence.

Blind faith was their mantra.

The Guglmänner also seemed to know how to stage a good publicity stunt. He found more pictures of them, from a few years back, marching through Munich carrying flaming torches. Once they sank balloons into Lake Starnberg printed with the slogan "It Was Murder." They also actively lobbied for a Bavarian euro coin featuring Ludwig, rather than Germany's eagle, saying the current coins were far too Prussian. Recently, they went high-tech on YouTube and released a fifteen-minute documentary that supposedly explained the true circumstances of Ludwig's death. The thing had over a half million views. To the Guglmänner Bavaria remained independent, outside of Germany, blessed with its own parliament, and it should be allowed to go its own way.

Seemed like a bunch of nuts.

Except for the fact that one of their own now possessed the book and they'd known all about both its existence and its whereabouts.

Prince Stefan would not be happy.

He enjoyed more of his food and beer.

And mulled over his options.

Decision, decisions.

COTTON STEPPED INTO THE COZY ROOM WHERE A FIRE raged inside a stone hearth. Heavy embroidered curtains lined with gold trim bordered tall windows. Bookcases filled one wall. Its owner apparently loved antiques. They were everywhere—chairs, tables, accessories, lamps, and desk. Clearly, no interior designer had cobbled this room together. No. This was a personal statement crafted by the castle's owner. He noticed an LED monitor on the desk, the screen split into four images, one of which was the wine cave where the man he'd taken down still lay.

"I do hope you didn't hurt him," his host said.

"It might leave a mark or two."

"It's his own fault. I told him to be careful. But it was exciting to see you in action."

He stared around, trying to gauge just exactly what he'd managed to get himself into. Paintings dotted the stucco walls. Monks in prayer, lords and ladies, the archangel Michael with his sword directing anxious wayfarers to heaven. A finely carved cabinet was filled with a collection of colorful drinking steins. Not everything was a period piece, yet it all fit. A mahogany clock with brass movements read 10:50 P.M.

"Is that my knife?" the man asked.

"I borrowed it. Hope you don't mind."

"Not at all. If it makes you more comfortable to hold it, then please do."

"Who are you?"

"My name is Marc Fenn."

"Is that supposed to mean something to me?"

"I am the grand master of the Guglmänner."

"And what is that?"

"Ah, the better question, Herr Malone, is *why* is that?"

CHAPTER 21

STEFAN FELT NO AFFECTION FOR THE HOUSE BESIDE Starnberger See. It bore zero connection to the Wittelsbachs, other than rising from land they'd owned for centuries.

But the lake was different.

It possessed a soul that had always affected the family's spirit, its waters a picture of peace and tranquility. The strongest wind barely ruffled its placid surface or disturbed what lay deep at the bottom of its heart.

Just like his family.

Ludwig II had loved the lake. Rose Island, the only splotch of land upon it, had been his favorite place. The king had spent a lot of time renovating and remodeling a small villa there into a refuge. The first rose blossoms came around mid-June, the second around mid-August, each lasting about a month, casting the tiny spit of land into a blaze of color. It was one of the few places Ludwig had felt truly at ease.

A place for him.

Fitting, it seemed, that he would die not far away.

He stood in the study and stared out at the dark water. The house, though dismal, offered the perfect base of operations. Not far from Munich, but sufficiently isolated to allow him to come and go without attention. His wife and daughters stayed at his upper Bavarian estate, deep in the Alps, not far from the Austrian border. His wife shunned the spotlight, preferring to live a solitary life, homeschooling their daughters. Surely she knew about his many dalliances. But, being the lady that she was, and reflecting the breeding that came from a long German heritage, she had never broached the subject with him.

She would make a good queen.

Quiet. Dignified. Satisfied.

He'd build her a castle.

Maybe he'd finally erect Falkenstein. At forty-one hundred meters, it was once Germany's highest castle. First erected in the thirteenth century, it had been razed four hundred years later. Ludwig II purchased the property in 1883, three years before he died, intent on replacing the ruin with a romantic castle in a dramatic, High Gothic style. Plans had been drawn, but the king died before work began and the site remained a ruin to this day. Thankfully, Ludwig's grand idea had survived, including drawings of the massive stained glass windows and Byzantine-like mosaic dome. It would make the perfect residence for Bavaria's new queen. The other three castles at Herrenchiemsee, Linderhof, and Neuschwanstein would remain the revenue producers that they were. Millions of euros came in from them every year, thanks to a horde of tourists. And every kingdom needed income. Falkenstein would be their private retreat, becoming the official summer residence of the Bavarian royal family.

God bless Ludwig II.

His great, great relative had possessed far more

sense than history bestowed upon him. He resented the label "mad," as his guests had liked to use earlier. Ludwig was far from crazy. More intuitive in a way his contemporaries could not understand.

Especially with how he dealt with the last kingdom. What a grand idea.

"Tell me, von Löher. What did you find this time?" Ludwig asked. "Do I have a new kingdom?"

I had just returned from another long journey. My first, two years earlier, in 1873, had taken me to Spain, the Canary Islands, along the northern coast of Africa to Constantinople, then to the Greek and Turkish islands. I closely inspected many differing sites, dealing with legal issues involved with any proposed acquisition, trying to pry vital information from suspicious people without revealing my mission. Along the way I'd endured unreliable steamships, horrible food, and terrible weather. Once, to not miss a boat, I traveled by horseback for fourteen hours across volcanic mountains, which I endured without complaining.

On Tenerife I found a place called El Palmas on the higher part of the island, a lonely area, covered with woodlands, but cultivable. The heights afforded a magnificent ocean view, the likes of which I'd never seen. A villa, belonging to an Englishman, was perfectly situated and handsomely appointed. Another, belonging to a marquess, was even more suitable. But neither was for sale, and the Canary Islands being a Spanish province meant that Spain would have to approve any transfer of land, which seemed unlikely.

On Samothrace among the Greek islands I found hot springs and the ruins of a Christos monastery. A vista of shrubland and trees, enlivened by the presence of finches, thrushes, and nightingales, stretched out from the shores. Woodland streams, like those found in the Alps, gushed to the sea. But the island was under Turkish control and the ruling regime was both lethargic and brutal.

When I made my first report in August 1873, I noted that the king should visit any prospective site before making a decision. But I also realized the impossibility of that happening. This whole undertaking is so full of novelty that, as soon as the tiniest hint of it leaked out, not only the German but also the foreign press would seize upon it with loud cries and lengthy pronouncements. Opportunistic entrepreneurs would thrust themselves forward. The acquisition of land and the entire project would be rendered much more difficult and costly. Yet, I must say, it remains an intoxicating idea, offering the precise combination of romanticism and fantasy that attracted people to life and ultimately sustained them. I am honored to be a part.

My latest expedition had been much more expansive, taking me to South America and the Pacific islands, all places I had never visited. Being a man in my mid-fifties, this type of adventure was arduous, to say the least, but I have endured the travel with remarkable good humor. On my return, in October 1875, I met with His Majesty, who told me about his own latest endeavor. In 1873, he'd bought Herreninsel Island, which lay on the Chiemsee, but only recently had started construction of something new.

"It will be my temporary new kingdom," Ludwig told me. "Isolated and protected. There will be paths, carriageways, even a railroad leading from the palace to the dock. The palace itself will be a copy of Versailles, only larger, better. The finest craftsmen in Europe will create it. Hedges and gardens will hide its walls until it suddenly appears with paths crossing grand avenues and canals. There will be orchards, pastures, and views of the mountains to the south. Belts of marshland overgrown with reeds will extend outward from the shore, adding further protection. Flora and fauna will grow everywhere. Can you just see it, in all its glory?"

I actually could.

"My dream will at least be partially real," the king said. "But tell me, von Löher, of your journey."

I recounted that nothing suitable was located on the southern continent. That land is wild and untamed, its politics highly volatile. But once leaving South America, rounding Cape Horn and heading north into the Pacific Ocean, I found a set of islands of unimaginable beauty. The British, French, Russians, Japanese, and, more recently, the Americans had battled for control of them. Once they were a loose confederation that fought among themselves. But, in 1810, a conqueror arose among them and suppressed all rebellion, proclaiming himself king. Over the reign of six monarchs since, all his descendants, the islands had slowly emerged into the Industrial Age. But their independence and cultural identity were threatened by greedy and powerful men, immigrants who control the economy and want the land brought within America's sphere.

On my visit, we anchored in a calm bay of turquoise-colored water. The mountainous landscape was heavily dotted with grass huts and carefully tended agricultural plots. We were greeted by long canoes paddled by a handsome, swarthy people who were friendly and welcoming. Europeans first visited nearly a hundred years ago when an Englishman, Captain James Cook, laid claim to what he called the Sandwich Islands. They are currently ruled by a man named David Kalākaua. The famous American writer Mark Twain wrote nine years ago that

> David Kalākaua, who at present holds the office of King's Chamberlain, is a man of fine presence, is an educated gentleman and a man of good abilities. He is conservative, politic and calculating, makes little display, and does not talk much in the legislature. The current king, Kamehameha V, has the power to appoint his successor. If he does such a thing, his choice will probably fall on Kalākaua.

Yet it had not. Kamehameha V died without naming a successor. According to the local constitution it fell to the legislature to choose a king, and they picked another man. But he died just over a year later without naming an heir either. In 1874, Kalākaua was chosen. From my personal observations Twain was correct in his assessment of a younger version. This is a wise and learned monarch.

Stefan laid the narrative aside.

It was from the journal of Fredric von Löher, composed in 1889. Thankfully, his great-grandfather long ago had kept a copy, as the Americans had pilfered Bavaria's secret state archives in 1945, taking whatever they wanted, including the original journal. It was probably now stashed away in some government records vault. Perhaps even the one still located in Bavaria and maintained by the United States. That, of course, would end when he assumed the throne. He'd toss the Americans out and, to return the favor, would retake possession of everything they had on file.

And why not?

Most of it had belonged to his family to start with.

His two German visitors were gone. Good riddance. He despised politicians. Churchill had been right. *A politician needs the ability to foretell what is going to happen tomorrow, next week, next month, and next year. And to have the ability afterwards to explain why it didn't happen.*

He shook his head. Three days.

That's all he had.

And Ludwig's tomb was empty. His brother no help at all. Thankfully, stealing the book from Herrenchiemsee had worked out.

He sat in his study and nursed another whiskey.

What he really needed was some companionship. But this day was about over. Going out was not an option. And never would he bring any of his women-for-hire here. A buzz disturbed the silence. His phone. He found the unit and noted the caller.

Christine Ertl.

He answered and listened to her excited voice as she told him the book was gone, her apartment burglarized.

Finally, something had gone right.

CHAPTER 22

DERRICK REENTERED THE CHARLES HOTEL. HE'D STAYED here simply because Prince Stefan had occupied one of the larger upper-floor suites. His room, a modest forty square meters, sat on the third floor. But it came with an impressive view of the park just beyond the hotel.

Stefan would have no idea anyone was watching him, nor would he know Derrick or his position with the United States government. From all of the intel collected on this ambitious Wittelsbach, Stefan von Bayern seemed an arrogant narcissist who thought himself far smarter than anyone around him. Apparently the complacency that came from being the second born in a former royal family bred a level of indifference that obliterated good judgment. Regardless, he'd been told that Stefan had checked out hours ago.

It was all up to Luke Daniels now.

Thankfully, few people knew much of anything about *das letzte königreich*.

The last kingdom remained one of those mysteries from another time that survived World War II and stayed hidden thanks to a classified designation. The CIA, in its infancy, back in the late 1940s and into the 1950s, had dealt with it for a while, then abandoned all further efforts, focusing instead on overthrowing governments and assassinating anybody that stood in America's way. The agency had been like the Wild West, doing pretty much anything to anyone, until 1961 and the disastrous Bay of Pigs, when their mission statement was altered, their charter forever changed. New laws restricted what they could and could not do. The freewheeling days ended and the march to the beat of a new drummer began.

Everyone forgot about the last kingdom.

But that did not mean it ceased to exist. Like a million other secrets, it languished within files long locked away. Derrick had tried to gain access to the American archive in Bavaria through a contact, a month back, but all of the information he'd received came heavily redacted. Further attempts had been thwarted by Langley.

So he was, in essence, flying blind here.

He took the elevator to the third floor and found his room. He was waiting on a report from Luke as to what happened at St. Michael's. With midnight approaching, the call was actually overdue. That second boat out on the Chiemsee was still giving him concern, and he'd already dispatched two assets to find out what they could, especially what happened to its occupants.

He'd never liked the unexpected.

He worked long hours as routine, always a hundred details on his mind. The political appointees above him rarely grasped more than a fraction of what was happening, and they always seemed to focus only on what *they* regarded as important. But it all mattered.

And if intelligence work were a cult requiring devotion and sacrifice, then he was one of its spiritual leaders. Normally, he worked out of a nondescript office building in Brussels in a space that was sparse, old, and unpretentious. Tonight he was in the field. On the move. Making things happen. Staying awake on a cocktail of caffeine and adrenaline.

Which he loved.

Thankfully, Malone was on board. He'd given the retiree some crap back at the convent. But truth be told, he admired professionals who knew how to get the job done. And Cotton Maloney could certainly do that. They would talk first thing in the morning, and he had some people Malone needed to meet. After that, he'd turn the man loose and hope for the best.

He stepped over to the phone and found the room service menu. He was hungry. The day was over. A new one about to begin. Luckily, the Charles offered a delicious late-night selection. He was about to place an order when his cell phone buzzed. No number appeared on the screen. Only a code. One he knew. From the deputy national security adviser.

Trinity Dorner.

He answered.

"I thought you might like to know that I've been appointed the next director of the National Counterterrorism Center."

An odd way to start a conversation, so he took the bait. "The president made a good choice."

That meant she would be heading the national clearinghouse for intelligence on terroristic threats.

"I thought so too," she said. "What are you doing in Germany?"

The direct question reflected her reputation for no nonsense. Trinity Dorner was a striking woman with steel blue eyes, long dark hair, little sense of humor, and a penchant for avoiding small talk. She was an accomplished listener, thinker, and watcher, not only hearing what people said but deciphering things they didn't even know they were saying. She was an expert at political weather forecasting, practical and pragmatic, attuned to the slightest change in the breeze. Her stoicism was legendary. During briefings she'd always sat in the back of the room, out of the way, so nondescript that people who didn't know her would ask afterward, *Who was that other one in the back?* So many asked the same question that the tag stuck.

The other one. TOO.

Truth be known she liked the nickname, but true to her nature she never expressed an opinion one way or the other. She shunned politics, covert ties, or anything remotely related to bias. The fact that she'd led with a compliment to herself seemed meaningful. She was sending him a message. *I'm leaving. Don't screw with me.*

So he gave it to her straight. "The Chinese are here."

Silence on the other end. He could almost hear her analytical mind processing.

"Doing what?"

"Making a deal with the Germans. And the Germans are making a deal with the Bavarians. Neither one of which is good for us."

More silence. More processing. She'd never ask him if he was sure, knowing he would not have said so if he wasn't.

"We're aware of some of this," she finally said. "The White House told the CIA to stand down sixty days ago, as other people would be handling it."

Other people? That was news.

More honesty. "Langley did stand down." He paused. "I didn't."

"Are you actually going to fall on your sword for this one?"

"I prefer not to, but will if need be."

"Remember what happened the last time you did that."

"So good of you to remind me."

"Somebody has to."

Maybe so. But he still didn't like to hear it.

"Derrick, you're at the end of your time. We both know you're not going to Langley. You're divorced. No kids. No life. What are you going to do once your career is over?"

He had no idea.

"Take some advice from an old friend. Don't make it end sooner than it needs to."

That was a lot of words for TOO.

This was indeed serious.

"They have to be stopped," he said. "You know that."

"I do. But, like I said, others have this. The CIA was ordered to stay out of Germany's affairs. Bad enough what Danny Daniels did a few months back. The president was furious."

"This is different."

"How so?"

"I have someone on the inside. I can make this happen."

More silence.

"You're leaving me no choice," she said. "The president will have to be informed." She paused. "And you recruited Cotton Malone."

"You have eyes and ears right on me, don't you?"

"It's the name of the game."

That pissed him off. "Tell who you want."

"I plan to do just that."

He'd always liked her. She was a savvy player. And never stupid.

"I called as a courtesy to our friendship," she said. "My time here at the White House is ending."

"You can't look after me anymore?"

"Something like that. You're a big, giant pain in the ass. But you're also usually right. I'll be back to you shortly."

"Can I keep going?"

"That's your call. As you say, this one is all on you."

"I'm prepared to take the hit."

"And, if you're successful, somebody else will take all the credit."

The call ended.

He stood in the room and stared out the window. At least everyone's cards were on the table. No more surprises. TOO was right, though. He had no life other than work. His wife left him fifteen years ago, tired of excuses and living alone. They'd tried to have kids, but no luck. Something with his sperm count, and he'd been too busy to put in the extra effort needed to compensate. Which only added to her growing resentment. Jody was a good woman and deserved better. She remarried quickly and now had a daughter. He was happy for her. But him? He was a career spy, caught in the middle of a political vise.

So what else was new?

His phone buzzed again.

He recognized the incoming number and answered.

"We need to speak," the male voice said. "Now."

"Go ahead, speak."

"In person."

"Tell me where and when."

CHAPTER 23

COTTON SAT IN A COMFORTABLE LEATHER CLUB CHAIR. He owned one himself back in his apartment in Copenhagen, among the few things he'd brought with him when he resigned from the Magellan Billet and moved from Georgia to Denmark. That shift had been a clean break. One life left behind, another looming on the horizon. He'd purposefully brought along as little as possible. Foolishly, he'd thought the past would leave him behind. But he'd come to learn that the past never stopped coming. The trick was to learn how to deal with its relentlessness. He'd fought it at first, trying to resist, but the past never took no for an answer.

His host sat relaxed in another club chair. A dapper middle-aged man with short, iron-gray hair brushed straight back exposing a broad, dignified brow. A mustache and goatee framed the face, the jaw bold, the eyes soft, the skin reflecting the rosy color of good living. He'd decided the knife was unnecessary and laid it on a side table.

"Do you like my home?" Marc Fenn asked.

He stared around at the general atmosphere of

genteel dignity that definitely belonged to another time. "Hard not to like a castle."

"It dates from the thirteenth century but, contrary to its look, it was never a fortified locale, more a *ritterschloss*."

Knight's castle, he silently translated.

"Its last noble owner died a long time ago, leaving no heirs. Sadly, all this fell into decay and ruin and squatters occupied it. Can you imagine? A century of wind and weather had its way. Then I came along."

"Lucky for this place."

"My thought exactly. I am a connoisseur of collecting. Objets d'art. Antiques. Books. Paintings. My former house outgrew my obsession, so I bought a location large enough to hold all my treasures. I also gave it a name."

He waited.

"Charmantes Schloss."

Charming Castle.

"Do you like it?" Fenn asked.

"So far, so good. Though I could have done without the tour of the wine cave."

"I do apologize for that. But I am so glad you like this place. I planned it all down to the finest detail and personally supervised the renovation."

"A man of means, I assume."

"Of course. Of course. I have a great deal of money."

"And lots of people in your employ."

Fenn waved off the observation. "They are not in my employ. Quite the contrary. Instead, we are bound in a brotherhood, loyal to ourselves, each other, and our fallen king."

He recalled Koger had said that he needed to talk to some people in the morning. "Are you working with the CIA?"

"Did Herr Koger mention me?"

"Hardly. He just said there's some additional help coming my way."

"Quite right. That was to happen tomorrow. But, after what you found at the palace, I decided that now would be better."

"Your man could have simply asked."

"Oh, now what fun would that have been. Far more interesting to bring you here surreptitiously, then watch you perform. It was marvelous. Quite a show. I was enthralled."

Hard to peg this guy. Was he just weird or acting? "Any chance you might enlighten me as to what the hell's going on?"

Fenn chuckled. "It can sometimes be quite confusing to enter the theater late in the second act."

"You could say that." He glanced around the room again. "Let's start with those black-robed men I saw."

"I was hoping you would find your way to the fire. They are part of the Guglmänner. I have many brothers at my disposal."

"I can see you're really proud about all that, but you're going to have to tell me, what is the Guglmänner?"

"Five hundred years ago it was a German tradition for men in pointed hoods and black robes to accompany the dead to their graves as living symbols of death. It was regarded as a great honor if the black hoods chose to walk with your coffin. There are paintings and books with sketches that show them quite clearly. In 1886, a delegation of black-cowled figures marched in Ludwig II's funeral procession, each holding crossed lances and carrying the royal coat of arms. It was they who adopted the name and look of the medieval version, and re-formed into a new brotherhood, devoting themselves to Ludwig *to the last and beyond*." Fenn paused. "He was murdered, you know."

"And you have evidence? That point has been debated for a long time."

"I find that when someone dies at precisely the right moment they need to die, suspicions are in order. Interestingly, the cause of death was left blank on his autopsy. Why do you suppose that was? Nearly all of the documents related to what happened when Ludwig was deposed were destroyed. Even the king's watch, found on his body, which noted the time it stopped in the water, disappeared, never to be seen again. One thing that has survived was what a Prussian envoy, who was there and helped with the search for the body, wrote. He noted clear marks of strangulation on von Gudden's neck." Fenn shrugged. "But, you are right, who knows? The fact is, Ludwig's death suited all of the political powers around him. His disgruntled ministers. His family. His uncle, the prince regent. And above all, Bismarck, who had cause to doubt Ludwig's loyalty to the German Empire."

Granted, the problem of a forcibly deposed king, popular with the people, had resolved itself within one day with a timely death

But murder?

"History tells us that everyone around Ludwig was Reich-friendly," Henn said. "His ministers, and the government as a whole, wanted a close relationship with Bismarck. But Ludwig was always against Bavaria losing its identity to a unified Germany. That uncertainty became a real danger for Bismarck. He had no intention of losing the federation he had so painstakingly cobbled together. Shortly before he was deposed, Ludwig wrote that 'this wretched German Empire is gradually but surely moving towards barbarism.' So his intent was clear. He wanted out. But Bismarck could not allow that to happen."

Fenn seemed to believe every word he was uttering.

"Of course, it is difficult to turn back the wheel of history," Fenn said. "Especially since there have been two world wars that altered Germany forever. But we still have to ask a hard question. Does Bavaria really belong within the Federal Republic of Germany?"

"You're a secessionist organization?"

Fenn nodded. "That is one of our contemporary purposes. Periodically we stage publicity events to keep the message alive."

"How is that working for you?"

"Not all that well," Fenn said. "But those displays occupy the brothers. They so like being a part of them. I like them too. Protests have their place. But what I like even more are results."

He'd dealt with his fair share of people like Fenn. The old saying was right. *A fanatic is one who can't change his mind and won't change the subject.*

"I have a problem, Herr Malone. One I need America's help with."

"Seems this is my night for helping."

"Ah, yes, Herr Koger told me about his recruitment of you. He called me when you left the convent. I was truly hoping that mine and America's interests might align. And perhaps they now have."

Since he had no idea what Koger was after, he did what had always served him best. Faked it. "That all depends on which interest of ours concerns you. We have several."

"First and foremost, I want Ludwig's body found."

He shrugged, as if nothing about that statement surprised him, then he pivoted. "We might disagree on that."

Fenn shook his head and pointed a finger. "This is not a matter for the United States or the Chinese. I told Koger that. This is a Bavarian issue."

That's a new one. The Chinese? He decided to shift gears, making a mental note to circle back to that one. "Why is the envelope I found so important?"

Fenn reached beneath his jacket and produced it. "I had a man inside the palace waiting for the right time to open the other compartment. If there's one there in that desk, surely there were two. And I was right. Prince Stefan apparently only had information relative to the book. Not this. My man watched as you found the other compartment. Quite a clever one, you are. That's what facilitated this little chat. I assume you read what was inside?"

"What kind of an agent would I be, if I hadn't?"

Fenn chuckled. "So true. Any thoughts?"

His eidetic memory recalled the lines.

> Where Matthias Strokes the Strings
> Edelweiss Over Black Forest
> No Water Cold
> Pulpit, Cross, and Garland
> Northeast the Crown
> Ends of the Dance

"I've been a bit indisposed to think on it," he said.

"And I again apologize for the inconvenience. Thankfully, I have many thoughts on the matter. Most formed while I waited for you to rouse from your forced sleep. You still seemed a bit irritated by what happened. Does it help to know that the man you took down in the wine cellar is the same one who rendered you unconscious?"

Actually, it did.

Fenn rose from the chair and stepped over to a striking antique desk topped with an intricate wooden inlay. Atop it was an unfolded Michelin map of Germany. "Please, come closer."

Cotton stood and walked over.

"We have a great mystery here. The prince regent, Luitpold, was faced with some difficult decisions. One nephew, Otto, had been declared insane and institutionalized. The other had been deposed and suddenly died. Both were kings. Ludwig died in 1886. Otto lived until 1913, and Luitpold ruled in his place. To his credit Luitpold never declared himself, nor asked to be declared, king. He simply did his duty as regent. Many say that Ludwig II's opportune death is explainable. He and his doctor drowned after a violent encounter with each other. Of course, my brothers and I believe otherwise. For us, murder is the only possible explanation."

"A bit single-minded, wouldn't you say?"

"Perhaps. But if we are wrong, why was Ludwig's body hidden?"

More news. But keep faking it. "I wasn't aware that it was."

"Oh, yes. It's been gone a long time, and there are several possible explanations. Luitpold, in 1886, could have never placed the king in his tomb beneath St. Michael's. But I don't think that's correct. Too many eyes were on what was happening. And surely someone involved with such a covert sequestration would have talked. Another explanation is that it happened between 1886 and 1913, when Luitpold served as regent. That could have been a more controllable move, utilizing a few trusted people." Fenn shook his head. "But, for me, there's a better explanation."

He waited.

"I've always believed that it was Ludwig III, before he was deposed in 1918, who moved the body."

A new player in the game.

Another Ludwig.

Seemed a popular name.

Fenn explained that the prince regent, Luitpold, died in 1912, after having lived a long life. His nephew Otto, still king since his brother's death in 1886, remained alive but institutionalized. Luitpold's son, also named Ludwig, became regent. But, in November 1913, the Bavarian legislature amended the national constitution to include a clause specifying that if a regency, for reasons of incapacity, had lasted for ten years with no prospect of the king ever being able to reign, the regent could assume the crown himself.

"In essence," Fenn said, "a 'let us have a new king' law. The day after this measure was approved, Luitpold's heir proclaimed the end of the regency, deposed his cousin Otto, and declared himself King Ludwig III. But he did not reign long. World War I changed everything, and by November 1918 Ludwig III was forced to relinquish the throne. He and his family thereafter were welcomed in Bavaria as private citizens, but only so long as they did not act against the people's state. Nearly eight hundred years of Wittelsbach rule ended."

Which had to be tough.

"A new republican government was formed after Ludwig III left, headed by a man named Kurt Eisner," Fenn said. "But in February 1919 Eisner was assassinated. Thinking he might be next, Ludwig fled to Hungary, later moving on to Liechtenstein and

Switzerland. He finally returned to Bavaria in 1920 and died in 1921. He was given a state funeral that drew one hundred thousand people and was buried in the Frauenkirche."

"Why do you think Ludwig III hid his cousin's body?" he asked.

"I cannot explain all that I know. Suffice it to say that the evidence points to Ludwig III."

"Why is any of this important?"

"Legend says that something was hidden away with Ludwig II's body. Something that has now become quite valuable."

"Which is?"

Fenn tossed him a curious look. "You seem a little short on facts."

"As you said, I just joined this party, and I was supposed to be briefed in the morning."

Fenn smiled. "That is all true. And so you shall. For now know that many have searched for Ludwig II's body. Hitler and the Americans at the end of the last war are two notables. Several of my predecessors as grand master launched efforts. His tomb beneath St. Michael's has been violated on multiple occasions. Hitler opened it. As did the Allies after the war. Then, earlier tonight, Prince Stefan opened it one more time, learning, as those before him, that it is empty."

"You know that for a fact?"

"Oh, I do. He was most surprised. He will be even more surprised once he learns that my brothers have retrieved the book he stole from Herrenchiemsee."

Now he got it. "You have a spy on him?"

Fenn nodded. "A good one."

"You've been busy tonight."

Fenn chuckled. "That I have. Planning is always the difference between failure and success."

So true. But he wondered what the book being gone meant for Luke.

"One of the reasons the Guglmänner re-formed in 1886 was to keep King Ludwig II's memory alive," Fenn said. "Part of that has long included working for an independent Bavaria. That has proven difficult, to say the least. But opportunities arise. One such has now arisen, which makes finding Ludwig II's remains vitally important."

"And what does this opportunity bring?"

"Freedom."

An odd reply. "For who?"

"Bavaria. Just as Ludwig II and Ludwig III would have wanted."

Now he was intrigued.

"The prince regent, Luitpold, is noted by historians as a man who transitioned Bavaria away from monarchy and toward a parliamentary government," Fenn said. "But he was first and foremost Bavarian. In his heart he wanted an independent nation. His son Ludwig III definitely wanted that. Every Duke of Bavaria since has wanted that. We have long believed that Luitpold and his son both may have honored those desires by respecting something known as *das letzte königreich*."

Those words again.

"You know what I mean?" Fenn asked.

"Koger mentioned it."

"Excellent. There were two things in that desk. A book and the envelope. Prince Stefan von Bayern went after the book—"

"And did not know about the envelope?"

Fenn nodded. "That's right. Now we have the book and the envelope. With both, I think we can find Ludwig II."

CHAPTER 24

Derrick entered the former royal Residenz.

He'd walked over from the Charles Hotel, a fifteen-minute stroll in the late-night cold, keeping a close watch on the few people moving along the broad sweeps of pavement. More snow was coming and the flurries had begun to fall in earnest during his trek. The call from Trinity Dorner still bothered him. Somebody on the team had ratted him out. Somebody obviously currying favor. Ass-kissers. He hated 'em. Call him what they will. Difficult. Tough. Single-minded. But nobody had ever accused him of kissin' up to the brass.

Quite the contrary.

He'd fallen on his sword during the whole water-boarding/torture debacle. What had TOO taunted? *Remember what happened the last time.* Like he'd ever forget. His loyalty had cost him everything. *Don't make it end sooner than it needs to.* An ominous threat. But reality. He did not want to lose his job. Not yet anyway. He appreciated Trinity's understanding.

And knew why.

She'd been there. All those years ago when he was

raked over the coals. He'd taken the heat, but he'd also changed things. Sure, for years he and others had tortured people thinking it the right thing to do. *Bad guys deserve bad things.*

But the more he did it, the less he liked it.

So he'd engaged in a little show-and-tell.

He'd called in the brass—an assortment of senior intelligence officials, mostly political appointees and career CIA who each brought a sense of duty, urgency, and long-windedness to the job—all of whom loved torture. Of course not a one of them had ever actually seen it done, except in reenactments. Which, like books made into movies, were nothing like the original. So a prisoner was selected. An Afghan terrorist who'd been waterboarded over sixty times. Incredible. Sixty times. He'd been in jail for years, the effects of the dim grainy light, stark corridors, stinky air, and noise wearing on him. They'd hauled him into a hot smelly cell, strapped him to an inclined bench, then elevated his feet. He'd told those watching that having the head below the legs prolonged the agony. A porous cloth was draped across the forehead and eyes. Water was then poured onto the cloth. Then the saturated cloth was lowered until it covered both the nose and mouth, restricting air flow.

More water was added.

In two varying doses.

Twenty seconds or forty seconds, depending on how bad you wanted to make it.

The wet cloth prevented nearly all air from getting to the lungs, and during that time of induced suffocation more water was applied. So much that the effect was the same as drowning, only you were on dry land. Finally, the cloth was lifted away and the prisoner was allowed to breathe.

Two, maybe three breaths.

That's all.

Then it started all over again.

The technique came from the friggin' Spanish Inquisition. They'd favored it since it left no marks on the body. Intelligence officers who'd subjected themselves to it lasted an average of fourteen seconds before capitulating. His audience that day watched for a half hour. A few started to cry. Two turned their heads, but he told them that was not an option. *If this is what you want done, then have the guts to watch.* Trinity Dorner had stood impassionate, her eyes never wavering. She'd been merely an assistant deputy director then. A person low in the chain of command. There because her boss had wanted her to come. But he saw that she agreed with what he already knew.

Torture was bad.

He'd done it so much he'd come to feel sorry for the prisoners, though some of them were really bad people. Many times he had to tell himself that punishment and revenge was not the objective. Ascertaining useful intel was the goal. But most of what you learned from torture was unreliable. "They'll say anything," he told the onlookers when it was over. "It's like they're being killed in a mock execution. Last I looked, that was illegal under international law."

A whole host of notables had loved waterboarding. The Pinochet regime in Chile. The Khmer Rouge. The British army in Northern Ireland. The South African police during apartheid.

Add the United States government to the list.

Finally, it was banned in 2009. But it still lingered. Quietly. In the background. Popping up every once in a while. He was proud that he'd had a small part in at least curbing its use. Unfortunately, all those political appointees and career intelligence officers whom he'd tried to intimidate never forgave him. No promotions came his way. No meaningful advancements. Nothing but a career stalled in neutral. Trinity Dorner went on to climb the ladder at Langley, eventually settling into a position where she could change things. And she had. Then, just after his inauguration, Warner Fox had brought her to the White House as a deputy to the national security adviser. Now she would head the counter-terrorism force. Definitely high up in the pecking order now.

And with a personal interest in what he was doing.

He could not decide if that was good or bad.

The Residenz sat just off the pedestrian-only zone, on a street that accommodated Munich's high-end shopping. Chanel. Louis Vuitton. Prada. Hermès. Prior to 1918 the Residenz had served as the seat of government and home to the Bavarian dukes. But it had been over a hundred years since the last vestige of royalty had walked its halls. He knew that much of the building had been destroyed during the Second World War. But it had been rebuilt into one of the largest museum complexes in all of Bavaria.

A massive tourist attraction.

The call he'd received a short while ago was a request for a meeting and he'd not refused. The caller had been the one to involve him in the first place, alerting him to the Chinese presence and the threat that the United States could face. He'd reported all that through proper channels with a recommendation that the CIA intervene, but, as TOO had so astutely noted, he'd been ordered to stand down. He'd lied to the attorney general in order to obtain the services of Luke Daniels, saying it would be for an operation in the Czech Republic.

He certainly could not use any CIA regulars. That misrepresentation had clearly been discovered. He'd wondered how long it would be before the assholes at Langley found out about Cotton Malone. That move would definitely get him into even more trouble. The three operatives he'd used tonight were all freelance, not on the company payroll, but one of them was clearly a snitch.

He stepped inside to a warm foyer and was escorted through a series of dimly lit corridors. Room after room opened to his left and right, many of them dark to the night. A few of the cleaning crew could be seen and heard as they worked.

He entered the Hall of Antiquities. A magnificent barrel-vaulted rectangle, every square inch ornately decorated, the walls lined with Roman busts. An older man sat at the far end on a raised dais. Not a throne, which had once surely been there. Just a mock representation. He walked the two hundred feet from one end to the other, down a checkerboard tile floor, past all of the sculpted busts, stopping short of the dais at a gilded wooded railing.

An exotic, musky scent hung in the air.

"Welcome," Albert, Duke of Bavaria, said.

CHAPTER 25

Cotton was leery of Marc Fenn.

Definitely someone clearly in the know. But a little strange.

Odd. Out of kilter.

"You still haven't said why Ludwig's body has to be found?"

"The story of the last kingdom is replete with hyperbole that has grown over the past hundred years. Tales of a vast treasure. Ludwig's missing personal property—"

"What property?"

"After he was deposed, much of Ludwig's effects—his books, papers, clothes, keepsakes, things like that—vanished. No one knows if they were stolen by servants, intentionally hidden away by the prince regent, or a combination. Only some of his correspondence survived. A great deal of it was destroyed by him shortly before he was arrested. The story goes that most of his belongings were hidden away with him."

He got the message. "And you know better?"

"Here's where we delve into the realm of speculation."

He caught the crease of amusement on Fenn's face. "Which you enjoy."

"That I do."

So he indulged the man. "I do, too, actually."

"Luckily, we now have the book and the envelope, so we can begin, in earnest, the search."

He pointed at the map open on the desk. "Do you know what those lines of text mean from the envelope?"

Fenn nodded. "I think I do."

He wondered if he was going to regret this. Yogi Berra was right. *You've got to be careful if you don't know where you're going, because you might not get there.* Ain't that the truth. But what the hell. "Tell me."

Fenn seemed pleased with the invitation. "I was so hoping you would be interested. I know I am. The envelope you found inside the desk is a most vital clue." Fenn reached down for the sheet of paper that the envelope had contained. "These lines are hand-written. I believe by Ludwig III himself. Thankfully, many examples of his penmanship exist. I plan to have a comparison made tomorrow. I have translated these words into English, though I understand you speak German."

"You seem to know a lot about me."

Fenn waved off the observation. "An eidetic memory. What a trait to possess."

"A gift from my mother's side of the family. Who told you?"

"Herr Koger. But not to worry. I was curious about who I would be working with, so he provided a few details. It's one of my smaller obsessions."

Yeah, right. Along with owning a castle and heading a brotherhood of guys who run around in black robes.

"Where Matthias Strokes the Strings. Edelweiss Over Black Forest. No Water Cold. Pulpit, Cross, and Garland. Northeast the Crown. Ends of the Dance," Fenn said. "The first line is easy. Matthias Klotz was a famous violin maker. He lived in Mittenwald. Here."

Fenn lifted a pen from the desk and circled the town, which was located in the extreme southern portion of Bavaria, in the Alps, right on the Austrian border.

"The second line is a bit of a paradox. 'Edelweiss Over Black Forest.' Let's leave it for a moment. The third line, 'No Water Cold,' is easy. Baden-Baden. A spa town. There are numerous hot springs there. The region has for a long time, dating back to the nineteenth century, advertised itself as having 'no cold water.'"

Fenn circled the town, located in the southwestern part of Germany, at the northwestern edge of the Black Forest, against the French border, west of Mittenwald.

"The fourth line, 'Pulpit, Cross, and Garland,' is Glücksburg. Here. The far most northern settlement in Germany, against the Baltic Sea. In its main church is a famous pulpit adorned with a cross and garland. The fifth line, 'Northeast the Crown,' is here. *Krone*, German for 'crown,' a small village that sits against the Polish border, to the northeast. Fenn circled both Krone and Glücksburg. "All in all a fairly simple riddle to decipher. So we have to assume that whoever crafted it wanted it solved."

Cotton noticed that the four towns were roughly situated with one in each quadrant of the compass. He watched as Fenn, with the pen, connected the northwest to the southeast, then the northeast to the southwest, forming an oblong-shaped X. At the center point, where the lines crossed, lay another town.

Eisenach.

"And the last line, Ends the Dance?"

"I think it's exactly as it says. The end of the message."

"What about the line you disregarded?"

Edelweiss over Black Forest.

"It has meaning. But what?" Fenn shook his head. "That remains to be seen."

"And the random letters?"

"Obviously, an anagram of some sort."

He agreed. Letters capable of being rearranged, used only once, to form a word or phrase.

HLNESRNTANME.

"Lucky for us," Fenn said, "there are computer programs these days that can find all of the possibilities."

"In German?"

"Of course. That was the language Ludwig III would have used. I have already sent the letters to a friend who is running that program as we speak."

If he was going to help Stephanie, he had to help Koger. But to do that he had to deal with this nut job. "I assume you're telling me all this for a reason?"

"We need you to investigate."

Really? "What about your brothers?"

Fenn laughed. "They are fine for parading—"

"And chloroforming people."

"That too. But this task requires a professional of your caliber."

"You still haven't told me what I'm after."

"Herr Koger did not share that information?"

"He left that off the recruitment pitch. What's so

damn important that you, Prince Stefan, the Chinese, and the CIA all want it?"

Fenn smiled. "Herr Koger had set up a meeting tomorrow where we would speak on this. Can we wait until then? I have violated enough of his confidence already."

Not going to happen. "Either you start talking or I start walking."

"I could stop you."

He chuckled. "Your brothers could try."

Fenn shook his head. "Herr Koger will not appreciate this."

"That makes it all the more better."

"Ah, that it does. I like your rebellious streak. We look for that in all of the brothers."

"You're stalling."

"All right," Fenn said. "Come over here, have a seat, and I will tell you something amazing."

Millions of years ago plumes of black molten rock emerged from the Pacific Ocean, steam hissing off the surface and announcing its arrival into open air. Slowly, over many more millennia, the rock expanded to eventually form dry land and high, jagged mountains. Over even more time seeds blew in on the trade winds, plants sprouted, trees grew, and it all turned green, bursting with life, forming one of the most remote island chains in the world.

Polynesians from the south first arrived around the third century after Christ. By the eighteenth century, Spanish, Dutch, Chinese, and Japanese ships had all visited. But it was James Cook, in 1778, who placed the islands on the map. He named them Sandwich, after his patron and friend, the Lord of Britain's Admiralty, the fourth Earl of Sandwich.

Over the next hundred and twenty years the islands

underwent nearly constant change. For centuries the inhabitants warred among themselves. Chiefs fighting each other in never-ending civil war. But by 1795 one warrior, Kamehameha, had conquered Hawaii, Oahu, Maui, Molokai, and Lanai, proclaiming himself king. In 1810, the remaining two islands, Kauai and Niihau, voluntarily joined what came to be called the Hawaiian kingdom. Over the next ninety years two dynastic families would rule. The House of Kamehameha and the House of Kalākaua. The former reigned through five kings until 1872 with the death of Kamehameha V. The Kalākaua's time ended in 1893, after two kings and a queen.

Missionaries first arrived in 1820.

Presbyterians, Congregationalists, and Dutch Reformists from New England. They came at an auspicious moment. Kamehameha I had just died. His son, Liholiho, had become king. One of his first acts was to abolish the ancient kapu system, a code of conduct with strict laws and regulations. A kapu offense, regarded as a threat to spiritual power and goodwill, often involved human sacrifice. Breaking one law, even unintentionally, often meant immediate death. With that code gone, and no alternative belief system created to replace it, a door opened for Christianity. And the missionaries seized the moment, ingratiating both themselves and their mores with the local society.

Succeeding companies of missionaries kept coming, increasing their numbers. Many eventually returned to the mainland. But many more stayed and influenced religion, education, and the organization of government. They also became traders, farmers, shippers, wholesalers, and retailers. Sugarcane, nut, pineapple, and coffee crops flourished. They, and their descendants, built a massive financial empire.

One they wanted to keep. So they engineered a coup.
Which happened on January 17, 1893.

The insurgents were nearly all foreigners, mainly American. Hawaii had been recognized by the United States as an independent kingdom since 1846. As such, the sovereignty of the islands should have been respected.

But it wasn't.

Instead, the overthrow of the monarchy was supported by a United States government minister, John L. Stevens, who ordered US Marines to come ashore from ships in Honolulu harbor. This bolstered the insurgents, who promptly arrested and imprisoned the last of the House of Kalākaua, Queen Liliʻuokalani, in her palace. The Marines never fired a shot, but their presence intimidated the royalist defenders. The queen herself wanted to avoid any loss of life, so she ordered her forces to surrender. That evening the chairman of the Committee of Safety, Henry E. Cooper, addressed a crowd assembled in front of the royal palace and read aloud a proclamation that formally deposed Liliʻuokalani, abolished the Hawaiian monarchy, and established the Provisional Government of Hawaii under President Sanford B. Dole, a descendant of the missionary community.

Hawaii was formally annexed by the United States on August 12, 1898.

"You essentially stole that sovereign kingdom," Fenn said. "The American pineapple and sugarcane plantation owners were terrified that the Hawaiian monarchy was about to make a deal with Great Britain. One that would have brought the islands into the British Commonwealth. To stop that, they staged a coup. One that America sanctioned, supported, and greatly benefited from. Today Hawaii is your fiftieth state. But it was acquired by ill-gotten gains."

Cotton was not unfamiliar with that part of American history. "Not our finest moment."

"Clearly."

He was wondering about the point of the story.

"Any chance you're going to tie all this into now?"

CHAPTER 26

DERRICK STEPPED UP ONTO THE RAISED PLATFORM AND approached the duke. "You look comfortable on that fake throne."

"This place was once the ancestral seat of my family's power."

He smiled and bowed. "And I have responded to your royal summons."

He'd known the duke for a long time. They first met about two decades ago, and had remained friends. He'd come to know that this man was highly educated and exceptionally well informed on both German and European affairs. He'd often used him as a sounding board. But his old friend looked tired. Fatigue showed as dark smudges beneath even darker eyes. Anxiety had turned the voice, usually strong and firm, to a dry croak.

Cancer was taking its toll.

"What happened at Herrenchiemsee?" Albert asked.

"You haven't heard from your brother yet?"

"Oh, yes. But he failed to mention anything about the book. I, of course, could not inquire since I am supposed to know nothing."

He told the older man about what occurred, including the unexpected boat on the lake firing at Stefan's thieves. He left out the part about his recruitment of Cotton Malone, which did not require sharing.

"So my brother was successful at the palace, but not so much at the family crypt," the duke said.

And he listened as Albert told him about the empty tomb.

"Why did you want Stefan to have the book and open the tomb?" Derrick asked.

Albert shrugged. "Both kept him occupied."

The duke had been the one who warned him about the pending raid on Herrenchiemsee. Albert knew that the CIA had planted an asset close to his brother, the idea being to keep an eye on what Stefan was doing. The duke just did not know the name or any other details.

"And as to the something else in that desk," Albert said. "In another compartment on the other side. Was I right? Was anything there?"

"I sent a man back to determine just that. I should have that information soon."

"That's good. Excellent. Now, I want to show you something."

The duke stood and walked behind where the throne sat to an exit portal. Derrick followed and they left the hall, passing through a grotto-like chamber. Arcades, slender marble columns, tuffs, crystals, shells, and a fountain cast an outdoor feel.

"All of this was bombed in 1944," Albert said. "Destroyed. This is a mid-twentieth-century re-creation."

"It's stunning."

They kept walking, passing through another garden hall, and entered what a placard identified as the Ancestral Gallery. The walls were paneled and gilded, dotted with portrait after portrait.

"A hundred and twenty-one images of my ancestors," the duke said with a sweep of his arm. "All Wittelsbachs except that one there, at the end. Charlemagne himself."

He admired the paintings, the eighteenth-century equivalent of pictures stored in the cloud. He followed the older man to a display cabinet, white-paneled and glazed, with a mirrored back. It contained a few small vases, plates, and statuettes, along with ornaments and medals.

"These are some of Ludwig II's personal items that have survived from his time. There's not much, so these are quite valuable." Albert opened the cabinet. "I had the curator unlock it earlier. One of the privileges of being duke."

Albert reached inside and removed a small black box. Sitting atop it was an octagonal silver star, with a companion cross, suspended from a faded red-and-white ribbon.

"This is the Knight's Grand Cross. The badge of the Royal Order of Kamehameha I. A silver Maltese cross surmounted by the Hawaiian crown."

He studied the medal. A white-enameled disc on the cross bore an elaborate golden K at its center. The blue-enameled band surrounding it was inscribed "Kamehameha I" in gold letters, together with two golden laurel branches.

"King Kamehameha V created the Royal Order on April 11, 1865. He named it in honor of his grandfather Kamehameha I, who united the Hawaiian Islands and created the first kingship. Both Hawaiians and foreigners were eligible for membership. For the former it was given for distinguished service to the king and the people of Hawaii. For the latter, the medal was part of an outreach by the Hawaiian monarchy to the rest of the world. That Royal Order still exists today, though the kingdom ended long ago."

It was a beautiful medal.

No question.

"Medals were awarded to foreigners fifty-seven times. Between 1865 and 1881 the kings of Siam, Belgium, Spain, Italy, Portugal, and Serbia were given the honor. The emperors of Germany, Austria, China, Russia, and Japan, along with the sultan of the Ottoman Empire, also received it, as did the Queen of England. One of the first to be given the medal, though, in 1865, was the young, newly installed king of Bavaria, Ludwig II. This is his."

He was amazed. "How would the king of Hawaii, who lived ten thousand miles away, even know of the king of Bavaria? And why would he give him a medal?"

"The Hawaiians were not heathens. Far from it, in fact. Their society was highly evolved. Foreigners who came there, though, thought them ignorant pagans. The Royal Order and the medal was their way of making themselves known on the world stage. Kings connecting with other kings. The better question, my old friend, is why was Ludwig one of the *first* to receive it. He was but the king of a small, insignificant land. Not an emperor or a ruler of a large power."

He waited for an explanation.

"The answer to that question can be learned from what happened not far from here, on a beautiful summer night in 1881. When this medal was worn for the first and only time by the king of Bavaria himself."

Ludwig sat across the table and assessed his guest. Torches provided both flickering light and a degree of warmth to the night mountain air. His feet rested on the carpet that covered the alpine grass.

He'd patiently waited as the carriage had approached through the woods, finally stopping along the shores of the Walchensee. His guest was, he'd been told, pure Hawaiian in blood. Now, sitting across from King David Kalākaua, he saw that the man was excessively stout, the skin the darkest of brown, the nose aquiline, the lips thick and full. The face sported muttonchop whiskers and a bushy mustache, along with curly, almost wool-like hair. He wore a dress uniform adorned with epaulettes, stars, and braided cords, along with high boots and a feather-fringed helmet. Both little fingers displayed gold rings. He spoke in perfect French, without the hint of an accent or intonation. Von Löher had told him that Kalākaua had studied law and loved the military, along with all its assorted pageantry.

On that point they differed.

"Majesty," his visitor said in French. "It is an honor to meet you."

"I assure you, my fellow king, the honor is mine."

"This is a lovely place you have chosen. We have mountains, too, but not with the cool crispness of this wonderful dry air."

"I understand you are touring the world."

Kalākaua nodded. "I have been to Japan, China, Southeast Asia, India, Egypt, Italy, England, and now Germany. I intend to become the first monarch to travel around the globe. Nearly three hundred days I will be gone from my kingdom when I finish. And all so that this meeting may occur with no one being the wiser."

He appreciated the subterfuge. "Who manages the government in your absence?"

"My sister and heir, Lili'uokalani, is regent while I am away."

"Sadly, I have no sister and my brother is not fit to rule."

"I was told of your brother's mental disabilities. You have my sincere sympathy."

He appreciated the sentiment.

"I see you wear the Knight's Grand Cross," Kalākaua said, pointing. *"The badge of the Royal Order of Kamehameha I."*

"I considered it a great honor when it was bestowed upon me."

"Have you ever wondered why you received it?"

Not particularly, but he indulged the man anyway. *"I have. In 1865, I was but twenty years old, new to the throne, my kingdom just a small place in a large world."*

"But Kamehameha V knew of you. He was a wise sovereign, educated and accomplished, and tried hard to do well by his people. He dressed plainly and poked about night or day on his old horse, unattended, visiting with his subjects. He was popular, greatly respected, even beloved. He was told of both you and this place by visitors to our islands. He became fascinated by a magical kingdom in the mountains, along with its tales of dwarfs and elves and its young ruler, whom the people there also loved. Those romantic images appealed to him, so he selected you to be one of the first to receive the medal."

"I remain honored to this day."

Kalākaua pointed. *"When von Löher there came to visit, he and I talked more of you and your kingdom. He told me about your own nocturnal visits in the mountains and the love the people have for you. It seems as you grow older you become more like Kamehameha V. As I listened, I, too, became fascinated, especially about your desire to leave this place. To have a new kingdom. And now, here I am, sitting with you."*

Attendants brought goblets of wine and a tray of sweets, which they left on the table before retreating back across the grass into the darkness beyond the torches.

Only von Löher stood within earshot.

"The American newspapers," Kalākaua said, *"are writing that my world journey is for the purpose of finding a buyer for my kingdom. They lament about all of the extensive American interests on my islands and how important they are to them. One editorial was quite emphatic, proclaiming that the world should be notified that any attempt to acquire the Sandwich Islands, by purchase or otherwise, would be regarded by the United States as an unfriendly act. They apparently do not realize that all of those islands they speak about belong to me. And they are not called the Sandwich. That was a British name bestowed upon them."*

He was liking this man more and more. "I have the same impertinence here. Ministers who fail to comprehend that this is my kingdom, not theirs. I am constantly questioned about everything I do."

"When von Löher visited, I realized how much we are alike," Kalākaua said. *"Both dreamers. I have seen photographs and drawings of your many castles. Quite impressive. I wish I could visit them. But, alas, my presence here must remain secret. We have nothing like a castle on my islands. We do not build much with stone. Then there is your flying machine."*

Only a few knew of his idea, von Löher being one of those. A cable car, decorated like a peacock, held aloft by hot air and powered by steam, to take him across the Alps.

"It sounds amazing," his guest said. *"Quite visionary. I, too, like to invent. I conceived of a submarine torpedo to fly through the water and take down a ship with explosives. An improved bottle stopper to preserve the contents within. And electricity utterly fascinates me. My palace has that marvel, along with indoor toilets and a telephone."*

"I have heard of the telephone. Does it work?"

"I can talk to people many miles away, with my voice transmitted merely over a wire."

The thought of such excited him, though it would only mean his ministers could find him even faster.

"And, like you," Kalākaua said, "I am heavily in debt."

He was surprised by the admission.

"I owe a large sum to a man named Claus Spreckels. He is from Germany, but now possesses Hawaiian citizenship. He owns many sugarcane plantations. My opposition says I am his puppet. That he owns me."

"Does he?"

Kalākaua laughed. "I suppose he does. As much as your creditors own you. But I face a much graver danger than a greedy merchant. Three thousand Americans handle all of the money, carry on all of the commerce and agriculture, and dominate the religion and education of my lands. On the one hand they bring order, wealth, and prosperity. But on another they want it all for themselves. My fear is that they may well succeed. Thankfully, my family's hold on power depends solely on my naming a designated heir."

Exactly as von Löher had reported.

Once chosen, that person inherited it all, without question.

A sadness filled Kalākaua's brown face. "We once had a bird, the mamo. A lovely creature. My ancestors would lay snares to catch them. Once caught, they carefully plucked out only the golden feathers. There are but a few on each bird, right behind the wing, among its many black feathers. Once those features were removed, though, the birds were released back to the wild to live, reproduce, and make more golden feathers. It took eighty thousand golden feathers to create one cloak for the chiefs. What a magnificent garment. I own one. But not with feathers from birds that still exist. The foreigners brought in a horrible little animal called a mongoose to control the rats in the sugarcane fields. The mongooses eat the mamo's eggs. The birds are now nearly all gone."

He did not know what to say.

"My kingdom is likewise disappearing," Kalākaua said. "Sugarcane, cattle ranching, and pineapple plantations are replacing the taro patches, fish ponds, and forest. I have traveled to the American capital and met with presidents. I saw it in their eyes. They want my islands. They want free tariffs on goods in and out. They want to use one of my bays, a place we call Pearl Harbor, as a military outpost. To obtain these concessions, they ridicule me in their press. Insult me and my people. One newspaper called my home a playhouse kingdom."

He shook his head. "That is insulting."

"To say the least. These people who live on my land have high-handed ideas of taking my property, as if it were theirs. The American newspapers call me ambitious. Dangerously flighty. Capable of being manipulated by merchants and planters. They arrogantly think that I wish to sell my kingdom. What they do not realize is I have no intention of doing that. I prefer instead to give it away."

CHAPTER 27

Cotton was impressed at Marc Fenn's knowledge of history. He doubted many Americans knew how the fiftieth state came to be.

"Within two days of the 1893 overthrow, every nation with a diplomatic presence in Hawaii, except for the United Kingdom, recognized the new provisional government," Fenn said. "The arrogant usurpers officially declared the Republic of Hawaii on July 4, 1894."

He was curious. "The Hawaiians did not retaliate?"

"Oh, they did. With a four-day uprising in January 1895 intent on restoring the monarchy. Blood was shed, but it failed. Poor Queen Liliʻuokalani was arrested again, this time tried by a military tribunal, convicted of treason, and imprisoned in her own home. It was then she abdicated, formally ending the Hawaiian monarchy."

He had to admit, this subject fascinated him. The first adult fiction novel he'd ever read, at age sixteen, was *Hawaii* by James Michener. He loved Michener's work. He was his favorite author. He recalled the massive epic spanning the centuries, recounting in story form the arrival of the Polynesians, the missionaries, the Japanese, Chinese, and Filipinos who all came and left their mark. The book had been published in 1959, at the same time that statehood was granted.

"When the overthrow of the Hawaiian monarchy occurred, to his credit, President Grover Cleveland called for an investigation," Fenn said. "A congressional report concluded the United States diplomatic and military representatives had abused their authority and were directly responsible for the change in government. The American minister was recalled and your military commander there was forced to resign. Cleveland stated publicly that a substantial wrong had been done, which should be undone. He told Congress in his 1893 State of the Union address that 'upon the facts developed it seemed to me the only honorable course for our Government to pursue was to undo the wrong that had been done by those representing us and to restore as far as practicable the status existing at the time of our forcible intervention.' Of course, that did not happen. Instead, the islands were brought within the American sphere, and annexed by the next president, McKinley, in 1898."

"Like I said, not our finest moment."

"And then there was the apology," Fenn said.

That he knew a little about. In 1993, on the one hundredth anniversary of the overthrow, Congress passed a resolution offering an apology to native Hawaiians on behalf of the United States for its involvement in the overthrow.

"The Apology Resolution," Fenn said. "Signed by your President Clinton. It acknowledged that the overthrow happened with the active participation of agents and citizens of the United States. Quite an admission for America. It then went further and said that the native Hawaiian people never directly re-linquished any of their claims of sovereignty. Instead, they were simply taken away."

"And the point of all this?"

"It's quite simple, Herr Malone. In the early morning hours of August 8, 1881, at Altach, near the cold waters of the Walchensee, a deed was executed in proper legal form whereby King David Kalākaua of Hawaii deeded away his kingdom to Ludwig II."

"So what if he did? A lot has happened since that deed was executed. As you say, a coup d'état occurred in Hawaii and Bavaria ceased to be independent."

"But the Apology Resolution contained a curious clause. Section 1, paragraph 6. Let me read it to you." Fenn stood and walked over to his desk where he lifted a sheet of paper. "'The Congress validates any and all actions and decisions by the kingdom of Hawaii that occurred prior to January 17, 1893, as legitimate and lawful, with nothing that occurred during the illegal overthrow to affect those actions in any manner whatsoever.' This language implements what Grover Cleveland said in 1893, that 'the only honorable course for our Government to pursue was to undo the wrong that had been done by those representing us and to restore as far as practicable the status existing at the time of our forcible intervention.'"

Now he saw the point.

"The king of Hawaii owned the islands in their entirety," Fenn said. "The land was his. Whatever he had sold to third parties prior to that night in 1881 was conveyed and gone. But whatever remained as of the date of the deed was conveyed to Ludwig. We've checked. That was a substantial part of the Hawaiian Islands. The vast majority of the land, in fact. So if Kalākaua deeded away his kingdom then, under Hawaiian law that existed at the time, that deed takes precedence."

His mind quickly filled in the gaps with what little Koger had told him.

"Bavaria ceased to be a kingdom and became part of the Weimar Republic in 1918," Fenn said. "All claims and ownership, along with any claims the Wittelsbachs may have had, were transferred to the republic, all of which was ultimately seized by the Third Reich. Then, after the war, those claims were vested in the new Federal Republic of Germany, where they have remained. The current German government would now be the valid successor in interest to any deed that may have existed between Ludwig II and King Kalākaua. At a minimum, even if that claim is deemed dubious, the current Duke of Bavaria would clearly be that successor."

He could not believe what he was hearing. "We're after a hundred-and-forty-year-old deed?"

Fenn nodded. "One that meant little to nothing until the mid-twentieth century. The Nazis knew about the last kingdom and they searched for the deed. They wanted to use it as a bargaining chip with the Japanese, who wanted ownership of the Hawaiian Islands. But they found nothing. The Allies, after the war ended, searched for a while too. But found nothing. Now Prince Stefan of Bavaria is on the hunt."

"To do what?"

The room's doors burst open and two men rushed in.

"We are under attack."

CHAPTER 28

LUKE HAD FOLLOWED THE BEARDED MAN NAMED Frederick from the beer hall, through the snowy streets of Munich, to an apartment building not far from the main train station. The older man had walked at a leisurely pace, seemingly unconcerned if anyone might be interested in him. The book from earlier was tucked away inside a coat pocket, safe from the elements. At least he knew who the man was and where he lived. And he'd managed to snap some clear images of the book that he'd already forwarded to Koger.

All in all, not a bad day's work.

Time to head back to his hotel and get some sleep.

He hunched into his coat against the raw cold that folded around him and rubbed his face with gloved hands. He was just about to leave when two figures caught his eye. Across the street. Under one of the streetlamps. Dark coats and caps gave them an air of menace, their faces set in determination. No one else was around in the early morning mist and he'd not noticed them before. They must have been hidden down the narrow alley next to the apartment building.

He kept his gaze locked on them as they both drew weapons and started to run.

His way.

That couldn't be good.

He darted off in the opposite direction.

First the shots on the Chiemsee from God knows who. Now this. He'd had no opportunity on the lake to turn things around.

Not this time.

He kept moving, leading them down a dark side street between two buildings, careful with his footfalls on the frozen cobbles. It would be easy to slip, though the soles of his boots were grippy rubber. He kept going, twisting left and right, peering ahead for any signs of more trouble. He turned a corner and spotted a metal fire escape that right-angled up a three-story building. He decided the high ground would be preferable, so he increased his pace and leaped up, grabbing hold of the bottom rung about eight feet off the ground. Momentum swung his body forward and he pivoted upward, grabbing the next rung, and pulled himself onto a metal platform.

He stretched out flat and lay still.

Waiting.

With the air of a spider about to ambush a juicy insect.

His two pursuers rounded the corner and slowed their pace, surely wondering where he'd disappeared to. Darkness was his ally and he used it to maximum advantage, his face pressed against the cold steel mesh of the platform flooring. The two shadows approached closer. His body was primed and coiled, his brain calm and controlled, both ready to strike.

Then another form appeared.

Behind the two men with guns.

Rounding the corner, rushing ahead, attacking from the blind side, driving a foot hard into the spine and sending one guy stumbling forward. Before he could recover, the form spun on the ball of the left foot and rammed a fist into the second guy's throat.

Sweet move.

The one who'd taken the throat chop gasped for air. The neck was a complex structure. Lots of blood vessels. A windpipe. Esophagus. Vocal cords. Thyroid gland. A whole bunch of stuff that could not take a hit. His hand-to-hand combat teacher in the Army defined the throat punch as a "rapid, unexpected knuckle thrust into the larynx of a douchebag who is pissing you off."

How true.

The guy below him was discovering just how awful a knuckle thrust could be.

The second pursuer had recovered from the spine kick and whirled to face the threat. But the new-comer did exactly what you were supposed to do and attacked. The form moved quickly, slamming a fist into the left side of the jaw. Luke heard a few agoniz-ing croaks. The newcomer jerked the man forward, wrapping an arm around the neck, digging an elbow into the gut, whipping the head back sharply. A crack signaled something broke. Which had to hurt. A kick to the pit of the stomach and the guy's breath was expelled with a sharp whoosh. He stumbled sideways, but the newcomer continued the assault, driving the left arm, like a battering ram, into the chest. The man dropped to the ground, his gun clattering away.

The newcomer spun toward the first man, who was still trying to breathe. Not missing a beat, the new-comer's right leg shot upward in a vicious arc, driving heel to shin hard, sending the guy to the ground.

The form stood, at ready, arms extended, switching attention between the two downed men. But neither moved.

The newcomer relaxed.

"You can come down," a female voice said.

One he recognized.

Lexi Blake.

DERRICK LEFT THE RESIDENZ.

He'd spent an hour with the duke, listening to a full report of what Stefan von Bayern had been doing for the past twenty-four hours, and what could be reasonably anticipated to come next. Albert had promised to keep him informed, and Derrick assured his old friend that things would keep moving forward on his end.

He'd read about the Kamehameha cross in a few of the old CIA reports. But seeing it. That made a difference. This crap was real. The deed could well be waiting out there. Somewhere. But plenty of people were looking for it.

He was tired.

Sleep would be welcome.

He was getting too old for all-nighters.

He stopped under a lit stoop and checked his phone. It had been on silent mode for the past hour. An email had come from Luke, with images attached. Pages from the book stolen earlier, along with a message that they would talk in the morning.

He looked forward to that.

The walk back to the Charles Hotel would take about fifteen minutes. Munich was settled in for the night, an icy-edged wind clearing the streets of all but the hardiest pedestrians.

He stepped ahead and walked.

This whole thing was becoming complicated. Nothing with the Chinese was anything but. Long ago, as a young recruit, he'd been told a parable. Supposedly, if a beach was an espionage target, the Russians would send in a submarine. Frogmen would steal ashore in the dark of night and collect several buckets of sand to take back to Moscow. The Americans would target the beach with satellites and produce reams of electronic data. The Chinese, though, would send in a thousand tourists, each assigned to collect a single grain of sand. When they returned, they would hand each grain over. And, in the end, they would know far more about the sand than anyone else.

That relentlessness was hard to beat.

In fact, it took everything you had.

He was already walking a tightrope, playing the White House against Cotton Malone and vice versa. This might be his last chance to strike pay dirt and get something he could bargain with. He hated having to resort to this. But the game had been established a long time ago. The rules simple. Those with power get power. Those without got nothing. He'd tried to work his way up the ladder, obeying orders, doing the right thing, and all that bullshit. Which had literally got him nothing. Luckily, most of the time he'd managed to remain above the gray gas of professional depression. Now he felt like it had engulfed him. So he was going to force the issue.

But first he had to find that deed.

If it even existed.

He came to the end of the commercial way, which drained into the ring road that encircled Munich's Old Town. A black velvet sky provided a contrasting backdrop to the steady fall of snow. He sucked in the cold air, trying to rid his lungs of the staleness of anxiety. His nerves were stretched taut. Cars passed sparingly. The bells of a distant church burst in the night like drumfire aimed at his stubborn soul. He waited for the traffic signal and permission from the lights to cross the four-lane boulevard.

Before he could, a dark sedan pulled to the curb.

His senses sprang to red alert.

The rear door opened.

Trinity Dorner stared out at him. "Get in."

CHAPTER 29

COTTON STEPPED CLOSE TO THE COMPUTER MONITOR as Marc Fenn adjusted the multi-window mode to focus on the cameras atop the exterior castle walls. Three vehicles were parked at odd angles before the main gate. Six men with automatic weapons stood near them.

Fenn reached for the phone on his desk and stabbed a button. "Are the main gates closed?" A pause while he listened. "Good." Fenn slammed the receiver down. "Come with me."

He followed his host from the study, through the castle, to a vaulted entrance foyer. Richly colored stuccos were reflected in the shiny marble floor. There, a steward waited with a heavy coat and gloves, which Fenn donned before stepping out into the cold. They trudged across the cobbles, careful with their steps as ice had formed in places, to a staircase that wound upward against the outer wall. Fenn climbed with quick, determined pounds on the wooden risers. They reached the top of the ramparts, where sentries once patrolled, and stomped down the battlement walkway, the crenellated outer wall to their right.

"What are you doing?" he asked Fenn.

"Dealing with a problem."

They made their way to a spot above the main gate. The six men with weapons stood below in the wash of the floodlights. But a seventh, unarmed man had joined the group, at the forefront with both hands stuffed into the pockets of a long wool coat. In the distance, among the trees, the raging pyre from earlier still burned.

"My name is Jason Rife," the man called out from below in English.

"Am I supposed to know who you are?" Fenn asked.

"Not at all. I understand we're searching for the same thing. I've come to make sure that we don't get in each other's way."

"And you require six armed men to have such a conversation?" Fenn said, his breath evaporating around his face in bursts of a gauzy haze.

Rife chuckled. "I wanted to make sure you understood the seriousness of the situation."

Considering the firepower, that was an understatement.

"There is the matter of the stone walls before you. Those guns will do little damage to them. And—" Fenn motioned with his left arm. Four men farther down the battlements assumed positions between the crenellations, their own automatic rifles aimed down. "There is this."

"Interesting how the private ownership of firearms in Germany is severely limited," Rife said. "Yet we have all these weapons."

"A fortunate twist of fate for us both," Fenn said. "What is it I need to understand?"

"I'm after the deed. *Das letzte königreich.* And I intend to get it. Please do not interfere."

"I was not aware I was."

Fenn was playing it close, trying to receive more than he gave. Smart.

"Are we going to be coy with one another?" Rife said. "I thought perhaps a frank, honest, face-to-face conversation might be productive. I've always preferred the direct approach."

"As do I."

"Then this should be easy. I'm asking, with all due respect"—and Rife bowed a little for emphasis—"that the Guglmänner not involve itself in this matter."

"It is a Bavarian issue."

"It *was* a Bavarian issue. Now it is an international issue."

Cotton stood silent behind Fenn, out of sight from below. He now knew that Ludwig II had acquired a deed in 1881 to the sovereign kingdom of Hawaii, a deed that would still carry legal significance thanks to a 1993 resolution of Congress. A resolution, though, is not a law. It's just a statement of legislative intent. But to ignore or contradict that resolution would make the US a hypocrite. Even worse, if the king of Hawaii had deeded away his land, that deed would have other legal consequences outside of the congressional resolution, ones that could vest regardless of any revolution, annexation, or statehood that may have come after.

His legal mind went to work, thinking like the lawyer he'd once been, prior to joining the Magellan Billet.

It would be like a man who secretly deeds away five acres to his brother. Then, years later, after he dies, his heirs go to claim those same five acres. The brother produces his deed, records it in the public records, and assumes ownership. The heirs challenge that. But they lose. The deed, properly executed and recorded, takes precedence regardless of the fact that no one knew about it. Same thing here. Only a bit different. Here an absolute monarch conveyed away his entire kingdom. Which was his right at the time. Any subsequent deeding away of portions of that kingdom by others would be invalid, as the grantor to those deeds would own nothing. Once the deed had been executed, the kingdom was gone. And, clearly, the German government would be the valid successor in interest to anything that Ludwig II, as grantee, had acquired. Even if that were in question, as Fenn had noted, the direct descendants of Ludwig would definitely be in the chain of title. Hence why Prince Stefan von Bayern was involved.

All of that made sense.

But who was the guy below with his mini-militia?

And what did he have to do with anything?

"Find out more about him," he whispered to Fenn, who did not flinch, keeping an impressive poker face.

"Who exactly are you?" Fenn asked. "You seem to know a great deal about my business."

"In my former profession it was vital that I knew everything about the people I dealt with," Rife called out. "I am intent on finding that deed. It is important to me. I am asking, gentleman to gentleman, please do not interfere."

"I am this order's grand master," Fenn said. "It was created to protect the memory and legacy of Ludwig II. That deed is part of both. You are asking me to disregard my duty."

"If you don't, some of your brothers will die. We will take whatever measures necessary to accomplish our mission. I assure you, we are not afraid to kill. Can you say the same?"

Fenn stood silent.

Cotton glanced left and watched the four brothers with their weapons aimed below. Not one of them moved. All stood ready.

"We are prepared," Fenn called out defiantly.

Rife motioned and the six men opened fire, sending their rounds into the stone of the castle walls. They all ducked for cover, but it seemed no attempt was made to aim upward at the battlements and Fenn motioned, preventing his men from returning fire.

The staccato from the automatic weapons ended.

They cautiously stood.

"Next time," Rife called out, "it will be flesh those bullets find. Don't say I didn't warn you when you, or some of your brothers, end up dead."

The six men with guns kept watch as Rife retreated back to one of the cars and climbed into the front passenger's seat. They then joined him and entered the other vehicles.

All three drove off.

"Quite a show," Fenn said.

"Is this worth dying for?" Cotton asked.

"That will be a decision for the brothers. Follow me."

CHAPTER 30

LUKE ROLLED OFF THE FROZEN PLATFORM, ALLOWED HIS body to hang down by his outstretched arms, then let go. The jolt came quick to his cold shins as his boots pounded into the pavement. He faced Lexi. "You want to tell me who you are. And it's not Lexi Blake."

She stood in the shadows, her hair, lustrous and coiled, falling wildly to the top of her shoulders.

"My name is Toni Sims."

"And which agency do you work for?"

"You're here for the CIA. I'm here for the White House."

"I wasn't aware that the White House employed intelligence agents on its own."

"It doesn't. I'm on loan to the NSC."

The National Security Council? The president's advisory council on foreign policy matters? That was a bunch of policy makers, not an action committee. "On loan from where?"

"The ASIS."

Australian Secret Intelligence Service? That was a new one. He'd never met anybody from there.

"The White House went looking a long way for you."

"Good things are hard to find."

Touché. He said, "Let's save that one for later. Right now, who are these guys?"

And he pointed to the two still forms lying on the snowy pavement.

"Your tails. I've been on you since you left the beer hall earlier and headed to Professor Ertl's apartment."

"And these two?"

"They've been on the man you followed from the beer hall. The one with the book. My guess is they would have taken that book. But, for some odd reason, you became more important."

Clearly, she'd known about him from the start. So the NSC planted an agent with the prince? Before he was involved. Extraordinary. But what did that mean? Did Koger know?

He doubted it.

"Don't you think working together might have been better?" he asked.

"And miss that great exhibition you put on in Herrenchiemsee? Shooting high. Did you involve Malone? Or Koger?"

"That would be me. He's a friend."

"And then your put-down of Christophe. Priceless. He didn't appreciate it at all."

"Like I care. He's an idiot."

She chuckled. "That he is. He's also been trying to get closer."

"Any success?"

"Wouldn't you like to know. Would you have really pounded me if I'd gone for the gun?"

He recalled the fight onshore. "Probably."

"Now that would have been fun."

"You know, opening that compartment in the desk was not your finest hour either," he said.

She shrugged. "That was Christophe's problem. Like you said, he's an idiot. I didn't really care if he failed."

He got it. "You wanted others to come after you left and get the book."

"Something like that. Of course, I didn't know then that you had the same idea with Malone."

He pointed. "Who exactly are these two guys?"

"Local help."

"That's not an answer."

"They were hired by a man named Jason Rife, who is ex-CIA."

The dark helped him keep his best poker face so as to hide his surprise. Ex-CIA?

What the hell was happening here?

He crouched down and checked out the two guys on the ground. Both wore black ski masks, gashes of white skin for eyes and lips. He removed the masks and saw they were each late twenties, European, wearing boots and jeans, their impressive physiques certainly courtesy of Soloflex. He found no keys, ID, or anything besides two cell phones, which he pocketed. They might prove informative. He then retrieved both weapons that had scattered across the pavement. "You want to tell—"

A car roared around the corner at the far end of the alley and screeched to a halt. Two men emerged and aimed guns his way. Luke never hesitated and fired two shots at the car with the weapons he held. Toni had disappeared behind him, the wash from the headlights illuminating her speedy retreat into darkness. He had to give her cover. So he sent more rounds at the car.

The men slipped back inside and slammed the doors.

He used the moment to retreat himself.

He heard the engine rev and the vehicle sped straight for him, running over the two bodies in its path. Which spoke volumes as to their intentions. He turned a corner and saw Toni to his right, pressed to the wall of a building.

Ready. Waiting.

"Let's take 'em," he said.

And he tossed her one of the guns, then darted left and assumed a position against the opposite building, waiting for the car to emerge from the alley. When it did, they sent bullets into the windows.

Which shattered.

He took out the driver. She shot the passenger.

The car kept going, barreling ahead, crossing the empty street and crashing through the front of a closed shop.

"That's a mess," he said.

Her shoulders rose and fell in concert with her rapid breathing. "One we don't need to clean up."

"I agree. Let's get out of here."

Luke stepped from the cab.

They'd found one a few blocks away from the chaos and used it to get far away from what was surely going to be an active crime scene. He didn't care for killing. Never had. Nothing about it was good. But sometimes it was necessary. Part of the job. A means of survival. And the two in the car had been intent on finding trouble. In fact, they'd charged right into it. He'd simply obliged them. And Toni Sims?

She'd fired without a moment's hesitation.

They were back in the Marienplatz, standing before

the new town hall, a richly decorated building the length of a football field, illuminated by an array of strategically placed arc lights. The square that fronted the building was clear of people but full of closed booths from the Christmas market. Snow was falling, but not heavy, lightly accumulating on the frozen ground. He stuffed his hands into his coat pockets and braced himself from the cold.

"Have you ever been inside the town hall?" she asked him.

He'd not pressed her on the journey over, deciding to let her set the tone. After all, she'd been tacitly in charge ever since he arrived on the scene. No sense changing things now.

"Never had the pleasure," he said.

"I thought you might be a history buff. I saw the way you studied the crypt beneath St. Michael's. There was interest in your eyes."

During his mandatory downtime Stephanie Nelle required from all her agents, which occurred roughly every sixty days, he usually hibernated in his DC apartment and read histories.

He loved 'em.

She pointed upward. The walls and cornices were peopled with figures of baroque statuary, all resting on narrow ledges. "The statues along the front show almost the entire line of the House of Wittelsbach from eight hundred years of reign. There, in the middle of the main facade, is Prince Regent Luitpold. He ruled Bavaria in place of Ludwig II, and his brother, Otto, until 1912. He's part of the reason we're here."

She apparently was far more informed than he was, and the background was appreciated. Still—

"What did you mean about those guys back there being hired by someone who was ex-CIA?"

"Do you know what a scythe is?"

"It's a tool. A sharp curved blade fastened to the end of a long handle. You cut grass or wheat with it."

She nodded. "It's also used by the Grim Reaper to harvest souls."

True.

"A year ago, before Warner Fox's inauguration, during Danny Daniels' final three months as president, there was a purge within the CIA. About two dozen longtimers were forced out. Some in high positions. Others field officers. They did not take it lightly."

He imagined not. Nobody liked being fired. Especially spooks who thought themselves invincible.

"They formed a group," she said, "called the Scythe. And they're about to wreak havoc."

"Does Koger know? He didn't mention any of this."

"He will know shortly. All of this is why the NSC is involved. For obvious reasons, the White House could not rely on the CIA. They've got an internal security problem. So I was brought in to work it from a different angle, just like you are doing for Koger."

He stared up at the clock atop the town hall.

3:00 A.M.

"The boat that shot at you on the lake," she said. "It was the Scythe. They wanted that book."

Every instinct told him to stay cautious. This plot had just thickened to molasses and he had zero in the way of proof for anything she was saying. Could be real. Could be not. His adrenaline surged, carrying with it suspicion, fear, vigilance, and mistrust. But it also fueled excitement. That chill of danger he found all so enticing. He had to resist that urge and use good judgment. That was one thing he'd learned from Cotton Malone.

"I want to hear more about all of this. But could we

do it after some sleep? The prince is going to want to see us in a few hours. That tomb was empty. He was definitely surprised by that, and we need to be awake and alert."

She smiled. "I should say so."

"I'm going back to my room," he said. "See you in a few hours."

He turned to leave.

"Want some company?" she asked.

That caught him off guard. It seemed the night of surprises.

"You've been trying hard the past few weeks to get my attention," she said, adding a smile. "Okay. You got it. And besides, I've been ordered to fully brief you and we can't go to my place. Christophe knows where I'm staying."

He didn't have to be told twice. "Can't argue with that logic."

And they walked off.

CHAPTER 31

DERRICK SETTLED INTO THE REAR SEAT AND STARED ACROSS the car at Trinity Dorner. Her being here, and not at the White House, signaled a big problem. Obviously, when she called earlier TOO had been right here in Munich. Typical of her. Keeping everything close.

"And to what do I owe the honor?" he asked.

"Your crap hit the fan."

He did not like the sound of that. He opened his mouth to speak but she silenced him with a raised hand.

"Not a word. For your own benefit."

He decided to take her advice and they rode in silence across a nearly deserted Munich before finally entering the gated compound for the US consulate.

Back on American soil.

Something about that brought little comfort.

Trinity led him inside the building, which was quiet given it was nearly 4:00 A.M. He wondered if they were here to see the consulate general. He knew the man. A recent political appointee of Warner Fox, closely aligned with the president. He'd made a point to keep his distance, though a CIA liaison worked in the building. They ended up in an empty conference room with a big-screen monitor, which came alive with the face of the president of the United States. Trinity motioned for him to sit, then left the room.

"We've never met," Warner Fox said. "But Trinity tells me you're somewhat of a maverick. In that we are alike. I want to tell you a story. I'm told you like stories."

He stayed quiet, for once, like a good boy.

"When I was little, my nanny liked to take me to the park. Yes, I know. A nanny. But I was a rich kid and my parents were not the warm and fuzzy type. But my nanny. She was an angel. I called her Baba. I truly loved that woman. There was a lake in that park and many times, when we'd go, an old woman would be there, beside the lake, with a metal cage. Baba told me it was a trap. And, sure enough, one day, I saw two small turtles in that trap. A third was in the old woman's lap and she was scrubbing the shell with a brush. She told me that she was cleaning off the algae and scum. Too much of that reduces the turtle's ability to absorb heat and makes it tough to swim. It also corrodes and weakens the shell.

"I thought that was really great of her to do that. She said that it was her way of helping the little guys out. Making a difference. But me being me, I had to ask her, 'Don't those turtles live their whole lives with algae and scum on their shells?' 'That they do,' she told me. I came from a family where every minute mattered. Where your whole damn life is about making money and getting ahead. So I had to ask if her time could have been better spent. She's only cleaning a few of the millions of turtles that exist. How was she making a difference?"

Fox pointed a finger at him.

"She just laughed and finished cleaning the turtle in her lap. Then she told me, 'If this little guy could speak, he'd tell you I just made all the difference in the world to him.'"

Fox went silent. Seemingly considering a pleasant memory.

"The moral of the story, Derrick, is that we can change the world. Not all at once. But definitely one turtle at a time. What we do has to make a difference. It's why I ran for this job. I know you hate my guts. I also know you're looking for your own turtle shell to clean relative to me."

He decided to be direct. "Is that why we're talking? You afraid of what I might find?"

"We're talking because this country is facing a crisis. A really serious crisis. And I'm the damn president of the United States. My job is to protect this country. I love this country. I'm told you love this country. Can we agree on those two truths?"

"Absolutely."

"Good. Let's put aside your ill feelings toward me, and the fact that you disobeyed a direct White House order regarding Cotton Malone, and focus on the crisis."

He was silent with bemusement, then, remembering certain courtesies, he said, "I agree with that, too, Mr. President. That's always been my goal."

"Trinity said you were a practical man."

"I can be. When you say 'crisis,' are you referring to what they call the last kingdom?"

"What do you know about that?" Fox asked.

"Enough that the Federal Republic of Germany may have a valid claim to the Hawaiian Islands. The brother of the current Duke of Bavaria is after that deed. I was asked by the duke to help find it first."

"People have been looking for that deed a long time. Hitler wanted it. Truman went after it. Eisenhower. What makes you think you can find it?"

"I'm good."

Fox chuckled. "Trinity also said you were modest. Are you the one who enlisted Malone to help?"

"Not at first, but I came to believe it was a good idea."

"Because he hates me too? Comrades in arms? What did you promise him? That he could save Stephanie Nelle?"

"Something like that."

"Hate is a powerful motivator. Trust me, I know. But, Derrick, I'm just an imperfect man, hiding behind a self-made myth, one I've cultivated hard for years. Say what you want about me, but I don't pretend to be what I'm not. Like Popeye, I am what I am and that's all that I am. But this isn't about me, or you, or Malone. This is far bigger. This is about this country's future. And it's our duty to protect it."

Through the years he'd become quite good at deciphering the silences between words, the thoughts speech disguised. That talent was telling him now that Fox was not posturing. He detected no lies, no embellishing flourishes that added a stronger feeling of truth. Nothing but sincerity.

Which he had to respect.

"I've learned something from my short time in office," Fox said. "An admission that may shock you. This job demands a more moderate personality than mine. A diplomat as well as an administrator. Somebody to inspire trust, not controversy. A father figure with a determined voice that doesn't offend. Unfortunately, none of that is me. I'm a bull in a china shop. I've always been the loudest voice in the room."

He didn't know what to say.

So he kept silent.

"Three months ago," Fox said, "the NSC advised me that the Chinese were actively negotiating with the Germans, all in cooperation with a prince in Bavaria. They all want something and, in the end, that something will cost us dearly."

Exactly what the duke had reported when Albert enlisted his help. But he still did not know all the details. "Why are the Chinese so interested?"

"When I was first briefed about their involvement, I asked the same question."

He watched as Fox motioned to someone off-screen.

A moment later the door behind him opened and Trinity entered and handed him a folder.

Then she left.

"In that file is the answer I was provided," Fox said. "Read it. Then you and I are going to have a serious chat."

The following information is provided as an operational overview to bring the current situation into a proper perspective.

BACKGROUND

Rare earths are a collection of 17 elements from the periodic table that possess magnetic and conductive properties. They are: cerium (Ce), dysprosium (Dy), erbium (Er), europium (Eu), gadolinium (Gd), holmium (Ho), lanthanum (La), lutetium (Lu), neodymium (Nd), praseodymium (Pr), promethium (Pm), samarium (Sm), scandium (Sc), terbium (Tb), thulium (Tm), ytterbium

(Yb), and yttrium (Y). Despite their name, rare earth elements are relatively plentiful in Earth's crust. What makes them rare is that they are widely dispersed, not found in economically viable concentrations.

Until the mid-twentieth century, most of the world's rare earths were found in India and Brazil. In the 1950s South Africa became the main supplier. Through the 1960s until the 1980s, California made the United States the leading producer. Since the turn of the twenty-first century, China is the number one supplier, producing 70% of the world's rare earth supply. More importantly, China supplies the United States with 80% of its rare earth needs.

POLITICAL LANDSCAPE

Beginning in 2006, China levied duties and implemented quotas on the export of rare earth elements. A dispute arose when those export quotas were cut by 40% in 2010. China argued that the quotas were necessary to protect the environment. Overmining was causing concerns. But the United States asserted that it was protectionism, as the difference in price for rare earths inside and outside China gave an unfair advantage to Chinese firms.

In 2010 China banned all exports of rare earths to Japan during a diplomatic standoff between the two countries after a boat collision incident. That showed China was not above using its near monopoly as leverage.

The United States filed a case with the World

Trade Organization's Dispute Settlement Body against the Chinese export restrictions. The European Union and Japan also joined. The panel ruled against China. And an appellate review board upheld the ruling. China dropped its export restrictions in January 2015. Since that time, prices for rare earths have fluctuated in a steady up-and-down progression, literally at the whim of the Chinese.

SUPPLIES

The search for alternative sources of rare earths is happening in Australia, Brazil, Spain, Canada, South Africa, Tanzania, Greenland, and the United States. Prior mines in all of these countries were closed years ago when China undercut world prices in the 1990s. It will take years and billions of investment dollars to restart production. In addition, there are environmental restrictions that will come into play in all of these locales, regulations the Chinese do not impose on themselves.

Increased demand has strained supply, and there is growing concern that the world may soon face a shortage of rare earths. Within five years demand for the elements will exceed supply by 40,000 tons annually, unless major new sources are developed. Recycling of electronic waste is one method for obtaining new supplies. Recycling plants are currently operating in Japan and France. Some recycling is done here in the United States, but nothing at levels that will produce significant new amounts.

RARE EARTH USES

Rare earths are heavily used in the production of high-performance magnets, alloys, glasses, and electronics. Some are used as catalysts for petroleum refining and diesel fuel additives. Others are important in magnet production, critical for electric motors, generators, disk drives, portable electronics, microphones, computers, phones, and speakers. Still more are used to make fuel cells, batteries, flat-screen monitors, fiber optics, and lasers. They are even used in agriculture to increase plant growth, productivity, and stress resistance. Rare earth feed additives for livestock have generated larger animals and a higher production of eggs and dairy products. None of the portable electronics, which the world has come to depend on, can be made without rare earths. In addition, their presence is vital to maintaining the national defense, as nearly every weapon system we have requires them.

CURRENT SITUATION

Lying off the coast of Hawaii, within its territorial waters, are one hundred billion tons of rare earth minerals. Estimates are that just one quarter of a square mile of these deposits would be able to provide one-fifth of the current global annual consumption. The minerals lie at depths of 11,500–20,000 feet below the surface. Deep, but not insurmountable for mining. Much of it is in the form of nodules, about the size of a potato, each packed with nickel, cobalt, and other rare earths. There are trillions of these nodules, just waiting on the ocean floor to be gathered. Their appearance on the market would alter not only China's near monopoly and end our reliance on foreign suppliers, but it would also lower the price for these elements worldwide.

CHAPTER 32

COTTON WALKED WITH FENN AS THEY FLED THE battlements and reentered the castle, the four men with rifles in tow. Fenn led the way through the ground floor, out a rear door, and into a dimly lit courtyard.

Fenn took him off to one side.

"Herr Malone, I have to do this without you. But *bitte*, please go to my office and access the camera marked 'Grand Hall.' I want you to see and hear what is about to happen."

He decided not to argue and nodded.

"You know the way?" Fenn asked.

He smiled. "I can find it."

Fenn headed off with the four armed brothers and Cotton re-entered the castle, quickly hustling to Fenn's study. On the LED screen was a ledger for the cameras and he clicked on the one marked "Grand Hall."

The screen filled with the image of a brightly lit space with about fifty figures inside, all ages, shapes, and sizes. Each wore a black robe, like the ones he'd seen earlier, with a hood. At the far end was a raised platform. A sole figure entered from the right and walked up onto the platform, staring out through eye slits in the black hood at the assembled. He wore a gold sash across his breast, the only one with such an adornment.

The figure spread his arms out wide and said, "It is now the appointed hour for us to assemble in council. None but members in good standing are entitled to remain during our deliberations."

Fenn's voice.

Speaking German.

One of the assembled stepped forward. "Master, the gates to the castle are secure, the doors locked, the sentinels are on watch, and all those present are entitled to remain."

Fenn nodded. "Good brothers, upon you devolves the work of the Order. You hold, each in your allotted sphere, so much of the peace and prosperity of the realm in your hands. Prove that you are worthy of the confidence reposed in you. Be wise in counsel, courteous in demeanor, firm and vigilant in duty, and careful and considerate in debate, lest an excess of zeal and strong convictions betray you into unguarded expressions, and the peace and prosperity of our Order be thereby endangered. And brothers all, remember the pledge of secrecy to the outside world as regards the business transacted at this council."

Another hooded man entered the hall at the far end and paraded to the platform. The group parted to allow him a clear path. He stopped before the dais. "Master, I find a stranger at the outer gate, under guard of the sentinel."

"Return at once and learn the purpose of this intrusion."

The black hood nodded, turned, and left the hall.

Fenn said, "Good brothers, eternal vigilance is the

price of peace and security. We should be ever on guard, whether the one who approaches be friend or foe. A friend will rejoice in our unity and strength. A foe will dread them. Let all, then, do their duty, as if the welfare of all depended upon each alone, and the visitor will find us a fraternal band united by no common tie, but loyal, brave, and strong. This should be the front we present to all who approach our castle gate. Master-at-Arms, prepare our brothers to receive the visitor."

One of the men yelled out, "Form in a double column."

The hooded men lined up in rows on two sides, leaving a passage between them. At the far end a figure entered wearing a white robe with hood, flanked on either side by black hoods. They each held their charge by an arm. The three marched down through the open ranks and around the hall twice. Nothing about it seemed forced. White Robe walked freely.

The assembled sang an ode.

> *Our brothers strong,*
> *Are mingled here in a happy throng,*
> *To welcome friends, with bumper and song,*
> *And with music's sweetest strain.*
> *We'll proudly greet and gladly extend,*
> *A welcome warm to every friend,*
> *Who'll bear a lance and our cause defend,*
> *And in our service remain.*

The whole thing appeared to be some sort of initiation ceremony. The guy in the white robe apparently was a new member. The three men stopped their parading before the raised platform. The assembled group formed a semicircle behind the newbie several men deep.

"Sentinel, what report have you to make of this stranger?" Fenn asked.

"I found him at the moat, unarmed and bearing a branch of olive, when he hailed me with a friendly greeting. He now awaits the pleasure of you, My Master."

The sentinel handed White Robe a sprig of evergreen. "I present you to the grand master, standing here clothed in a stranger's garb. Take this branch of olive. Otherwise, your life and mine would be in peril. Yours as a hostile intruder, and mine for admitting you here."

Fenn stepped to the front of the platform and lifted a sword from a small table. "What is the purpose of your presence here?"

White Robe said, "To solicit a conference, with a view of enlisting in your cause."

Fenn raised the sword. "Your name and purpose are in part revealed. Good reports have been brought concerning you. True, you come as a stranger, but we have reason to believe you to be true and honorable, and worthy of acceptance in our Order. We are a brotherhood established by good men and true for the advancement of those great principles as first established by our departed sovereign, Ludwig II. Friendship. Loyalty. Aid. Protection. Were you fully advised of these purposes before entering the castle?"

"I was."

"Are you in sympathy with them?"

"I am."

"Not all who come with professions of friendship, and bearing in their hands olive branches, are friends. Hence we have a test that proves the true and condemns the pretender. Once you have passed the ordeal, and are admitted to full fellowship with the loyal brothers of our Order, we will grapple you to our souls with the links of the mystic chain. But not until then."

A blindfold was tied around White Robe, covering the eye slits in the hood.

"You come among us clothed in the garb of a stranger," Fenn said, "in which there is a typical significance. We see you as in the broad glare of a noonday's sun and you appear fair enough. White being emblematic of innocence, truth, and virtue. We do not expect you to be perfect. But it is only those who strive with honor and courage to attain the highest excellence that we admit to full fellowship among us."

The lights in the hall dimmed.

Fenn approached the table and lifted a gold goblet. "When duty calls, we obey. If you are true and courageous, no harm will follow. But if you are a spy, and have evil designs against this Order, this liquid will at once reveal your true character. It is a charmed distillation, discovered by an ancient sorcerer, its ingredients unknown, save to one who shall be nameless here. It has battled all the arts of the chemist. 'Tis bitter as wormwood to the taste of one who is false at heart. But if honest, true, and brave, it is in sweet accord with both the blood and the palate. As gentle as spring water. If you are what you profess to be, fear not to drink and all will be well."

The goblet was handed to the blindfolded initiate who raised it to the ceiling, then sipped its contents.

Nothing happened.

"Well done, my son," Fenn said. "The poison is only

in a guilty conscience, which shrinks from the touch of what is pure. Your truth and courage stand approved. Good brothers of the Order, in the name of purity, I pronounce this friend true and brave, and worthy of the honor and confidence of our goodly realm."

The assembled group broke out in loud applause.

The blindfold was removed and Fenn raised the sword. "You have done well and we welcome you to our Order." The blade was brought down to gently touch the top of the head, collapsing the hood point. "You are now a member of this Order with all the rights and privileges appertaining thereto."

The sword was removed.

"There being no further business before our council, we will proceed to close for the evening. We shall retire outside to the fire and enjoy some time of fellowship. But first, let us clothe our new brother properly."

The white robes were removed, then the hood taken away. Black robes were handed to the new member, who began to don them.

Cotton saw the face.

The thief from Herrenchiemsee.

The guy with Luke.

Who worked for Prince Stefan.

CHAPTER 33

DERRICK LOOKED UP FROM THE TWO PAGES HE'D READ, mentally sorting through the situation, searching for options. Instinct and training cautioned him against saying too much. Was he being played? Manipulated? Hard to say. These folks were way ahead of him. So be smart, give as little as possible, and see what came from that. That always worked in the past. Rash feelings and quick emotions rarely led to anything but trouble. Good choices demanded smart judgment, discipline, and, above all, timing.

Yep. Timing.

"You thought this was just about helping out a friend, protecting our fiftieth state, and getting some leverage on me," Fox said through the monitor. "Now you know why that deed is vitally important to this country."

Oh, yeah. He got it.

"Amazing, really," Fox said. "When the king of Hawaii decided to give his land away, none of it really mattered beyond the simple control of the islands themselves. But, now, that kingdom is a state. A political entity. And if China could somehow wrestle control of that state, they would also have claim to those rare earth deposits. The only reason those minerals haven't been plucked from the ocean is that they sit in our territorial waters. Believe me, China, Russia, and Japan all want them. But only China discovered an inside track and now they're trying to exploit that to the fullest."

"Is this mysterious deed valid?"

"It may not matter. We told the world in 1993 that we stole the Hawaiian kingdom and we apologized. We also said that its monarchy was legitimate and we would respect whatever it did, prior to the coup. Sure, we could take that back, but we'd look like a fool on the world stage. And that we cannot afford. We've been challenging Bejing's dominance over the South China Sea for over a decade, arguing in every tribunal that China's claim to those waters is void because they have no writings to back anything up. So far, we've won that argument. What do you think will happen once all this is revealed?"

He knew the South China Sea dispute was complicated. It involved territorial claims by Brunei, China, Taiwan, Indonesia, Malaysia, the Philippines, and Vietnam. It was important because trillions of dollars' worth of goods passed through those waters each year. One-third of the global maritime trade. Eighty percent of China's energy imports and forty percent of its trade floated across the South China Sea. Fishing and oil drilling rights were also at stake. Control those waters and you controlled all that trade. Right now they were deemed international. But China had become creative and started building islands to gain a foothold. The United States objected and a United Nations tribunal ruled against China's staking a claim. He recalled a CIA briefing memo on the subject that specifically noted that not a shred of documentary evidence existed to support China's ownership of those waters.

Now, here they were, on the hunt for a document that could establish a valid legal claim to Hawaii.

Fox was right.

This stink would be hard to get off your shoes.

"They'll ram everything we've said about the South China Sea down our throats," he told Fox.

"Precisely. We'd be the world's greatest hypocrite. I can already hear it. 'America says one thing, does another when it's their nuts in the vise.' Not to mention the legal implications that deed will have on every land title in Hawaii. Our real property laws are clear. You need an unblemished chain of title. That deed is a fatal break in the chain. The litigation will be endless. When the Hawaiian king deeded that land away, he owned it all. It was his personal property to do with as he saw fit. That's one of the joys of being a king."

None of that sounded good.

"The Germans are a thorn in our side," Fox said. "They'd love to stick it to us. We can't allow them to make a deal with the Chinese. They already are too close for comfort. If they make this happen, both China and Germany will be impossible to deal with."

"So we need to put a burr under their saddle?"

"Something like that."

He stared at the screen. "What do you want me to do?"

"I want you to forget about screwing with me. It's not worth it. You have literally brought a knife to a gunfight. I'll save you the trouble. Do this, win this, and I'll be in your debt. How you want to use that debt is up to you. I'm not going to insult you with a promise of a promotion. Let's do this for the country, then see where we go from there."

Okay. That made sense.

"I read your personnel jacket," Fox said. "And

Trinity told me all about you. You've had a great career. What you did to stop torture is admirable. I never was in favor of any of that. Pointless. Impose enough suffering on someone and they'll tell you whatever you want to hear."

He was surprised at the admission.

"People think they know me," Fox said. "They don't. I can be an ass. Tough to deal with. Sometimes full of myself. But I'd never torture anybody for any reason. I agree with Obama on that one. You did good helping to end it."

"It cost me."

"I'm sure it did. Anything worth having has a price."

"What's the price here?"

"Your self-respect."

Good point. And he felt a little foolish. Which, he assumed, was the whole idea. All of the intel on Fox painted him as a man who sucked every atom of oxygen from every room. Not a man accustomed to being dismissed, ignored, or one-upped. Much more a talker than a listener. But he'd not figured this man to be reasonable.

And a solid patriot.

"You disobeyed my direct order," Fox said, "and involved Malone. Any other time that would rub me the wrong way, and there'd be hell to pay. But this is not ordinary. Anything but, in fact. So I'm giving you a pass. I know why Malone is involved. He wants to help Stephanie Nelle."

This man was irritatingly well informed.

"Let me make this easy for you both. Contrary to what Malone believes, I have respect for both him and Nelle. Malone saved my life. Did he tell you?"

Not a word. Typical.

"On Inauguration Day. The whole thing is stamped

top secret. Nobody knows. Stephanie Nelle played a big part too. I owe her, and Malone. Yes, they both get under my skin and rub me the wrong way. But I don't like owing people, Derrick."

No, he assumed not.

"Recently, I rode Malone and Nelle pretty hard," Fox said. "That was my mistake. What they did in Germany and Poland was the right call." The president went silent a moment. "I got a man killed, Derrick. A friend of mine. I pushed too hard and underestimated what I was dealing with. I should have let Malone handle it the way he wanted. I screwed up. I hate screwing up, Derrick. The damn press labels me wild, impulsive, willful, and arrogant. Somebody who can't accept a mistake. Maybe some of that is true. But nobody calls me stupid. At least not to my face. Except Malone."

Fox paused, seemingly in thought.

"But I deserved that one. I'm being straight with you, Derrick, because Trinity says you're a straight shooter. I'm not going to make the same mistake again. Too much is riding here. My job is to protect this country. I plan to do that. Succeed here and I'm going to owe you. We—you, me, Malone—are going to have to stop this. It's imperative we stop this. We have no choice. This country runs off electronics. Everything we do is dependent on them. I can't allow the Chinese, who already control nearly all of the rare earths on the planet, to assume total dominance. Our national defense will be in jeopardy. The Chinese could literally shut us down. We're stockpiling all we can of rare earths, but we can't store enough. We have to win this fight."

Fox motioned again to someone off-screen. The door opened and Trinity reentered, sitting at the table across from him.

"He's all yours," Fox said. "Tell him the rest, and please, both of you, don't make me regret any of this."

"I won't," she said.

"There is something I need," he said to Fox.

"I'm listening."

"Access to the classified military archives here in Bavaria. What I was able to see a few weeks ago was limited. I need all of the information. Unredacted."

"For what?"

"I doubt we're the first to follow this path. I've found that you can learn a lot from trailblazers."

"I agree. I'll get you access. And Derrick, everything we just talked about is between the three of us here. Nothing to Malone. He stays out of the loop. I don't want him to know I'm involved. In the end, Malone will get what he wants with Stephanie. But he doesn't need to know how or why."

"Got it."

The screen went dark.

"He's not as bad as you think he is," she said.

"I never said a word about him."

"You didn't have to."

Icy fingers of apprehension clutched his gut. Everything about this was hazardous. *Naked* was the word used in the trade parley, meaning little organizational backup, no team, no diplomatic cover. On your friggin' own. But what did he care? His career lay in tatters. And he knew the score. If he failed the White House would disavow him and Langley would fire him. But if he succeeded, he might actually have a shot at making up his losses and regaining the initiative. Still, "What's the rest I need to know?"

"It started a few months ago and it's now reached a boiling point. They're called the Scythe, and they want you dead."

CHAPTER 34

COTTON SAT ON THE EDGE OF THE BED.

The meeting of the Guglmänner had adjourned an hour ago. Fenn had offered a place to sleep for the night and he decided to accept that hospitality. Why not? He was tired and needed time to think. A lot had been coming fast. Which was par for the course.

He should call Koger and report that he'd made contact with that "additional help" he'd mentioned. Also with Jason Rife, whoever the hell that was. Koger needed to know. First impression? Rife talked like an intelligence operative. He'd said an ex, so the likely suspect was again the CIA. All the more reason Koger should be informed. He had to admit, Fenn stood his ground against those guns. That took guts. But for what? An ideal? A memory? A corpse that had been hidden away long ago? A legend? A story? The whole thing was nuts. Was he dreaming? No. His dreams were rational. Even his nightmares carried more reasonable content than all this. He considered himself a solid listener. Someone who absorbed details, cataloged them in proper order, then made good decisions. Sure, he'd made his share of mistakes. But decisiveness had always kept him alive. He liked to adhere to three basic rules. First, organize. Second, gather your strength. Third, test that strength before using it. None of that seemed possible here.

Everything seemed jumbled.

But that did not include the bedchamber he'd been assigned, which was anything but a hodgepodge. Part of it jutted into one of the round turrets, the ceiling coffered with huge crossbeams that framed out elegantly carved panels. The poster bed was enormous with bulbous Jacobean legs. A lovely baroque mirror with a brace of flying angels carved around it held sconces that lit everything with a warm glow.

He found his cell phone and located Cassiopeia's number in his favorites. He tapped the screen and the phone dialed. He didn't expect her to answer. It was the middle of the night. He just wanted to hear her voice when asked to leave a message. It always calmed him. Hard for him to admit that he needed someone. He was pushing fifty, living alone, and constantly in the middle of this or that. Thankfully, Cassiopeia was equally restless. They made a good team. She got him.

And he her.

Where he and his ex-wife butted heads more than they should, he and Cassiopeia seemed to work things through. Neither pushed nor threatened the other. The emotional walls that had been so tall and thick in the beginning of their relationship had withered to nothing more than faint gauze. They'd both overcome their fear of need. Instead, longing brought comfort.

And they loved being together.

Should he marry her?

That was a question he'd been asking himself more and more lately. He'd not been all that great a husband the first time. There'd been infidelities on both their parts. And a son came out of that betrayal. He loved Gary. The boy was growing up fast, soon to be out of high school. He was still talking about joining the Navy and making the military a career.

Like his dad.

And granddad.

His ex-wife wasn't happy about the choice, but realized there was little she could do. The boy may not be a Malone by blood, but he was in every other way that mattered.

He ended the call without leaving a message.

A knock came to the door.

Fenn entered, carrying a laptop. "I apologize for disturbing you, but I saw the light on and thought you should see this."

They'd not had an opportunity to speak earlier as Fenn had quickly hustled him off, away from the brothers.

"Why did you want me to watch that initiation?" he asked. "It seems that would be a private matter, not for outsiders."

"Ordinarily, that would be true. But you needed to see that one."

Now he understood. "You know that guy works for Prince Stefan."

Fenn nodded. "I do. He has set himself up as supposedly our spy within the prince's ranks, but I know better. He's a double agent, with his true loyalty to the prince. I've allowed him to ingratiate himself with us, and I allowed the initiation. But he is no brother of ours."

"We call that rockin' someone to sleep."

Fenn nodded. "That would be accurate."

"He's the one who alerted you about the book theft?"

"*Ja.* He also set up a scenario where we could steal the book back. But I am not fooled. I suspect the prince wanted us to take the book and solve its significance for him, with his spy telling him all we learned."

"That would mean Stefan is seriously uninformed."

"He is. He and his brother, Albert, are not close. I doubt Stefan has much more than bits and pieces of the puzzle. He's hoping we have more."

"So the spy will not learn of the envelope?"

"Not at all. That information stays with us. I did make clear, though, in his presence, that we intend to go after Ludwig's body. What I did not want him to know was anything about you. The four men earlier on the battlements with us are totally trustworthy. They will reveal nothing." Fenn sat on the bed with the computer balanced on his lap. "As I mentioned, I had the twelve random letters from the message digitally analyzed to see how many words could be formed."

Cotton saw them at the top of the screen.

HLNESRNTANME.

"I had the program focus on German," Fenn said. "As you can see, quite a few words came from re-arranging various combinations."

He studied the list and saw that to be true.

"But only two words were formed by rearranging *all* of the letters," Fenn said. "They are there, at the bottom."

Ernst Lehmann.

"So we have a name," Fenn said. "And a place that came from the crossing lines on the map earlier. Eisenach."

"I'm assuming you know what that means?"

"Of course. I am an expert on Ludwig II. I have read every book published on him and have most of them downstairs in my library. I also own some of his surviving correspondence. Ernst Lehmann was a lawyer. He practiced law from 1868 until his death in 1929. His office was located in Eisenach. These clues were left to send whoever found them to Ludwig's lawyer."

"Lehmann?"

Fenn nodded. "He represented the Wittelsbach family during Ludwig II's reign, then while the prince regent served, and also during Ludwig III's short time as king. He was their personal lawyer. For Ludwig II, he did much of the legal work associated with the king's building projects. He arranged for deeds to land, loans from third-party lenders, construction contracts. Whatever was needed. His name appears on countless legal documents I recall seeing."

"Unfortunately, all that was a long time ago. Lehmann's been dead for nearly a hundred years."

"Ah, but, Herr Malone, that is the wonder of this whole thing." Fenn tapped the keyboard on the laptop, then pointed to the screen.

He saw a website.

For Lehmanns.

He read a short intro beneath the logo.

Lehmanns is the world's largest law firm with over 8,000 lawyers in 57 countries, generating over four billion euros in annual revenue. The firm maintains regional headquarters in Beijing, London, Dubai, Washington, DC, and Hong Kong. Its main headquarters is in Munich. The firm was founded in 1873 by Ernst Lehmann. His three sons inherited ownership on their father's death in 1929 and began a meteoric growth that has led to the modern global firm of Lehmanns.

"I checked," Fenn said. "Ernst Lehmann's heirs still

occupy senior leadership positions and own a majority of the firm. One of his granddaughters is the current senior managing partner."

He got the message. "You want me to pay her a visit?"

"Please."

"Why do you think there is anything there to find? All this happened a long time ago."

Fenn smiled. "That's the whole point. This entire mystery was created for posterity. For those who came after to find. We have not been sent to Ernst Lehmann for the trail to run cold. Whatever was there a hundred years ago may still be there."

"And it all could be bullshit too?"

"Faith, Herr Malone. Have some."

"Why don't we go together?"

"Because my presence would detract from your inquiries. I am regarded by many as a mere amusement. The antics of the Guglmänner bring attention to our cause, but they also generate ridicule. I have to confess that I have allowed our activities to lean toward the absurd—but what has happened as of late has shown me that there is a deadly seriousness to things."

"Jason Rife?"

Fenn nodded. "That man is a killer. A type of person you are far more familiar in dealing with than I or my brothers. I can help with puzzles and clues and history. But I do not want any of my people harmed."

He admired the man's sincerity and dedication to his comrades.

"So please, go to Munich. Visit Lehmanns and see if there is anything to find. My instincts tell me there is."

As did his own. But there was still the matter of

Luke, who remained embedded, and what Koger was doing. "I need you to do something."

"Of course, what is it?"

"Prince Stefan's spy has been useful, but he could prove a problem. Take him out of the picture. Make it splashy and public, but nothing traceable back to you. His usefulness is minimal, but I need an open field to run in without worry of being caught. It's time to get the prince out of your business."

Fenn smiled. "Consider it done."

CHAPTER 35

JASON RIFE ENJOYED HIS BREAKFAST OF BELGIAN WAFFLES along with a few strips of crisp maple bacon. The Germans knew how to make a waffle, he'd give them that. And fry some bacon. But beyond those two particular talents, he didn't really care for Germans. And why would he? They tried to conquer Europe twice in one century.

Talk about ambitious.

He finished off the waffle and emptied his coffee cup. The server promptly appeared and offered a refill, which he waved off. The service here, at the Strada, was top-notch. One of Munich's finest hotels. Nothing like the budget-rate dumps he'd been forced to endure while still with the CIA. Contrary to what Congress and the general public thought, the spy business did not include an open checkbook. James Bond ordering the most expensive bottles of champagne and caviar? No way. There were rules. Per diems. Oversight on what you spent. And consequences when you didn't follow the rules. Thankfully, he was not subject to those any longer.

Thirty-four years he spent with the CIA.

A lifetime. A career.

Then he was fired.

No warning. No reason. Just *it has been determined that your services are no longer needed and your employment is hereby terminated, effective immediately.*

He, along with forty-five others, were there one day, gone the next.

He'd suspected politics as the main culprit, the agency using the opportunity of a change in presidential administrations to purge itself of what it regarded as "problems." He'd risen to the level of a senior field officer and had handled some really delicate situations. Sure, he'd had his share of mishaps. Who didn't? But he also was no fool. So it seemed a bit naive that his superiors thought he would just accept the termination and move on. Amazingly, a few of those fired had done just that. But another group of fourteen men and women decided that if the company had no loyalty to them, then they would return the favor.

So they formed the Scythe.

They'd debated on where and when to first strike, deciding that their initial objective would be centered on Germany and something known as the last kingdom. He'd heard tales about it back in the days when his services were needed. And he knew that Derrick Koger was here working an operation relative to it. He also knew that the White House was involved, through the NSC, having dispatched their own operative. Thank goodness for friends in high places. Have enough of those and secrets were hard to keep.

The last kingdom was a remnant from the past, one of many hidden away at Langley. The CIA was so big, so compartmentalized, its past riddled with so much crap, that no one could ever exhaust the information in its files.

But the real secrets—the ones that mattered—
Were never, ever, written down.

He left the hotel and drove from Munich twenty
miles south to the Alpine foothills. Every turn in
the road found a new wintery vista. A succession
of broad wooded valleys accommodated the highway,
a backdrop of snow and evergreens stretching to a
distant blur. He half expected to see dancing elves
and kobolds. Traffic was moderate, the morning rush
hour still lingering, so it took nearly an hour to find
the cluster of snow-topped wooden chalets with stylish canted roofs. The whole thing looked like some
Christmas card, snug and serene among the woods.
This area was full of blue-collar, working families,
most earning pensions at the manufacturing plants
not far away. The locale was also the base for a team
of his Scythe associates who'd assembled there over
the past week. One of three locations scattered across
southern Bavaria with men and women awaiting
assignment.

He eased his rental car off the highway, slowing
and turning in through an opening in a low wooden
fence. He'd called on the way and informed the
occupants he was coming. The day was cold, the sky
sunny and cloudless, the morning mist already gone.
Being higher in elevation here, south of Munich, the
snow from last night had accumulated in respectable
amounts.

He stepped from the car.

The front door opened and one of his associates
exited.

Terry Knight.

His old friend was fifty-three, short and stout
with a moderate amount of wiry brown hair dusted

with an equally moderate amount of gray. They first met fifteen years ago. Knight had many areas of specialization. Safecracking, forgery, surreptitious entry, electronic surveillance, sabotage, and just about anything else a field officer might require to get the job done. He'd worked for Technical Services as one of their "handymen."

"How are the other two?" he asked Knight, a curl of smoke issuing from the chimney stack.

"Still sleeping. They said that was really cold water."

He chuckled. "I bet it was. It's time for you to go to work."

"I'm ready. What do you have?"

He liked that his old friend's spirits were always buoyant and eager, with a hint of mischief.

"The listening devices you installed throughout Fenn's castle paid off," he told Knight. "After we rattled the cage last night I got an earful. Cotton Malone is there."

The attack on the Chiemsee had not gone according to plan. The idea had been to kill the thieves and retrieve whatever had been taken from the palace. But his men out on the lake had been forced to abandon the effort and escape into the water after the ferryboat interfered. Luckily, they'd both worn neoprene suits against the cold, which had allowed them to swim back to shore and escape hypothermia. The move with the ferry had been a carefully orchestrated act, done by someone who'd known precisely what they were doing.

Somebody like Malone.

Who'd apparently made quick contact with Marc Fenn.

Which had surely been Koger's doing.

"After my visit, Grand Master Fenn was a busy guy,"

he said. "He deciphered the clues Malone uncovered, then talked at length about them with some of his black-hooded brothers. This morning, Koger came to the castle to get Malone. He, Fenn, and Malone had a long chat." He paused. "We've caught a break. Koger and Malone are meeting with Paul Bryie and Randy Miller in a few hours. Koger set the meet up."

He saw that Knight seemed as pleased as he'd been. Some of those friends in high places had told him about the meeting, along with its time and location.

"Our adversaries need to know what they're facing," he said. "I don't think they consider us much of a threat."

Knight smiled. "I always did like to be under-estimated. What do you have in mind?"

"It involves a helicopter and you."

"Since you're the pilot, what's my part?"

"The meet is at Meridian Technology. Bryie and Miller are en route there now."

"I know the place."

So did he. "Get me access from the rooftop heli-copter pad."

"When?"

He told him the approximate time. Then reached into his pocket and removed a phone. "I'll text you on this. When I do that roof door needs to be open five minutes later."

"You're asking a lot," Knight said, "for only a few hours from now."

"You can handle it."

Knight laughed. "To get these bastards? You bet your sweet ass I can."

CHAPTER 36

Luke awoke.

The other side of the bed was empty, the shower in the bathroom running with the door open. He glanced at his watch. 8:40 A.M. He and Toni had been in his hotel room for nearly five hours. Some of that time had been spent talking, her bringing him up to speed, the rest in more personal endeavors. They'd both seemed to want an escape into some irresponsible ecstasy. But, what the hell? They were both grown adults. The sleep part had been for the past two hours. A quick nap before a new day began. Normally, right after waking he worked a swift, vigorous ten-minute exercise regimen of squats and push-ups followed by a hot shower and shave. Not today. Perhaps he'd join her? The water switched off.

Too late.

She emerged from the bathroom with one towel draped around her toned frame, another wrapping her wet hair.

"About time you wake up, soldier."

"Aren't you the bright-eyed and bushy-tailed thing in the morning?"

"Best time of the day."

He rolled out of the comforter and sat up on the side of the bed. "I'm more a night person."

She tossed him a smile. "Yeah, I gathered."

He'd switched his phone to silent when they'd arrived back, wanting a few hours of quiet. He now saw that Koger had been calling. No message or voice mail. Not the guy's style. He liked to dial a number and speak to a live human being. And he kept calling until that happened.

"What do I tell Koger about you?" he asked Toni.

"I think he knows all about me by now."

He could tell she was still more in the know than him. Which he didn't particularly appreciate. He unlocked the phone and punched in the number.

"There's a woman here in Munich," Koger said, "working with the prince, who's from the NSC."

"I'm aware. She and I have become acquainted."

He reported all that happened and explained about the book, its journey through the night, and the images he'd forwarded. He also told Koger about the attack and the four dead men.

"You're quite the badass," Koger said.

"I had help."

"Is she good?"

He glanced her way. "I would say so."

"Everybody is on the same team," Koger said. "Which I'm sure your lady friend knows all about. What's her name?"

"She has two, but the real one is Toni Sims. An ASIS agent."

She tossed him a mock salute, then went about dropping the towel and dressing, not the least bit concerned about modesty. He watched as she slipped on her undergarments, then slid her trim legs back into tight jeans.

"An Aussie?" Koger asked.

"She doesn't talk like one, if that's what you mean."

"Make sure she's in the loop," Koger said.

"I think she's already fully in the loop," he said. "It's you and I who are not."

She offered him another smile, which he liked.

"I agree," Koger said. "Have her tell you about the Scythe. You need to know. It's a new day, new game, with new players. And Malone is still in this."

That was a shock.

"Was that him last night in the ferryboat?"

"Yep. I recruited him after that. Stay safe and keep me informed."

The call ended.

He was curious. "Care to enlighten me on the Scythe?"

She pulled the sweater down over her chest. "Absolutely. Over breakfast. Koger mentioned them?"

He nodded.

Both of their phones dinged.

He checked the screen.

A text.

From the prince.

STEFAN STOOD IN CHRISTINE ERTL'S APARTMENT.

The place had clearly been rifled, books tossed about, the front door violently damaged. She'd called him a few hours ago to tell him about the intrusion, but he'd waited until a little before 9:00 A.M. to summon his people. Christophe had already arrived and confirmed that he dropped the book off to Ertl immediately after leaving the church last night. Ertl confirmed that fact, telling him that she'd locked the book in her desk before going out for the evening. When she'd returned her door was hanging off its hinges and the book was nowhere to be found.

"Did you tell anyone about the book?" he asked Ertl.

The older woman shook her head. "*Nein*. No one."

He turned to Christophe. "Did you tell anyone?"

"Only Lexi and Smith knew. I brought the book straight here."

Outside in the hall he heard footsteps climbing the stairs. A few moments later Lexi and Smith appeared in the doorway. He'd texted them the address and told them both to come immediately.

"I want to know if either one of you revealed anything about the book to anyone?"

They both shook their heads. What else were they going to say?

"What happened?" Lexi asked.

"The book was stolen," Stefan told her. "And I seem to have a spy working for me."

"I agree," Lexi said. "And I know who it is."

CHAPTER 37

DERRICK TURNED OFF THE STREET AND SPED THE CAR DOWN a concrete ramp into the garage beneath the office tower. Malone sat on the passenger's side. He'd picked him up south of Munich at Marc Fenn's compound. He was upset that Fenn had moved unilaterally. That had not been the plan. And he'd apologized to Malone for the unexpected violation. He'd insisted on a full report of everything that had occurred, which Fenn provided and Malone corroborated, adding what else was found in the desk, along with Fenn's deciphering of the message. Trinity had given him a full briefing on the Scythe, which included an identification of its leader, Jason Rife. Considering that Rife had gone to the trouble of making personal contact with Fenn, along with a demonstration of firepower, he'd decided that the chain of command should be informed. Once done, and after answering a lot of questions about what he was doing, he'd requested a meeting with agency officials, which Langley had approved.

They took a freight elevator straight to the eighteenth floor, which Derrick accessed with a code punched into a keypad. When the doors parted they walked through a crowded storage room and down a maze of wide carpeted corridors, lined with offices, to a far corner. Tall glass doors led into a world of partitioned walls, false ceilings, and bright lights. A cube farm, fully equipped with desks and computers.

"This is officially Meridian Technology," he told Malone. "A company that provides software for text analytics in over forty languages. Which can be really helpful, I might add. Unofficially it's funded by the CIA, and sometimes we use these offices to coordinate our local activities. Everyone was told to come to work at noon today. That gives us a couple of hours of privacy."

Cooperative corporations often provided cover for the CIA. Historically, that was usually offered by them to win favor for profitable government contracts. Electronics and software firms were the agency's favorites.

The main workroom flowed through another wall of glass into a smaller area containing two mahogany desks. A door marked PRIVATE led into a large furnished office, the two outer walls tinted glass, one of the inner walls clear glass. The morning sun spread a bright brocade of light everywhere.

Waiting for him were two men. One was potato-nosed, with sagging jowls, pouched cheeks, and lusterless gray hair. The other was all spit-and-polish in a dark suit, white shirt, and silk tie, with a long neck like something seen at the zoo. The bigger man wore pleated dark trousers, an understated striped shirt, no tie, and suspenders that bulged from his massive girth.

"You look like crap, Derrick."

"And you look like the broad side of a barn, as usual."

The big man laughed. "So what else is new?"

"The pork roast is Randall Miller, CIA station chief here in Germany," he told Malone. "The spare rib is Paul Bryie, from counter-terrorism."

Malone introduced himself and they completed a round of perfunctory handshakes.

"Let's have a seat," Derrick said. "We have a problem, and I want to know everything you know about the Scythe."

"Where'd you hear about that?" Miller asked, clearly a little perplexed.

"Let's say I have a good source of intel. I'm head of special operations, yet I wasn't told a word about it. Why?"

"It's being handled," Bryie said. "By counter-intelligence. We're dealing with it quietly."

He'd never liked Bryie and the feeling was mutual. Counter-terrorism was akin to internal affairs at a police department. Part of its job was to find the bad apples. And if that effort squashed a few good ones along the way? Too bad. They'd squashed him once.

But not today. "Explain to me, and my associate here, how you're handling it."

Bryie shook his head. "That's above both of your pay grades. Langley sent me here not to brief you, but to clean up your mess. And Malone should not even be part of this. You know the orders on him."

"Malone is my problem. Not yours."

He allowed his icy gaze to bore into the wiry little man. He was in a bad mood. A lot was happening around him that he knew little to nothing about. Long ago he'd learned how to deal with the sluggish obstinacy of petty bureaucrats. Especially ones like Paul Bryie who'd never worked the field. Bryie had been an analyst. Every aspect of his life neat and precise, everything tallied in tidy columns, each minute planned. A desk jockey. Always had been. Always would be, preferring the world neatly arranged, like paragraphs on a page. TOO had told him to do what he did best. *Raise hell.* And the White House would stand behind him. So he allowed his sullen features to take on the frozen expression of a death mask.

And withdrew his revolver.

Which he aimed straight at Paul Bryie.

COTTON WATCHED THE SCENE PLAY OUT.

He could feel the tension and sensed there was a history between these three men. Yet Koger seemed different. Calm. Measured. Empowered?

Bryie straightened up in his seat.

No matter who you were, no matter how much experience you possessed, having a gun pointed at you was unnerving. He knew that from bitter experience. Doubtful Koger would pull the trigger, but that was the thing about having a gun pointed your way. You just never quite knew what was coming next.

"We're here all alone," Koger said. "This floor doesn't open up for another two hours. Do you get my drift?"

Bryie said nothing.

The gun stayed aimed.

"You going to kill me?" Bryie asked.

"More wound you, with some enormous pain."

No one said a word.

"I called for information," Koger said. "Langley approved my request for a briefing and sent you two. I don't need a lecture on how to do things. What I need is information. This Scythe interfered with an ongoing operation last night. They fired on my people. They then tried to intimidate some German nationals with more gunfire. Of course, I had no idea the group existed until a little while ago. Otherwise, I would have been prepared. I don't like being unprepared."

"It isn't going to happen," Bryie said. "You're not being brought into the loop on this one."

The gun fired, its retort loud and startling. The bullet had zoomed past the wiry man and pinged off the inner glass wall, which apparently could take a hit as bulletproof.

"Holy crap," Bryie called out as he shrank down in the chair. "Are you out of your mind?"

"I'm not screwin' around here," Koger said. "The next one is going to send you bleeding to the hospital."

"You're nuts," Bryie called out, trying to regain his composure. "A pain-in-the-ass loose cannon."

"No. I'm aggravated, and I need intel."

"I'm counter-intelligence," Bryie said. "You know what I can do to you."

"If I shoot this piece of crap in the knee," Koger said. "What are you two going to say?"

Miller shook his head. "Looked like an accident to me."

Cotton knew the right answer, too, and held up both hands in mock surrender. "I'm not even supposed to be here."

Koger grinned. "Looks like you're outnumbered, Paul."

Bryie seemed to register the gravity of his situation. "All right. Put the gun away and we'll talk."

Koger laid the weapon on the table within easy reach.

Bryie seemed to regain control of his nerves. "You're nuts. Totally and completely nuts."

"I've been called worse," Koger said.

"I'm sure you have." Bryie paused, grabbing a couple of quick breaths. "In the waning days of the Daniels administration his CIA director cleaned house. Forty-six field officers, analysts, and managers were fired. Across all divisions, in every part of the world. Don't get me wrong, each one of those let go had a long history of disciplinary issues. One problem after another. For me? They all needed to go. Not a one of them worth keeping."

"But not everyone at Langley agreed?" Koger asked.

"Hardly. Some thought it all political. Selective firings to settle old scores. Daniels' people, doing at the end what they didn't have the balls to do earlier. And there's some truth to that. The firings were all appealed to Fox's new CIA director. But, to everyone's surprise, she affirmed the firings. Every. Single. One of them. That bred a civil war within the agency that's still raging. And now it's boiling over right here in Germany."

"Why haven't I heard a word about this?" Koger asked.

"We've gone to great lengths to keep things under wraps," Bryie said.

Randy Miller's pudgy lips formed a smirk, one Cotton thought might have fooled many people to their detriment. "We have to be careful. The Scythe have lots of friends left in the agency. Those fired agents had all been around a long time."

"Which means," Bryie said, "that we are leaking classified information like a sieve. All of those terminated agents had access to super sensitive stuff. We regularly police against outside access and moles.

That's our job. But from the inside? From a bunch of people who'd been trusted? That's a new one. Bottom line is we've got forty-six agents who are pissed off."

"And the Scythe?" Koger asked.

"About a dozen of them, we don't know the exact number, formed this group," Miller said, "and gave themselves that catchy name. Up till now, they've been relatively quiet. We've been watching, but not much of anything has happened."

"Until last night," Koger said. "They are obviously interested in me."

"Which is what?" Bryie asked. "I checked. There are no sanctioned ongoing operations here in Bavaria."

"The Scythe were way ahead of me," Koger said. "They knew where I was and what I was doing."

"Unlike Langley," Bryie added. "Like I said, Derrick, they have friends in high places and we're hemorrhaging information. You're a tough guy here with your gun. But this is going to be a two-way street or no street at all. Pick one. I'll either stay and tell you more, or leave, depending on your choice."

Cotton watched as Koger considered his options, the best of which seemed a no-brainer. "I'm just a utility infielder in this game, but you need to know what they know."

Koger seemed to get the message. Loosen up. Turn on the vacuum cleaner. So he briefed them on the Duke of Bavaria's request for help, the presence of the Chinese, the interest of the German government, and what happened last night, ending with, "The last kingdom is a fairly obscure piece of intelligence that has suddenly become the flavor of the day."

Koger then explained about a huge deposit of rare earths sitting on the bottom of the ocean in Hawaiian territorial waters that China wanted.

Miller nodded. "That all makes sense. The Chinese are Germany's closest foreign ally. They do over two hundred billion euros in trade with them every year. And, unlike us, they do it nearly balanced with as much exported to China as is coming into Germany. It's Chinese demand for German products that has fueled Germany's strong economy for some time now. When everyone else was barring Chinese equipment for a new telecom network on national security grounds, Germany resisted and bought the stuff. The largest share of imports into Germany every year is from China. There's also an enormous amount of collateral investment. Berlin and Beijing have a mutually beneficial cozy relationship. We have to watch that constantly. And you're right. We've known for a few months now that the Chinese are working some sort of operation in conjunction with the Germans. What that is has been hard to pinpoint. The Germans don't particularly care for us, so it's been difficult learning details. We do know that the chancellor's chief of staff and the head of the German parliament met with Prince Stefan last night."

"About what?" Koger asked.

"I don't know."

"Find out," Koger said. "It could be crucially important."

Cotton knew that Germany's relationship with the United States had been strained for a while. It started with the Daniels administration, but escalated with Warner Fox. Recently, he'd found himself right in the middle of that tension with the latest national elections.

"Fox doesn't give a rat's ass what the Germans think of him," Miller said. "He likes keeping them at arm's length. Which, I might say, is not a bad strategy.

But this new German coalition government is fragile and they're looking for international partners wherever they can find them to shore up their power. China wants to be that partner. That much we do know."

Koger nodded. "Duke Albert told me that Stefan wants the deed so he can bargain it to Germany in return for the German parliament granting Bavaria a secession vote. Stefan believes the Bavarian people will vote to leave the Federal Republic. And he may be right. If that happens, Albert becomes king. But that isn't going to last long. The duke is dying with terminal cancer. Maybe a few months left, at best. Then Stefan takes over. Hence his interest in all this. I'm guessing the Germans have already made a deal with the Chinese to assign the deed to them, in return for God-knows-what. Everybody wins, except us."

"And now you have a group of renegade ex-CIA after the same thing," Cotton said. "But why?"

"To ram it down our throats," Bryie said. "Or sell it to the Germans. The Chinese. Or blackmail us. The list is endless. But whatever their intentions, they're not honorable."

"Who's leading them?" Koger asked.

"Jason Rife."

Cotton stared at Koger.

"What is it?" Bryie asked. "What do you two know?"

"Those German nationals I mentioned who were contacted last night. That came from Rife personally," Koger said.

He told the other two about Rife and the six men with guns.

"That's confirmation," Miller said.

Bryie nodded.

"The Scythe are definitely here."

CHAPTER 38

RIFE PRESSED THE CONTROL STICK FORWARD AND THE MD-520N chopper knifed through the cold lucid air twenty-five hundred feet above Munich. He'd leased the helicopter from a local airport, glad one was available. The two-seater was used routinely by police departments around the world because at five hundred feet the blades could barely be heard over street traffic.

Extensive flying lessons had been a part of his CIA training, including helicopters and all sorts of military aircraft, and he marveled at the responsiveness of the high-tech machine's sensitive controls. The lack of a tail rotor was unusual, but the pressurized air that passed out the boom provided excellent directional control and further lessened noise.

He sped across downtown Munich. Ribbons of high-way, rooftops, office buildings, apartment complexes, and hotels raced by below. He left Old Town and headed for the northern edge and the more modern section, high-rises rolling by in succession beneath the undercarriage.

Ahead lay the building. Twenty stories of multi-use

space, mainly corporate offices, law firms, accountants, and a multitude of other businesses. Among them was a suite of offices on the eighteenth floor that belonged to a Belgian corporation, which was a wholly owned subsidiary of a Dutch entity. He'd been inside several times and was familiar with the building's layout.

As was Terry Knight.

Like any large office complex, there was security that provided controlled access to the employees of the various tenants or their acknowledged guests. Nothing fancy. Just what one would expect in today's day and age. Which allowed the CIA to work out of the building with a high degree of anonymity and a moderate amount of protection.

He looped the chopper up and over the roof, circling from above. He stayed high and used the morning sun and altitude to further conceal the turbine's soft staccato. He spotted the rooftop landing pad and reached for the phone, sending the text already typed in for Terry Knight.

And counted down five minutes.

LUKE WAITED TO HEAR WHAT WAS GOING TO COME OUT of Toni's mouth next. Her admission as to knowing who the spy was among the prince's minions shocked him.

So he readied himself to react.

"Explain," Stefan said to her.

Toni pointed at Christophe. "He's a black hood."

STEFAN EVALUATED HIS THREE EMPLOYEES.

Christophe he'd known for a long time. But the other two? They were strangers, hired on Christophe's recommendation after background checks had been run. He knew that Smith was ex-military, dishonorably discharged. A man with the requisite skills and a bad attitude. Perfect. And, so far, Smith had worked out fine. Lexi Blake? She, too, had passed a check. As he recalled, she was a freelancer who'd worked for a variety of private corporations doing things they could not do openly. A person-for-hire, with no particular allegiance other than to more-than-fair compensation. He couldn't hold that against her. Greed was not unusual for people with the skills he desired. In fact, it was a trait he could easily work with.

"Three days ago, I followed him," Lexi said. "Something didn't ring right. I saw him meet with men I traced to the Guglmänner."

He watched Christophe, who stood silent.

"What motivated you to follow him?" he asked her.

"I don't like people who ask a lot of questions," she said. "And this one is extra nosey. Not to mention a little handsy."

Stefan chuckled. "Who could blame him."

"I don't like handsy," she said.

"Fair enough. But he's in charge. It's his job to ask questions."

"You don't seem surprised by the accusation," Smith said.

"I'm not surprised. In fact, we wanted the Guglmänner to take the book."

LUKE GLANCED AT TONI.

Who seemed as surprised as he was by the admission.

"This is a complicated matter," the prince said. "The Guglmänner have been around a long time. They are perhaps the best source in Germany on Ludwig II."

"What about your own family?" Luke asked.

"You would be surprised how little we know about our ancestors. It comes from a hundred years of indifference and complacency."

"You sound bitter," Toni said.

"I am. Which is why you are all here. The Guglmänner are not going to willingly disclose any information to me. I've tried before and failed to get them to open up. So Christophe became involved with the group months back, when I first began to plan this operation. A few hours ago he was welcomed fully as a member. He has led them to think that he is their spy among my ranks. So I had the book delivered here and Christophe informed them of the opportunity. To their credit, they came and stole it without delay."

"To do what with?" Toni asked.

"We don't know," Christophe said. "Not yet, anyway."

"We have not had a chance to see what they will do," the prince said. "But I believe they know more about the book's significance than I could ever learn. So what better way to become educated than through them."

"Okay," Luke said. "I get all that. And it's really clever. But last night you were genuinely surprised with the tomb being empty."

"I was hoping that the rumors were wrong." The voice was low, but steady and sure. "Again, I think the black hoods can lead us straight to Ludwig."

"Is what you're after here?" Toni asked.

Good question.

"I believe so. It's the only place it could be. Christophe's job will be to keep us informed on the black hoods' progress."

"You sure they'll go looking?" Luke asked.

Stefan smiled and faced Professor Ertl. "Tell them."

The older woman smiled.

"That is the one thing we know for certain."

CHAPTER 39

COTTON SEARCHED HIS MEMORY FOR DETAILS ON JASON Rife, but he could not recall a thing. Which was a bit unusual for him. But he'd simply never come in contact with the man before, nor heard anything about him.

So he asked, "Tell me about Rife?"

Bryie shook his head. "You're not even supposed to be here."

Koger reached for the gun.

"Okay. Okay," Bryie said. "He was career CIA. Worked India, Lebanon, Syria, Sudan, Morocco. He also did a stint in the old Yugoslavia. Then he was sent to Iraq in the late 1990s to stir up opposition to Saddam Hussein. He had to be recalled after we found out he was plotting to kill Saddam. In retrospect, not a bad idea, but we don't assassinate people anymore."

He caught the last two words, knowing that in its early days the CIA had routinely utilized assassination.

"Rife urged the Clinton administration to back an internal Iraqi attempt to overthrow Hussein," Bryie said. "It was organized by a group of Sunni military officers, a few members of the Iraqi National Congress, and the Kurds. We were to supply covert CIA assistance. Needless to say it turned into a fiasco. The plotters were all caught and executed. That's when Rife was sent to Latin America."

"Which was even worse," Miller noted. "He worked as a supposed military attaché out of our embassy in Buenos Aires. Then he became chief of station in Panama, Mexico, and the Dominican Republic, and eventually chief of the Latin America Division. But he had to be removed from there, too, after he intervened to help a friend who'd been arrested on drug charges in Mexico."

Cotton smiled. "Sounds like he doesn't like rules."

"To say the least," Bryie said. "I assure you, Rife has a long and storied personnel jacket. In the right scenario, from another time, that type of lone-rangering would have been appreciated. Not anymore. The world is too complicated, too interrelated. Rife never gave a damn about consequences. Unfortunately, those do matter."

Cotton got the picture. "And now he's organized some angry ex-agents into a fighting force, one that's here, screwing with Derrick."

"Apparently so," Bryie said. "Frankly, we didn't view this Scythe as any real threat…until today."

"They were definitely a threat last night," Koger said. "And you should know that one of my people killed four men here in Munich. My guess is they were Scythe, or hired by them."

"I'll need the details," Miller said. "I can check it out through my sources here in Munich."

"Luke's doing?" Cotton asked.

Koger nodded. "He took 'em out."

"Is he okay?"

"Not a scratch." Koger faced Bryie. "Is counter-intelligence monitoring the Scythe?"

Bryie shook his head. "These guys dropped off the grid when they were fired. We made an error in not watching them. But I'm going to get people on it immediately."

Cotton had long ago discovered that in life you get out in proportion to what you put in. He sensed something from Randy Miller so he asked, "What else do you want to say?"

"Who says I do?"

"A long time working the field."

Miller tossed him a long stare.

"What is it, Randy?" Koger asked.

"You need to keep your mouth shut," Bryie said.

Koger lifted the gun from the table and pointed it. "Shut up, Paul."

"Screw you, Koger. That's it. I don't have to take this anymore." Bryie rose from the chair and pointed a finger at Miller. "What you're about to do is going to get you fired. Maybe even arrested. Bad enough Malone is here. I'm not going to be a part of this. Contrary to you, I abide by rules. My superiors told me what I could and could not say. Randy's did too. I've already broken those parameters. But not anymore. You're on your own, Randy."

And Bryie stormed from the office.

"That was a lot of drama," Koger noted.

"He's by-the-book," Miller said in a low voice. "Always has been. And he's right, we were told to not be so cooperative. Listen. Ask questions. But don't talk too much."

A flicker of uncertainty showed in Miller's eyes, which only added to the mounting tension in the room. Everyone seemed to be testing each other, seeking out strengths and weaknesses, assessing tactics.

"What is it you have to say?" Cotton asked.

"I've been looking into *das letzte königreich* for a few years now."

"And you're just now mentioning this," Koger said.

"It was only a side project. But lately it's turned into a whole lot more. I've studied it in detail. The OSS and the CIA, both during and after World War II, looked into it."

Miller undid two buttons on his shirt and revealed something hanging from a neck chain. "This was in the archives from World War II."

Cotton saw it was a small brass ward key.

Koger leaned in close. "What's it open?"

Miller shrugged. "I don't know. I'm still working on that. I don't even know where it came from. It was just part of one of the old files."

"Why did you take it?"

"I thought it would be safer with me."

"Are you the one who had all the stuff I ordered redacted?" Koger asked.

Miller nodded. "I did. But I can see now that this whole thing is bigger than I imagined."

"Bryie didn't want you to tell us this?"

"Langley didn't want me to tell you. But I thought you had to know. I have a lot more info on this at my apartment. You're right. We can't let the Chinese get that deed. What was for me a historical curiosity has become something far more important. Rife approached me a few weeks ago and wanted to talk all about it. I told him to go to hell."

"You report that contact?"

Miller nodded. "Of course."

"Let me guess," Cotton said. "To Bryie?"

The big man nodded.

"You have eyes and ears in my team, don't you?" Koger asked.

Miller nodded. "I've been keeping up with you."

Koger was clearly agitated. And with good reason. His employer was withholding information and playing games. Big-time. Even worse, they were looking over his shoulder. But for some reason Koger did not seem all that concerned. Any other time there'd be an explosion.

But not here.

Which made Cotton wonder.

Who was pulling the big man's strings? It had to be higher than the director of the CIA. Which left only one option.

The White House.

Koger gestured with the gun and bore his predatory eyes into Miller's. "I need you to tell me everything you know. Right. Now."

CHAPTER 40

RIFE MANIPULATED THE CHOPPER'S CONTROL STICK AND started his descent. The concrete landing pad was roughly twenty feet across and bisected by a huge red X. Thankfully, plenty of bright sunlight illuminated the spot. He touched down softly and switched off the turbine.

The blades whined to a stop.

He grabbed a vinyl bag from the passenger's seat and slid open the plexiglass hatch. A cold wind buffeted the top of the still-twirling blades, but the pad was shielded by a short wall that capped the roof. He climbed out of the chopper and headed straight for a metal door with BUILDING STAIRWAY—KEEP CLOSED stenciled in German on the gray exterior.

The door opened.

"Just like you wanted," Terry Knight said. "Five minutes."

He entered.

Gray featureless walls wrapped the warm rectangle at the top of a lighted stairway. He peered over the railing down the center space that faded twenty floors below. Fluorescent panels illuminated each landing, where concrete steps turned one hundred eighty degrees. Knight was dressed as a security guard.

"How'd you manage that?" he asked.

"Opportunity presented itself. I took it."

He'd have expected no less. "Anybody dead?"

Knight shrugged. "Do you really want to know?"

No, he didn't. "Are they still on the eighteenth floor?"

Knight nodded. "In the main office. You know where."

Yes, he did. Having been there several times before himself back in the supposedly good ol' days. "Anybody else on the floor?"

"Not that I could see. I found out no one was to report until noon. My guess is Koger commandeered things for a while."

"Is the stairwell door open on the eighteenth?"

Knight displayed a set of keys. "I unlocked it myself on the way up."

"Does one of those keys control the elevators?"

Knight nodded and identified the right one.

He searched through the vinyl bag and removed a short-barreled automatic rifle, draping the sling around his left shoulder. Then he found two sound-suppressed automatic pistols.

He kept one and gave the other to Knight.

"Stay here and watch the chopper."

Then he advanced two floors down to the unlocked door marked 18. He clicked the steel door's handle to open it and peered through a tiny slit into the hall beyond. He knew there was no closed-circuit TV monitoring. The last thing the CIA wanted was for someone to have the ability to electronically observe anything that happened on the floor. The security for this place came from anonymity.

No one was in sight.

He slipped through the doorway and turned the corner, heading toward the elevator bank. There, he pressed the down button. Thirty seconds later the car arrived empty. He used the key Knight had procured to shut off the elevator. He exited and pressed the up button. A minute later the other car arrived, which he also disabled. He knew about the freight elevator on the other side of the floor, but it stayed locked with restricted access. Koger might have access, so he had to make sure it did not become an avenue of escape, along with the four stairways.

His targets waited across the floor at the south end.

He re-gripped the semiautomatic, his finger loose on the trigger, and stalked ahead. Along the way he passed dozens of closed doors. He tested a few knobs. Locked. Good. At a corner he inched his head around the edge. The main office was straight ahead. Suddenly, Paul Bryie pushed through a hinged sheet of glass and headed in his direction, apparently for the elevators.

He quickly backtracked.

On the way he passed a recessed door labeled MEN'S ROOM. He pushed through and waited. Bryie passed a few seconds later. He slid the semiautomatic around to his back, resecured his grip on the sound-suppressed pistol, and followed. At the corner he stepped around and confronted Bryie at the elevators.

The thin man turned around and faced him. "Do it."

He nodded. "Knight's on the roof with the chopper."

"I'm leaving the way I came. Good hunting."

Bryie entered the stairway and left.

He headed back for the office.

CHAPTER 41

Cotton gazed out the windows at the buildings in the distance. They were west of downtown, near the old Olympiapark. Not far from where, in 1972, Palestinian terrorists killed eleven Israeli athletes and local police killed five of the eight terrorists during a failed attempt to rescue the hostages. The other three were captured. Which only led to the hijacking of a Lufthansa flight a month later, when the West German government released the three in an exchange. But the Israelis eventually tracked down and killed every single Palestinian suspected of involvement with the massacre.

If you wrong us, shall we not revenge? Shakespeare was right.

And that's exactly what was happening here.

Tit for tat among spies.

Randy Miller stood near the windows, Koger was still seated, both men talking, debating what to do next. Koger had put away his weapon. He felt like a third wheel on a date. Through the open doorway back to the inner secretarial area, he noticed movement. The glass doors leading to the outer work area opened, then closed, and a man entered cradling a semiautomatic weapon. Unusual? This was a CIA front. But the face, hard and determined with eyes locked ahead, he'd seen before.

Last night.

Jason Rife.

Before he could utter a sound, Rife burst through the office doorway. The first salvo of bullets strafed Randy Miller, pricking his enormous frame like a dartboard, bouquets of blood roses erupting across his bulging white shirt. The retort sounded like a dot matrix printer spitting ink, only louder. Another salvo smacked the thick glass windows, but did not break them. Miller slammed against the outer wall, the window reverberating from the impact like ripples on a dark pond. A final volley finished Miller in the head, bullets slicing and dicing flesh and bone, ricocheting off the glass, blood splattering like paint on a bright canvas. Koger reached for his gun as Rife sent a burst of rounds his way. Cotton reacted and lifted the nearest armchair, hurling it toward the shooter. Its flight and impact provided the few seconds needed for he and Koger to rush for the only other door out, which led into an adjacent conference room.

They entered and slammed the door.

No lock. He hoped the damn thing was solid.

"Get down," he yelled.

They dove to the carpet just as the first blast of bullets pounded into the wood on the other side of the apparently solid wooden door. Adrenaline poured through him. He stood and slid the heavy conference table across the tight carpet toward the door, the armchair at the far end leading the way, the rest of the chairs sliding by the wayside. The armchair slammed into the closed door, followed by the table.

That should slow some forward progress.

He yanked open the door at the far end of the conference room, readying their escape. Their pursuer pushed on the other door, immediately realizing something blocked the way.

The door slammed forward several times.

The table inched back.

"You see the face?" he asked Koger.

"Loud and clear."

And they both ran from the conference room.

RIFE SLAMMED INTO THE DOOR AND THE BARRIER ON THE other side finally slid back. He squeezed through and surveyed the conference room. Chairs were strewn all over, the rectangle empty, the door at the other end closed. He backtracked through the main office toward the outer secretarial space. Along the way he made sure Randy Miller was dead.

Good riddance.

Last thing they needed was for this guy to shoot his mouth off.

He left and spotted Malone and Koger slipping out the glass door into the open office area.

He pointed the gun and fired.

Bullets peppered the glass, but the transparent wall did not shatter.

KOGER WHIRLED AROUND.

Thirty feet away, across the expansive cubicle area,

flames shot out the end of a short gun barrel. He silently thanked someone at Langley for the foresight to use bulletproof glass.

"Move it," he said, and they tore down the hall, turning the corner.

They needed to take a stand. No way was he going to cower down to these traitors. But it was always best to choose your ground wisely.

"Any ideas?" he asked Malone.

They came to an intersection of hallways.

"Bryie set us up," Malone said.

"I got that. And I'll be dealing with him. Right now, we have a more immediate problem."

"I'll draw him my way," Malone said. "You shoot him."

"Done."

RIFE STOPPED HIS ADVANCE.

He'd come to kill not only Randy Miller, but Koger and Malone. Miller had been part of the internal review board that recommended not only his own termination, but also those of all the other forty-five people too. He and Miller went way back, their relationship anything but cordial. No surprise the bastard refused to help him when approached a while back. He assumed Miller had garnered a great measure of satisfaction from recommending his termination. Hopefully as much as he'd just found by gunning the big man down. Now he had to end Koger and Malone. Too much was at stake for these two to stay around. They were not like Miller. No. They were competent field officers, and he could ill afford to have to deal with them, considering what lay ahead. One or both of them were surely armed. And they weren't the type to flee a fight.

Just the opposite.

So he had to assume they were waiting for him.

Good.

He'd not gone hunting for a while.

CHAPTER 42

Cotton swung around the corner and kept moving.

Somewhere ahead Rife was waiting with an automatic rifle. Considering he was unarmed the odds were not good if they came face-to-face. Koger had headed in the opposite direction, the idea being for them to force their attacker to choose his poison.

He turned a corner.

Rife appeared.

Fifty feet ahead.

He dove back into the corridor he'd just exited as a burst of rounds obliterated the drywall. His escape ahead was a long corridor. Lots of open space. No way he could make it to the end of the hall before Rife arrived and took a shot. He spotted a nook with a restroom door on either side, a water cooler in between. Men's room to the left, ladies' to the right. He sprang to his feet and slipped into the men's room, peering out through the cracked-open door. Ten seconds later Rife appeared, leading with the gun, flashing his eyes around the corner, surely wondering where his prey might be and if he was armed. More importantly, where was Koger? Hopefully the gunfire had alerted him. Or at least he had to assume that was the case.

Cotton needed to draw attention to himself.

The next time Rife snuck a peek, he pushed the door out, then allowed it to ease shut. Another quick millimeter of opening and he confirmed that Rife was coming straight down the hall toward the men's room.

He surveyed what was behind him.

Fluorescent light illuminated a black marble counter with a double sink and pewter fixtures, a wall mirror throwing light out into what was apparently an employee washroom. The floor was black marble, the four toilets separated by stone partitions. Surely Rife was proceeding with caution, which should give Koger time to move. Now he knew what the fox felt like.

Not good.

He decided the best defense was an unexpected offense. So he stood near the exit door, watching the crack of light at the bottom darken. Rife would have to grab the handle and yank the door open, his way.

He readied himself.

The shadow at the bottom reached its apex of darkness.

Rife was just on the other side.

Go ahead, you SOB. Do it.

The door moved.

He anchored his body with his left foot and slammed the sole of his right shoe into the door, propelling it outward.

RIFE WAS PUSHED BACK, OFF BALANCE, THE GUN UNSTEADY in his grip.

The door exploding outward had startled him.

He'd not expected Malone to be that aggressive, but he should not have been surprised. He staggered for a few steps.

Regained his balance.

And worked to level the gun.

Cotton lunged from the doorway and tackled Rife, propelling his body into the other man before he could fire.

Together, they hit the carpet.

He needed to disarm Rife but the gun's shoulder strap prevented that from happening. So he opted to pound his right fist into Rife's face. He rolled his body to be on top and noticed that Rife had come prepared, wearing a Kevlar vest.

Good for bullets.

Not so good for a fistfight.

Koger hurried toward the gunfire, which had come from the other side of the floor.

He heard sounds of a struggle.

One he was drawing closer toward.

Rife pivoted upward and tossed Malone off. He used the moment he'd bought to roll onto his side and regripped the weapon, intent on obliterating his attacker. But Malone seemed to realize his dire predicament and scampered immediately toward the bathroom door, yanking it open and disappearing inside. Before it fully closed, he sent a volley of rounds into the wooden panel.

Footsteps were approaching.

From behind.

He swung around and aimed the rifle. If Malone had been armed, he would have used the weapon.

No.

The real threat was coming.

KOGER'S EARS PERKED AT THE SUDDEN SILENCE.

There was a struggle, then gunfire, then nothing. And all just around the corner ahead. He approached the wall edge and peered around.

Nothing.

Empty.

"Malone. Where are you?"

COTTON HEARD KOGER CALL HIS NAME.

He'd flattened himself across the black marble floor, anticipating Rife's attack. The threat must now be gone. He came to his feet and opened the door. The other side was riddled with weapons fire.

"Here."

Koger appeared from around the corner at the end of the corridor and rushed his way. "You okay?"

He nodded. "I'll live."

"We need to find that bastard."

He agreed.

They headed off in the only direction Rife could have gone, following the corridors until they came to the elevator lobby.

Koger pushed the button for down and both car doors opened. "He didn't go that way."

They stared at the stairway door.

Koger eased it open.

Footsteps pounded.

Above them.

※

RIFE SCAMPERED UP THE CONCRETE STAIRS TWO AT A time toward the roof. He'd taken out Miller, and tried for Koger and Malone, but failed. No need to risk any more. Those two were trouble. Better to fight another day.

Knight waited at the top of the stairs.

"Change in plan," he said. "I couldn't get Malone or Koger. We need to go."

He handed over the rifle and rushed out onto the roof, jumping into the helicopter and firing up the turbine.

"Be ready," he said to Knight.

※

COTTON ENTERED THE STAIRWELL.

Koger right behind him, gun in hand.

Two floors above a door opened, then closed. He vaulted up the stairs to a solid metal door. Blades whirled outside. He cracked open the metal door. The chopper sat with its plexiglass bubble cabin pointing straight at him. The rotors wound fast and the helicopter slowly started up, the skids clearing the pad.

He pushed open the door a little more. A cold wind buffeted. Rife was at the controls. Another man inside the cabin swung open the hatch door and aimed a gun

their way. He fell back into Koger and allowed the
metal door to shut, dropping to the concrete floor.

Rounds pinged the outer facade.

The rotors grew louder.

Then faded.

He came to his feet and opened the door.

The chopper was flying away.

CHAPTER 43

Stefan tried to enjoy his breakfast.

He'd dispatched Christophe to head back to the Guglmänner. The time had come to play his hand with those fanatics. The current incarnation of the brotherhood had existed for about seventy years, restarted in the 1950s during Germany's postwar rebuilding as a specialized social organization. An amusement in the media every once in a while. The only thing making them relevant at the moment was that they possessed a wealth of information passed down from the time of Ludwig II's death and in the decades after. Much more than his own family possessed.

"I want you to know, Christine, I appreciate your help here."

He and Professor Ertl had left her apartment and walked to a nearby café. The Guglmänner had moved quickly on the book, exactly as Christophe had predicted. He'd made Ertl aware of his plan and she'd agreed to be the bait. That's why she'd accepted the book from Christophe, locked it in her desk, then left for the evening, providing the perfect opportunity. Now that the black hoods controlled the book, perhaps they could solve the mystery. The one Christine had researched as best she could. The same one his father and uncles barely mentioned.

At least to him.

They were dining on fresh bread, strong coffee, and some delicious Danish ham.

"I glanced through the book when Christophe first brought it," she said. "It's an 1875 edition. *Tannhäuser und der Sängerkrieg auf Wartburg.* Not a mark on any page. The correct seal was there, though. The embossed swan with a break in the neck."

King Ludwig III had owned an impressive private library. A few thousand volumes, each one embossed with a swan as a personal mark that denoted ownership. He'd adopted it from his cousin Ludwig II, who'd loved swans. Odd, really. In German lore swans were an ill omen. Yet images of them adorned all of the castles and palaces. So many that Ludwig II acquired a nickname. The Swan King.

"There are other volumes from Ludwig III's library in the national archives," she said. "All with the same embossing on the title page."

Good to hear the book was absolutely authentic.

Ertl was an expert on late nineteenth-century Bavaria, post Ludwig II, during the time of Luitpold's regency and Ludwig III's brief reign. They'd met a decade ago when he first began to show an interest in that period. He'd rekindled their relationship a few months back and she'd seemed eager to help.

"We need to find another copy of that book," he said to her. "Can it be done?"

She nodded. "Now that we know what we're looking for, I should be able to locate another in one of the state libraries."

"Please do that. And quickly."

Ertl's knowledge, like his own, of the legend surrounding Ludwig was hampered by a disturbing lack of information. But she had discovered among Ludwig III's papers a reference to a possible hiding place in the desk. So he'd sent his people to investigate, which had resulted in success.

"Marc Fenn and his brothers now need to go to work," he said to her.

"They will. It's their whole purpose."

Fenn was an interesting fellow. He inherited his wealth from his grandfather, who founded a household cleaning products company in the late nineteenth century. His father turned it into a global chemical empire that eventually had close ties with the Nazis. But, like so many other entities that had been needed after the war to rebuild a destroyed Germany, their sins were forgiven and the company flourished. Smartly, Fenn diversified in the 1990s and started making cables, antennas, and receivers for cell phones. He was a billionaire several times over, with all the time and money in the world.

Which he envied.

Once king, he would deal with Marc Fenn and all of the other industrialists who wanted to profit from *his* Bavaria. There'd be a price to pay for the privilege. Just like the old days.

"It is the Guglmänner's move," he said to Ertl. "We have supplied them with all we have. Now they need to use it."

He'd already told her everything that happened last night.

"If there's a chance they can recover the body, they will," she said. "They have long peddled theories of Ludwig II's murder. The body, if found, along with modern forensics, will give them the first opportunity to actually prove their beliefs. A way to possibly legitimize themselves. Have you seen their video?"

He had. A thirty-minute exposé on the death of Ludwig II, with everything pointing to murder. Lots of supposition. Not much evidence. They'd posted it online two years ago, garnering over two million views. That's a lot of interest in a bunch of obsessed men wearing black robes and hoods.

"No one has ever had the opportunity to study Ludwig's remains," she said. "The autopsy done at the time of his death was totally controlled by the government, who had an interest in suppressing the truth."

"Do you believe he was murdered?"

She shrugged. "It's doubtful. That secret would have been too difficult to keep. More likely he died at just the right moment through his own fault. He was a foolish, reckless man."

He agreed.

But he was still counting on Marc Fenn to move forward.

In fact, it was his only play left.

COTTON WALKED DOWN THE HALL, PAST THE RESTROOMS that had served as a lure and back to the main office. Koger followed. The glass partitions bore dozens of bullet scars. Everything seemed morbidly quiet, a fitting backdrop to the carnage. Randy Miller lay on the carpet, propped semi-upright against the outer glass wall, blood splatters smeared across the clear surface, bullet shatters spreading like spiderwebs. The overweight frame had contorted in death, the smell sickening from all of the body fluids shed.

"We needed him alive," Koger said of Miller.

"Which explains why they shot him."

He held his breath and crouched down close to the body. The shirt had been shredded and frayed from the entry wounds. A glimmer caught his eye through the cloth on the bloodied chest. The chain with the ward key. He loosened Miller's tie, opened the shirt at the neck, and yanked the chain free.

"We may need this."

He pocketed the key.

"And there's one more thing." Koger crouched down and rifled through Miller's pockets, finding an ID card and a ring of keys. "I need this to get into his apartment and the archives."

Cotton checked his watch. "I'm going to go to that law firm and see what there is to find, if anything."

"I'll call in a cleanup team. This is a mess. In more ways than one."

He agreed.

"You realize that if Rife knew we were here, he might know about that law firm too," Koger said.

"The thought had occurred to me."

"Watch yourself."

CHAPTER 44

LUKE WAS SURPRISED THAT THE PRINCE HAD INSISTED that he accompany Christophe back to the Guglmänner. Toni had been a little put off not to be included, but the prince had made clear that the black hoods were an all-boys club, always on the lookout for new recruits. "Herr Smith should make a great addition to their ranks," he'd told Christophe. "Which will give us two among the ranks."

"The grand master is a man named Marc Fenn," Christophe told him as they walked. "He's wealthy, smart, and obsessed."

"Apparently not smart enough to know he has a double agent working for him."

Christophe smiled with a confidence he'd come to detest. "Maybe I'm just good."

Back home in Tennessee, this cocky ass would definitely qualify for redneck status. Which wasn't bad, by any means. He'd proudly worn the label all through puberty and into his teenage years. Even now he occasionally was tagged. Which he liked. But that didn't mean he enjoyed dealing with 'em. Like one of his buddies used to say, *You can pick your friends and pick your nose, but you can't wipe your friends on your saddle.*

"Maybe you are that good," he said, giving the idiot the credit he wanted and hoping it would loosen his tongue. "Where exactly are we going?"

"Fenn wants to see me. They're moving forward with things, just like we hoped. It's our job to get involved with these idiots as deep as we can."

They were walking the streets of Munich, the sidewalks packed with people. Christmas loomed two weeks away and the city was all decked out in anticipation. His watch read a little past 10:00 A.M. The pale orb of a wintry sun glimmered in a cloudy sky, coaxing the world to light. All of the animosity from last night on the Chiemsee seemed to have waned. That was another thing about rednecks. Short memories. New battles to fight. Toni had gone with Stefan and he wondered what else might be on the prince's mind. The background info he'd been briefed on noted that the guy was a bit of a ladies' man. He doubted he'd make much headway with Toni since she seemed more than capable of handling herself, but for some reason he didn't like the thought of him trying.

They turned off the sidewalk into an outdoor market. A painted sign above the entrance, adorned with fresh pine boughs, read MITTELALTERMARKT. Entering was like stepping back in time to the Middle Ages, complete with the flying of colors, period dress, food, drink, and olden crafts. Everything was buzzy and festive. Dancers were garbed in Renaissance attire. Vendors role-played medieval characters. Blacksmiths crafted swords. Glass was being hand-blown. A pig roasted on a spit. The apple fritters at one of the booths looked delicious. Christophe stopped at another vendor and ordered two meads.

"What is it?" Luke asked.

"Fermented honey wine. Time you learn to drink like an ancient German."

The brownish liquid came served in red clay mugs that seemed awfully fragile, their thin handles just begging to be snapped off. He sipped the mead, thick and sweet with hints of fruit and spice. Not his thing, but he wasn't going to let anyone know that. So he followed Christophe's lead and downed the whole mug.

They walked across the market to one of the larger booths where two men in colorful vestments were crafting medieval leather shoes. They passed through the booth and then a thick curtain that opened into a covered tent. Some sort of work area. Waiting for them was a man in his mid- to late fifties with short iron-gray hair brushed straight back. He wore a stylish cashmere knee-length overcoat with a dark Louis Vuitton scarf.

"This is the guy I told you about," Christophe said to the man in English. "Jonathan Smith."

The older man made no effort to shake hands, so Luke kept his own stuffed into his coat pockets.

"This is Marc Fenn, the grand master of the Guglmänner," Christophe said.

"I am told you're not fluent in German," Fenn said.

"American, through and through," Luke noted. "But I am good at what I do. Christophe says you need some...specialized help. I can do that." He paused. "For a price."

"Everything is for a price with Americans," Fenn said.

"It's called capitalism. We like it. Makes the world go round."

He had no intel on this guy, and he was a little

suspicious that the head of the brotherhood was taking the time to meet with a total stranger. He'd learned long ago that the owner of a place rarely did the hiring. That was left to others lower on the organizational chart. So what was this about? Maybe Christophe was not nearly as good as he thought he was.

"I am also told you might like to join our ranks," Fenn said.

Luke shrugged. "I'm not much of a joiner, but my friend here says there are benefits. I like benefits."

"We cherish the bond between the brothers. It is something we all hold dear."

He could not decide if the words were pandering or he meant them down to his core.

"I have a job that needs doing," Fenn said. "And it comes with…benefits. It is a job for which I prefer not to involve the other brothers."

"He's a brother," Luke said, pointing at Christophe.

"He is special, since he also works for the prince. He is our spy. Christophe said you would understand the necessity of that duplicity, as you, too, work for the prince."

"I understand euros and dollars. And I don't owe the prince a thing."

Fenn nodded. "You owe me nothing either. But I will owe you when you complete the job I need done."

"I like the sound of that."

"We can handle it," Christophe said, eager.

"I require something," Fenn said. "But it will be difficult to obtain."

"I assume the benefits are in proportion to the risk?" Luke asked, playing the part of what was expected.

"Twenty-five thousand euros each, if you succeed. And all for just a few hours' work."

"And if we don't succeed?" Christophe asked.

"You'll probably end up in jail, at which point I will disavow ever knowing you."

Christophe shrugged. "Nothing new there. I'm in."

"Me too," Luke said.

STEFAN DID NOT LIKE THE FACT THAT NO ONE recognized him.

Few knew, or cared, about a Wittelsbach. Once they were among the most elite royalty in all of Europe. The sovereigns of Bavaria, a fairy-tale-like place that everyone admired. Now they were nothing. His brother possessed a bit of notoriety, but not much. Albert had long withdrawn from the public, preferring to stay cloistered at Nymphenburg with his stamps. When death finally came he doubted anyone would give the Duke of Bavaria much thought. No elaborate state funeral. No accolades. Little to nothing. Just a body hauled down into a crypt and sealed away. Of course, everything would be different if he could find that deed and make a deal with Berlin.

Kings were definitely treated differently.

He and Lexi Blake were on the move. Christophe and Smith were making contact with the black hoods, further ingratiating themselves with the brotherhood. It was important that close contacts be maintained there, especially since he'd allowed the group to take the book. Ertl was working on securing another copy, just in case it might be needed. She was right. Marc Fenn and his cohorts would move ahead. No question. And, thanks to Christophe, he knew they possessed far more information than he could ever amass. That spoke volumes regarding the level of knowledge and interest within the Wittelsbach family, which amounted to practically nothing. He'd kept Lexi with him since it never hurt to have a capable pair of eyes and hands around. And it didn't hurt that all that came inside an attractive package.

Earlier, he'd received a call from a contact within the Residenz palace. Albert had visited there during the wee hours of the morning, along with another man. Tall, thin, gray hair, American. They'd started in the Hall of Antiquities and ended in the Ancestral Gallery. Stefan had not visited the Residenz in a long time. It had little relevance to the family. Most of it was a late twentieth-century re-creation. Little remained from the time of his ancestors, the whole thing just a tourist attraction.

Which definitely had its place.

He and Lexi entered the Residenz through a side door used by employees. His friend was waiting and walked them both upstairs to the Ancestral Gallery and one of the glass-enclosed display cabinets.

"The duke was interested in that," his spy said, pointing.

The medal he knew about. It had been awarded to Ludwig in 1865 by the king of Hawaii. He'd been unaware, though, that it had been returned to public display.

"How did it come out from storage?" he asked.

"The duke requested it be placed back on display," his spy told him.

Troubling. On many levels. What was Albert doing here? And why show off this medal? Last night his brother had, as usual, shown no interest in anything. Yet, for some reason, he'd come here after their encounter and met with an American.

For what?

"The man who was here with the duke. Any idea who he might be?" Stefan asked.

His spy smiled. "I have no name, but one of the custodial staff recognized the duke and snapped a picture of the two of them."

What a break. "Do you have it?"

"I do."

CHAPTER 45

COTTON STEPPED OFF THE ELEVATOR AND INTO THE expansive lobby of Lehmanns. He'd taken a taxi across town to the high-rise building that sat in the heart of the more modern part of Munich. He'd also taken Koger's warning about Jason Rife to heart and been careful on his route and on full alert once arriving.

On the way over he'd used his phone and learned more.

Though the firm still carried the name of its founder, Ernst Lehmann, its ownership was diverse, spread across several hundred equity partners. It employed thousands of lawyers worldwide, specializing in bankruptcy, real estate, tax, immigration, health care, litigation, estate planning, employment, and business law. A full-service institution with lawyers in fifty-seven countries. Depending on the situation, it could either parlay favor or do battle. Its extensive array of legal talent was surely supported by an army of secretaries, legal assistants, clerks, office managers, and bookkeepers, themselves supported by thousands of square feet of office space, volumes of research materials, and all the other varied and assorted tools needed to get the job done. One internet site noted that revenues last year topped four billion euros. A far cry from the solo practice of the late nineteenth century.

The floor bustled with activity among a sumptuous ocean of white in a sleek minimalistic, modern decor. Lots of acrylic, metal, and glass glazed with a mirror-like black shine. Not a ninety-degree angle in sight, everything smooth, curved, and sloped. Warm-toned paints mimicked elements of stone and wood in shades of gray and violet. The polished pine floors were equally bright and airy. Two large impressionistic lithographs consumed one wall. He approached a receptionist counter and a crystal vase brimming with fragrant flowers. Three people worked behind it tending to phone lines and dealing with visitors. Bright sunshine filled the space from exterior walls of glass, which, understandably, made him a little nervous. A bright-eyed young man in a light-colored suit with a thin tie approached and asked in German if he could be of assistance. Cotton had already learned the name of the senior Lehmann, who remained the titular head of the firm.

"I would like to see Dianne McCarter," he said in German.

"Are you expected?"

He had to play this just right. "I am."

"*Bitte*, your name, please."

"Harold Earl Malone."

He decided his full name would be better here.

The young man tapped a keyboard a few times. "So sorry, but you are not on her appointment list for today."

Big surprise. But it was worth a try.

Time for plan B.

On the way over he'd thought about the six lines from the riddle. *Where Matthias Strokes the Strings. Edelweiss over Black Forest. No Water Cold. Pulpit, Cross, and Garland. Northeast the Crown.* All of them led to a specific point on a map except the second part, which really made little to no sense. *Edelweiss over Black Forest.* Edelweiss was a mountain flower, like a daisy. Found mainly in the Alps. So why was it *over* the Black Forest?

Maybe the line served another purpose.

As gatekeeper.

"Tell her, *Edelwei Über Schwarzwald.*"

The guy tossed him a puzzled look.

"She'll understand what it means." The guy did not look like he was going to take the bait. So he added, "Trust me, you want to pass on this message."

Or at least he hoped that was the case.

Twenty minutes passed before an older woman in a dark wool suit approached him as he sat in the busy reception area. The young man from the desk had told him to wait while he made inquiries. Since he had zero places to go, he'd obliged the request.

While waiting he read up on Dianne McCarter with info from his phone. She was eighty-three years old, the youngest daughter of Ernst Lehmann's second son. She'd been a lawyer for nearly sixty years, inheriting the senior management reins when her brother and two cousins died in a 1986 plane crash. She had two daughters and a son, along with grandchildren and great-grandchildren, some of whom were lawyers too. Her accomplishments were notable, even serving in the Bundestag for a time representing Bavaria. She no longer actively practiced, though she did maintain a Munich office and the title of senior executive partner. Probably more of a rainmaker, there to keep the big-name clients paying big fees. It seemed she spent most of her time now lecturing at various universities on law and politics.

"Herr Malone," the woman said to him.

He stood.

"I am Frau McCarter's personal assistant," she said in German. "If you would come with me."

Apparently, his hunch had proven correct. If Ludwig III had written the lines to direct someone to Ernst Lehmann in Eisenbach, it made sense that there would exist a method for Lehmann to know if that person was authentic. What better way than to leave some specific, but not obvious, words that had to be uttered. Simple, yes. But sometimes the simple things worked best. Of course, when all this was conceived nothing close to what was at stake now existed. What had once been a way to just find the body of a dead king had turned into an international race for much more.

He followed the woman onto the elevator where she pressed the down button. After a few stops along the way they walked off into an underground parking garage. A black Mercedes coup waited with the engine running and the rear door open.

The woman beckoned. "*Bitte.*"

"Are we going somewhere?" he asked.

"I'm not, but you are."

"And where would that be?"

"To speak with Frau McCarter. She is waiting for you."

CHAPTER 46

DERRICK DECIDED TO START WITH RANDY MILLER'S apartment, but first he swung past Luke's hotel and retrieved a package that had been left for him. Inside the manila envelope were two cell phones that had been retrieved from the men who'd attacked Luke last night. He'd have them dumped to see what they might reveal. Hopefully, if those guys were connected to the Scythe, the phones might provide a trail to Rife and his people.

Randy Miller had been German station chief for a few years and had settled down in Munich. He was divorced and lived alone in an apartment on the city's east side, not far from the A99 outer autobahn. Malone had been right about Paul Bryie. That man leaving so abruptly had not been happenstance. Bryie had to be connected to Rife, part of those *friends* Miller had stated still existed for the Scythe within the agency. If not, why didn't Rife gun him down on the way to the office? Surely the two passed each other.

The cab deposited him at the apartment building.

What a mess.

Here he was, standing in the cold, doing what exactly?

If you told someone you worked for the CIA, the first reaction was usually wonder, then disbelief. *Really? You serious? How cool is that?* The revelation always conjured up images of every Hollywood stereotypical spy. But reality was so different. No tuxedos, fancy gambling tables, or jet-setting around the globe. The CIA's job was to simply collect and analyze intelligence data. That mainly came from studying books, journals, industry bulletins, newspapers, websites, tweets, Facebook posts, television, and radio. Anything and everything that offered information. From all that reading reports were generated by the thousands of pages. Most were hardly read and simply filed away as reference material. Ninety percent of the agency worked in cubicles, like the ones back at Meridian Technology, sitting before computer screens. Nothing about any of that was glamorous or exciting. Just analysts who hated their supervisors, supervisors who wanted to be assistant directors, and ADs who thought they'd make a great director. So why did he want an office at Langley? A reward? Recognition from his peers for a job well done? Crap no. He wanted it simply because he deserved it.

A final success.

To go along with all of the failures.

His marriage seemed the worst of all. It took a lot for your wife to walk out with only her clothes after twenty years of marriage. No goodbye, take care, or go to hell. Just gone. Without a word. It was said that the eyes of a lover resolve like an eagle's, spotting the smallest of things. That had been Jody. Nothing slipped by her. Everything came under her glare.

But he'd made it easy for her.

He'd been uptight, constantly preoccupied, and perpetually moody, rarely offering her his undivided attention. Foolishly, he'd thought she'd never leave. That they were in it forever. But he'd been wrong.

There'd not been another woman in his life since, as no one could ever take her place. If only he'd told her that—just once—maybe things would have turned out differently.

He hated sports and cared little for games, so he buried himself in work, his closest companions books, movies, and museums. In that order. He lived a solitary life and constantly told himself that one day he'd be happy. *Life, liberty, and the pursuit of happiness, right?* Wrong. More like life, disappointment, and more disappointment. He'd long struggled to find meaning in the wild swings of good and bad fortune that constantly came his way. But fate seemed to have finally shined a light on him.

He was involved with something big.

And he had the president of the United States as an ally.

He'd worked every hot spot in the world, dealt with every kind of lowlife imaginable. Now he was director of special operations. But not much "special" ever happened in Europe anymore. The Cold War was long gone, his post regarded as a nothing job where you really could not get yourself into much trouble. Which spoke volumes as to what the CIA brass thought of him. Trinity might be right. His time was ending. So why not go out with a bang. Do something that made a difference. Decades in the field had taught him patience, planning, and guile. But, most of all, to always play for keeps—

Or don't play at all.

He paid the cabbie and stepped into the apartment

building, trudging up the stairs to the third floor. He'd been provided the address on the way over by secure text after reporting Miller's death. There was nothing particularly special or attractive about the building. Just one of a zillion nondescript multi-housing projects located all around Munich. Over 1.5 million people lived in the city. Another 4.5 million in the outlying areas. A huge, sprawling metropolis. Easy to get lost in. Even easier to be forgotten in.

He approached the apartment and his senses sprang alert.

The door hung partially open.

He looked around, saw no one in the hall, and found his weapon. Not a sound came from inside. He pushed the door open with his right foot. The place was a wreck. Somebody had tossed it. Not a book, file, or computer in sight.

He inspected every room.

The same.

Whatever had been here was long gone.

Only one explanation.

The Scythe.

CHAPTER 47

Rife was pleased with the day so far.

He'd taken out Randy Miller, nearly killed Malone and Koger, and managed to retrieve everything that Miller had accumulated on the last kingdom. Once Koger called for the meeting, Paul Bryie had learned from Miller about the German station chief's interest in Bavarian history. Especially the last kingdom. Miller had told Bryie a lot, especially what he'd managed to uncover at the military archives in southern Bavaria among documents that had been there forgotten since the war. Hundreds of thousands of pages of German and American military records. Of little interest now, other than to historians.

Miller had collected a fair amount of material, mainly reports from an OSS team that had been dispatched to Bavaria in 1945 to look into the last kingdom. The Office of Strategic Services was the precursor to the CIA, operating during World War II as America's primary intelligence agency. It was headed by General William Donovan and mainly coordinated espionage activities behind enemy lines for all branches of the services. At its peak, tens of thousands of people worked for it. Truman dissolved it in 1945, but a lot if its personnel and leaders morphed, two years later, into what became the CIA.

Earlier, he'd sent a team to Miller's apartment, which removed everything relating to the last kingdom. He'd ditched the helicopter in an open field outside of the city, then he and Terry Knight had headed back to the house south of Munich. His men had delivered what they'd found from Miller's apartment, reporting that no one had beat them there.

That was good.

As he fully expected Derrick Koger to head straight for it.

"I tried to tell Miller to keep things to himself," Paul Bryie said, who'd driven south from Munich to join them. "He was hell-bent on telling Koger everything."

Hence why the big man had to die. "It's not a problem anymore."

"You missing Koger and Malone is a problem," Bryie said.

Like he needed reminding. "I got it. But I'll deal with them. Right now, we're at least three steps ahead and, thanks to Miller, I think we can get even further along the road."

He'd already paged through the old files Miller had removed from the archives. Lots of brittle paper with fading ink. But a few, with varying dates, had been intentionally isolated by Miller into a separate file marked "Important," each on stationery with the letterhead "Office of Strategic Services. Interoffice Memo. Secret."

TO: General William Donovan
FROM: Lt. Mike Burke

SUBJECT: Germany/Japan Cooperation
DATE: April 5, 1943

1. New intelligence confirms that relations between Japan and Germany are deteriorating.
Both countries' war plans are failing. They
each want the other to join their respective
fights. Compounding this, it has become routine for their representatives to exaggerate
minor victories and minimize losses to the
other. We have confirmed intelligence that
Germany consistently downplays every defeat
of the German army. They claim the Soviet
offensive will soon run out of steam and that
anywhere the Wehrmacht can be sent on
land, it is sure to win. But where the army
has to be taken overseas it becomes somewhat more difficult. That is clearly a direct
reference to Germany's resistance in becoming involved in the Pacific land conflict.

2. Japan has consistently refused to disclose
to Germany its actual strategic position in the
Pacific. Japan has also refused to interfere
with American shipments being off-loaded at
Vladivostok, allowing large numbers of troops
and material to be transported from East
Siberia to the Soviet Union.

3. Sources confirm that Hitler and the German
high command are incensed with Japan's
refusal to intervene with those American
shipments, which is allowing a continued re-
inforcement of Soviet troops from the east.
Hitler is quoted as saying about the Japanese,

"They lie right to your face and in the end all their depictions are calculated on something which turns out to be a deceit afterwards."

4. Part of the friction between Japan and Germany centers around Japan's continued interest in the Hawaiian Islands and Germany's inability to assist with that interest. Multiple sources have mentioned a document that Germany has searched for since 1939, which relates to the Wittelsbach family. Details are uncertain. We are still working to develop more.

Apparently, Japan wanted Germany to find that deed. In return, they dangled the possibility of more cooperation to the Axis in Europe. But it seemed that the OSS, at least in 1943, knew few facts. He read another of the separated memos.

TO: General William Donovan
FROM: Lt. Mike Burke
SUBJECT: New Operation Authorization
DATE: January 9, 1944

1. Sources close to the German high command have confirmed that there is an ongoing search within Bavaria for a document relating to the Wittelsbach family that could impact the United States. The current Duke of Bavaria, Rupprecht (Robert), lives in Italy, having been exiled by the Nazis in 1939. It is impossible to make direct contact with him at this time as he is the personal guest of King Victor Emmanuel,

residing in Florence. His wife and children live in Hungary.

2. Rupprecht opposed the Weimar Republic and, like his father, Ludwig III, never renounced his claim to the Bavarian throne. Upon his father's death in October 1921, Rupprecht declared himself king, noting that his father had never formally renounced his crown either.

3. Rupprecht never joined nor supported the German far right, though Hitler tried to make that happen with promises of a royal restoration. Sources confirm that neither man likes the other. Rupprecht is currently barred from returning to Germany. He very much wants a restoration of the Bavarian monarchy. He has even proposed an idea of a union with Austria to form an independent southern Germany. He wrote a memorandum in May 1943 where he stated his belief that Germany would be defeated in the war. He also proposed the idea of him taking the German crown, which had been held by the House of Wittelsbach in the distant past.

4. The main friction between Rupprecht and Hitler seems to center around a document from the 1880s involving Ludwig II, which the Germans want. They have been actively investigating its whereabouts all across Bavaria but have yet to find anything. Rupprecht has refused to offer the Germans any assistance.

We are working on securing more details and
request permission to certify a new active
operation dedicated to this purpose.

It seemed that Randy Miller had culled through
the crap and found the gold. Three other memos
mentioned more of the Nazis' efforts in Munich,
and across southern Bavaria, during the spring and
summer of 1944. Then he came across another report,
this one from General Donovan himself, marked
"Top Secret."

TO: General Dwight Eisenhower
FROM: General William Donovan
SUBJECT: Ongoing Operation report
DATE: October 24,1944

Information has come to my attention that
for some time the Nazis have been conducting
a wide-ranging investigation across Bavaria.
We have learned that they are searching for
a document that belongs to the Wittelsbach
family, one that dates to 1881 and involves
the former king, Ludwig II. Due to the extremely sensitive nature of the information
I am requesting time to brief you in person.
My recommendation is that occur as soon as
possible, given the urgency of the situation.
So far, to our knowledge, the Germans have
yet to find anything of substance, but their determination is troubling. Please advise when
we may talk.

Rife's reading was interrupted by the buzz of Bryie's
phone. The other man answered, listened a moment,

then thanked the person on the other end and ended the call.

"Malone has a cell phone," Bryie said. "We have it pinged."

He smiled.

God, he loved technology.

"Tell me where."

CHAPTER 48

COTTON ADMIRED THE BUILDINGS OF LUDWIG MAXIMILIAN University. They were grouped around two large squares on Ludwigstrasse, a royal avenue named after Ludwig I, a former king who created the route as the city's grandest boulevard, a place for magnificent Italian Renaissance buildings, state parades, and funeral processions.

The car from Lehmanns had woven a path through late-morning traffic. He wondered if they were headed to the university but saw that the destination seemed to be another building—long and tall with one arched window after another spanning a city block—bearing the name Bayerische Staatsbibliothek. Bavarian State Library. His driver stopped in front. Another man waiting at the curb opened the door and beckoned for him to exit.

He entered the library.

Curiosity got the best of him and he hesitated a moment to catch a few lines of a placard that stood in the foyer, which noted that the institution had been founded in 1558 as the court library for the House of Wittelsbach. Today it was the central state library and repository for the Free State of Bavaria. Total holdings of 33 million units, among those more than 10.7 million volumes, 57,000 periodicals, and 138,000 manuscripts, making it one of the most important centers of knowledge in the world.

Impressive.

His minder waited ahead and motioned for him to follow. They found an elevator on the far side, which he rode up alone to the third floor. Waiting for him was an older woman, with a narrow waist, and an elaborate styling of her nearly white hair that made her small, delicate features look even smaller. Her cheeks were pinched and sunken, her blue eyes misty under hooded lids. She wore a stylish black pantsuit with boots and pearls.

"I understand you have some words for me," she said in perfect English.

"Edelwei Über Schwarzwald."

Edelweiss over Black Forest.

"I sincerely believed I would never hear them."

He stepped from the elevator. "You are Dianne McCarter?"

"I am. It's nice to meet you, Herr Malone. My office found me when you appeared downtown. My assistant, like me, has waited a long time to hear those words. Please. Come. I have much to share with you."

LUKE ENTERED THE FRAUENKIRCHE, MUNICH'S GRAND Cathedral of Our Dear Lady. It occupied a prominent spot in Old Town, not far from the Marienplatz. A plain redbrick building, its details lost in a mighty ensemble of mass and space, the obligatory external buttresses needed to support the towering walls hidden within its interior. Twin towers marked the outside, each topped with a copper dome, their bulbous image a distinctive city landmark. He and Christophe had walked over after spending nearly a half hour with Marc Fenn. The older man had told them what he wanted done and when.

Which would be no easy task.

Before him stretched a long, high nave. A double row of towering octagonal pillars stretched right and left its entire length to the main altar. None of the exterior side walls could be seen. Only the columns. Everything was too polished and shiny to be old, most likely post–World War II re-creations. A knot of people was stopped a few feet away admiring something in the floor.

A footprint embedded into one of the tiles.

He listened as a tour guide explained in English, "It is said that the devil made a deal with the builder of this church to finance its construction on the condition that it contain no windows."

Staring down into the inner hall, no windows could be seen.

"By the time the devil came to inspect, the church was finished and consecrated. So the demon could not fully enter. Instead, he stood here, in the foyer. But the clever builder tricked the devil by positioning the columns so that the windows in the outer walls were not visible from here. Once he learned of the deceit, the devil stomped his foot so hard that he left a footprint."

He smiled at the clever story. What folks won't do to keep the tourists coming. Christophe was studying an interior diagram of the church.

He walked over.

"It's beneath the chancel," Christophe said, pointing ahead.

The interior bustled with visitors admiring the decorations and taking photographs. But with no flash, as several placards warned. An organ banged out deep bass notes that bounced off the stone walls. They followed a small herd of people toward the main altar and a massive crucifix that hung from the upper vault. On the far side they came to an open iron gate with steps that led down to the crypt. Fenn had told them that an array of Wittelsbach ancestors were buried beneath the cathedral, some dating back to the thirteenth century. One in particular was Ludwig III, the last of the family to hold the title of King. Both he and his wife were there, not in adorned tombs created especially for them. Instead, their remains were enclosed inside wall vaults with little pomp or circumstance.

They descended into an underground chapel with walls of more plain redbrick and found six vaults embedded into one of the brick walls. Each a perfect rectangle that together with the others formed a large square. Crisp dark seams delineated each tomb. Five had their occupants identified on the stone slabs. Four women. One man. Konig Ludwig III von Bayern.

They both stared at it.

No one was around.

Fenn had told them what had to be done.

I need you to break into the tomb of Ludwig III and retrieve an engraved pocket watch.

Neither Luke nor Christophe had questioned why, both seemingly satisfied that twenty-five thousand euros each would satisfy any of their curiosity.

"How do we open that?" Christophe whispered.

Luke stepped close, examined the stone, and decided to be helpful. "I don't think it's going to be a problem."

CHAPTER 49

COTTON FOLLOWED THE OLDER WOMAN ACROSS THE library's third floor to a reading room. Bright sunshine flooded in through the windows. Tomes were stacked high on two long oak tables.

"*Bitte*, Herr Malone, take a seat."

Old habits were hard to break, so he could not help noticing the books. Many were older leather-bound volumes. From the size, shape, and binding, he knew they were nineteenth- and early twentieth-century editions. Each time period came with advances in how books were bound. A trained eye noticed those differences and could easily date the works. Being piled indicated these were not rare or precious. Stacking cracked the bindings and depreciated value. So rare books were always dealt with individually.

"Are you a fan?" she asked, pointing to the table.

"I own a rare bookshop in Copenhagen."

"A bibliophile? How wonderful. I, too, love books. My family has maintained an extensive private library for generations. I so enjoy volunteering my time here in retirement."

"From what I saw, you're still in charge of one of the largest law firms in the world."

She chuckled. "Not in charge anymore. But I do own a large interest."

"How did I rank a meeting with you?"

"In good time, Herr Malone. First, please tell me who you are, and how you came into possession of the words you uttered."

"Forgive me, but your last name. It's not German at all."

"I had the great fortune to fall in love with a big, stout Irishman. My father wasn't pleased, but Kevin was the love of my life. Sadly, I lost him a decade ago. But I have his name, and three of his children to give me comfort."

He liked this woman.

She seemed sincerely genuine.

So he told her about the theft at Herrenchiemsee and the discovery of the book and envelope, including what he knew about Prince Stefan, Marc Fenn, and the Guglmänner. He only left out any reference to the mysterious deed.

"The black hoods are somewhat of a paradox," she said. "Careful with those people. Fanatics can be unpredictable and dangerous."

"The thought had occurred to me."

"You have yet to explain your interest in all of this."

"I'm here for the United States."

And he told her who he was and exactly why he was involved. Deception seemed counterproductive.

Her olden face stayed like granite. After a few moments of silence, she said, "The Americans want the deed, don't they?"

He was surprised. "You know about that?"

"Of course. The Americans and Germans both

searched for it during the last war. But the Germans lost the war and the Americans gave up. So neither ever made it as far as you have."

"Your father dealt with that?"

She nodded. "The Nazis swept across Bavaria searching for what Ludwig III hid away. Thank goodness he was clever and they were inept." She paused. "Not as smart as you seem to be."

"Prince Stefan knew about the book hidden in the desk. If he knew, why couldn't the Nazis find out too?"

"That is easy to answer. The Wittelsbachs hated Hitler. They would have shared nothing with the Nazis, nor would they have ever cooperated with them. My father told me that Duke Rupprecht, the head of the house at that time, knew precious little about what his father, Ludwig III, had done. It seems the two of them were not close, and his father took what he knew to his grave. Rupprecht tried to bargain with both the Nazis and the Americans to regain his throne, but neither cooperated. Which was probably best since Rupprecht never knew much of the *Rätselspiel*."

He translated. "The mystery game?"

"Ah, you speak our language."

He nodded.

"*Ja*, the mystery game. That is what Ludwig III named his quest."

He was curious. "You're being quite open with a perfect stranger."

"But you are not a stranger. Ludwig III left precise instructions with my grandfather long ago. Cooperate with whoever utters the words you spoke. They vouch for your authenticity. Which means you have solved the first part of the game. So it is my duty to follow those instructions, not to question or change them."

He got it. "I'm a lawyer too."

"Then you understand what I am saying."

"All too well."

She pointed at the books on the table. "I caught the interest in your eyes. During the last war, though much was evacuated, over a half million volumes in this library were lost. Nearly ninety percent of this building was destroyed by the bombers."

"What do you do here?" he asked, genuinely wanting to know.

"I make things right."

A curious comment.

"I head the restitution project for illegally acquired materials." She reached across and lifted a volume sheathed in plastic. "This book is a good example. The library bought it innocently at auction in 1973. We now have learned it was stolen by the Nazis in 1940. We are working to find its owner, or at least the descendants of its owner, so it can be returned. My law firm funds that research."

She seemed proud of that fact.

"We are checking all of the collections for illegitimate purchases. So far, about sixty thousand books have been examined. From what we have found, the acquisition of nearly five hundred could be regarded as unlawful. We have managed to return over half of those to their owners."

"That's important work." And he meant it.

She smiled. "It does give me a great satisfaction. And it occupies an old woman's busy mind."

She was trying hard to be disarming, and he wondered why.

"There are so many mysteries here," she said. "A few years ago an Italian scholar discovered among our Johann Jakob Fugger manuscripts an eleventh-century

Greek codex containing twenty-nine ancient homilies, previously unpublished, by the theologian Origen of Alexandria. Can you imagine? What a treasure."

She was definitely posturing, feeling him out. Lawyer to lawyer. Trying to learn what she could without seeming interested.

So he obliged her and asked, "How long have you been waiting for somebody to say those words?"

"All my adult life. My father passed the duty on to me, as his father did to him. No one came to any of us, until today."

"What is going on here? Why all this secrecy?"

"My grandfather had the honor of being the personal lawyer for King Ludwig II, then the prince regent Luitpold, and finally King Ludwig III. The late nineteenth and early twentieth centuries were an exciting time in Bavaria. So much happened. Some good. Some wonderful. Some awful."

"You haven't answered my question."

"*Nein*, I have not."

"I suspect you had me brought here to see what I know." He hesitated. "And, too, perhaps, to satisfy your own curiosity. Despite the fact you're supposed to be a disinterested lawyer. A mere messenger."

The old woman grinned. "Perhaps you may be right."

RIFE STARED OUT THE WINDSHIELD AT THE BAVARIAN State Library. Terry Knight drove the car as they sped down the wide expanse of Ludwigstrasse, heavy with midday traffic. Malone's phone was still centered at the library's location. From what he'd been able to learn, the building itself was massive, shaped like a closed *H* at the top and bottom. Tens of thousands of square feet over multiple floors, and, contrary to television and movies, no amount of remote tracking could narrow down the search to one particular spot within that building. And though he knew where Malone was, he had no idea why he was there.

Which was even more troubling.

He knew what Koger would do. Search for Paul Bryie, knowing Bryie had sold him out. Which he had. But good luck finding the man and proving anything. Bryie had gone to ground and would stay there until Koger was dead. Then he'd bask in the protection from his friends within the agency. Friends who did not care for Koger, and who would work with him to hold Koger responsible for what happened to Randy Miller. Thankfully, the issues with Miller were solved and all of the materials he'd managed to accumulate on the last kingdom were now confiscated. The archives definitely needed a visit and a purge, but he could not worry about that right now. Malone was the immediate threat. He'd not counted on this level of involvement. Everything he knew about Malone pointed to a highly competent, well-trained field officer who could definitely hurt you. Koger stumbled into that stroke of good luck on purpose.

One or the other on their own seemed containable.

Together, they were a problem.

Time to deal with Malone.

COTTON SETTLED IN THE CHAIR AND LISTENED AS DIANNE McCarter told him what she knew.

"Ludwig III was, in many ways, a sadder individual than his dead cousin Ludwig II. He ruled but five years, from 1913 to 1918. When the First World War started in 1914, Ludwig proclaimed Bavaria's solidarity with Germany. He was committed to a German victory. As the war progressed he showed more and more loyalty to Germany, which Bavarians began to resent. Finally, the German Revolution emerged near the end of the war. The kaiser was overthrown and proportional representation was implemented everywhere. Ludwig III was forced out. On November 12, 1918, he reluctantly signed the Anif Declaration and abandoned his kingdom."

He recalled what Koger had told him. "But it wasn't an abdication. He just released the military and ministers from their oaths and walked away."

"Precisely. Which makes him especially sympathetic. And, like Ludwig II in 1886, he had no choice. But, unlike his cousin, Ludwig III was in full possession of his faculties and did not die a day after losing his throne."

Good points.

"Ludwig III died three years later. Thankfully for him, he married well. His wife was wealthy. They owned estates in Bavaria, Moravia, and Hungary. They had thirteen children, one of whom is the grandfather of the current duke, Albert. From 1919 to 1921 Ludwig III worked every day to regain his kingdom, but it was not to be. My father told me that, at some point, Ludwig III became aware of his cousin's efforts, decades earlier, to secure another kingdom. A last kingdom. How did he learn this? My father never said. But it was Ludwig III who hid away the body of Ludwig II."

"And left a mystery game on how to find it?"

The older woman nodded. "Exactly."

He was puzzled. "Why do that?"

"Ludwig III felt a great connection to Ludwig II. It is easy to see why. They both suffered the ultimate failure of being deposed. The former chose the wrong side in a world war. The latter lost a grip on reality. From what my father told me, Ludwig III wanted to make sure that the memory of the family never waned, especially the memory of Ludwig II. He also wanted a way for his family to perhaps one day reclaim what was rightfully theirs. He'd watched as the world erupted around him in the madness of total war. It makes sense he would think ahead, to posterity."

"Where does the Guglmänner fit in?" he asked.

"I truly do not know. But my father was a member."

He told her, "They know a great deal about this mystery game."

She considered the information for a moment, her pale blue eyes staring off into the room over half-moon spectacles perched on the tip of her nose. "Probably from my father. He was not good at keeping secrets."

"That's not a good trait for a lawyer."

She chuckled. "Quite right. But who knows? It may not have been him. That is the problem with this whole endeavor. Only bits and pieces of the puzzle have survived, scattered across multiple places and varied sources. No one has the entire picture. It was a secret kept close, perhaps too close, and it has not been passed down without parts of it, perhaps, being lost."

"We discovered a book."

And he told her about the copy of *Tannhäuser and the Minnesingers' Contest at Wartburg* found in the desk at Herrenchiemsee, something Prince Stefan had definitely known about.

"You see," she said, "there is another piece I was

unaware of, but the Wittelsbachs apparently knew. I have to say, Ludwig III made a bit of a mess of things."

"Maybe we clean up that mess."

"That seems your task. Am I right?"

He nodded.

"All right, now that you have found me and uttered the correct words, and we have spoken and you seem sincere, I have something to give you." She pointed to an envelope lying on the table. "That is for you. My father prepared it a long time ago. I had my assistant bring it over after you appeared at the office. It has rested inside a locked safe for a long time."

"You don't know what it says?"

"Of course not. Unlike my father, I am good at keeping secrets. My task was only to pass it on to the person who uttered the right words."

CHAPTER 50

STEFAN ENTERED THE BUILDING THAT HOUSED THE consulate general of China. It was located on Romanstrasse, just outside the gates of the Nymphenburg Palace. It represented one of the 104 foreign governments that maintained a diplomatic presence in Munich, which showed the city's importance. He liked that Bavaria hosted such a variety of international connections and he planned to do nothing but expand on those once he was king, elevating that presence into full-fledged foreign embassies.

He was taking a chance coming here, but a call earlier as he was leaving the Residenz had requested his presence, in person, at noon. And, considering who made the call, and what was at stake, he could not ignore the summons.

He'd brought Lexi Blake with him.

For two reasons.

First, to impress upon her his importance to all that was happening. And, second, to somehow lay the groundwork for having her. She was both physically stunning and professionally capable. Something about beautiful dangerous women. Perhaps that's what attracted him to working girls. It took guts to give yourself to a stranger night after night, all the while making them feel special. It was acting on a grand scale, and the women he frequented were more than skilled in both the art of lovemaking and convincing their clients that they were something more than a revenue source. Lexi Blake offered all that and more, since she was not for sale.

Or maybe she was?

All he had to do was determine the price.

Didn't everyone have one?

"Wait here," he said to Lexi as they stood in the consulate foyer.

She nodded and took a seat across the room.

He announced his presence to the guard.

Stefan sat inside a spacious, bright exterior room adorned with woodwork, cabinets, and tables, all of fine Chinese workmanship. A silk painting, stiff and textured with gold characters, hung from one wall. Several bronzes and some exquisite jade carvings sat atop one of the larger redwood tables. This seemed a place to make a visitor feel as though they were in China. And, legally, they were, as the soil beneath him was part of the People's Republic. Which was a bit of a joke. Since the country was not a republic in any way and the people had zero power.

A white-jacketed attendant asked if he wanted anything to drink, but he declined. A moment later a middle-aged, austere-looking man with a thin, aesthetic face entered. He wore a trim-fitting dark blue suit and walked with a limp, leaning on a red-lacquered cane.

Stefan stood out of respect.

"So good of you to come," the man said in perfect German.

He studied his host, whose face betrayed nothing, noticing the eyes. Dark. But gentle. Like the voice. Which raised alarms.

"And you are?" he asked.

"My name is irrelevant." He pointed to a blue-and-white porcelain vase. "Call me Ming, in honor of that beautiful work of art."

No hand was offered to shake.

Fine by him. He didn't particularly care for the Chinese. Just a necessary evil, with an emphasis on *evil*.

"I am aware of your conversation last night with two prominent members of the German government," Ming said. "In light of that, I thought it best that we have a personal chat. The situation has changed."

He did not like the sound of that. "Since last night? I was told I had three days to work with."

"And you still do. But information has come to my attention that the American Central Intelligence Agency is now involved. They are after the same thing you are."

He was shocked. "Why?"

"Your brother brought them in."

Albert? "You can't be serious."

"The duke is a personal acquaintance of a CIA agent named Derrick Koger." Ming removed a cell phone from his pocket. He tapped the screen and displayed the image of a man nearing sixty. "Have you ever seen him?"

Yes, he had. In the photo that his man at the Residenz had shown him a little while ago. He nodded and explained, then asked, "Why are the Americans dealing with my brother? He's dying. He only has a few months left to live."

"He's alive at the moment, and definitely interested in what you are doing."

Okay. So what? "I can handle him."

Ming tapped his cane to the hardwood floor twice. The door opened and a man entered. Chesty, thick blond hair whitened at the temples, jowls expanded, the nose slightly pugged, a jaw prowlike and combative. He strutted like someone who'd been around and knew the world.

"This is Jason Rife," Ming said in English. "Formerly of the CIA."

"You are working with the Chinese?" Stefan asked, keeping to English.

Rife shrugged. "The enemy of my enemy is my friend."

"I wanted you both to meet. Jason has informed me about Derrick Koger and the CIA's interest." Ming faced Rife. "Tell him."

"Washington is definitely in your business," Rife said. "Lucky for you, I'm in your business too. At this moment an operative by the name of Cotton Malone is doing something at the Bavarian State Library. Did you know that?"

He shook his head.

"Isn't it good I do? I have a man there right now, ready to deal with Malone. I also know that you have a spy in your midst. You know him as Jonathan Smith. His real name is Luke Daniels, an American intelligence officer. He was placed there by Koger to monitor your activities."

That couldn't be.

"Can you see now," Ming said, "how complicated this has become?"

He did.

Ming explained to Rife about Koger meeting with Albert at the Residenz last night. Exactly as his man there had reported to him earlier.

"And you had no idea about the connection between your brother and Koger?" Rife asked Stefan.

He shook his head. "None at all."

Rife grinned. "Then it's a good thing we've joined forces. We also have the Guglmänner to deal with."

"I have a spy there," he told them.

Rife seemed impressed. "Do you now?"

"What do I do about this Luke Daniels?" he asked. "Kill him?"

Ming raised a halting hand. "Not at all. There are other ways to deal with the problem. But first there is something else you need to know."

"And you're not going to like it," Rife said.

CHAPTER 51

C OTTON OPENED THE OLD ENVELOPE, THE SECOND ONE like it in two days, removed a small piece of paper, and read the typewritten words in German, silently translating.

> When Good Friday falls on St. George's Day, Easter on St. Mark's Day, and Corpus Christi on St. John's Day, all the world will weep. But where the minstrel aims his praise, and Parsifal points his gaze, the seer and dove offer help from above. Faithfulness keeps guard by day and night, though the gateway opens and closes with Wagner.
>
> krty ognm isql nbcd zioh lwdp dsgr aloc
> 050 16 19 2

More riddles.

He showed the note to McCarter. "Couldn't they just tell us in straight language? Why all the subterfuge?"

"That would have been impractical," she said.

"The idea was to make the mystery game a challenge. Only those with the right knowledge could solve it. Of course, its creators never anticipated the internet. You must remember that Ludwig III lived in a most turbulent time. Germany had been defeated in war, then politically dismantled. The kaiser was gone. A revolution had taken place and monarchy abolished. Bavaria as an independent kingdom ended. He had no one he could trust. Even his wife, perhaps the one person he was closest to, died in 1919, just a few months after he was deposed. He was a man lost, with nothing but an empty title as king of Bavaria. So he clung to the past and hoped for a future. Part of that involved hiding away his cousin's body, along with who knows what else, none of which was overly important until the 1940s."

"It sounds ridiculous."

"Perhaps. But, as people like to say, it is what it is."

"There's no guarantee that the deed was hidden away with Ludwig II's remains."

"*Nein*, there is not. But it seems like the most logical place, provided the deed even still exists. It could have been destroyed long ago."

That's true. He pointed to the page. "Any idea what this latest riddle means?"

A smile creased her lips.

"I think I may be of some help."

KOGER WAS BACK IN DOWNTOWN MUNICH, HAVING LEFT Randy Miller's apartment with nothing. He'd yet to hear from Malone and decided that a trip south to the military archives would be a waste of time. He was in a taxi, headed to meet with Malone, who'd texted to say he was on the third floor of the state library and would wait for him to arrive.

His phone buzzed.

The screen noted Unknown as to the caller.

He answered anyway.

"I have some information for you." Trinity Dorner.

"I'm listening."

"Malone's phone has been pinged through the CIA. Our people there just reported it. Rife's friends within the agency did it for him. We're going to purge them all when this is over, but for now we need to use them."

"Fox's idea?"

"Absolutely. On this he and Danny Daniels agree. The CIA has a cancer that's fast growing. Daniels cut out some. We're going to excise the rest."

Not his problem. "What did the ping reveal?"

"Malone is at the Bavarian State Library."

Right on.

"So is Terry Knight," Trinity said.

He smiled. "Good for the goose and the gander?"

"Something like that. We can ping phones too. I thought you should know. Watch yourself, Derrick."

The call ended.

The taxi turned onto Ludwigstrasse and passed the university. He settled back in the seat and told the driver to slow down and go past the library building, then round the block and return. Plenty of cars filled the busy boulevard on both sides. A red light stopped them just before the library. He used the opportunity to scan the opposite side of the street.

And spotted Terry Knight.

Crossing.

Headed for the library.

"Check that," he said. "I'll get out here."

COTTON WAITED FOR MCCARTER TO EXPLAIN.

"King Maximilian, Ludwig II's father, died on March 10, 1864. My father told me that he spent his last day on this earth talking to his eldest son, wishing that Ludwig would die as peacefully as he was about to. He also recalled a sixteenth-century prophecy from Nostradamus. *Quand le Vendredi Saint tombera sur le jour de Saint George, Paques sur le jour de Saint Marc, et la Fete Dieu sur le jour de Saint Jean, tout le Monde pleurera.* Her French was excellent, and he easily understood.

When Good Friday falls on St. George's Day, Easter on St. Mark's Day, and Corpus Christi on St. John's Day, all the world will weep.

The same words as on the sheet.

"The prophecy had long been uttered across Bavaria by the superstitious," she said. "Maximilian himself was quite superstitious. He repeated those words to Ludwig right before he died. My grandfather was there and heard them."

"It's obviously a reference to the calendar."

"And the year where all those dates simultaneously aligned was 1886."

He connected the dots. "The year Ludwig II died."

She nodded. "Precisely. The prophecy fulfilled."

But he was still baffled. "That's all fascinating. But do you have any idea why your grandfather and father chose that year to add into this mystery game?"

She shrugged. "The prophecy became closely identified with the Wittelsbachs, long before there was a Ludwig II. Why? No one knows. But everyone thought it amazing that Ludwig died in the exact year the prophecy predicted. If this helps, my relatives would have known that the solution to the prophecy was well known. 1886. So the actual year is not all that important. But rather, what to do with those numbers seems, to me, far more relevant."

He liked her logic. It made sense. "And the other parts of the message?"

She grinned and shrugged. "Those I will leave for you to decipher."

"You don't know? Or won't say?"

"Part of the duty of the one who utters the words you spoke is to decipher the game on their own. My telling you of the prophecy is meaningless. That is a well-known fact from history. But the rest? That is for you to discover." She paused. "Or not."

"I bet you were a good lawyer," he said.

"I was, actually."

"You miss it."

"Not in the least. My children and grandchildren run the firm now." She motioned with her hands. "I stay here, among the books, trying to right a wrong. And you, Herr Malone, what do you do besides own a bookshop?"

He thought of Stephanie Nelle, his former boss and current friend. She was in big trouble and needed help, but was too proud and too stubborn to ask.

"Me too," he said. "I try to right wrongs."

CHAPTER 52

Derrick was careful as he entered the state library through its main doors, stopping in the outer foyer before another set of interior doors, concealing himself, and spotting Terry Knight through the glass, who'd assumed a position farther inside where he could easily see the exit and elevators.

People were coming and going.

Plenty of traffic to keep Knight's attention.

The damn fool was waiting for Malone. They'd pinged the phone and here he was. Rife tried to take them both out earlier. Had Knight come to finish the job? You bet. But first they were probably wondering what Malone was doing.

He kept out of Knight's sight and watched.

Less than five minutes later Malone stepped off the elevator and walked straight for the exit doors, hands stuffed into his coat pockets. Derrick retreated into an alcove that accommodated two foyer restrooms, slipping into the men's room but keeping the door cracked open. Malone pushed through the inner set of glass doors and kept walking through the foyer for the outer set. Knight stayed back, but was clearly following. Derrick retreated farther into the bathroom and found his phone, texting to Malone that he had company.

A few seconds later a reply came.

I know.

RIFE HAD FINISHED HIS DISCUSSION WITH PRINCE STEFAN and left the Chinese consulate. After they'd revealed all that they knew and decided on a joint course of action, he'd taken his leave, driving back into town. Earlier, he'd left Terry Knight at the state library to find out what Malone was doing. Knight had texted to say Malone was on the move, walking down the east sidewalk on Ludwigstrasse, heading toward the university. Luck had smiled on him today as he was driving in the same direction, on the same side of the street.

Then he saw trouble.

Derrick Koger, staying back on the sidewalk, following Knight.

COTTON KEPT WALKING, NOT SURE WHERE HE WAS GOING or what his next move would be. He desperately wanted to corner the man on his tail. Koger had texted back and said he was following and the man's name was Terry Knight. Ex-CIA. Surely part of the Scythe. When he'd stepped off the elevator in the state library he'd done what he'd always done as an active agent. Assessed the room. Which had been busy. But a quick scan had revealed a face he recognized. The man who'd been shooting at them from the helicopter as it flew away. He never, ever forgot a face.

Thank goodness.

He'd kept walking out of the library, casting the impression that he was oblivious to anyone who might be interested in him. Koger's text alerted him to the fact that they now had Knight sandwiched. Ahead he spotted a towering church facade with twin steeples that accommodated bells, which were ringing the 1:00 P.M. hour. People came and went through tall arches that led toward what appeared to be entrance doors. He turned and scampered up the shallow, broad stone steps, passing through one of the arches and entering the nave.

Time to spring a trap.

DERRICK SAW MALONE VEER RIGHT AND ENTER ST. Ludwig's Church. He'd driven by it a million times, just never been inside. Maloney was a pro, realized he was being followed, and knew he had backup. So he had to assume he'd turned into that church for a reason.

And Knight followed.

But tires screeching caught his attention.

RIFE WHIPPED THE STEERING WHEEL TO THE RIGHT and hopped the curb, stopping the car fifty feet in front of Koger on the sidewalk. His gun lay on the passenger's seat. He grabbed it as he popped open the door, keeping his eyes locked on Koger through the side window.

People on the sidewalk scattered in surprise and shock.

He rolled out into the midday sun, stood upright, and leveled the gun, keeping the car between him and Koger.

※

DERRICK WAS ONLY MOMENTARILY CAUGHT OFF GUARD by the car appearing ahead. He'd learned long ago that surprise never got you. It was the rebound that mattered. And he was a hell of a rebounder. Besides, with Knight around, he figured Rife would not be far away.

And here he was.

He reached beneath his coat, found his pistol, and freed it from the holster. People were between him and the car. Rife was out, bringing his weapon level. He'd never backed down from a fight. Not ever.

Not now.

He ticked off two rounds.

But his aim was affected by the people in the way, several of whom dove to the pavement. One shot shattered the passenger's-side window. The other ricocheted off the open driver's-side door.

Rife recoiled, seeking cover.

Clearly, the SOB wanted him dead.

Okay.

Go for it.

※

RIFE SWUNG BACK UP FROM HIS CROUCHED POSITION, using the car for cover, and aimed.

But Koger was gone.

DERRICK DARTED RIGHT AND SOUGHT REFUGE INSIDE A recessed doorway. People were still scampering every which way, some even seeking safety out in the busy street among the passing cars.

Traffic began to congeal.

A couple more rounds Rife's way seemed like a good idea, but his better judgment told him no. People could get hurt. Instead, he yanked open the glass door in the alcove and entered a building.

RIFE SHOULD GO AFTER KOGER.

But the wail of sirens drawing closer cautioned otherwise. He'd taken a chance with a surprise attack, the idea being to distract Koger, take him off the trail, and give Knight time to act.

Which worked.

Hopefully Knight would be successful with Malone.

CHAPTER 53

COTTON ENTERED THE THREE-AISLED NAVE. MAYBE A couple of hundred feet long and a third of that wide, the overhead vaults alive with religious paintings, their depth and richness impressive. A massive fresco of *The Last Judgment* hung behind the high altar, reminiscent of the Sistine Chapel. A number of people milled about inside, admiring the stunning artwork. He had only a few moments before Knight arrived, and he soon spotted what he'd hoped would be there.

Confessionals.

Two wooden booths with a center compartment, all three with louvered doors. Above one of the booths a small red light burned, indicating it was occupied with a penitent. The other booth bore a green light. Several people were kneeling in nearby pews in silent prayer, perhaps waiting their turn. He'd grown up Catholic and had, on many occasions as a child, taken confession. Always a strange experience. Kneeling in the dark on an incredibly hard wooden prie-dieu without a stitch of padding. He could still feel the ache in his knees. But that was the whole idea. The experience was not meant to be pleasant. The priest sat comfortably in the center compartment on the other side of a lattice opening that concealed faces but allowed voices through. Not his favorite way of spending a Saturday morning. But you had to go to confession before taking Communion at Sunday morning Mass.

That was the rule.

The confessionals here were nothing elaborate, a bit of a counter to the overall architectural scheme, simple and unadorned, occupying a back corner. He stepped over, opened the door to the empty booth, and entered. Through the louvers he was able to watch as Knight entered the nave and surveyed the surroundings.

A panel slid in the wall.

He glanced back.

The priest had opened the lattice portal.

He knew what was next. He was supposed to say, "Please bless me, Father, for I have sinned. It has been like thirty-five years since my last confession and here are my sins."

Bet that would go over great.

He decided to say nothing.

Knight walked down the center aisle toward the main altar, his back now to him.

"May I help you?" the priest asked in German.

"Not today, Father."

He opened the door and slipped out. Knight was fifty feet away, facing the altar. The floor was polished stone. Perfect for concealing footsteps, provided you trod carefully.

And he did.

He swept up behind Knight and tapped him on the shoulder. When the man turned, he decked him with a hard right to the jaw. Which hurt his knuckles. Knight was built like a fire hydrant, surely accustomed to "takin' a lickin' and keepin' on tickin'." But nobody likes to get blindsided. Knight rolled his body over on the floor and reached beneath his coat.

No way.

Cotton kicked the gun from Knight's hand. "Are we really going to do this?"

The visitors scurried toward the exit. Those praying also seemed shocked by the violence. Knight froze. He'd expected more of a fight. Then he noticed that the man's gaze seemed to focus past him. He turned. Koger stood at the end of the aisle, near the confessional, gun pointed.

The priest emerged from the confessional.

"What is the meaning of this?" the older man said in German. "This is a sanctuary."

Knight sprang to his feet.

"Stay right there," Koger said. "Or I'll shoot your sorry ass."

Cotton found the gun he'd kicked away, a 9mm, then assumed a position behind Knight so there was nowhere to go except right or left into the pews. Little good that would do. No escape was possible.

"I am calling the police," the priest said in English.

"No need," Koger noted. "We're leaving."

The priest seemed unfazed and stuffed a hand into his cassock, removing a cell phone.

Koger stepped over and took it away, saying, "Sorry, Father. But we don't need the police."

"Move," Cotton said to Knight, pointing the gun.

The main doors swung open and four uniformed officers rushed inside. Koger saw them and they saw his gun, the police reaching for their own weapons.

"Hold on, big fellows," Koger said.

But the officers were not listening. They leveled their pistols and yelled in German for Koger to drop his gun. Then they noticed Cotton's weapon and issued the same command.

"I don't think we should argue with them," Cotton said.

Koger slowly laid his gun and the phone on the floor, then raised his hands. Cotton followed suit, stepping forward so they could see he was cooperating. Knight, who was unarmed, raised his hands, too, drifting back toward the altar with slow, even steps.

"On the floor," one of the policemen yelled. "Face-down. All of you."

He glanced at Koger, who shrugged. *Like we have a choice?*

And he agreed.

"Do it," Cotton said to Knight, and he slowly descended to his knees.

But Knight bolted toward the altar.

Cotton realized what was coming and flattened out on the floor. Shots rang out. Knight dove forward, his momentum sliding his body across the slick marble like a ballplayer gliding into second base head-first. Rounds thudded into the wooden pews. Knight body-crawled forward, the pews offering excellent cover.

Cotton started to rise, intent on going after him.

"Don't," Koger yelled.

He turned back and saw that it was good advice. The other officers' weapons were trained on him and Koger.

They'd fire the moment he stood.

Knight was still on the floor, crawling forward toward a curtain that separated the nave from the rear of the altar, where the priests and attendants prepared themselves for Mass. Two of the police rushed forward, trying to find a better angle through which to fire. More shots. But the pews still blocked them. Knight disappeared through the curtain.

"Stay down," the police ordered again. "Don't move."

Two of the uniforms rushed ahead toward where Knight had gone.

He stared at Koger.

Who shook his head.

Dread swept through him like water emptying from a sink.

This was not going to be okay.

CHAPTER 54

STEFAN'S HEAD SPUN.

A lot had come his way during the visit to the Chinese consulate. The CIA? Spies within his ranks? His brother's duplicity? He'd never seen any of that coming. But thank goodness he had new allies. People with brains, guts, and resources. *The enemy of my enemy is my friend.*

Absolutely.

He'd left the consulate and driven the short distance over to Nymphenburg and the Wittelsbach residence. His brother was not there, having gone out, but was due back shortly. He'd sent Lexi Blake off to meet up with Jonathan Smith and Christophe, dealing with whatever Christophe was working through with the Guglmänner. The ex–CIA agent, Jason Rife, had made that suggestion after telling him that Jonathan Smith was not the only person planted within his ranks. Lexi Blake was a spy too. Smith from the CIA. She from the White House.

"Why is the president of the United States interested in me?" he'd asked Rife.

"He doesn't want you to have the deed. He doesn't want Germany to acquire that deed from you. And he certainly does not want the Chinese to have it."

Apparently he'd come to the attention of people in really high places. Both troubling and gratifying. How disappointing about Blake. He'd had plans for her. Not anymore.

"Just get her to Smith and your man Christophe," Rife had said. "I'll take care of the rest."

He wondered what that meant but had not probed any further.

No sense arguing with good fortune.

He heard the front door open and close, then one of the stewards offering a greeting and taking his brother's coat.

A moment later Albert walked into the study. "Come to upend another table and destroy my stamps?"

"Why are you undermining me?"

A puzzled look came to Albert's wizened face. "In what way?"

"You brought the CIA and the Americans into my affairs."

Albert sat in one of the chairs, slow and easy. "I just came from the doctor. The news is not good."

They'd never been close. The age difference between them had pushed them apart from the start. He'd been a small child when Albert was a teenager. He was a teenager when Albert left university as an adult. Their lives had always been divergent. Different interests, friends, social circles, politics. Albert had always leaned right, while he considered himself a progressive. No. More a radical. Change was good. Still—

"What did the doctor say?"

"As if you care. Other than as to the time of my coming demise, when you will become duke."

"If you did not want me to ask, why mention it?"

His brother looked fatigued.

"Christmas is two weeks away. I will see it for the last time. I will then become progressively worse and bedridden. I am told that the pain will be enormous and will require heavy sedation. Doubtful I will be able to speak or communicate in any way. Most likely I will lapse into a coma. By the Epiphany, I will be dead."

January 6.

The day set aside to commemorate the three magi visiting the Christ child, bringing gifts.

Less than a month away.

"Brother," he said to Albert, "contrary to what you think, I do not wish death upon you. Fate has placed that burden. Not me."

"And you are merely taking advantage of that fate."

"I am simply trying to restore to our family what is ours by right. What was taken from us by force and coercion. Is that so wrong?"

Albert said nothing.

"Is it?" he asked again, voice rising.

"No. It is not."

The admission shocked him, along with a flicker in his brother's eyes that seemed, for the first time ever, sympathetic?

"What are you saying?" he asked.

"I will not live long enough to see if our family's birthright can be restored," Albert said. "But you will."

"Do you know what I am doing?"

Albert nodded. "The Americans briefed me. You seek the deed for the last kingdom. I confess to not understanding all of the politics, but it seems the price we have to pay to get the Germans to give us the secession vote. I told the Americans that the deed might not even exist."

"Do you believe that?"

"I truly don't know. But finding Ludwig II seems a good start at finding out."

"Do you want me to do this?"

"I didn't, at first. But now I do."

He was shocked. "Why did you involve the Americans?"

"To do what I could not and stop you. But now I believe they can actually help us, though they'll never realize it. They have access to resources and information we do not."

First, revelations about spies in his employ. Now his brother, whom he'd always considered with nothing but contempt, had become an ally?

This seemed a day for the unexpected.

"I have been thinking a lot about Grandfather and Father," Albert said.

Neither had been king. His grandfather Rupprecht died in the 1950s a bitter man. He'd never known him. Unlike Rupprecht's father, Ludwig III, who'd supported Germany in the First World War, Rupprecht and the House of Wittelsbach had actively opposed the Nazis. And they paid a price. His grandmother, Rupprecht's wife, had been arrested and imprisoned at Dachau. She survived that horror, but left the country after being freed, vowing never to return to Germany. Rupprecht had lobbied the American liberators hard for a restoration of the Bavarian monarchy, but received no support. Amazingly, during his lifetime, his grandfather bore witness to the independent Kingdom of Bavaria, the German Empire, the Weimar

Republic, Nazi Germany, Allied-occupied Germany, and the establishment of a divided, West and East Germany. Along the way Rupprecht fathered eleven children, one of whom was his father.

Who'd lived a full life too.

Like many in the family, though, he'd been a dour man, reveling in solitude, keeping mainly to himself, preferring, like Ludwig II long ago, mountains to cities, trees to people. He'd loved to hunt and breed dogs. He died at Berg Castle, alone, buried in an abbey beside Lake Starnberg. The highlight of his life had been presiding over the eight hundredth anniversary of the founding of the House of Wittelsbach. Little bits and pieces. That's what his father and grandfather had enjoyed of royalty.

Stefan wanted it all.

"Don't worry about the Americans," Albert said. "They believe themselves on our side. And they are. We just cannot allow them to keep the deed if it is found. We need to use them, but not allow them to succeed."

Albert stood.

"Come, brother. I want to show you something."

CHAPTER 55

RIFE SWUNG THE CAR AROUND THE CORNER AND SPED down the street a few blocks over from Ludwigstrasse. He'd received two texts from Terry Knight detailing his location. Ahead, he spotted Knight on the sidewalk and eased to the curb.

Knight hopped inside.

"What happened?" Rife asked.

"The damn police showed up. They got Malone and Koger. I managed to get away."

He smiled, knowing the one thing the CIA detested more than anything was notoriety. By definition, the agency worked under the radar, and the last thing it wanted was the locals to know they were around. If Malone and Koger were in custody, there was a good chance the Bundesnachrichtendienst, the BND, Germany's Federal Intelligence Service, would be alerted. That would bring lots of attention, which should jeopardize Koger's entire operation. He knew the BND and the CIA did not get along. Never had. And given what he now knew about Koger and the White House, the last thing either wanted was attention. America had stuck its nose into Germany's business. In a major way. And got caught. There'd be hell to pay.

He'd been involved with compromised operations before and knew how messy they could become. And the White House? That was a new one. Rarely did intelligence operations directly involve the president. That was why God had allowed the invention of the CIA. And every president since 1948 had made use of that political insulation. But not Warner Fox. He'd jumped in headfirst and had *his* National Security Council dispatch *their* own operative. That meant only one thing. This was really, really important.

And, actually, it was.

"Let's hope the BND does our work for us," he told Knight as they drove away. "We have a lot to do and don't need Koger's aggravation."

Randy Miller was dead. Malone and Koger in custody. The spies within Prince Stefan's entourage were being dealt with.

Things were looking up.

DERRICK RESTED ON HIS KNEES, HIS HANDS ON HIS HEAD, fingers intertwined. Malone was in the same position about fifty feet away, three-quarters of the way closer down the church's main aisle to the altar. Three German state police kept guard. One each on him and Malone, both armed, the other talking to the priest with his gun reholstered. The others had fled the nave. They'd already radioed in that the situation was contained and requested additional help. Hopefully, that was going to take a few minutes.

His gaze caught Malone's.

And saw his old friend was thinking the same thing.

Now or never.

He gave a slight nod of his head. Then bellowed out a loud, unexpected yell. Which had the desired effect, causing a moment of surprise for their two minders. He released his hands from atop his head and swept the legs out from under the cop nearest to him. The man's arms went high as his butt pounded the floor hard. The gun was the main concern and Derrick punched the man's right wrist, which caused his fingers to relax their grip.

The gun clattered away.

He swung again, pounding his big paw-like fist into the side of the man's face. The body went limp and lay still on the floor.

He realized that the cop with the priest was his next concern, so he leaped for the gun on the floor.

COTTON REACTED THE MOMENT KOGER YELLED, SWINGING his right arm up and around, snatching the gun from the policeman's grip. He then lunged upward, sweeping his right arm in an arc, driving the gun's hard metal into the man's right cheek. Stunned, the policeman staggered back. Cotton hopped to his feet and sent the man to the floor with another blow to the head with the gun. He swung around and saw that Koger had the third policeman contained with a weapon pointed straight at him.

"You done?" Koger asked him.

"I think so."

He retrieved the cop's gun, breathing hard from the exertion.

"Don't die on me," Koger taunted, advancing toward the priest and relieving the policeman of his gun and radio. "I'm not interested in hurting anybody. So how about you two get into the confessional, one each in a compartment, and close the door. And Padre. I still need your cell phone."

The priest retrieved it from the floor and handed it over.

The two men stepped inside the booths and closed the doors.

Koger motioned.

He knew what to do.

Knight had disappeared through the curtain. Apparently, there was another way out. One they could take too.

They both rushed that way.

RIFE SPED OUT OF MUNICH.

He and Knight were headed south toward the house in the alpine foothills where Knight and the others had been staying. Bryie should still be there too. He'd turned over the driving to Knight so that he could read more of what Randy Miller had amassed, especially the one file of specially culled memoranda. He'd imaged them on his phone before leaving earlier, and was anxious to restudy one in particular.

TO: General Dwight Eisenhower
FROM: General William Donovan, OSS
SUBJECT: Confidential TOP SECRET
DATE: July 18, 1945
We have interrogated 19 prisoners relative to Operation Last Kingdom. Nazi high command was definitely searching for documents relative to the possible deed you and I spoke

about. One prisoner informed us that the tomb of Ludwig II was breached, but found to be empty, the king's remains gone. We have yet to ascertain why that is significant, but it seemed so to them. The current members of the House of Wittelsbach have offered assistance to us but, in return, they want a restoration of the monarchy and an independent Bavaria. That is impossible under the current political scenario, as Germany is divided into distinct quadrants under Allied control. There is no practical way to separate Bavaria. The current Duke of Bavaria, Rupprecht, who is the senior member of the Wittelsbachs, flatly refuses to offer anything useful until those two conditions are met. We will have to proceed without his assistance. In my opinion we may be stymied to make any further progress without the family's help. The German prisoners knew little more than we already know. It might be that the best course is to allow whatever may be out there to stay hidden. The war itself may have muddied the trail to the point that nothing can ever be located. That would not be an unacceptable outcome, considering the risk of exposure. For now I am suspending Operation Last Kingdom until something, if anything, more substantive surfaces.

CHAPTER 56

STEFAN FOLLOWED ALBERT ACROSS THE GROUND FLOOR of the schloss to his parents' former bedroom. He and Albert had occupied first-floor bedchambers, but his mother and father had preferred the ground floor. They both died a long time ago, but their room had remained relatively unchanged. Since Albert lived alone, and Stefan had no intention of ever occupying this dreary place, the makeshift memorial had remained untouched.

They entered the bedroom and Albert switched on the lights. He caught the musky scent of his father's stale tobacco that still infected all of the fabrics. The room was spacious, with an eclectic mixture of Bavarian furniture and personal items special to his parents. The same rich velvet portieres draped the tall windows, another wall dominated by an oil painting of Kaiser Wilhelm II in full imperial regalia. His father had been a fan. Family photos dotted one of the side tables. Images of his mother, father, aunts, uncles, Albert, and himself. Different places and time periods. Lots of whiskers, choker collars, and Iron Crosses. Several of the images were quite old, the men dressed in uniforms cut in the style of the kaiser's day, the military officers wearing spiked nickel helmets, their breasts encrusted with ribbons. Others were of the family. The Wittelsbachs were noted for large clans. Eight-plus children per marriage was not uncommon. But in his immediate family there'd been only two.

Albert stepped over to Kaiser Wilhelm's portrait and swung it out on its hinges. Behind was a wall safe. His brother spun the dial and worked it left and right. Stefan knew of the safe, but had never been privy to its combination. Why would he? Second sons were not included in such things.

He'd not lived here in decades, leaving on his twentieth birthday to start a home of his own. Thankfully, his wife's family possessed great wealth and made sure she brought a huge dowry with her. Mainly cash. He had a knack for investments, and it helped that he employed one of the savviest financial firms in Germany. He'd escalated that initial dowry into a substantial fortune. Once he was king he'd also control all of the confiscated Wittelsbach property, both real and personal, which he planned to repatriate to the family with the same vigor in which it was taken.

Albert finished entering the combination and opened the safe.

The only thing inside was a single volume of what appeared to be a writing journal, its leather bindings singed by time.

"This was our great-grandfather's journal."

"Ludwig III's?"

Albert nodded. "He started it after relinquishing the throne in 1918. It was meant only for the family and passed to Grandfather, then to Father, and finally to me."

The message came clear.

Only for dukes.

"You will soon be duke, perhaps even king," Albert said. "So it's time you become aware of what is in this journal."

He was beginning to understand. "This is how you know the secrets?"

His brother nodded. "Firsthand information."

"So Father never told you a thing about Ludwig's tomb being empty."

"All he knew came from this journal." Albert laid the book on the bed and untangled its leather straps. "I will not live long enough to see the fruits of your labor. But that does not mean I do not want you to succeed. Quite the contrary, in fact."

He was a bit unnerved. He and Albert had never experienced anything remotely considered brotherly, except the sharing of parents. Their entire lives they'd remained aloof. Normally, he would never even be in line to succeed. But Albert had broken with Wittelsbach tradition and not married.

Which was rare, indeed.

"What are you saying?" he asked, listening with careful concentration.

"I have not the strength, nor the health, to mount this fight. You chastised me last evening for not wanting to be king. You are wrong. I would have loved to be king. Regaining what is ours is important to me. But achieving that goal is now up to you."

Stefan could not believe what he was hearing.

"Why did you chastise me for opening Ludwig's tomb? Why not simply show me this journal beforehand?"

Albert gently laid a hand on his shoulder. "Brother, please do not take what I am about to say in the wrong way. But I always considered you vain, arrogant, manipulative, and incapable of accomplishing anything other than satisfying your own personal wants and desires. You are married to a good woman, yet you cheat on her continually. Your daughters are precious, yet you hardly know them."

He kept the growing anger within him in check.

For once.

"But last night," Albert said, "when you toppled that table I saw, for the first time, a glimpse into your soul. You love Bavaria. You want it back, as it was for so long, as an independent vibrant nation. You want what belongs to our family restored. The injustices heaped upon us reversed. I saw all that clearly in your eyes."

He did want all that.

"That's when I knew that it was time we work together," Albert said. "I have not the life left in me to achieve much. But you, brother, can do it."

"Is it possible to succeed?"

Albert nodded. "It could very well be. That is why I involved the Americans. That deed to Hawaii was meaningless in 1886. But, by the time of Ludwig III, in 1918, it had become quite important. Inside this journal, Ludwig recounts how the American government inquired about that deed. Hawaii was, by then, one of their protectorates. Land they wanted to keep. Then, in the Second Great War, both the Nazis and the Americans searched for the deed. Our grandfather tried to barter it to the victors in return for our kingdom, but they refused. So he kept the secret. And it has stayed secret all these decades. Until now."

"The Chinese want that deed," he said, deciding to be honest. "Badly."

"I know. There is much at stake for them, for America, for Germany, and, most of all, for Bavaria.

They are all tied together, though their ultimate interests are quite diverse."

"We have to compel the Bundestag to grant us a secession vote," he said. "It's the only way to make any of this happen. That's what I have been working for."

"I know, brother. I know. And I apologize for being an impediment. But not any longer. You must know what our great-grandfather knew. It is my hope that with such knowledge, and your own will and determination, we can be successful and find that deed for ourselves."

Albert pointed at the journal.

"It is yours now."

CHAPTER 57

COTTON LED THE WAY AS HE AND KOGER ENTERED A REAR vestibule. They'd have only a few moments. Each looked at the other and knew what had to be done. The way ahead was unlit and Terry Knight could be lying in wait. But the immediate threat was behind them and Cotton had an idea. He spied a gold-colored braided rope with decorative tassels at each end and snatched it off a wall hook. Probably used to close off one of the openings in the stone railings that encircled the main altar.

They passed through an archway and he motioned for Koger to huddle to one side and he crouched down at the other, tossing one tasseled end across while holding the other. They each stashed their weapons in coat pockets and he motioned for the rope to stay on the floor. Koger seemed to understand exactly what he had in mind. Say what you want about the big man, he was cool under pressure.

Footfalls could be heard coming their way.

The two officers would have to proceed with some caution and not just rush past the curtain. Surely they realized their targets were armed. And nobody would just rush right in—

Except these guys.

Who pushed through the curtain and ran into the dimly lit vestibule, coming straight for where the rope lay. He and Koger timed their movements perfectly and brought the line taut just as the officers made it to the archway. The legs of the first one came out from under him as he tripped and plunged forward. A collision from momentum then brought the second officer down. Cotton took one of the policemen and Koger the other, both delivering punches to the face that sent the two to the floor, lying still. They each reached for a weapon the policemen were carrying.

"We've got a lot of guns," Koger said. "Now let's get out of here."

He agreed. "I'd say we have about a minute or so before this church is full of trouble."

They hustled ahead and found a rear door that exited to an alley on the church's far side. Probably the same path Knight had taken. They rushed out and kept moving, finding a busy street a block over and dissolving into the crowd. The guns rested within their coats, out of sight. They kept moving, putting as much distance as possible between themselves and the church, mindful of cameras that were surely everywhere.

After a few minutes Koger stopped by a trash bin. "Shut your phone off and give it to me."

He did, then handed it over. Koger shut his off, too, then tossed both to the ground, grinding the sole of his shoe into each one. Repeatedly. Cotton had already determined how they were being tracked.

"The damn things are like homing devices," Koger said.

Cotton retrieved both phones off the ground and

tossed them into the bin. He also added one of the guns he'd retrieved.

Koger tossed a gun in too. "What did you find out at the library?"

And he told Koger all that Dianne McCarter had said. In turn, Koger reported what he'd discovered at Randy Miller's apartment.

"We have another piece of the puzzle," he said. "But we need help."

Koger seemed to get what he meant. "Back to the crazies in black hoods at the castle?"

Cotton smiled. "Yep."

LUKE SAT IN THE PEW WITH CHRISTOPHE.

Toni had called and said the prince wanted her to work with them, so he'd told her where they were.

Why not? The more the merrier.

They were still beneath the Frauenkirche in the crypt chapel. People had steadily come and gone over the past hour as they'd sat and planned. The wall crypts holding Ludwig III, his wife, and three others rose across the chapel in one of the brick walls. Hardly anyone stopped to take note of their final resting place. He wondered what it was like to be so famous, yet so unknown. The man had been a king. But few, outside of historians or some die-hard Bavarians, knew he ever existed. He hoped his own life would have more meaning and stand for something. Teddy Roosevelt said it best. *It is not the critic who counts, not the one who points out how the strong man stumbled or how the doer of deeds might have done them better.*

You got that right.

The credit belongs to the man who is actually in the

arena, whose face is marred with sweat and dust and blood. Who strives valiantly. Who errs and comes short again and again.

He knew all about that.

Who knows the great enthusiasms, the great devotions, and spends himself in a worthy cause. Who, if he wins, knows the triumph of high achievement, and who, if he fails, at least fails while daring greatly, so that his place shall never be with those cold and timid souls who know neither victory nor defeat.

Unfortunately, Ludwig III seemed to have been one of those timid souls.

Christophe stood across the chapel, milling about, trying to fit in. They were waiting for Toni. Koger had told him to stay close to the prince, report what was happening, and work with Sims. That was one thing. Now he was involved with the black hoods, working the other side. Which was a whole other thing. What worried him was how readily the guy Fenn had accepted him. Sure, Christophe was a known commodity and there was a job that needed to be done. And he'd seen stranger behavior before when people hired whomever without checking things out, thinking money bought loyalty. But something seemed off. Even worse, there was nothin' he could do about it. Like what his father used to say, "If frogs had wings they wouldn't bump their asses when they land."

Yep.

Christophe walked over and sat beside Luke on the pew. More people drifted in and out of the chapel, negotiating the stairs back up to ground level and the main nave.

"We need to get into that tomb," Christophe said.

"My mother would say the only way to do that was through prayer."

"Sounds like a devout woman."

"She's a saint." And he still called her every Sunday, no matter where he was in the world.

"Since neither one of us prays all that much," Christophe said, "what are you thinking?"

"When I was younger, an uncle died," he said, keeping his voice to a whisper. "They buried him in one of those vertical mausoleums, above ground, inside a vault like the ones over there. I hung around after the coffin was slid inside and watched a friend of mine seal it up. The front looks like it's part of the wall." He shook his head. "It's not. Like a wine bottle cap with a stopper, there's a part that slides into the vault nice and tight. But it will also slide right back out. I'm bettin' these vaults are the same."

Fenn had told them that the church closed at four today for a special service, presenting a good opportunity to take a look.

Christophe pointed. "There's a corridor over there, past the altar, that leads to a room. Can you pick a lock?"

"Can't you?"

Christophe said nothing.

"I can get it open," he finally said.

Toni appeared at the bottom of the stairs and caught sight of them. She bounded over and sat in the pew in front of them. "What are we doing here?"

Luke smiled. "Grave robbin'."

CHAPTER 58

STEFAN WAS AT A LOSS.

He sat slumped in a chair, feeling crushed and humiliated, staring blindly into the semi-darkness, confusing thoughts tumbling around in his tired mind. The journal seemed a treasure trove of intimate information about his great-grandfather.

Ludwig III was born in Munich, a descendant of both Louis XIV of France and William the Conqueror of England. He was named after his paternal grandfather, King Ludwig I of Bavaria. He grew up in Munich, inside the Residenz. At age sixteen he was commissioned a lieutenant in the Bavarian army. At seventeen he entered university and studied law and economics. When Bavaria went to war with Austria in 1866 he, along with many others, enlisted. Young, green, and sparsely trained, many of them did not survive. Ludwig was wounded, taking a bullet to his thigh, and received the Knight's Cross First Class of the Bavarian Military Merit Order. But the ordeal cemented a lifelong aversion to the military, and there were entries in the journal that attested to his dislike.

He lovingly wrote of his marriage to Maria Theresia, Archduchess of Austria-Este. They had thirteen children, one of whom had been Stefan's grandfather Rupprecht. It seemed a loving marriage, and when she died in February 1919 the entries that came after were all tinged with deep sadness and regret. One entry, written in the curious non-cursive style of the rest of the journal, caught his eye.

As I sit here and contemplate the fate of myself and the fate of my kingdom it strikes me that I may be the first monarch to ever be bestowed four separate titles. First, as a young man, while my father lived, I was His Royal Highness, Prince Ludwig of Bavaria. Then after my father's death I became His Royal Highness, the Prince Regent of Bavaria. For a short five years, after my cousin Otto was legislatively deposed, I reigned as His Majesty, the King of Bavaria. That title I quite enjoyed. But once deposed, I became merely the Duke of Bavaria, a title held only in pretense, meaning nothing.

He could sympathize with that lamentation. It truly seemed an empty title.

Albert had left him alone in their parents' bedroom, offering him the solitude to take in the journal. He'd noted one page had been bookmarked with a strip of torn paper. An entry from October 1918.

The great world war is lost, of that I am sure. Now revolution is spawning, infecting all of Bavaria. The time is coming when I will be forced to leave. My goal has always been to maintain some sort of balance between Bavaria and Prussia, all while trying to preserve the glorious German empire. But that is now lost too. I fear that nothing will be sacred here. That all from the past will be extinguished as a way to compel the people to move forward under some sort of radical modern parliamentary rule. Kings and Wittelsbachs will be forgotten, their memory intentionally purged from the public consciousness. I am no longer in a position to lead the government. My people are lost. But it is my duty to protect our family's past. Sadly, it seems I will be the last of the Wittelsbach kings. My fervent hope is that one day our family might regain what will soon be taken away. When that day might arrive is impossible to know. Perhaps it never will. My deceased cousin, King Ludwig II, had a great dream. A grand plan. He wanted a new kingdom, a place where he could rule as kings were meant to rule. To his credit he found that dream, but its reality never came to pass. A last kingdom. What a marvelous thought. Sadly, it will not come to pass for me either. But I have created my own personal version. A place where our family might rest in peace with its memories and accomplishments. It waits in a safe place, watched over by the Sängerkrieg, protected by the Rätselspiel, waiting for a time when we are once again revered.

Cryptic words for sure. But enough to make the point.

Was the deed there?

Possibly.

"The Sängerkrieg" was a clear reference to the legendary minstrel contest at Wartburg, which supposedly took place in 1207. Nobody knew if the event was real or imaginary, but poets had been dealing with it for centuries. Supposedly six minstrels competed against one another before the count and countess of Thuringia, all to determine who could best sing the praises of the prince. One, named Heinrich, became the most eloquent and earned the envy of the others, who tricked him into receiving a death sentence. But Heinrich gained the protection of the countess and garnered a one-year reprieve, during which he traveled to Hungary and sought the assistance of a sorcerer. The *Rätselspiel*, or mystery game, was the subsequent poetic duel between one of the minstrels and the Hungarian sorcerer.

An epic tale.

Uniquely German.

Which the composer Richard Wagner adapted to an opera.

Tannhäuser und der Sängerkrieg auf Wartburg.

The printed version of which had been waiting inside that desk at Herrenchiemsee.

Now he knew.

Ludwig III created his own mystery game. Complete with cryptic clues and gallant quests. To embark upon it required a knowledge of the world around you, similar to the Sängerkrieg and its battle between the minstrel and the demon.

Wittelsbachs had always been enamored with romantic notions.

Most times to their downfall.

But maybe not here.

Albert re-entered the bedroom.

"Did you mark this page?" he asked his brother.

Albert nodded. "I wanted to be sure you read it. Father told me of the book in the desk. Unfortunately, he never mentioned any of the other steps to this Rätselspiel. I doubt he knew them. But others are ahead of you, brother. Far ahead. I was just on the phone with a contact who told me that the Americans are now fully aware of the mystery game and are closing in. Time is running out. It is imperative that we assume control."

"Are you serious about helping me?" he asked Albert.

His brother nodded. "I am."

"Then tell me what we need to do."

CHAPTER 59

DERRICK SAT IN THE FRONT PASSENGER'S SEAT, MALONE in the rear seat by himself, of the G-Class Mercedes SUV driven by Marc Fenn. They'd hired an Uber driver to ferry them from Munich south to Fenn's estate. They'd had to wait nearly ninety minutes for Fenn to return to the castle. When he did they'd explained all that had been learned and asked his advice.

Which he'd provided.

"The lyric 'where the minstrel aims his praise, and Parsifal points his gaze, the seer and dove offer help from above' is clever," Fenn had said. "You have to have some intimate knowledge to understand it. But that was surely the whole idea."

"Any chance you could explain without the hyperbole?" Malone asked. "We're in a hurry."

"Come now, gentlemen," Fenn said. "This is quite marvelous. A true revelation. What was heretofore legend is now becoming fact. Ludwig III's Rätselspiel."

"You know about that?" Malone asked.

"I have always believed he devised this entire scheme. And now we have proof. The lawyer

Lehmann, Ludwig III's private counsel, has confirmed it all to be true."

"So what does the riddle mean?"

"For that we need to take a drive. Not far. But I can show you."

They were now deep into the alpine foothills, speeding down a black line of asphalt that cut a path through snowy meadows. Scattered icy white petals floated down from an ever-blackening sky, visible in the car's headlights. They rounded a bend in the highway and a spectacular sight came into view a couple of miles away.

Neuschwanstein.

Shimmering in the crystalline late-afternoon air.

One of Ludwig II's three spectaculars.

Towers, turrets, castellated walls, all seemingly inaccessible, glowed from spotlights that fired an incandescent blast of dazzling brilliance onto its white marble walls. It sat three thousand feet high, rising from its rocky summit with the stately grace of an old-world German knight's castle. Its symmetry seemed anchored in the artistically arranged graduations of height and the pinnacle-covered roof, all the personification of ancient defiance and lordly power, satisfying any and all conceptions of what a royal stronghold should be. Which had probably been Ludwig II's whole intent. What had he read once about indulging passions? *The appetite increases the more it is fed.* Ludwig's certainly seemed insatiable. Easy to see how Walt Disney became inspired in the 1930s to create Sleeping Beauty's castle after paying this place a visit.

"Is that where we're going?" Derrick asked Fenn, pointing to the castle.

"It is. I am close friends with the curator. He's waiting for us."

"To do what?' Malone asked.

"Everything you have found so far," Fenn said, "leads to the last place Ludwig II occupied before being deposed. His final redoubt. Where they took him into custody. This castle. I dare say that Ludwig III chose the elements of his mystery game with a great amount of symbolism."

They kept speeding down the darkened roadway, rolls of snow lining its edges. Fenn slowed as they came to a cluster of gift shops, hotels, and parking lots that accommodated the crowd of visitors. Few were around. Definitely not tourist season. But Christmas was evident from the colorful decorations and evergreen boughs on the quaint buildings and light poles. They passed a horse-drawn carriage that contained six people huddled under wool blankets.

"Normally you walk up, take one of the carriages, or take a shuttle bus," Fenn said. "We've been granted permission to drive."

Fenn turned left and headed up a narrow, steeply ascending road. They passed a few other intrepid visitors who were walking down. Light snow continued to fall. Finally, Fenn parked in a cul-de-sac, surely where the buses and carriages turned around on their trips up and down.

"We walk from here," Fenn said.

They stepped out into the cold, dry air and Derrick buttoned his coat and turned up the collar. Malone did the same. Neuschwanstein rose high above them. No moat or outer protective wall offered any security. Instead, the impressive edifice screamed a proud, kingly glory, seemingly unassailable on all sides from invaders. They trudged up an asphalt path and Derrick saw that on three sides the rocks descended steeply down to a deep gorge. Only the south side of the mount, where they were walking, was approachable. The sound of falling water could be heard, but not seen, in the distance.

He stopped and listened.

"The Pöllat gorge accommodates a waterfall about fifty meters high," Fenn said. "Maximilian, Ludwig II's father, constructed a wooden bridge across it and named it after his wife, Mary. Ludwig II rebuilt that bridge out of iron when he started construction on Neuschwanstein. It crosses ninety meters above the gorge."

"It's not lit?" Malone asked.

"In summer. But not this time of year. The view of the castle from it is most impressive."

They walked more.

"In Ludwig II's day, where we are standing was a graveled path," Fenn said. "The commission that came to take the king into custody was confronted by armed locals right here. Ludwig watched from up there"—Fenn pointed—"in the principal tower."

"You know this stuff," Derrick said.

Fenn nodded. "It has been an interest of mine for a long time. I am just glad that my knowledge can now prove useful."

They kept walking, climbing up the steep path.

"It took thirteen years to build this masterpiece," Fenn said. "It cost a hundred twenty million gold marks. That was an enormous sum. A stupendous fortune. It placed a huge financial hardship on Ludwig, since he used his own money. Contrary to popular culture, Ludwig did not drain the Bavarian treasury building castles. He used the money allocated to him each year for his household upkeep, along with borrowed money, to build his dreams. But what irony, that what bankrupted Ludwig now produces millions of euros in revenue every year for Germany."

Derrick stared up at the gatehouse's redbrick facade, richly ornamented by the cupolas of arched windows, battlements of projecting balconies, leaning roofs, and side fighting towers. The Bavarian coat of arms hung above the main gate. A couple, walking arm and arm and huddled in thick coats, strolled out.

He turned back and stared out at the dark countryside. In the dim light, the view extended for miles to the west, lights dotting the vista, some stationary, most likely houses or farms, others cars moving down the highway they'd navigated on the way in. The hushed silvery landscape glowed here and there with its own luminosity. The glow from the moving cars seared into his retina in a confusing white swirl of brightness and movement.

He thought about earlier in Munich.

And Rife's attack.

Were any of those vehicles bringing trouble?

CHAPTER 60

RIFE SHIFTED THE CAR INTO FOURTH GEAR AND SPED down the highway. Apparently Koger and Malone had figured out they were tracking them through their phones, as both units had gone dark. But Marc Fenn's remained active. The listening devices within Fenn's castle had revealed that Koger and Malone had appeared, learned a lot of information, then they and Fenn had left, headed south, apparently to Neuschwanstein. The latest ping showed that Fenn's phone was right on top of the castle's location.

Terry Knight sat beside him.

He'd also placed, then received, a call from Prince Stefan, who'd stated that he would be heading south, too, along with his brother, Albert, who had now joined forces with him.

Good.

Things were progressing.

The unexpected alliance between Koger and Malone had presented a threat. Not to mention the two spies in Prince Stefan's midst. Then there were the four men who'd been killed last night. Two were hired help. Two were Scythe. The hired help had been run over by a car. His men died from bullets to the head. They'd been sent to deal with Luke Daniels, but apparently Daniels had dealt with them. Which served as a warning.

Enemies abounded everywhere.

Nothing new, though. He was accustomed to a rough playing field. The good thing here was that he was unrestrained by any rules or lines of authority. No one was looking over his shoulder or telling him how to handle things. He could literally do whatever was necessary, and he planned on doing just that. All of the clues that had been unearthed so far apparently pointed the way to the fairy-tale castle that now came into view through the windshield. Seemed a bit ironic, considering the carnage he was about to unleash.

A familiar feeling surged through him.

One that said things were about to come to a head.

STEFAN WAS STILL ASTONISHED BY WHAT HE'D READ IN his great-grandfather's journal, welcome insight from a bitter seventy-four-year-old man. Clearly, Ludwig III had tried to preserve what he could of the Wittelsbach legacy. The horrors of World War I, then the German Revolution, and finally his loss of throne and kingdom had exacted a heavy toll. It made sense that he would take affirmative steps to protect his family's heritage.

Rätselspiel.

Mystery game.

Indeed.

He was sitting in the passenger compartment of a Eurocopter EC135, the sleek aircraft's cabin adorned with Hermès signature fabrics and butter-soft leather.

A glass partition separated the cockpit from the cabin, providing a high degree of privacy. When he'd asked Albert what needed to be done, his brother had told him they must head south. Now. Albert had been equally cryptic when questioned about the helicopter's owner, merely saying that the aircraft was at their disposal.

His brother looked tired.

All this exertion had to be hard on him.

"You should have allowed me to handle this," he said to Albert. "You are not well."

"I appreciate your concern. But I would like to be a part of this, however small that might be. I have long thought that Neuschwanstein would be key to the quest. Though only partially completed when he died, it remains the most enigmatic of Ludwig II's three castles."

They were speeding fast through the cold air. Daylight was nearly gone, the low ceiling of cloud shedding a steady fall of light snow. A row of fierce peaks ripped the southern horizon into jagged strips. Below stretched a sea of snow broken only by dense patches of forest, the occasional house or farm, and the open expanse of frozen lakes.

Neuschwanstein sat near the ancient town of Füssen, only a kilometer from the Austrian border. The town's claim to fame had long been violin making, but Ludwig II made the location famous. The future king had been raised at Hohenschwangau, another castle just outside of town, where he and his brother, Otto, spent their childhood. Later, after his father died, and Ludwig became king, he bought a nearby summit with an ancient ruin, which was leveled and Neuschwanstein constructed, all within sight of his childhood home. The two castles still remained.

One finished, the other never to be completed. One known throughout the world, the other basking in its shadow.

Like he and Albert.

In so many ways.

Strange, this new alliance. He and Albert's past conversations had usually been friendly, but never familiar. Always before they'd represented conflicting factions, the ideological chasm between them never closing. Two worlds, two eras, locked in confrontation. His represented reform and progression, Albert's more traditional in patience and satisfaction with the status quo, their priorities irreconcilable.

But not anymore.

"I always thought what Father told me," Albert said, "about *das letzte königreich* were simply stories. Fanciful tales of nonsense. But once I read the journal it became clear that Ludwig III took the notion quite seriously and actually created something real."

Yes, the old king had.

It waits in a safe place, watched over by the Sängerkrieg, protected by the Rätselspiel, waiting for a time when we are once again revered.

"Do you know what he meant by 'watched over by the Sängerkrieg'?" he asked Albert.

His brother smiled. "I don't. But there are people here that do."

CHAPTER 61

Luke checked his watch.

5:20 p.m.

He, Toni, and Christophe had taken refuge in an underground room, just past the chapel—a storage area for cleaning supplies and other equipment. He'd hoped that nothing inside would be needed and, thankfully, no one had disturbed their solitude. The cathedral had closed nearly ninety minutes ago for some sort of private ceremony. For the past fifteen minutes the organ above had been playing.

"Let's do it," he said.

Toni opened the door and carefully peered out. "Looks okay."

They fled the room and returned to the chapel. The music was louder, seeping down below from the stairway through the closed iron gate. Its deep bass tones should offer excellent cover for any noise they might make.

"But first," Luke said, "we need to find out if that gate is locked."

Toni climbed the stairs, hesitated a few moments,

then descended and shook her head. "Closed. But not locked."

Good.

Their escape route seemed okay. The idea was to open the burial vault and retrieve the pocket watch Fenn had said should be there. Also, if they came across anything else "out of the ordinary" they should remove that too. Really? Out of the ordinary inside a one-hundred-year-old decayed body? Everything about this screamed trouble. Yet Christophe seemed oblivious to anything. Toni, on the other hand, had tossed him enough looks that he realized she also smelled trouble. Regardless, once done, they should be able to leave by blending in with whatever was happening upstairs. The only glitch would come if whatever was happening included a visit down here.

"Okay," Christophe said. "You said this wasn't going to be a problem. Show me."

He stepped over to the five burial vaults.

"Give me a hand," he said to Christophe. "Lexi, keep an eye up those stairs for any visitors."

She nodded and remained at the bottom of the stone risers as he and Christophe turned their attention to the square engraved slab that sealed the final resting place of Ludwig III. He'd not been able to get extra close earlier with all the people around. But now he saw that his hunch was right. The stone was not mortared to the wall. Instead a gap existed, indicating that it was a separate piece. He saw that Christophe likewise understood. They each worked on a side, wedging their fingers into the gap and wiggling the stone outward. It took effort but there was enough play to allow them to work a steady back-and-forth until they could get a solid grip on the outer lid, sliding it out ever so slowly. Together, one on each side, they freed the cap and set it on the floor.

"That was heavy," Christophe said.

Yes, it was.

Luke stood back up and stared into the receptacle.

Empty. No coffin. No body.

Nothing.

Oh, crap.

This was worse than he'd thought.

COTTON STOOD AT NEUSCHWANSTEIN'S CRENELLATED gateway and noticed the stone figure of a dog above one of the doors. Beneath it was an inscription. BEI TAG UND NACHT, DIE TREUE WACHT. Faithfulness keeps guard by day and night. The phrase included in the riddle Dianne McCarter had provided to him.

"Looks like we're in the right place," he said.

"I knew that when you showed me back at my castle," Fenn said. "Those words pointed straight here."

That they did.

Beyond the gatehouse was a spacious, split-level inner courtyard devoid of people. He felt like he'd come face-to-face with a remnant of a fantastical world that had long been dead. Lights illuminated the open space. Turnstiles and ropes that formed a zigzagging queue stood empty. An uneasy silence passed around him in the icy air, which only made his breathing more noticeable. He hated the cold. He'd been bred in the heat and humidity of middle Georgia with lots of gnats, mosquitos, and onions.

The sound of a waterfall continued in the distance, somewhere out into the darkness. Fenn led the way inside to a gift shop where a man waited. He was short, with light brown hair and scowling eyebrows, a dark mole dotting his right cheek. He introduced himself as the curator, adding a smile that had all the charm of a durable-press shirt.

"We are old friends," Fenn said. "He is not Guglmänner. But definitely a friend of the brothers."

"Marc explained what is happening," the man said in a nasally voice. "This is quite exciting. I have always wondered if the stories were true."

Cotton smiled. "Why don't we find out."

LUKE INSTANTLY REALIZED THE SITUATION.

"Your buddy, Fenn, sent us here for a reason," he said to Christophe, "and it's not to get into this tomb."

Toni hustled over and saw the empty receptacle.

"Fenn said there was a body in here," Christophe said.

"Which ought to tell you something," Toni added.

"We need to get out of here," he said. But on the off chance that Fenn had truly not known the tomb was empty, he decided that replacing the cap would be best. "First, let's clean this up."

Together, all three of them lifted the capstone and slid it back into place. Then they climbed the stairs to the iron gate, which Toni slowly opened. He recalled the nave's geography and realized that the portal was toward the main altar, a long walk from there to the exit doors. And whatever special event was happening could make their retreat far from unnoticeable. But the chance would have to be taken.

They stepped out.

The organ continued to blare.

Acolytes were busy arranging the altar, about half a dozen young people in robes milling about. The pews were empty. Thank goodness. Whatever was happening had not yet started. Maybe they'd caught a break and could disappear fast. But his hopes were dashed when he stared back through the nave toward the main doors.

Five uniformed police entered.

Which confirmed this was a trap.

He and Toni turned, intent on finding another way out. But Christophe had other ideas, reaching beneath his coat, finding a gun, and firing in the cops' direction.

"This is not going to be good," Luke muttered.

CHAPTER 62

COTTON FOLLOWED KOGER AND THE CURATOR DEEPER into Neuschwanstein, admiring the mythical atmosphere. Flashes of another place and time flickered before his eyes. He half expected to see knights in armor strolling the corridors with their squires in tow. The building was now officially closed for the day so the place loomed empty.

At a spiral staircase they climbed up to the third floor.

"The throne hall is down there, to the right," the curator said as they exited the stairway. "But what you are after is this way." The man pointed down a long corridor, one side of which was an exterior wall with darkened windows. The other side opened, through Norman arches, into lit rooms. "The normal tour would start ahead at the throne room, moving through the dining room and the king's bedroom, turning on the far side and then coming back down this corridor to the stairs. But nobody is here, so we can cheat just a little and go in reverse."

The man seemed pleased at the possible mischief.

The curator led them down the corridor. The

rooms to his right were a flaming symphony of color, embellished with rare woods and decorated with exquisite murals, all from Wagnerian operas. Lustrous brass chandeliers contributed to the grand splendor. Cotton wondered how many wood-carvers, painters, goldsmiths, and needleworkers labored to create it. Everything was intensely quiet, like a mausoleum, illuminated by incandescent fixtures and shafts of weak exterior floodlight that filtered in through the mullioned windows.

Halfway, the curator stopped. "This was the king's study."

Like the rest of the interior, the walls were a warm, knot-free oak, stained walnut. A gold-plated brass chandelier hung from the center that accommodated electric candles that burned bright. A large writing desk and a high-backed chair with some charming embroidery sat beneath the chandelier. On the desk sat a large inkstand and two bronze lamps. Behind the desk a set of closed double doors led into another room. He breathed in the warm air, heavy with the waft of dust and polish.

"Do you know what we're after here?" Koger asked.

The curator nodded. "Marc explained what you have learned. 'Where the minstrel aims his praise, and Parsifal points his gaze, the seer and dove offer help from above.' Quite a clever twist of words."

The same conclusion Fenn had come to, which made Cotton wonder.

Who came to it first?

"The king's desk once stood out here," Fenn said. "Against the window, in the corridor. Of course, Ludwig lived alone, so that would not have been an issue. He only slept here for about a hundred and seventy days total. When he did, he would sit at the desk and stare out at the panorama of regal old pines, birch groves, and wide valleys. Quite a sight that would have been. The desk was moved into the study a long time ago to accommodate the thousands of visitors who traverse this hall every day."

The curator pointed at the bright, colorful wall murals. "These were all painted by Joseph Aigner, an artist from Munich, on large canvases built into the wall. Aigner, though, worked too slow for Ludwig's patience. So he was eventually replaced with another painter. That so-called 'interference with his artistic vision' was said to have driven Aigner mad."

"Any truth to it?" Cotton asked.

The curator shrugged. "No one really knows. Aigner killed himself in 1886, five months before Ludwig died. But before he was fired, Aigner tried to curry Ludwig's favor." The curator approached one of the large murals that filled the top half of a side wall. He pointed, then explained, "These paintings tell a story. Once there was an itinerant knight, a singer named Tannhäuser, who fell in love with Elisabeth, the niece of the Landgrave of Thüringen. But their differing social status prevented them from marrying so, in despair, Tannhäuser traveled to a place called Hörselberg, where the goddess Venus resided. There he stayed for a year enjoying the pleasures of her decadent realm."

The curator pointed to more of the murals that illustrated what he was saying.

"Eventually, Tannhäuser grew weary of the goddess and moved on, arriving at the Wartburg, where a singers' contest was happening. He joined in, but shocked the other minstrels by singing the praises of sensual love. He was banned from the Wartburg."

The curator stepped before another of the paintings and pointed.

"In despair, Tannhäuser went on a pilgrimage to Rome seeking the pope's forgiveness, which was refused, so he returned to Venus's enchanted mountain. That entire saga is depicted here, in all its colorful glory. Wagner wrote a great opera that took license with the traditional story. What is here is not Wagner's interpretation of the Germanic legend. Instead, Ludwig wanted everything in this castle to more reflect the original story of the amorous crusading Franconian knight and the great song contest at the Wartburg."

Cotton could see that Koger was becoming impatient. That he could understand. His patience was also wearing thin. A lot was happening and too many bad guys were around to waste time on legends. But the curator and Fenn both seemed right at home in fantasyland. He decided to bring things back on topic. "The book that was found at Herrenchiemsee was of the Tannhäuser and the minnesingers' contest at Wartburg. That points to here?"

Fenn nodded and removed the volume from his coat pocket. "I brought it along, in case we need it. Both this book, and the reference we saw below to faithfulness keeping guard by day and night, definitely point to here. Along with one other thing."

He had no choice, so he asked, "Which is?"

"*Parsifal*," Fenn said. "Another of Wagner's operas that Ludwig II loved. It was loosely based on a thirteenth-century epic poem of the Arthurian knight Parzival and his quest for the Holy Grail."

"Ludwig was inspired by the poem," the curator noted. "As Wagner's patron, Ludwig encouraged the composer to create an opera based on the romance.

Which Wagner did. The Singers' Hall, up on the fourth floor, is decorated with tapestries and paintings depicting that story. Ludwig commissioned eight private performances of the opera just for himself." The curator stepped over to one of the larger murals. "Ludwig was enamored with opera. He loved the adventure, the romance, the battles between good and evil, love and hate. He liked to refer to himself as Parsifal. There are numerous writings, in his own hand, that have survived, where he referenced himself with that nickname. And then there is this."

The curator pointed to the upper left corner of the mural where Tannhäuser was singing in the contest. Eight spectators were watching the performance. Three seated. Five standing. All wore medieval clothes and cast a medieval appearance. Save for one bearded face. Right in the middle of the group.

"I told you that the painter Aigner fell out of favor with Ludwig," the curator said. "He tried to regain favor by including the king's image in one of his murals. This one. That face, there, with beard and mustache, is the king's."

Cotton stepped closer and took in the features. "It does look like him."

"It is him," Fenn said. "Parsifal himself."

The words from Ernst Lehmann flashed again through his mind. *But where the minstrel aims his praise, and Parsifal points his gaze, the seer and dove offer help from above.*

And he got it. He pointed. "Where the minstrel aims his praise."

The redheaded singer, standing tall, arm raised in a blue cloak, faced left.

"And Parsifal points his gaze."

Ludwig II also faced left.

He stepped to the right side of the mural. An ornate porcelain stove, in pale white and green, stood beneath the painting.

"Are they pointing to this?" he asked the curator.

Fenn smiled. "They are pointing to that spot. But not to that stove. It was added only a few years ago. Instead, what is important is what stood here in the early part of the twentieth century, when Ludwig III conceived his mystery game."

"You know what that was?" Koger asked.

Fenn nodded.

CHAPTER 63

RIFE AND TERRY KNIGHT USED THE DARKNESS FOR COVER as they approached Neuschwanstein. Snow had begun to fall in a steady burst, emerging out of the blackness as gleaming flakes in the castle's bright floodlights. Swaths of frost-feathered pines rose around them. The time was approaching 6:00 P.M. He and Knight had driven up as far as they could, parking beside another vehicle, which had most likely brought Fenn, Malone, and Koger. Hopefully, most of them would not have a need for a return trip home. At least not in a car. Maybe a hearse.

He stopped.

They'd passed no one on the short walk up the twisting asphalt incline, the castle surely closed for the day. But there would be employees still inside, closing up the place. Cameras too. Probably lots of them. Outside as well.

So they had to be careful.

He led the way as they rounded the final bend and approached the main entrance. A large court-yard extended past the gatehouse, the white limestone and wall bricks illuminated by more bright halogen lights. Snow covered much of the cobblestones and iced the roof tiles. Several doors were visible, along with a multitude of windows, most dark. To his right he saw lights through a set of glass doors and caught movement beyond.

Employees.

He pointed ahead.

Knight headed up a flight of stone steps to an upper courtyard. Rife followed, keeping a watch out for anyone. They hustled over and climbed another set of exterior stairs that led to double wooden doors. The iron latch opened. They slipped inside and, before closing the doors, a quick scan of the courtyard revealed that all was quiet.

"What now?" Knight asked.

He'd taken some time earlier and studied a rough schematic of the castle's interior. They were inside a vaulted hallway, dimly lit, that led deeper inside. A spiral staircase should be at the end of the corridor, one that would take them to the third floor.

"We wait."

But first.

Rife found his phone and sent a text to a man he'd posted in the distance, keeping a watch on the exterior for anything unexpected.

A moment later came the reply.

They're here.

He turned to Knight and whispered, "We're good. Come with me."

STEFAN STEPPED FROM THE HELICOPTER OUT INTO THE cold. Albert followed him, struggling to climb down. They both moved away as the blades wound down.

They'd landed on a lit concrete pad, dusted with snow, among the trees not far from Neuschwanstein. The pad was there to accommodate high-profile visitors, like the Duke of Bavaria and his brother, the prince. Albert led the way as they headed for a trail outlined by a string of low-voltage ground fixtures. He knew they were beyond the castle, on another rocky mount, the roar of the waterfall in the Pöllat gorge close by.

Snow crunched beneath their shoes.

He felt like Ludwig II, parading around in some nocturnal adventure, thinking that darkness somehow provided security. If anything, the night allowed threats to move about more easily, unnoticed. And yet here he was parading through an alpine forest, atop a rocky crag, with a sibling he'd long resented, headed for a castle one of his ancestors had struggled to erect but never finished. That seemed the Wittelsbachs' fate. Emperors, kings, and dukes in a nearly constant struggle to succeed. Yet always failing. Every. Single. Time. Amazing that the family held on to Bavaria for eight hundred years. But it had been gone for a little over a century. Maybe a reprieve might be in the making. One orchestrated by two Wittelsbachs working in concert. One in the twilight of life, the other in his prime.

They emerged from the trees to a spectacular sight of Neuschwanstein, a couple hundred meters away, carefully placed lighting revealing the castle in all its glory.

"Ludwig possessed a great vision," Albert said. "One that can only be appreciated in this day and age."

He agreed. But there was a more pressing matter. "Are we going inside?"

"Not yet," Albert said.

He was curious. Ming had told him on the phone to get here. Fast. "What are we waiting for?"

"I am quite close with the castle's curator and he told me to wait until he called."

"For what?"

"I'm not sure." Albert motioned. "While we wait, let us take in the view from the bridge. I've always enjoyed that sight."

He was cold and the snowfall seemed to be increasing. But he did not want to do anything to spoil his newfound partnership.

Especially on such a trivial matter.

"Okay. Why not."

CHAPTER 64

LUKE COULD NOT STOP CHRISTOPHE, WHO RAISED HIS weapon and fired two shots at the incoming police. The uniformed officers all dove to the vestibule floor, which bought them a few seconds to race off in the opposite direction.

"He's going to get us killed," Toni said to him as they ran.

"You think?"

The acolytes readying the high altar all fled in a panic toward the far end of the nave. Luke glanced back. Christophe lagged, alternating his attention between what lay ahead and behind. The police had returned to their feet but were not rushing ahead, conscious of the fact that at least one of their targets was armed. Luke quickly absorbed the local geography. The interior was divided into three sectors. Each appeared slim and confined due to their impressive height, but there was actually lots of room to maneuver.

Too much, really.

What he needed was another way out and he spotted that off to his left, a set of huge doors beneath a darkened stained glass window. Toni saw it, too, and headed for it. Christophe had yet to catch up. Which mattered not since that guy was radioactive. Sure, Fenn may not have known that the tomb was empty and the police just happened to show up here at precisely the right moment. But like his mother would say when he tried some cockamamie story on her to explain his way out of trouble. *Coincidence is God's way of staying anonymous.* Bless her soul, but this was not God's work. No. Fenn had set them up to take a fall. The police were here for a reason.

And it wasn't good.

Toni reached the door and grabbed the heavy iron latch.

Which opened.

She rushed out. Luke followed.

Christophe caught up and exited with them. The side doors led to a small landing, then a few stone risers dropped down to a compact plaza ringed by dark multi-story buildings. Three breezeways led out through the buildings. Two police cars, blue and red lights strobing, motored through one of them and screeched to a halt. Officers poured out, reaching for their sidearms.

Crap. These guys were serious.

Christophe leveled his weapon and fired a round toward them. Luke knew what was coming and dove toward Toni, taking her down to the cold pavement as the officers sent a barrage of bullets their way.

Several found Christophe.

Thudding lead caused muscular convulsions.

A look of surprise filled Christophe's face and he staggered forward a few paces, struggling to keep his balance, then toppled backward, hitting the pavement hard.

"Crawl. Fast," he told her.

She seemed to know that staying low could work as the police were focused on the more immediate threat. They belly-crawled forward using a series of large stone planters for cover. Another of the breezeways opened to their right. Twenty feet away. The cops were a good thirty yards behind them. Darkness loomed, broken only by a few freestanding amber light fixtures. His Ranger training kicked in and he recalled the six steps to save your ass. First and foremost, keep out of harm's way. Then, take cover fast. Don't panic. Think clearly. Keep reassessing. And, most important, be smart before moving.

So far he'd adhered to the first five.

Time for number six.

"Stay flat and use that last planter as cover, then roll into the breezeway."

Toni nodded, never hesitating or flinching. She was damn good under pressure. He risked a glance back and saw that the police were reassessing the situation, probably making sure Christophe was no longer a problem. Toni wiggled forward to the next planter. Luke followed, both of them trying not to make a lot of noise. The stone steps leading up to the cathedral's side door gave them a bit of cover since the police were on its other side.

They both made it to the last planter.

He rolled onto his back and saw that the police had yet to advance.

"Do it. Now," he said.

She came to her knees, crouched low, and bolted for the blackness of the breezeway. No shots came their way. She disappeared into the darkness. He rolled over and readied himself. Noise from behind caught his attention. He started forward, staying low.

A shot rang out and a bullet pinged off the concrete. Real close.

"Haltepunkt."

He didn't need to speak German to know what that command meant.

"Hände in die luft."

"No *deutsche*," he called out.

"Hands in the air. Now," another voice called out.

No choice. He raised his arms, showed his empty hands, and stood. The four policemen were on the stone steps, guns aimed his way. Toni was nowhere to be seen or heard. Hopefully, she got away.

"Down on your knees," came an order.

He hesitated, trying to decide if he could out-maneuver these guys. Doubtful. They were ready to unload on him. At least one or more of the rounds would find their mark. Christophe had not moved. Surely dead. Arrest seemed preferable to that alternative. But it would most likely end his involvement with this operation. Once compromised, rarely did an intelligence officer reenter the game. Instead, they were sent off to join another.

Suddenly, the entire plaza was ablaze with light.

Atop the buildings ringing the open space, banks of floodlights dissolved the darkness and lit the world in a bright glow. Not halogens. These were the old-fashioned bulbs, springing to life at full intensity. The police reacted by shielding their open pupils from the glare with raised arms. Luke fought the urge to squint. Instead, he closed his eyes, turned, and rushed for the breezeway. He made it inside to the welcome darkness and saw Toni standing beside an open electrical box.

"My father was an electrician. I know my way

around a circuit box. I was hoping the switches worked."

"God bless Thomas friggin' Edison. Those cops aren't going to hesitate long."

"I agree."

And they both ran off.

CHAPTER 65

Cotton stared at Marc Fenn and waited for an explanation.

"Within a few years of Ludwig II's death, this castle was opened for tours by the prince regent, and people flooded in to see what their dead king had created. At first, things were left as they were, out of respect. But that gradually became more and more difficult to achieve." Fenn stepped from the study and back through the arch to the corridor. "Much of the furniture and Ludwig's personal items had to be removed and stored away to give people room to walk."

A whistling wind rattled the window casement, pressing on the panes.

"Downstairs," the curator said. "In the basement. That's where things are stored. In the same room the Nazis used during the war to hide stolen art."

Fenn pointed at the desk. "As I mentioned, that writing table was out here, in the corridor, under the window. The oak cabinet, there on the right wall, stood on the left, where the ceramic stove is now."

Cotton stepped across the study to the cabinet.

"It's a storage unit," the curator said. "Ludwig kept the architectural plans and sketches for the castle inside. It dates to 1881."

"The king personally used that piece of furniture?" Koger asked.

Fenn nodded. "One of those rare pieces that has survived."

"More important," Cotton said, "did Ludwig III use it?"

The curator nodded. "It was here during his short reign. Our records indicate that he visited this castle quite often."

Cotton inspected the front of the oak cabinet. Four arches with beautifully carved panels and capitals supported an elaborate head piece, the front of which was constructed of seven entwined, carved columns. The panels of the cupboard doors were ornamented with artistic fittings, the top crowned by pinnacles, gables, towers, and crosses.

"It's beautiful," he said, examining the craftsmanship. "Who made it?"

"A man named Hofmann," the curator said. "He also crafted a desk that is displayed in the study at Herrenchiemsee."

He caught the connection. That desk he knew.

"We are most definitely in the right place," Fenn said.

He agreed. Then his mind recalled Lehmann's message. *When Good Friday falls on St. George's Day, Easter on St. Mark's Day, and Corpus Christi on St. John's Day, all the world will weep.* And the second part. *But where the minstrel aims his praise, and Parsifal points his gaze, the seer and dove offer help from above.*

"So the minstrel and Parsifal point to this chest, which in the early twentieth century stood on the other side of the room, right where the images in the painting are looking."

But he wondered how the seer and dove would help from above.

He stepped close to the cupboard and opened the four cabinet doors. The two at either end accommodated shelves spaced about a foot apart with nothing on them. The two middle doors protected a series of small drawers, stacked atop one another in rows of four. Each was marked with an engraved number, starting with 1 in the upper left and ending with 32 in the lower right.

"What are these?" he asked.

"The best guess," the curator said, "is that they were places for trinkets, supplies, other small things."

Koger shook his head. "What are we supposed to do?"

Cotton smiled. "It's a puzzle."

"Which I have little patience for."

"Thankfully, I do."

Koger shrugged. "Okay, Maloney, work your magic."

He returned his attention to the cabinet. Fenn was right. Every clue pointed right here. So the answers had to be *here*. "The first part of the message Lehmann left is a year. The second part has to involve this cabinet."

1886. The seer and dove offer help from above.

He stepped away from the cabinet to the writing table and lifted the heavy straight-backed chair that sat to one side. He brought it over and used it to gain height and study the carved ornamentation from above. The top was loaded with intricate filigree, crosses, and towers, along with, lo and behold, two doves. One left of center, the other to the right. Both carved of oak, perched with their long necks high and straight. Invisible, unless you stood high.

He reached over and touched them. Both rotated freely on a center axis with no resistance. Round and round, squeaking ever so slightly. He stepped off the chair and stared at the numbered drawers.

1 to 32.

And ran through the possibilities.

1. 88. 6?

18. 86?

188. 6?

None of those worked. But 18. 8. 6? That made sense. In fact, it was the only combination that did, given the double eights in the middle of the other four. He opened the drawers marked with those numbers. All three were empty. But what had he expected? Think. *The seer and dove offer help from above.* The same guy who made this cabinet also made the desk with the two hidden compartments at Herrenchiemsee.

He stepped back onto the oak chair and grabbed a dove with each hand. Immediately he noticed that they no longer spun freely. Both were stationary with just the tiniest of wiggle room. He twisted left and right. Nothing. Only one direction left. So he pulled them upward. They came free of the oak top, each attached to an iron bar that groaned as it became more exposed. At about six inches there was no more rod and he heard a click.

A panel in the lower left side of the cabinet opened.

The others saw it, too, and came close.

Cotton stepped down.

"I'll be damned," Koger said. "You found it."

CHAPTER 66

STEFAN FOLLOWED HIS BROTHER AS THEY CAREFULLY made their way across a graveled path that led to the Marienbrücke. Normally, on a summer's night, people would be everywhere, the line to walk across the Queen Mary's Bridge long, since it offered the best spot for photos of Neuschwanstein. The bridge itself dated to Ludwig's time, named for his mother, still sporting its original railing and largely unaltered arches. But tonight no one was around, the bridge unlit, stretching unseen in the wintery darkness.

"Remember when we came with Father," Albert said.

He did.

Albert was twenty-five, attending university. He was a boy, not even yet a teenager. Their father had brought them south to the mountains in the only journey they all three had ever taken together. It had been his first visit to Neuschwanstein, which they'd toured one evening privately, without tourists. He'd been amazed at the intricate woodworking and the array of color from the gilding and countless murals. The grotto had really intrigued him. Set near the king's study, it was an artificial dripstone cave with wondrous colored lighting, all made of papier-mâché to resemble icicles and stalactites, even a real stream of water splashed down from the make-believe rocks. It had all seemed so unreal. So magical. Looking back, that was perhaps the first time he thought of himself as royalty.

Now he may become king.

Albert stepped from the rocky ground onto the metal span, the grates thick with fresh snow. Easy to see why visitors were not allowed this time of year. Together they walked about halfway across its thirty-five meters of length, ending about where they'd stood with their father all those years ago. Ninety meters below was the Pöllat gorge, its raging water from the mountains unfrozen and crashing down in a steady thunder. A stinging draft of icy air took his breath away and bit the skin through his woolen trousers where unprotected by his overcoat. They stood together, the two highest-ranking members of the Wittelsbach family. Its current number was somewhere around five hundred individuals. Just a small portion lived in Bavaria. Most were spread across Europe, Asia, the Middle East, even the United States. Only his family and Albert were directly supported by the main estate. The rest fended for themselves.

"Ludwig II would have the castle's rooms lit with twelve hundred candles," Albert said. "Then he would come right here, and stand over this chasm, gazing for hours at the fairy-tale brilliance he created."

They stood a few moments in a strained silence.

The chill, though bitter, seemed invigorating.

"What will you do with it?" Albert asked, pointing to the illuminated castle, seemingly floating in the darkness.

"Nothing," he said.

"I would finish it."

He was curious. "Why? It generates millions of euros in revenue and provides the people with something to see and appreciate. Just as it is."

"But it also represents failure. As does Herrenchiemsee. They both require completion. They scream for a period at the end of their sentences. If for nothing else, I would do it simply to validate Ludwig II's grand dreams."

He could appreciate that sentiment. "But it would cost hundreds of millions of euros and accomplish little."

"Really? Think of the result." Albert pointed at the Neuschwanstein. "That is perhaps the most famous castle in the world. Its design has been replicated and adapted countless times. When it was built all called it folly. But here it is, over a century later, still serving the nation."

Another true statement.

"It deserves completion."

He wondered about Albert's laments. They were unlike him. His brother had always been pragmatic to the point of indifference, collecting his stamps and doing little to nothing of anything else. The family had never mattered to him. So he wanted to know, "Is that your illness talking?"

"No, Stefan. It is the Duke of Bavaria talking."

He felt vibrations beneath his feet, which signaled someone else was on the bridge. He turned to see two dark forms detach themselves from the shadows and walk toward them.

Then he realized.

"You were expecting them?" he asked Albert.

"I believe you know one of them."

He waited until the forms drew close.

"Good evening," Jason Rife said.

He did not know the other man.

"This is my associate, Terry Knight. We came to deal with what's happening inside the castle."

"Ming sent you?" he asked Rife, curious.

"No. He"—and Rife pointed to Albert—"sent for me."

"I had no idea you were connected with my brother."

"I imagine there's a lot you have no idea about," Rife said.

He did not appreciate the rebuke.

"It's time you know the truth," his brother said. "About many things."

They all stood suspended high in the cold night air. Exposed. Vulnerable. But also surprisingly private. Had that been the idea?

"Dear brother," Albert said, "I think we will, this night, have the deed for *das letzte königreich*. Once that occurs, I will give that document to Herr Rife, who will then provide it to the Chinese. In return, Berlin will grant Bavaria the opportunity to vote to be free. Which the people will overwhelmingly support. A win for us all." Albert paused. "Then I will be king."

He was puzzled. "That will not happen in time for you."

"But it will, Stefan. For you see, I am not dying. In fact, I am in perfect health. I created that story, with the help of my doctor, to spur you along, for I knew your ambition could be put to good use."

He was astonished. "You are not ill?"

Albert shook his head. "I manufactured that story so you would be sufficiently motivated. And you were. Just the thought that you might be king was enough for you to do what I could not."

"You used me?"

Albert chuckled. "Of course I did. I had to know if Ludwig's tomb was empty. There were stories, entries in the journal that indicated such, but I had to be sure. I also needed that book from Herrenchiemsee. So I made sure certain information came your way. Enough to spur you forward. And you did not disappoint me. You see, brother, I know you all too well."

He felt the fool.

"Originally, I planned to carry this out much further," Albert said. "I thought its resolution would take more time. But circumstances have accelerated. More progress has been made, in a short time, than I thought possible. That is good, and it has led us here."

"What has happened?"

"The CIA did its job," Rife said, "and solved the mystery."

"I thought you were ex-CIA, now working with the Chinese."

"I am. But you gotta admire their get-up-and-go."

The other guy, Knight, stood silent, never moving. A bit unnerving. In fact, the whole scenario was horribly uncomfortable.

"I'm leaving," he said.

He turned, but Knight immediately blocked his way.

"No, Stefan," Albert said. "You are not going anywhere. It is time we come to an understanding."

CHAPTER 67

LUKE AND TONI FLED THE BREEZEWAY AND HEADED back onto a crowded street that stretched past the cathedral's rear. His eyes were once again accustomed to the gloom. The time was approaching six-thirty and Munich was alive with its nightly Christmas activities. The streets overflowed with people radiant with joy. He could hear the music and crowds from a few blocks away where the main market stretched for over a mile. He'd passed through it many times over the past week, coming and going on the prince's business, never really taking things in. Now it offered the perfect place to disappear among the thousands who would surely be there.

"Let's get to the market," he said, glancing back and seeing the police emerge from the breezeway, searching ahead. One caught sight of them and pointed. "And fast."

They shouldered through the pedestrians and turned a corner, breaking into a run down the middle of the pavement, as traffic was not allowed. The street emptied into the main thrust of revelers, all enjoying the craft stalls, food vendors, and *glühwein* sellers.

Festive music rose above the noise. Some nearby brass horns. He looked back and saw the police were still coming and he recalled an old adage his father told him right after he obtained his driver's license. You can't outrun their radios, son. Not that he hadn't tried a few times. But his father had been right. He never once escaped them.

"Any ideas?" he asked Toni as they kept moving.

"Head for the Marienplatz. It should be packed."

They turned left and followed the flow toward the central square that extended out from the old town hall, where they'd ended up late last night, long after the people had all gone home. At this early evening hour it was a sea of activity, all of the booths open for business. A triangle of an evergreen, festooned with lights and decorations, rose thirty feet. The source of the music came from a stage near the town hall.

He stopped. "I get the feeling we're being herded."

"I agree. Those cops are not pursuing us like they should."

He recalled from last night that there were a myriad of ways into and out of the plaza, side streets and alleys. Which not only offered them choices but also provided the police with just as many opportunities. Several thousand people engulfed them enjoying the lively market, but he felt extremely exposed.

"If we start to leave, they're going to be waiting for us," he said. "Just like they were back at the cathedral." He told her about his suspicions. "Fenn had to know that Christophe was working with the prince. He sent us there to get arrested, or worse—which happened to Christophe."

The guy had been a bit of an asshole, but he'd not wanted to see him dead.

"Does Fenn know about you?" she asked. "Or me?"

"Hard to say. I just met the man today. But it's way too much of a coincidence that we were both sent with Christophe."

"That would mean the prince and this man Fenn are working together."

"I know. It makes no sense. But there's no tellin' where anyone's allegiance lies. Until they show themselves."

"Does that include me?"

Her windswept curly hair billowed about, her cold chin tucked into the collar of her wool coat.

"How about present company excepted."

She smiled. "I'll take that."

Luke scanned the crowd, hard to see much beyond the press of bodies. So he stepped over to another concrete planter and hopped up, gaining three feet in height. Which helped. In the bright lights that illuminated the square he caught sight of uniformed officers entering the plaza on the far side and fanning out. He already knew there were police behind them.

He hopped down. "We've got lots of company coming this way."

"Then let's enlist the crowd."

He caught the twinkle in her eye and agreed.

Why not?

STEFAN WAS TRAPPED, HIS MIND IN TURMOIL, HIS thoughts uncharacteristically paralyzed with apprehension. But there was nothing he could do other than play this out and show no weakness. So he turned back from Knight, who still blocked his way to leave.

"You have always been impetuous," Albert said.

"Lots of hotheadedness, temper, and tantrums. Brooding and hatching one impractical scheme after another. There is simply nothing new, nothing unexpected, nothing to discover about you. But I am curious, what made you think you could ever be king?"

"You did."

"*Ja*, I did. But before I revealed myself. What were you thinking?"

He stiffened his spine and stood tall. "I thought I was the only Wittelsbach with a backbone. You cared only for your stamps and your next meal. I wanted more for Bavaria."

"No, Stefan. You wanted more for you."

"I don't make any secret of the fact that I would like to be king. Who wouldn't? Other than you."

"But I do want it. Very much, in fact. Which is why I have worked so hard to spur you along. Do you really think you would be a good king?"

"Of course. Better than you."

"That's where you are wrong. Being a king takes more than the desire to be one. It takes competence. Intelligence. And, above all, patience. This country will face enormous challenges once it votes to be free. The economy will be challenged. People will expect a high level of services. We will have to take our place among the world's nations. I have thought about those challenges for a long time. Have you, Stefan? Have you given a single thought to anything, other than your coronation?"

He resented the condescending remarks. "Go to hell, Albert." He faced Rife. "What was all that talk about at the embassy? All the plans. What you wanted me to do. More for show?"

"Not exactly. At that moment we needed you to keep moving forward as a necessary distraction. But my old pals at the CIA have worked fast. They are inside that castle, right now, solving the puzzle."

"They have the deed?"

"Maybe," Albert said. "But, at a minimum, they will point the way. Now it is time."

"For what?" he asked.

"For you to cease all your efforts. For me to take charge. I promised Father on his deathbed that I would succeed, where all others failed, and bring Bavaria back to the family. I have been patiently waiting and waiting for the world to change."

A curious statement.

"That deed Ludwig II managed to obtain, one that granted him ownership of the obscure Hawaiian Islands, was meaningless in 1881. Those islands lay thousands of kilometers away in the middle of the Pacific Ocean, only important to the United States and Great Britain. Bavaria and Germany were more concerned with European domination, and tried twice to conquer the entire continent. But they failed, and the deed was nearly forgotten."

"Not by our family," Stefan declared.

"True. Our great-grandfather Ludwig III seemed quite interested in it. But our grandfather and father always thought it was an interest coupled only with a desire to preserve our legacy past the ruins of the First World War. He wanted the family to survive. He wanted our memory to be preserved. Revolution had taken over. People wanted to erase the past. So he secluded away the remains of Ludwig II, and his brother, Otto, along with much of our family's heritage. What that may include is hard to say. Father always thought the deed was there, waiting for us. Officially, we say that most everything the Wittelsbachs had disappeared when the kingdom fell in

1918. Stolen or plundered. But that is a lie. Much was deliberately hidden away."

"By who?"

"The Guglmänner accomplished the task."

That shocked him. "They were involved?"

"They have always been loyal to Bavaria and to us so, yes, they were definitely involved. They carried out Ludwig III's express wishes, and in the chaos of the Great War and Revolution that followed, it was easy for them to accomplish the job. But the secret of *where* died with the precious few who knew the location. That happens when secrets are actually respected. Through the decades only bits and pieces of where to look survived. We knew some. The black hoods knew some. Others knew some. But no one knew it all, so no one could seriously search."

"Until the Nazis," he said.

"Quite correct. They tried but, along with everything else they attempted, failed. The Americans tried for a time too. But they also failed. Much of that is thanks to our grandfather, who would not allow the secret to be discovered. Eventually, Hawaii became the fiftieth state of America, and nobody gave that deed a thought until I learned something quite by accident."

Stefan knew. "Rare earths?"

"That's right," Albert said. "The Chinese want control of those nodules lying off the coast of Hawaii. And they're willing to seriously bargain to get them. They were our leverage with the Germans. But Herr Rife, here, offered me a quicker, faster way to results. The Chinese prefer to deal with him. So we are adjusting matters."

"The Chinese set me up?"

"No, Stefan. Your arrogance and pride set you up.

We all simply took advantage of those. Thankfully, the Germans need the Chinese and we need the Germans. In the end, the Bavarian people will decide if they want their country and king back. But I am certain they do."

As was he.

"You, though," Albert said, pointing, "will remain a prince. Never to be a king. That honor will be mine. It was granted to me at birth."

This couldn't be happening. He'd been used. Worse, he'd grossly underestimated his brother, who'd cleverly manipulated him.

"What if I do not want to remain a prince?" he asked.

Albert shrugged. "You have no choice."

He stared across the night at Neuschwanstein. Dammit. He'd come so close. Still. "You should step aside and allow me to take the throne."

"And if I don't?"

"I can make you. I'll go to the press and expose all of this."

Albert shook his head. "Sadly, I knew that would be your position. I was hoping perhaps we could come to a different understanding."

"Never."

And he meant it.

"Forgive me, Stefan."

Albert motioned.

Everything exploded into a star-shot burst of pain as the heel of Rife's hand drove into his nose. A spray of warm blood shot out into the air as the breath left his lungs. He'd never been struck in the face before. The sensation was both painful and surprising. Then he was grabbed at the waist and swung around, off balance, an arm vised around his neck cutting off air. His nose quickly swelled, blocking breathing even further. He was yanked back as Knight grabbed both ankles. He tried to resist, jerking his legs, but was unable to break free.

Together, they heaved him up and over the bridge's low railing.

It happened so fast that it took a moment to process that he was falling through the cold with a strange sensation of weightlessness. The sound of the waterfall drew closer and closer. Icy air rushed down his throat and seared his lungs. Adrenaline pumped through his system as a lifetime flashed through his mind. His heart thudded with a massive resonance, as if about to explode from his chest. Then he slammed into something hard.

Which hurt.

His body rebounded.

He hit it again.

Rocks?

Cold water rushed over him.

His mind went blank and bare.

And the world vanished.

CHAPTER 68

LUKE SPOTTED A TRASH CAN AND HEADED FOR IT.

He and Toni would have only a moment to sell things. He didn't really like the idea of what he was about to do, but had no choice. He approached the can, looked inside, then yelled in English, "Bomb. There's a bomb here. Run. Now. Run."

Toni took her cue and screamed, "Everyone get away."

They both flailed their arms and kept sounding the alarm. Hopefully, enough people around them spoke English.

And they did.

Only a few seconds were needed for the threat to become real. People rushed away in every direction, quickly crowding into one another. As things congealed and people began to feel trapped, panic set in. He added to the confusion by yelling again that there was a bomb.

The crowd erupted into full panic.

Exactly what they wanted.

What had been an orderly gathering for the police

to navigate was turning into an impenetrable wall of humanity.

"That should do it," Toni said.

"Oh, yeah."

RIFE STOOD ON THE BRIDGE AND STARED OUT INTO THE night and the falling snow. Prince Albert had watched impassively as his brother was murdered.

"He would have been a recurring problem," Albert said.

"Not anymore."

"No. That problem is solved."

"What about the body?" Knight asked.

"It will be found," Albert said. "Eventually. We will attribute it to Stefan's carelessness. Thankfully, he had a reputation for being reckless. Nothing now remains in our way."

Good to hear.

His deal had been with Albert all along. The idea being for the duke to involve Koger and all of the various resources the CIA could bring to the table. Once that played itself out, Koger would either be dismissed or killed, depending on what developed. He preferred the latter since he and the big man had never been buddies. Just one more debt he'd like to repay. All part of his new devil-may-care attitude toward life and law.

"We need to know what is happening inside the castle," Albert said, the voice sounding far away, the duke facing away.

"We should know shortly," he said.

"Then what?"

"Hopefully, depending on what's found, we can

kill Koger and Malone and this will all be over, and everybody gets what they want."

"You sound skeptical," Albert said.

He shrugged. "Bavaria has to vote yes on independence first."

"It will."

"You that certain?"

"I know this land and people. We have never felt a part of Germany. We crave independence. A recent candidate for German chancellor used the slogan 'Back to the Future.' It was ill-played for Germany as a whole, but suits Bavaria perfectly. The people want their king and kingdom returned."

"You're a ruthless SOB."

"That I am. Please do not forget that."

Sure. But who cares? All he wanted was payback. But he wondered. "No remorse about your brother?"

"He was never much of a sibling."

Albert glanced at his watch, bared between the tip of his coat and the end of his glove. Rife turned to leave and saw two men at the end of the bridge. Stout forms, toting automatic rifles. Not there before.

"They with you?" he asked Albert.

"More with the Guglmänner. But they serve me."

"Good to know."

He motioned to Knight and they started walking toward the forms and off the bridge.

"Where are you going?" Albert called out.

"To finish this."

COTTON STEPPED OFF THE CHAIR.

The others crowded around the cabinet with its

newly revealed secret compartment. Inside he spotted a small wooden container made of dark, satin-smooth mahogany, the corners strapped with dull brass. In the center was a brass plate engraved with "Konig Ludwig III von Bayern." Its lock, also clad in brass, demanded a ward key. He laid the box on the desk and fished the key from his pocket.

The one Randy Miller had kept around his neck.

"I think we now know what this opens," he said to Koger.

"Where did that come from?" Fenn asked, clearly perplexed.

Since that was none of the guy's business, he ignored the question, then inserted the key and turned. The lock freed. He hinged open the lid to reveal an inside divided by a row of wooden inserts that held ink, powder, quills, and wax.

"It is the king's scrivener's box," the curator said. "Quite common in the nineteenth and early twentieth centuries."

Cotton knew about these cases. He'd seen several before. This one, though, had been hidden away for a specific reason. Remembering what he could about them, he felt around and found a small metal catch that he released. The row of inserts swung forward to reveal a compartment beneath where writing paper would have been stored.

But none was there.

Instead, something else lay within.

Odd. Unusual.

"What is that?" Koger asked.

CHAPTER 69

LUKE KEPT PACE WITH THE CROWD.

People flowed out of the Marienplatz in a mad dash. He hoped no one was hurt in the chaos. That was always a risk with so many people around. He and Toni stayed among the masses, blending in. He'd caught sight of a few police, trying to advance their way into the crowd, but the collective panic was working perfectly, allowing them to exit the main plaza down one of the side streets. The crowds thinned the farther they went from the old town hall. Soon their cover would be gone and he'd already spotted police cars a few blocks away down another street. They were now beyond the pedestrian-only zone and traffic jelled, reacting to the unexpected flood of people.

"This way," he said.

And they headed down another street, past closed shops, the sidewalks becoming less and less populated. Around him became a patchwork of light and shadow. The next intersection emptied into a busy boulevard, thick with cars whizzing back and forth, and they waited for the traffic signal to change. Sounds of sirens echoed through the night, more flashing lights seen in the distance.

"There's going to be a lot of cops looking for us," she said.

"I need Koger," he said, and brought out his phone. He tried the number but all he got was voice mail. He tried Malone's number with the same result.

The light changed and they crossed to the other side of the four-lane street. Was he compromised? Had his cover been blown? Or was what happened at the cathedral all directed toward Christophe, who had, after all, played both ends against the middle? Hard to say. The most logical conclusion was that both he and Toni were compromised and that the prince and the Guglmänner were somehow working together. If that were so, then why allow the black hoods to steal back the book? Just give it to them. Procedure mandated that he report in, but that wasn't possible. Koger was his only contact. So he started to walk ahead, down the sidewalk, but Toni stood still.

He turned and faced her. "Is there a problem?"

"Where are you going?"

"I have no idea." But he had one possibility. "We need to find the prince and get some answers."

"I know where he is."

"Really, now?"

She produced her phone. "I received a text. He's at castle Neuschwanstein, along with Malone and Koger."

"Aren't you a wealth of information. When were you planning on sharing this?"

She shrugged. "I was enjoying watching you contemplate the situation."

"What are they doing there?"

"Their jobs, I assume."

"We need to get there."

She grinned. "I came to that decision about fifteen minutes ago."

A car turned the corner and came to a stop at the curb a little ways down from where they stood.

Toni did not seem alarmed.

"You expecting someone?" he asked.

Toni walked over. Luke followed. An attractive, middle-aged woman with long dark hair stared out at him from the rolled-down front passenger's-side window.

"Meet Trinity Dorner," Toni said. "Deputy national security adviser. My boss."

He shook his head. Surprise, surprise.

They both climbed into the backseat and the car motored away.

"I didn't know White House personnel engaged in active field operations," he said.

"And I wasn't aware that Magellan Billet agents worked for the CIA."

"We do when your boss is tryin' to shut us down."

"This has turned extra complicated," Dorner said, not bothering to turn around and face them.

"Care to elaborate?" he asked.

"Our sources have confirmed that the police were provided a tip that a theft was ongoing inside the cathedral. They were told about two men and provided physical descriptions."

"No woman?" he asked.

"Only two men. Which means whatever was set up was done before Toni was sent there, then something changed and she was added."

He told her about Christophe and his double agent activities, Marc Fenn, and the errand to the tomb of Ludwig III.

"The whole thing stunk from the start," he said. "But I had no choice. It became pretty clear when we saw the empty grave."

"And I saved his ass from being arrested," Toni added.

"Lucky for you, Mr. Daniels, that Toni was there," Dorner said.

"I count my blessings every day."

And he tossed Toni a smirk sideways across the backseat.

The car wove its way through the evening traffic, keeping a steady pace, finally turning onto the entrance ramp for the autobahn, heading south.

"Where are we going?" he asked Dorner.

"Are you always so inquisitive?"

"Only when I'm in a car with somebody who definitely doesn't seem to like me."

"Spoken like the nephew of an ex-president."

"More like the employee of a woman who's being tormented by your boss."

Dorner finally turned to face him. "For the record, so we're clear, I like Stephanie Nelle. I don't agree with what's happening to her. And why would you think I don't like you?"

"'Cause I've obviously screwed things up enough that you've decided to personally come save the day."

A slight grin came to the older woman's thin lips. "I can see why Toni likes you."

"I didn't know she did."

"That's the whole point of tonight, Mr. Daniels. There's a lot you don't know. So how about you sit back, shut up, and enjoy the ride."

He wasn't going to allow that rebuke to be the final word, especially since he now knew who'd texted Toni. "We're going to that castle, aren't we?"

"That's exactly where we're going."

Then he got it. "Koger and Malone are in trouble."

Dorner turned around, her attention back out the windshield where the wiper blades kept the snow at bay.

"I'm afraid they are."

CHAPTER 70

COTTON REACHED INTO THE SCRIVENER'S BOX AND REMOVED the object, which consisted of two concentric brass disks, each with the twenty-six letters of the Latin alphabet engraved clockwise on their face. The outer disk was a little over two inches wide, the inner just over an inch and a half. The two shared a common center post, which allowed both disks to rotate. The smaller disk carried an additional engraving of "CSA" and "S.S."

He knew what that represented.

Confederate States of America.

The "S.S."?

Secret Service.

"It's a cipher wheel, used by the Confederacy during the Civil War," he said.

Koger seemed impressed. "You sound like you know all about it."

"I do. My great-great-grandfather, on my mother's side, was a Confederate spy. A man named Angus Adams."

Cotton had seen several grainy, black-and-white photographs of Adams, who'd been short and slender with a bushy head of light hair and a thick mustache common for the time. Most remarkable was the resemblance Angus bore to him, there in the chin, eyes, nose, and mouth.

"As a spy, Adams led the first covert incursion into Pennsylvania with twenty other Confederates, posing as a Union unit in search of deserters. He obtained intelligence on troop movements, which Lee used in his march toward Gettysburg. He was then sent to Indiana to stir up insurrection, as a way to entice that state to join the Confederacy."

"Sounds like a resourceful individual," Fenn said.

"He was. And he almost succeeded in Indiana, but was captured and imprisoned in Ohio."

What happened after that evolved into legend. Supposedly, while in jail, Adams was reading *Les Misérables* and became inspired by Jean Valjean's escapes through the Paris underground. He then noticed how dry the lower prison cells were, with no mold, though they remained in perpetual darkness. That might indicate a constant source of fresh air. Sure enough, he dug down and found a masonry-lined tunnel, probably used for drainage. Adams and five others eventually made their escape through it, and he left a note for the warden.

"In French. *La patience est amere, mais son fruit est doux.* Patience is bitter, but its fruit is sweet."

The warden had not appreciated having his face rubbed in the insult of an escape, so a massive manhunt ensued. Adams fled south, heading for Kentucky. Near the Ohio River Union troops cornered him in a small border town. He found refuge inside a farmhouse where the owner lay ill with delirium. Escape was impossible, so he hid himself inside the mattress upon which the sick man lay. When soldiers inspected the house, they checked to see if Adams was the man in the bed, but never thought to look beneath the man, inside the mattress.

"He snuck out the following day," Cotton said. "When he made his report to his superiors one of them made a comment that Adams was apparently soft as cotton, since no one, not even the sick soul in the bed, had known he was there. And the name stuck. Cotton Adams."

Koger pointed. "And this disk?"

"There's one in a trunk at my grandfather's farm in Georgia. There are only five others known in the world."

"Now there is a sixth," Fenn noted.

"Which really means nothing. Reproductions are all over the internet for sale. The question is, what is an original doing here?" He turned the brass disk over. On his grandfather's were the words "F. Labarre, Richmond VA," for Francis Labarre, a goldsmith in Richmond, Virginia, who'd made all of the cipher disks. This one was engraved differently.

FOR KING LUDWIG II
IN HONOR OF HIS CORONATION.
1864 J.D.

"Ludwig was crowned in 1864," Fenn said. "What does the J. D. represent?"

"Jefferson Davis," Koger said. "What else could it be?"

He agreed. "This seems to be a gift from the Confederate president to the newly crowned king of Bavaria. If I had to speculate, I would say Confederate envoys were looking for European allies. So they curried favor with a new young king. Thankfully, they found precious little help anywhere for their cause."

"What is it doing here?" the curator asked. "Hidden away."

An excellent question. "The Confederacy used them to encrypt messages during the Civil War. Their use was damn effective, the codes nearly impossible to crack. So good they were used during the Spanish-American War and World War I."

"Ludwig was fascinated by codes," the curator said. "All his life he dealt with them. He loved sending secret messages."

"Which explains why Jefferson Davis made this a gift," Koger said. "But the question of the moment is, what does this have to do with what we're dealing with?"

CHAPTER 71

Rife made his way through the dark woods, down from the snow-covered rocky promontory and back toward Neuschwanstein. Knight followed, keeping watch on their rear. A bit unsettling to know that the Duke of Bavaria had his own private militia. Frankly, he'd not given the Guglmänner much thought until a few hours ago.

He and Knight finally arrived back at the gatehouse entry into the castle. Still no one around, the place conveniently quiet. They returned to the same exterior door at the top of the stone risers and reentered, making their way quietly up to the third floor. There, they carefully avoided the corridor that led to the king's study and scampered ahead, taking refuge in the throne room, a palatial space that stretched up two stories with rows of colorful pillars forming an upper colonnade. He knew that the corridor just outside would take them around the third floor through a series of rooms, eventually finding the study. He decided they should get closer so he motioned and Knight led the way.

He had to wait for confirmation before acting.

They'd eliminated the annoyance of Prince Stefan,

secured Albert's complete cooperation, and now only had to wait and see if Koger and Malone solved the puzzle. Why work when others would do it for you? Seemed like a good plan. But that was the thing about good plans. They could go to hell in two seconds.

Especially here.

The Chinese were impatient and unsettled, demanding immediate results. Nothing new there. Paul Bryie had checked with his people at Langley. They were aware of the attack in Munich and Randy Miller's death, all of which had been attributed to the Scythe. He realized that repercussions could come, but Bryie was providing enough misinformation to lead that hunt in a different direction. All he needed was a little time and he might well have that deed. The Chinese had first made a deal with the Germans, but once he came on the scene they saw that money would be far easier to part with than future political favors. Those had a nasty habit of becoming never-ending. Fifty million US dollars to him for the deed was one and out. So they'd accelerated the Germans' timetable to three days, placing pressure on them to perform. He'd assured the Chinese he'd have results before that. A solid payday. But the real payout would be sticking it up the asses of his former bosses. It would be the first of many insults he planned to inflict on the Central Intelligence Agency.

Oh, yeah.

They'd regret firing him.

Knight led the way as they headed through a series of rooms. He realized that the way the floor was designed, half the rooms ran down one side of the center, the other on the opposite side with connecting doors. They came into what had obviously been a dining room and he realized that the study was just on the other side of the closed double doors. He could hear the murmur of voices through the thick walls, but nothing specific.

He motioned for Knight to keep going.

But his partner turned into the table and jostled one side hard, causing the gilded bronze centerpiece to move across the top with a loud scrape.

Rife froze.

So did Knight.

DERRICK HAD A FAMILIAR FEELING.

One he'd honed over the years. Something was wrong. He could feel it. How? Why? Where? Those were unknowns. But his brain was on high alert, his eyes and ears assessing everything around him. The immediate vicinity seemed calm. But there was something about the whole setup that simply did not add up. Hard to say why. But he'd learned not to argue with the feeling. If he was wrong? Okay, he might look a little foolish. But if he was right and ignored it, he could end up dead. Bad enough he'd allowed Rife and Paul Bryie to get ahead of him this morning. He wasn't about to make the same mistake again. Both he and Malone were armed, which was somewhat reassuring. But this castle had the feel of a rat maze. Lots of room to run, just no place to go.

Malone was still examining the cipher wheel.

"Can you use that thing?" he asked.

"I think I can."

Fenn and the curator stood nearby, watching carefully.

"And what can you two add to this growing mess of mystery?" Derrick asked them.

"Many of Ludwig II's personal effects disappeared after his death," the curator said. "Through the years a lot of items have resurfaced. I have bought some myself for this castle's collection, as have other sites throughout Bavaria. But I have never seen anything like this before."

"You told me Ludwig III created this whole mystery game," Malone said to Fenn. "So how did he get this cipher wheel?"

"The family eventually took possession of Ludwig II's belongings," Fenn noted. "They were passed down to various branches. Some were donated to museums, some were kept. I can only assume that cipher wheel was retained by the prince regent Luitpold, who gave it to his son Ludwig III. It's not gold or silver, so it had no value back then. But isn't it marvelous? The Rätselspiel has come to life. It is real and we have the solution within our grasp."

"How do you figure?" Derrick asked.

"You don't see?" Fenn said. "All of the clues—the book, the note from Ludwig III, then the one from Lehmann, even the key you produced—they all point right here. I think, finally, we have all of the pieces in one place."

"How do you know that?" Malone asked.

"It is quite simple," Fenn said. "The wording. 'Where the minstrel aims his praise, and Parsifal points his gaze, the seer and dove offer help from above.' That happened. 'Faithfulness keeps guard by day and night.' That's here. Now we have only the final part to decipher. 'The gateway opens and closes with Wagner.' Along with those random letters and numbers. Tell us, Herr Malone, do they relate to the cipher wheel?"

Derrick could see Malone was hesitating with his

answer, and he could also read the look in his eyes. He stepped back out of the study, through the archway, into the corridor. He gazed left and right, the view extending fifty feet in both directions past other rooms. Nothing he saw caused alarm.

Then he heard something.

Like a scrape.

"What was that?" he asked.

"Could be one of the staff closing up for the day," the curator said.

Or it could be something else. Derrick caught Malone's attention. "Let me talk with you." He faced Fenn. "Excuse us."

They stepped from the study down the hall, out of earshot.

"Can you use that thing?" he whispered.

Malone nodded.

"Okay. Whatever you learn, keep it to yourself. These two are real Johnny-on-the-spots. I don't like friendly. We need to find what's out there before anyone else."

"I hear you, and agree. I don't think we're alone."

"Me either."

He turned.

Malone grabbed his arm. "Don't shoot the staff."

He smiled. "I'll try to be careful."

They returned to the study.

"Malone is going to see what he can do," Derrick said to Fenn. "I'm going to take a walk."

"Where?" Fenn asked.

He also hated nosey-Nellies.

"Don't know. Just a walk."

RIFE KEPT MOVING THROUGH ONE ROOM AFTER ANOTHER.
Lots of oak paneling, colorful wall paintings, and
beamed ceilings with carved ornamentation. He hoped
the misstep with the table had not been noticed, but
he had to assume it was since he was dealing with
two highly competent professionals. He also had to
be careful with his steps as the plank floor creaked
in places. Luckily, there were a multitude of rugs
that helped shield their steps. Placards identified the
spaces as bedroom and oratory. They finally stopped
in a parlor, heavy with recesses formed by arches
and columns. The rest of its decor consisted of bookcases, brass chandeliers, and candlesticks adorned
with Bohemian glass. Blue silk curtains embroidered
with lilies and swans hung before the windows. He
stepped over and parted the sheers, glancing down at
the inner courtyard and external staircase from which
they'd entered. He realized that they were at the
floor's farthest edge, pointing north, the opening to
his right leading to another corridor and the series of
rooms that ran opposite the ones they'd just traversed,
which included the study with Koger and Malone.

Knight had slipped into the next room.

He followed.

And was surprised.

It was not like the others. Some sort of faux grotto,
complete with stalagmites and stalactites and a dry
waterfall. Weird. A glass door opened to an upper
conservatory filled with plants. Knight stood to one side
of the doorway, gun ready, signaling for him to stop
and that trouble was approaching. Knight pointed back
toward the way they'd come and they headed there.

"What's up?" Rife whispered.

"Koger has good ears. He's coming our way."

Perfect.

CHAPTER 72

COTTON STARED IN WONDER AT HIS GRANDFATHER.

They sat in the attic, one of the many old trunks that littered the dusty space hinged open. He'd always been allowed free rein with the family's memories, rummaging through stuff that had been lovingly retained for countless decades. Clothes, photos, letters, books, knickknacks, newspapers, shoes, toys, a little bit of anything and everything. But his investigations had finally uncovered something extraordinary. Two brass wheels bound on a center post with the alphabet engraved into both along with the initials CSA and S.S.

"What is it?" he asked his grandfather.

"That belonged to Angus. He used it during the War between the States. It's a cipher wheel, for decoding messages."

He made the connection. "CSA is Confederate States of America?"

The old man nodded. "That's right. S.S. is for Secret Service, which was their spy agency."

"Do you know how to work it?"

His grandfather took the disk from him. "During the war, if a general wanted to send commands to his colonels and captains, he had to guard 'em with ciphers. That way they couldn't be read if the enemy captured 'em. But those ciphers had to be changed a lot, and those changes had to be simple and easy to do. Just enough to throw the enemy off guard."

The whole thing mesmerized him. Soldiers on the battlefield.

Secret messages. Codes.

His grandfather showed him the disk. "This thing allowed those changes to be made, and fast. Do you know what a cipher is?"

He shook his head.

"It's different from a code. With codes you take a bunch of letters or symbols and give 'em a new meaning. Like 'Little red riding hood' means 'attack at sunset.' You string together a lot of phrases that, if you know the code, reveal the message. But a cipher. Now that's different. With a cipher you have the whole message right in front of you. You then convert that message to random letters that appear to have no rhyme or reason at all. But it can't be read unless you have a way to decipher it." His grandfather held up the brass wheels. "Using somethin' like this."

"That thing can reveal a secret message?"

"If you know the key. With a cipher you have to choose the key first. If you don't know the key, you're never goin' to break a good cipher."

"Have you ever used that wheel?"

His grandfather smiled. "My daddy taught me how when I was not much older than you. Around fourteen, if I recall right. You want me to teach you?"

He nodded. "I do. I really do."

AND HE LEARNED A GREAT DEAL, ALONG WITH EVEN more from reading in the decades thereafter. Alphabet ciphers worked only when no letter in the cipher represented more than one in the original message.

Each letter had to be distinct so there'd be no pattern that could lead to its unraveling. The cipher wheel created that randomness. It also helped if the number of letters within the key word was small. That made it even harder to break the cipher. Finally, word sizes in the final message were usually concealed by grouping the cipher in a set pattern.

Like here.

Thirty-two letters, in groups of four.

KRTY OGNM ISQL NBCD ZIOH LWDP

DSGR ALOC

To really complicate things, sometimes the original message was reversed before being converted to a cipher. He and his grandfather had worked through many examples with the old Confederate cipher wheel. He'd never thought he would ever see another original one. Yet here one was, hidden away inside a German castle.

"Can you decrypt the message?" Fenn asked.

He removed the sheet that Dianne McCarter had provided from its envelope and laid it on the desk.

"The last part of the message says that 'the gateway opens and closes with Wagner.' Then there is 050 16 19 2."

His mind raced, thinking like a Confederate spy concealing an important message. *The gateway opens and closes with Wagner.* He stared at the book from Herrenchiemsee that Fenn had laid on the desk. The opera it depicted was reflected in the murals surrounding him. It was part of this for a reason. He grabbed the book and opened to its title page. "Tannhäuser und der Sängerkrieg auf Wartburg." Along with a byline for Richard Wagner. Toward the bottom of the page was Munich 1905, along with, as he translated in his mind

Printed by FRANZ HUMAR, MUNICH
Published by FRANZ SPEISER, PRIEN-AM-CHIEMSEE
050

There was the connection.

It had to be.

He told them what he thought.

"I agree," Fenn said, excitement in his voice. "Part of the mystery to all this was the need to have the component parts."

He turned his attention to the other numbers. 16 19 2. His grandfather taught him that books had many times been used to conceal a cipher key. A particular word somewhere inside, among the tens of thousands of words, which could be altered with each cipher. Books were not an unfamiliar item on the battlefield in the 1860s. He opened to page sixteen, then counted down to line nineteen and over to the second word.

Ehre.

Honor.

"That's the key," he said.

"Lucky for us," Fenn said, "that you know what you are doing."

Yep. Lucky for us.

DERRICK ENTERED A LARGE ROOM THAT OCCUPIED THE castle's north end, just past the grotto. A shadowy space anchored by massive furniture, bookshelves, and more of the colorful murals, only different mythical characters and scenes from the study. He crept in a slow, steady pace, conscious of everything around him, his steps sometimes revealed with a creak or groan from the wood floor. His right hand gripped the gun retrieved in the church.

A familiar void in his stomach heralded danger.

Hopefully, he'd come across one of the castle staff doing their job.

No harm, no foul.

But, if not—

He stopped at one of the columns that supported the ceiling. The capitals were decorated with images of Christ, some sort of king or emperor, a bishop, and a crusading knight. The whole damn place had the feel of a comic strip, one scrolling mural after another everywhere he looked.

But something was off.

Not right.

No employees.

The silence was broken by the occasional snatch of voices coming from Malone, Fenn, and the curator back in the study.

And something else. Ahead.

Low. But constant. A rumbling.

The waterfall?

He stared out of the room, into the next.

His right thumb engaged the gun's hammer.

RIFE HEARD A CLICK.

Clear. Distinct. A sound he knew signaled danger.

And close. Next-room close.

He signaled to Knight.

Bait taken.

They readied themselves.

CHAPTER 73

COTTON RECALLED EVERYTHING HIS GRANDFATHER taught him about the cipher wheel. The alphabet on the inner wheel was always for the actual message to be sent. The outer wheel's letters created the cipher text. The randomness of the key word made breaking the cipher next to impossible, as there were literally millions of words to choose from. Fenn and the curator watched him closely, which was becoming annoying. Koger had wandered off to check things out.

He stared at the cipher.

KRTY OGNM ISQL NBCD ZIOH LWDP

DSGR ALOC

"I need something to write on," he said to the curator.

The man hurried off, then returned with a pen and pad.

"Give me a few minutes."

And he sat at the desk.

Fenn and the curator drifted back out to the

corridor, beyond the archway, near the window. They conversed like two aspiring ventriloquists, lips barely moving, their voices pitched just enough for the other to hear.

He realized he was working backward. Not encrypting a message, but rather decrypting one that already existed. The first letter in the cipher was *k*, so he twisted the inner wheel until its *k* aligned with the *e* on the inner wheel. He could hear his grandfather's lesson. *That's your pointer. Don't forget.* Then he altered the wheels' alignment so the inner *k* now faced the inner *h* from *ehre*. He repeated that process each time with the cipher letters, twisting the wheels, finding a letter that corresponded with the matching letter from the key. *Ehre* was a short key. Which meant it would repeat itself eight times to match the thirty-two letters in the cipher text.

He kept working the wheels back and forth, occasionally allowing his gaze to drift to the two men standing twenty feet away. Amazing. Who knew that conversations between a boy and his grandfather would one day become vital? He'd loved that man. His father died when he was ten, lost in a top secret US Navy submarine accident. His grandfather became everything. They spent a lot of time together. He missed him. He'd been dead a long time.

It took a few minutes, but he ended up with a fully deciphered text. Which he locked into his eidetic brain. Then, while keeping his eyes on the two men who were still quietly conversing out in the corridor, he used the point of the pen to carve out the cipher and numbers from the brittle paper Dianne McCarter had provided. He then rolled that fragment into a tiny ball and swallowed it. Koger wanted the message secure.

Now it was.

He alone knew.

"Did Ludwig III speak English?" he asked the curator, grabbing the man's attention.

"*Ja*," the curator said. "He was quite fluent in several languages."

He wrote on the pad, tore off the top sheet, and held up the piece of paper. "Which explains why this was coded to English."

"Perhaps it was an added measure of security," the curator said. "Using an American cipher wheel, so why not create the message in English. In the early part of the twentieth century that language wasn't spoken nearly as universally as it is today."

"Do you have the full message?" Fenn asked.

He nodded and stood.

Fenn motioned.

Three men appeared in the corridor. Two were from the castle last night. They'd been part of the contingent of brothers who'd confronted Rife. Both held pistols. The third man was an older, sharp-faced, gnomish little man with patches of wiry hair fringing a balding top. He wore a charcoal herringbone wool coat and a homburg hat.

Fenn stepped into the study. "I will have that message."

He stayed still.

"Be sensible, Herr Malone," the other man said. "We do not want bloodshed. The message, *bitte*."

"And you are?"

"Albert. Duke of Bavaria. I am the one who involved America in this quest."

"Clearly, our services are no longer required."

"Quite correct. We will be ending our relationship shortly. The paper, *bitte*."

He hesitated another moment, then handed it to Fenn, who read the words.

"What does it say?" the duke asked.

"To infinity and beyond."

"That makes no sense."

Cotton smiled. "It did to Buzz Lightyear."

***

DERRICK ENTERED THE KING'S BEDROOM. LOTS OF CARVED oak panels, a stout central pillar, and a ceiling of joist woodwork. The paintings here were the same, but different, draping the top half of the walls. The canopied bed seemed some elaborate work of art, obviously hand-carved and loaded with richly ornamented finials. To his left, glass-paneled doors opened out to what appeared to be a balcony. One of them hung slightly ajar and he heard the waterfall in the distance.

Odd the door would be open.

***

RIFE STOOD INSIDE WHAT HAD ONCE BEEN SOME SORT OF interior closet. It opened through a panel in the bedroom wall that, when closed, completely concealed the entrance. He would have never known it existed but for his earlier review of the castle layout.

Now it provided the perfect lair.

He and Knight waited with guns ready, listening as Koger's footsteps inched across the outer hardwood floor, each one partially cushioned by a floor rug. He'd left the balcony door ajar as a way to draw Koger's attention and provide a few precious moments of advantage. The problem was that the door to the closet was solid oak with no openings, so he had no idea what was happening on the other side. Everything depended on timing.

He nodded at Knight.

Now.

He pulled open the panel.

The door leading out to the balcony hung half open.

As if someone had gone out.

But Koger was gone.

DERRICK WASN'T SURE IF HE WAS MORE ANGRY AT THE trap laid for him or that whoever laid it thought him that stupid. Once he'd seen the open door he'd retreated into a bay window alcove just to the left. Draperies framed out the opening and offered the perfect cover for him to retreat behind. And sure enough, just a few seconds passed before he heard the soft squeak of hinges, then quick footsteps.

"Where'd he go?" a man said.

Terry Knight.

Which meant—

Derrick stepped out, leveled his gun, and said, "Right here."

His first round took Knight down with a shot to the chest. His eyes surveyed the room and caught a half-opened panel in the wall to the left of the bed and a washing table. He readjusted his aim and fired two rounds into it.

The oak panel swung farther inward.

Then he finished off Knight with a shot to the head.

RIFE STEPPED BACK, REALIZING THAT KOGER HAD NOT been fooled. Two rounds pounded into the swinging oak panel. Luckily, there was room in the closet and he was able to get out of the way.

Then another shot.

Not his way.

A coup de grâce?

He paused and allowed the tense silence in the bedroom to linger, hoping Koger would think there was no one there. Hearing nothing, he stepped out with his gun aimed. Knight lay on the floor, bleeding from chest and head wounds. Koger was gone. He bent down and checked for a pulse.

None. Rage flushed through him.

"Damn you, Koger. It's you and me," he called out.

"Just the way I want it."

The voice came from ahead, past the next couple of rooms, back toward the vestibule with the spiral staircases.

"Too scared to face me?" Rife asked.

"I could say the same to you."

No way.

He stood and headed for the voice.

CHAPTER 74

Luke glanced over at Toni.

They were speeding south on the autobahn through the cold night. Trinity Dorner had not uttered a word for the past fifteen minutes. Two calls had come in for Dorner during that time. Both short. He'd taken her advice and shut up.

For now.

"Things are escalating," Dorner finally said. "The Chinese have joined forces with the Scythe and the Duke of Bavaria."

Fascinating, and good to know.

Dorner tossed a cell phone back over the front seat into his lap. "Push 3. And a piece of advice. Talk little, listen more."

He scooped up the unit. Toni watched him carefully. He decided to be a good boy and do as told. He pushed 3 and brought the phone to his ear. One ring and it was answered.

"Mr. Daniels, this is Warner Fox. May I call you Luke?"

"You can call me whatever you want."

Fox chuckled. "A prerogative of being president. I understand time is critical, so let me get to the point. Derrick Koger and I recently came to an understanding."

News to him.

"I'd like to come to one with you."

"About what?" he asked.

"Malone and Koger are out of pocket," Fox said. "We have no idea if they're making progress or not. Are you aware of what we're after?"

"Only that it's a document from the time of Ludwig II. That's all I was told. I take my orders from Koger. I assume he knows what we're after, and that's good enough for me."

"And me too," Fox said. "But if a situation arises that Koger becomes unable to move forward, I need you to take the lead."

Nothing about that sounded good. "What about your White House envoy? Both of them."

"I want *you* to take the lead."

"What about Malone? He's higher ranking than I am."

"He's retired. You're not."

Then he got it. "Meaning you can give me orders. And I don't actually work for the White House. So I can be trashed."

"Trinity said you were a quick one."

That he was. "So what am I looking for?"

"A deed between the king of Hawaii and the king of Bavaria, dated 1881."

That was a bit unusual. But he knew better than to ask why.

That was not his concern.

"Find it," Fox said, "and you'll have my and the country's gratitude."

"What makes you think Koger or Malone can't get it done?"

"Nothing, except that they've been out of contact nearly all day. An attempt was made on both of their lives this morning, which we know failed. They eluded the Munich police earlier, and have been on the run ever since. We also know they headed south, to where you're headed right now. The Scythe, the Chinese, and God knows who else is headed that way too."

"What about what happened with the Munich police with me just a little while ago?"

"We can only assume that you and my envoy were meant to die, as your German associate did. Either that, or be arrested, taken out of service. I don't think the Guglmänner really cared which. We've learned that they are complicit in this with the Duke of Bavaria, who wants the Chinese to have that deed."

The duke himself? "What about Prince Stefan?"

"He and the duke headed south by helicopter earlier. But we think the duke himself is running this show."

Lots goin' on.

"Watch yourself, Luke. I'm told the Chinese play for keeps. It's important we play a similar game."

"It's the only way I play."

"That's what I want to hear. Now, would you pass the phone to Ms. Dorner. I need to speak to her."

He handed over the phone. Dorner accepted it and listened. He noticed that they'd left the autobahn and were now on a two-lane highway lined with snow, the wipers continuing to brush new flakes from the windshield.

He glanced up toward the front seat.

Dorner was still listening. Finally, she said, "I understand."

She ended the call.

"You clear?" Dorner asked.

"Yes, ma'am," he said.

"He can be a great ally, or your worst enemy," Dorner said. "Your choice, Mr. Daniels."

"I have a pile of both of those. One more in either stack doesn't make a whole lot of difference."

"Unless that one can cause you immeasurable amounts of grief. Which, I believe, the president of the United States can do."

"I got the message," he said. "Loud and clear." He turned to Toni. "How about you?"

"I know my orders."

"We have company," the driver said.

Luke turned his head and stared out the rear windshield, which was kept partially clear by the black lines of an embedded defroster. Two headlights were framed out by the cleared oval.

"That car has been with us since we left the autobahn," the driver said. "Nice and steady. Never moving. I slowed down twice and it matched me."

"How far left to go?" he asked.

"Twenty minutes."

He stared out the remaining windows and the front windshield. Nothing but black on either side of the road, the asphalt threading a path through columns of dark trees.

"Something's happening," the driver said.

Luke turned back to see someone angle an automatic rifle out the passenger's-side window.

Oh, crap.

"Everybody down," he yelled.

Rounds thudded into the car's trunk, pinging off

the metal. One slammed into the rear windshield, spiderwebbing the glass. Another followed, shattering the web, spitting fragments out in the car's wake. Cold air rushed inside. They began to swerve, back and forth, on the roadway. He risked a glance at the driver and saw blood. The guy had been hit, but was trying to keep the vehicle under control. The car following revved its engine and sped up, passing them on the left side. A gun flew back over the front seat and landed between him and Toni as they crouched down, out of the line of fire.

Toni grabbed it. "Lower your window."

They were still swerving, their driver trying to slow to a stop. The other car drew parallel and he pressed the button for the window.

Toni came up and fired twice.

He saw that she took out the rear window on the passenger's side. The other car reacted to the attack and accelerated, speeding away. Their driver brought them to a stop. Luke popped open his door and hopped out into the cold, quickly opening the driver's door and assessing the situation. Toni was out with the gun leveled. The other car had stopped, maybe a half mile down the road, only its taillights visible in the dark.

"You okay?" he asked the driver.

The guy shook his head. "There's some glass in my skull and I'm not seeing things real good."

"We need to switch places."

He released the driver's seat belt and helped him out, gently placing him in the backseat. Dorner had yet to say a word, but was watching everything carefully with a face of granite. Talk about cool nerves. He wedged himself behind the wheel and refastened the safety belt.

Toni climbed into the rear seat.

"Nice move with the gun," he said to Dorner.

"I assumed you both knew what to do with it."

Their attacker's car turned around in the road, the rear taillights replaced with headlights. Which started coming their way.

"They seem to want a fight," Dorner said.

Luke slammed the gearshift into drive.

"Good. 'Cause I'm goin' to give 'em one."

CHAPTER 75

COTTON REACTED TO THE SOUND OF GUNFIRE BY grabbing the heavy inkwell off the desk and throwing a strike right at the two short, brawny figures with guns, trying to make a one-two split with those stout pins. The heavy chunk of brass thudded into one of the men, who deflected it, while the other ducked out of the way.

Which gave him the second he needed.

He lunged, the heel of his left shoe swinging up and slamming into the chest of the one who'd taken the inkwell, sending the guy staggering back. He then pivoted and slammed his right fist into the other guy's face, stunning him long enough to allow two more blows to the gut, which doubled him over. He'd guessed correctly that neither had ever been in a real fight, despite their size and fake temperament. He turned his attention back to the first one and took him down with a hard right to the jaw.

His immediate concern was the guns and he spotted one on the floor, which he moved toward, snatching it up with his right hand. Both men groaned and wheezed in agony. They were no longer a concern.

Fenn became the problem. The older man had found the other gun, which had clattered across the floor toward the desk.

He was quick.

But Fenn was quicker. "That's enough. Let your gun fall to the floor."

He hesitated, so Fenn aimed the gun straight at him. The curator had retreated to one corner, a look of fear on his face. The duke had never moved. Just watching. Cotton allowed the gun to hit the floor.

"You may leave," the duke said to the curator. "And please make sure we are not disturbed."

The man nodded and hustled away. The two minders recovered their senses and began to stand.

"Get your weapons," Albert ordered. "And try to stay alert and handle yourselves better."

The curator scurried from the room like a fiddler crab, but Albert stopped him for a moment and they exchanged a few whispers. Then the curator hurried off.

"Search him," Fenn said.

And they found the gun tucked at Cotton's spine, beneath his jacket.

"Keep watch," Albert told the two men with guns, who stepped back, able to view both the study and the corridor.

Then the Duke of Bavaria approached. "Herr Malone, I am hoping we can come to an understanding."

He shrugged. "I do pride myself on being easy to get along with."

The duke noticed the paper on the desk with an oblong hole in it. "The message from Lehmann?"

He nodded.

"And the cipher part?"

He rubbed his tummy. "I was hungry."

The duke stood impassionate, his features remaining rock-hard. "I am going to assume that you deciphered it. And that you and Herr Koger decided to keep that information to yourselves."

"Sounds like a good plan."

The old man finally smiled. "I would have done the same. But, unfortunately for you, I need that information." Albert hesitated, then said in a louder voice, "Please. Join us."

From around the corner, out in the corridor, a man appeared. Asian. Middle-aged. With a thin aesthetic face, dressed in a trim-fitting dark blue suit. He shuffled along with a limp, aided by a red-lacquered cane, in the measured walk of someone sure of his thoughts.

Finally. The shadow to all of this had taken form.

"What are you, Ministry of State Security? United Front Work Department? People's Liberation Army?" he asked, rattling off the various foreign intelligence arms of the People's Republic of China.

"How about all of the above."

"Which means you're pretty high up. You have a name?"

"Call me Ming."

"How charming. As in the vase?"

"What else?"

"And the purpose of your visit to this amazing castle on this winter's night?"

"I want to offer you a choice."

He was intrigued.

Ming reached into his pocket and removed a mobile phone. The older man stabbed the screen with his index finger and brought the phone to his ear.

"Please stand by," Ming said, then he hit a button, surely for mute.

He waited for the man to make his pitch.

"I anticipated you might be difficult," Ming said. "I have two men stationed outside the apartment where Fräulein McCarter stays while in Munich."

Ming paused, allowing his words to settle in.

"We've been busy today," Ming said. "After your visit to the state library we ascertained whom you met with. A witness told us that when you left the reading room, after meeting with such a respected attorney, you pocketed an envelope. We can only assume that your visit there related to what is happening here, and that what you were given is there, on the desk."

Cotton stayed silent.

"So here is your choice," Ming said. "You may either provide me the original cipher text, or my two men will kill Fräulein McCarter."

"As I said, I ate it."

"Come now, Mr. Malone, do not insult my intelligence. You have an eidetic memory. Which you just made excellent use of."

"Nice to know my reputation precedes me."

"Your reputation is quite impressive," Ming said. "Especially your involvement in our internal affairs a few years ago."

He shrugged. "Just another day at the office."

Ming chuckled. "Quite right. But back to your choice. And let me add something to the equation. If somehow you do not care if that old woman dies, then I will kill her and find someone else you do care about. Perhaps Cassiopeia Vitt? Or your son?"

They'd done their homework. He would have expected no less. And he had no reason to doubt that this man would do exactly as stated. Chinese intelligence was noted for its ruthlessness. But he wanted to know, "Where's Koger?"

"He and two old friends are in another part of the castle," Ming said. "Becoming reacquainted."

"So you made a deal with the Scythe?"

"Luckily for us both, our interests temporarily aligned."

He realized that he'd found the head of the serpent and that it was going to be difficult to leave without some sort of bloodshed, preferably not his. Was the threat to McCarter's life real? He had to assume that it was.

"All right," he said. "I know the deciphered message."

"That information would be most appreciated," Ming said. "But, of course, we have to know it is correct. So you will come with us as we discover that for ourselves. If you are wrong, then"—Ming motioned with the phone—"something unfortunate will occur. Do we have an arrangement?"

"Doesn't look like I have a choice. Besides, I'd like to see what's out there too."

Ming brought the phone back to his ear. "Stand by. If I do not check in with you personally every hour from this point on, do what we discussed." The man ended the call. "I am hoping we can both act civilized."

"Of course. Why not."

But he had no illusions, realizing that once this man had what he wanted, he and McCarter were both dead.

The trick would be to stay a step ahead.

CHAPTER 76

DERRICK INTENDED ON DRAWING RIFE TOWARD HIM. He'd fled the king's bedroom and an adjacent ante-room, returning to the long vestibule outside the throne room. The entrance to the spiral staircase used earlier was at the far end, another spiral staircase opening to his immediate left. He knew that Malone and the others were on the other side of the floor, so he decided up was the way to go. He climbed the stone risers, making no attempt to mask his steps. What awaited him on the next floor? He had no idea. But one thing was certain.

Rife would follow.

'Cause that's what fools do.

※

RIFE WORKED HARD TO CONTROL HIS RAGE.

He'd not been this angry since the day the CIA fired him. The insult of a lifetime. Out of left field. He'd never seen it coming. But others had. Which made the whole thing even worse.

Terry Knight had been loyal. When he'd asked him

to join forces, Knight had never hesitated. He was a dependable field officer, always getting the job done. No questions. No complaining. All you could ever ask for in a friend.

Now he was dead.

He stepped from the last room, back into a large vestibule area. Footsteps echoed to his left, coming from a spiral staircase.

Moving upward.

Koger.

Announcing his presence.

Typical.

He gripped his gun.

And followed.

DERRICK CAME TO THE TOP OF THE STAIRCASE FINDING himself on the castle's fourth floor. Much less lighting here, consistent with the building being shut down for the night. Four other portals exited out of the vestibule. One for the other spiral staircase at the far end, another to his left that led to the upper gallery of the throne room, and two that provided access to what a placard labeled as the Singers' Hall. He recalled the curator mentioning it earlier. More paintings, all of German legend and high Romanticism, lined the vestibule walls.

He seemed unable to escape them.

He turned right and headed for the Singers' Hall and entered a large rectangular space. Overhead a pinewood squared ceiling contained rich ornamental paintings and the signs of the zodiac. Its slanting sides rested on carved wooden supports loaded with images. Pillars rose periodically along the edges with more ornaments, arabesques, and allegorical representations. At the far short end was a dimly lit bower separated from the rest of the room by steps and three arcades, the murals behind it painted with a lively forest scene. Carved wooden benches with elaborate embroidery lined the long side walls, their coverings interwoven with gold thread. Gilded brass candelabra and chandeliers dotted the ceiling and parquet floor.

Big. Roomy. Old, but still decorous.

Perfect.

"Rife," he called out. "I know you can hear me. Let's settle this man-to-man. No guns. Just us."

RIFE STOOD JUST PAST THE SPIRAL STAIRCASE, ON THE fourth floor in another vestibule, and heard the challenge. The voice came from the open portal to his right, the one that led into what was identified as the Singers' Hall. He turned and entered, spotting Koger standing fifty feet away, inside a dimly lit cavernous space. The big man tossed his gun aside and held both arms outstretched at his sides.

"You and me," Koger said.

He tossed his own weapon away.

And accepted the challenge.

DERRICK CAUGHT THE HINT OF A SHADOW, THEN A BLACK figure slithered into view, slow, cautious, and, as he reminded himself, full of deadly skill.

Luckily he knew about a street fight.

Anything went. Break fingers, poke out an eye, bust up a nose. Nothing was off-limits since the other guy was definitely trying to kill you. That meant you had to get him first. It was a fight for your life, with no rules and no referee. He'd had a number of them over many different things. Defending turf. Taking down a problem. Self-defense. Proving a point. Once even after a fender bender, which the other guy started. All of them had been born out of anger by people unable to control their emotions. Most had involved some amount of alcohol. All of them had been fueled by quick outbursts of emotion.

Like a friend being killed by your enemy.

Rife came straight at him.

Like his daddy used to say. *There's gonna be two licks passed here. One when I hit you and the other when you hit the ground.* Derrick realized this man had surely participated in his own fair share of brawls.

But he'd had enough of this traitor.

And delivered a solid right jab to Rife's jaw.

Which stopped the advance.

But not the attack.

Rife rebounded and lunged, wrapping both arms around his chest, trying to take him down in a full-blown tackle. But there were advantages to being six foot one and two hundred and forty pounds.

He stood his ground.

And brought a knee into Rife's gut.

He heard the breath leave the man. Rife backed away, sucking in lungfuls of air. Steadying himself. A bruise had already formed on his right jaw.

"You're not that tough, big man," Rife spit out.

"Tough enough to deal with you."

Rife straightened up and raised his fists.

He accepted the challenge and stepped forward, his own fists balled and ready. They stood toe-to-toe like two prizefighters, circling around one another, each looking for a weakness, waiting for an opening. He'd learned long ago that it was better to draw your opponent in than go to him.

So he hesitated.

Rife took the bait and swung, landing a left jab into his ribs.

Which hurt.

More than it should.

Not good.

RIFE FELT THE RIBS CRACK.

Good.

Koger toted fifty pounds on him and a few inches more in reach, but he knew how to handle himself in hand-to-hand. He liked that they were settling their differences straight up. But he did not intend for this to go on for long. He was maneuvering Koger across the floor, ever closer to one of the guns. They each lay on an opposite side of the hall.

Just get there.

And one shot would end this.

DERRICK WINCED AT THE PAIN IN HIS RIGHT SIDE, HIS brow prickly with sweat. Clearly, he was not twenty years old anymore. Rife had landed a solid blow, then followed with two more jabs that he'd managed to block, but a third connected with his ribs again.

He doubled over in pain.

Rife shoved him back toward one of the many candelabra that dotted the hall. They were each thick, heavy, about eight feet tall and gilded, resting on a tripod of three legs attached to a marble base. He stumbled and staggered, his arms wrapped around his ribs.

Rife stepped back, breathing hard, savoring the moment.

Derrick hit the wood wall hard and slid to the floor. The room expanded and contracted before his eyes, his ribs aching with each breath.

Something had broken.

The guns lay on the floor about twenty feet away. Rife made no attempt to get one. Instead, he just stood, rubbing his sore jaw, assuming the role of victor.

"You should not have killed Terry," Rife said. "You should not have done that at all."

"He was…a…traitor. Like…you."

His left arm nursed the ribs, his right palm resting on the wood floor. A candelabra stood right in front of him. He kept breathing hard and made sure Rife knew he was in pain.

Which wasn't hard. 'Cause he was.

"You've always been a pain in the ass," Rife spit out. "But I'm goin' to do everyone a favor and end that right now."

Rife advanced on what he thought to be fallen prey. Derrick fought the pain and steeled himself. That was the thing about not being twenty anymore. You were a hell of a lot smarter. *Come on. Closer.* A drop of sweat slid in a slow track from his forehead to his chin, tickling his face.

Closer. Closer.

Every muscle in his body grew taut.

Rife came within range.

His right leg swung up and he planted the heel of his shoe on the stout gilded stem, shoving the heavy candelabra over.

Rife never saw it coming until it was too late.

The candelabra crashed into him. Rife tried to stop it, bringing both arms up, but its weight and momentum were more than enough to push back and take him down to the floor.

Derrick gritted his teeth, rolled, and came to his feet.

Rife wrestled with the candelabra, trying to get it off him.

Six steps and he found one of the guns.

Rife managed to push the candelabra away and tried to stand.

Derrick shot him in the chest.

The sharp bark echoed through the hall and hurt his ears.

Rife collapsed, his head lolled to one side, and a small gurgling noise seeped from his throat. A thin trickle of blood crawled down from the corner of his mouth. More blood spewed out in a violent exhale. A few spasms. A cough. The eyes glared at him, one moment with life, the next all gone. Muscle gave way and the flesh and bones settled on the floor.

In death.

End of problem.

He'd not even fired a gun in several years outside of range practice. But tonight he'd already killed two with one.

He needed to get back to Malone. Surely the shots had been heard. He turned and headed out of the hall by way of a long side corridor, one arm cradling his ribs. Windows opened to the castle's exterior facing toward the path they'd used to enter earlier. He stopped a moment and gazed out to the night. Bright halogen lights lit the castle walls and the path below.

He caught sight of people. Walking away.

Fenn. Two other men, following Malone at gun-point. The Duke of Bavaria. What was he doing here? And the last face. Chinese. Walking with a cane. Who was he? They all seemed chummy, except for Malone, and were leaving in a hurry. He shook his head. How-ever he placed the pieces on the board, they added up to the same conclusion.

He'd apparently been played.

They'd surely left him to Rife and Knight, thinking they would eliminate the CIA's involvement.

No such luck.

He was still on the board.

In play.

The curator was nowhere in sight below. The lack of response to the gunfire from anyone within or without the castle seemed to indicate a certain level of complacency. The man had certainly been cooperative with Fenn earlier. Derrick headed down the corridor toward the spiral staircase.

His side hurt. That much he'd not feigned.

But he'd live.

There was a job to be done.

CHAPTER 77

LUKE SLAMMED THE TRANSMISSION INTO GEAR AND floored the accelerator. The rear wheels skidded and the car spun, the back end swerving until the rubber caught the frozen pavement and they shot ahead. The other car was already coming straight at them. He adjusted his path and placed them on a collision course.

Playin' chicken was a rite of passage in east Tennessee. Everybody did it at least once after getting their driver's license. He actually did it a lot more than once. The idea? Drive your cars directly at each other. At some point you had to make a strategic decision. Either swerve out of the way, or keep straight. If one driver swerved while the other continued straight, the straight guy won. The prize? Simple respect. If both drivers swerved and avoided collision, both kept their honor. But if neither swerved, they both probably died. Respected. But still dead. He grew up in the day of no airbags, so head-on collisions were one hundred percent fatal. He'd been damn good at playin' chicken. Keeping focus. Where the only world that mattered was the one caught in the headlights.

He accelerated.

Ninety kilometers an hour.

A hundred.

The distance between the two cars was closing fast. Trinity Dorner sat impassionate. Not a sound. Nor a movement. Nothing from the backseat either.

He kept going.

The headlights ahead grew larger through the windshield.

No other cars were on this dark stretch of highway.

The steering wheel vibrated in his hands, signaling the tires were a bit out of balance. He still owned a vintage Mustang, his pride and joy, and he always made sure those four radials, with the shiniest chrome hubs you'd ever seen, were perfectly balanced.

He kept the car on a straight path.

When you played chicken in Tennessee there was an unwritten rule. Always veer right. That way nobody got in anyone else's way. But that presupposed the game was being played from the middle of the road. Which was not the case here. They were in the other car's lane. That meant he had room to go right, but the other car had nowhere to go except left. So if they flinched, they'd both be headed the same way.

That meant—

He pressed the accelerator harder.

One hundred twenty kilometers an hour.

The other car suddenly veered left, into the opposite lane.

He kept the steering wheel steady, the car traveling straight ahead.

The swerve by the other car at such a high speed came with consequences, which he'd witnessed before. The combination of deviation and momentum angled the car upward onto the driver's side's two wheels, like a stunt in some movie, only it did not stay there. In the rearview mirror he saw the car keep going, flipping over, slamming into the pavement, sliding across the asphalt, upside down, sparks spewing out in its wake.

DERRICK DESCENDED TO THE GROUND FLOOR. HIS BODY hurt from the unaccustomed abuse, especially his ribs. Each step down came with pain.

He saw no one on the ground floor. The curator had to be somewhere, so he found the gift shop. Empty. He stepped back outside to the inner court-yard. Lights burned in the gatehouse on the second floor. He located a staircase and climbed, locating a series of offices. He found the curator inside one of them, donning his coat, preparing to leave. He rushed in and jammed the gun into the lower part of the Bavarian's jaw.

"Where did they go?"

The man's eyes went wide with terror, his face a mask of fear. "Linderhof."

"Where is that?"

"About an...hour from...here. Another...of Ludwig's castles."

"Why there?"

"The cipher...pointed there. To the...Venus Grotto. Behind the castle."

"Do you have a cell phone?"

The head nodded yes.

"I want it."

It was quickly produced. Not a smartphone. Just a simple flip unit.

"Any security code?"

The head shook no.

He withdrew the gun. "Get out of here."

The man scurried for the door.

"By the way. There are two dead bodies waiting on the third and fourth floors."

The man stared at him in astonishment.

"That's your problem," he told the curator. "Not mine. Leave."

The man ran out the door.

He heard a new sound. The heavy rhythmic beating of a helicopter's rotor. Firing up, then fading away.

Derrick opened the phone and dialed.

LUKE WORKED THE BRAKE AND BROUGHT THE CAR TO a stop.

"You have quite the nerve," Dorner said. "How did you know he would go left?"

"I didn't. But it was his only option."

"Quite the risk-taker."

"I just do what has to be done."

Toni and the driver in the backseat said nothing. Not much to say. He shifted to reverse, swung the car around, and drove back to the other vehicle.

He and Toni exited.

They bent down in the darkness and looked inside.

Neither man was moving. But he noticed something. "They're Chinese."

Toni checked a pulse on one. "Not a problem anymore. Dead."

"What the hell are they doing here?"

The phone in his pocket vibrated. He found the unit and answered, though he did not recognize the number.

"Luke."

Koger.

"Where are you?"

He told him.

"That's good. We need to get to a place called Linderhof. It's about an hour away. Malone is captive and being taken there by helicopter." Derrick gave Luke his location. "Come get me. And fast."

CHAPTER 78

Cotton settled into his seat aboard the helicopter, which came with a luxurious cabin large enough to accommodate not only him, but the duke, Ming, and Fenn. The two black hoods with guns had stayed behind, Fenn taking over armed guard duty during the flight. But the threat to Dianne McCarter still loomed with Ming having to check in every hour. Regardless, he planned on being a good boy, since he had to see if the thirty-two-letter cipher led to pay dirt.

THRO UGHT HEVE NUSM OUNT TOTH

ERED OUBT

The first thing he'd noticed was the message had been conceived in English. So he'd fashioned his joke of a message in English too. Before he confronted Fenn earlier he'd mentally sorted the eight sets of four letters into words.

THROUGH THE VENUS MOUNT TO THE

REDOUBT

Which he'd finally told to Fenn, who seemed to instantly understand its significance. Once Fenn conferred with the Neuschwanstein's curator, he'd become convinced where they needed to go.

Linderhof.

Which sat about an hour's drive away.

By helicopter? Twenty minutes tops.

He sat back in the leather. Fatigue underlay his tension, but that was nothing new. He'd learned long ago how to deal with fear and apprehension. Ming was the only pro here. Fenn thought himself comfortable with the gun, but he doubted he knew what to do with it when the chips were down. Surely the guy felt emboldened after getting the jump on him back in the study. But he'd intentionally not resisted and allowed that to happen.

Which had got him here.

"Let me guess," he said over the rotors. "This ride is courtesy of the People's Republic?"

Ming smiled. "Of course."

The Chinese had taken control. Koger? That was the remaining mystery. He'd heard several shots while they were leaving and wondered if that was good or bad. Unfortunately, there was nothing to be done about it.

Koger was on his own.

DERRICK SAT IN THE BACKSEAT WITH HIS NEW BEST friend, Toni Sims, formerly of the Australian Secret Intelligence Service, now attached to the National Security Council, on special assignment for the White House.

Will wonders never cease?

Luke had found him at Neuschwanstein below the castle where Fenn had parked earlier. They'd descended from the craggy mount and found the highway south into Austria, which offered the fastest route east back into Germany and to Linderhof. They'd left the injured driver at one of the hotels. Trinity had called in the injury and people were dispatched from Munich to come and get him. Now, with Luke driving, and Trinity in the front passenger's seat, the four of them were headed straight for trouble. Trinity had insisted on coming, pulling rank, which he'd thought a bad idea. But, as usual, TOO did what she wanted. Luke reported what happened on the road and the two dead Chinese. He had to assume more assets were nearby.

"How far?" he asked.

"The blue dot on the phone says thirty minutes," Trinity said.

He did not regret killing Knight or Rife. Quite the contrary. They both deserved to die. Especially Rife. Arrogant bastard actually thought he could take him. A lot of people had made that mistake.

But his ribs still hurt.

Screw the pain.

Focus.

"What do we know about Linderhof?" he asked them.

LUKE KEPT HIS EYES FOCUSED AHEAD AND WOUND THE car through the tight turns characteristic of Alpine roads. Luckily, this one had been cleared by a plow, the asphalt only dusted with fresh snow, the edges piled high with the day's remnants. He was going as fast as he could, realizing that Malone was bare-ass-to-the-wind, without backup. Trinity and Koger had filled in the information gaps. Two of the Scythe were dead and the Chinese were full-on, finally making no secret of their involvement. Contrary to the movies, intelligence services did not routinely kill each other's assets. It happened. Sure. But only in the most extreme of circumstances.

Clearly, this situation had evolved to the extreme.

And Pappy was in trouble.

He whipped the car hard right and took the turn a little faster than he should have. The back end swerved, but he steered in the opposite direction and regained control. Thank the lord for the Blue Ridge mountains, which had roads just like this.

"We're looking for the Venus Grotto," Koger said. "I was told it's behind the castle."

Trinity was working on her phone.

"I have a schematic of the grounds," she said, "from the castle's website. When we get close, I can direct us."

"That helicopter is going to get there a lot faster," Luke said, keeping his eyes locked out the windshield.

"Malone's a pro," Koger said. "He can handle himself."

He shook his head. "I still don't like it."

"Neither do I."

"If they're headed to Linderhof," Trinity said, "that means Malone solved the cipher. The other two of Ludwig II's castles figured into the hunt, so it makes sense this one would also be included. I checked. That chopper handles four passengers and a pilot. My guess is the two with the guns didn't make the trip."

He agreed with that assumption.

"But there still could be assets all around," Toni said.

"Damn right," Luke added.

"If I know Maloney," Derrick said, "he's got things under control. It's just that nobody else knows it."

Or at least he kept telling himself that.

"That would be Pappy," Luke said.

"Does anyone call this man by his name?" Trinity asked.

"What fun would that be?" Luke said. "He might actually think we like him."

"How much farther?" Koger asked.

"Five minutes less than the last time I told you," Trinity said.

CHAPTER 79

COTTON GLANCED OUT THE HELICOPTER'S SIDE WINDOW and spotted Linderhof below. They'd taken a circuitous route, surely to avoid the high peaks that surrounded them, most stretching up hundreds of feet. The pilot seemed skillful, weaving a path over the valleys, then up and over some of the more respectable foothills. It had taken a little longer to get here than he'd first thought. He figured the flying distance had been about fifteen miles. The driving distance? Thirty miles, at least. But none of that was in a straight line. Lots of curves and zigzags. Probably forty minutes to an hour to make the drive. His hope was that Koger had dealt with whatever had been sent his way, then learned from the curator where they'd gone. That's what he would have done if the roles were reversed. So he had to assume the big man was on his way.

If not, then this was going to be his party alone.

He knew a little about Linderhof. The compact palace was Ludwig's version of the Trianon at Versailles, a favorite of Marie Antoinette. Not a replica, more another re-imagining. A rococo jewel, richly articulated by windows, balconies, banded pilasters, wrought iron, gilt, and crowns, all standing atop a lower story of rusticated blocks enclosed by a balustrade. Like at Neuschwanstein, floodlights illuminated the exterior, the white walls sparkling in the night. It sat off by itself, in peaceful repose, secluded in the alpine foothills among acres of trees, parklands, and gardens, miles away from any town. It had been Ludwig's favorite and the king had spent a lot of time there. The only one of his projects to come to completion. Though, to Ludwig, nothing was ever really finished.

The chopper touched down in a small clearing about a hundred yards from the palace. He'd noticed nothing but black as far as he could see on the way down. Which meant they were alone. Except for two guys waiting beyond the wash of the blades. Not Fenn's brothers. These were Chinese operatives, each toting an automatic rifle. The chopper's rotor wound down and they exited out into the cold. A profound silence once again overtook them, broken only by a frigid breeze.

"These men are here to make sure you behave," Ming said. "I have more on the way."

"As do I," Fenn said.

All good to know.

"Where are we to go?" Ming asked.

Fenn pointed off toward the north and the palace. "It's beyond there, up on the hill. The Venus Grotto."

"How do you know this is the right place?" Cotton tried.

"We just do," Albert said.

"There are cameras and security inside the palace," Fenn said. "Nothing much outside. No on-site security people, either, this time of year. We have the place to ourselves."

Also good to know.

So far he'd bought nearly an hour in time.

Was it enough?

***

DERRICK STUDIED TONI SIM'S PHONE, WHICH, LIKE Trinity's in the front seat, displayed a schematic for the grounds at Linderhof. About a hundred and twenty acres. That's a lot of real estate. Plenty of buildings, too, scattered all around. The curator said they were headed to the Venus Grotto, which, according to the map, sat at the extreme north edge of the property. It had been excavated out of the ground, watercourses altered, then a structure formed from iron, cement, and brown linen, the interior walls coated in antimony to simulate glittering stones. The layout had been modeled after a famous grotto on Capri, complete with an underground lake into which a waterfall emptied. The first electrical service in Bavaria had been installed inside to power a prismatic array of red, green, yellow, and blue lights that cast more of the illusion.

Sounded weird and expensive.

"What are they after there?" he asked himself.

"Malone had to lead them," Trinity said from the front seat.

"Thank you for those words of wisdom," he said. "They aren't much help. But I'm so glad we have them."

"You feel better insulting me?" she asked.

"I'll feel better when we're there. This isn't an office in DC or a Langley briefing room. This is friggin' real, and somebody's butt is on the line."

"I appreciate the reminder. I forgot about that."

He told himself to lighten up. He knew TOO cared

about the people who worked for her. But he felt so damn helpless. He should not have gone after Rife. That was a personal payback, which had left Malone exposed.

But it had to be done.

"We're almost there," Luke said.

Outside it was nearly pitch-black, only the scarcest of lights breaking the darkness. They were deeper into the Alps with their combination of highs and lows, speeding through one of the valleys toward some nineteenth-century castle built by a guy that many people called mad.

Looking for a hundred-and-twenty-year-old deed.

The whole thing sounded nuts.

He studied the schematic again. "We need to avoid the main entrance. There's a road that parallels the northern perimeter of the property that's close to the grotto."

"I already have it," Trinity said. "That's where we're headed."

He caught her tone. *Cut me some slack. I'm worried too. And, I'm thinking.* "You forgive an old fool for being a prick?"

"I can take a hit," she made clear.

"I know you can. I just shouldn't add 'em on."

COTTON HAD BEEN LED AT GUNPOINT ACROSS THE darkened grounds, through a trellis-walk devoid of plants to an open park, then up an incline, the going slowed by Ming and his cane. Everything was dusted with snow, all of the statuary and fountains boxed off with plywood for the winter. They'd followed a graveled path to a paved one. The presence of two trained assets added an extra element of risk to this endeavor. What had someone once said? *Gut instinct is your greatest critic. Listen to it.*

Oh, yeah.

He was listening.

"Ludwig II called this place *meicost ettal*," Fenn said. "It's an anagram of *L'etat c'est moi*. I am the state. He had such a sense of irony."

"He was a man ahead of his time," Albert added. "I've always found it gratifying how so many people admire him today."

Lots of ambition surrounded him. Ludwig's palace. China's drive to dominate the world. The duke wanting a crown and kingdom.

"So you're the kingmaker?" he asked Fenn.

"If that is what you want to call me."

"He has been a good friend to my family," Albert said. "Without his resources we would not be here."

"And your brother?" Cotton asked.

"He gets peace," Albert said.

They turned on the path and kept walking through the cold. Light snow fell in scattered flakes. Here he was again, taking chances, playing the odds, challenging the risks. He'd taken those for God and country, for his son, Cassiopeia, his dead friend Henrik Thorvaldsen, even his ex-wife. This time it was for Stephanie Nelle, whether she wanted his help or not.

So, in a sense, he and Fenn were similar.

Both were trying to elevate someone else.

But something didn't sit right. The Chinese rarely showed their hand. They were notorious for staying in the shadows. Yet here they were, front and center. Taking point on this advance into the unknown. No doubt existed that he'd be killed once the information he gave had been verified.

Ming stopped for a moment and made a call to his men bird-dogging Dianne McCarter, telling them all was good here.

So he'd bought another hour.

And he planned to make the most of it.

"There it is," Fenn said, pointing. "The Venus Grotto."

But he also saw something else.

Two more men with guns.

Standing guard. Waiting.

Great.

The odds just got even worse.

CHAPTER 80

Luke followed the directions Dorner provided, navigating the darkened highways through two well-lit intersections and finally coming to a driveway that led to a closed gate. He stopped the car. In the wash of the headlights he saw the flimsy fenced panel was padlocked with a chain.

"We don't have time for niceties," Koger said.

He shifted the car into reverse, backing up enough to give him a solid head start to gain speed. He'd busted down his fair share of barriers as a teenager. No sense allowing some gate to ruin a good time. He popped the gearshift back into drive and floored the accelerator. The car lurched forward and he sped straight ahead, ramming the front bumper into the gate, exploding it outward. Pretty damn flimsy, if he did say so himself. He'd destroyed a lot sturdier.

He brought the car to a stop. "That made noise."

They'd not seen the helicopter on the ride in, which meant it was already on the ground.

"How far are we from the grotto?" Toni asked.

"A few hundred yards," Dorner said.

Koger popped open the rear door. "We walk from here."

They all climbed out into the cold.

"What do we have?" Luke asked. "Two guns?"

He knew Dorner had one, minus a few rounds, and Koger had mentioned he was armed, though he'd used some of his bullets too.

"Open the trunk," Dorner said.

He pushed the trunk release on the key fob. They walked around to the illuminated compartment and saw an array of weapons.

"I wasn't sure what you might need," Dorner said. "So I brought an assortment, with ammunition."

"I doubly take back all the bad things I've ever said about you," Derrick told her, reaching for a rifle.

COTTON STARED AHEAD IN THE DARK AND SAW NOTHING but trees, rock, and bushes. One small section was illuminated by the amber glow of a pole light. Above that was something even more out of place. A steel structure, held aloft by tall girded struts that acted as some sort of temporary roof.

"Fortunate for us," Fenn said, "the grotto is undergoing an extensive, multi-year restoration. The structure was built to keep the rain and snow out while they work. There have been a multitude of leaks in the grotto ceiling, ruining the inside. Finally, the government did something."

"How lucky," Cotton said.

"Come now, Herr Malone, isn't this exciting?" Fenn said. "We may be about to solve a long-standing mystery, one that might reveal something extraordinary."

He pointed at Ming. "Something that could also alter the balance of power in the world."

"Let us not be overly dramatic," Ming said. "Rare earths are plentiful throughout the world."

Cotton chuckled. "Of course, years ago, with your government cutting prices to the bone, you shut down every other major producer in the world. It would take billions to reopen those mines and compete with China."

"Seems to me all of that is just a by-product of a free market. I believe you Americans call it capitalism."

"We actually call it predatory pricing and monopolization. It's illegal." He pointed ahead. "Can we get this over with?"

A sound broke the silence. Like a crash. Away, but not that far.

Ming seemed bothered and looked at Fenn. "Was that your men arriving?"

"Possible."

Ming pointed at two of his men with guns. "Investigate. It sounded like it was on the property."

The men hustled off into the night.

Following the paved path that led past the grotto.

Fenn motioned ahead. "Shall we?"

LUKE CARRIED BOTH AN AUTOMATIC RIFLE AND A sidearm. Toni and Derrick were likewise double armed. Dorner? She seemed content with one pistol, and he wondered if she knew how to use it. Crashing through that gate had generated plenty of noise to disturb this gigantic bowl of quiet. They were advancing down a paved path that led deeper into the forested grounds. On their left a building appeared, marked by a sign as the Moorish Kiosk. Lights burned near it, illuminating what looked like a miniature mosque, complete with a gilded dome. Snow clung to the evergreens all around like frosting. They kept moving, flanked out on the path. Luke led the way on the right, Toni behind him. Koger and Dorner on the left.

Something caught his sharp eyes ahead.

Forms emerging through the darkness.

He raised a clenched fist and signaled stop.

DERRICK WAS ANNOYED THAT TRINITY HAD INSISTED ON actively participating. That was foolishness, but she outranked him. She'd been pleased when he'd told her about Rife's and Knight's sudden demise. Not a moment's concern for two dead Scythe. That woman was all business. But she beat the hell out of the paper pushers he routinely dealt with, all fond of nitpicking and finding problems that didn't exist.

He noticed something ahead. Blackness moving. Luke had seen it, too, and signaled stop. He reached back with his left hand and halted Trinity. They all stood rigid. The forms ahead were not moving either.

He didn't like the feel of things.

Not at all.

LUKE SCOURED THE DARKNESS WITH HIS GAZE, FOCUSING off to one side, while concentrating on his peripheral vision. It somehow helped to bring things in the dark into clearer perspective.

Especially movement.

He'd learned the trick long ago while hunting deer.

"Somebody's there," Toni whispered in his ear.

She'd apparently seen it too. "Yep."

"They're standing. Watching. Maybe thirty yards away."

Then he caught new movement.

Down.

To their knees.

He motioned a warning to Koger, then swept his left arm back, taking them both off the path.

Just as gunfire erupted.

CHAPTER 81

Cotton stepped through the doorway into the Venus Grotto. The inside was warm. Too warm, actually. And they all removed their coats and gloves.

The corridor beyond was adorned with huge stalactites dropping from the ceiling. Rock surrounded him on all sides. He touched the wall and realized none of it was real. All faux. Created in the nineteenth century to satisfy the peculiar whims of Ludwig II. He'd read about this fantastical place, though he'd never visited.

The two armed men stood behind him, just out of reach, Ming and the duke ahead. Fenn disappeared around a corner. They followed. Suddenly, the place came alive with bright light, revealing a vaulted space about thirty feet high, more ceiling stalactites achieved through an artful use of canvas, cement, and paint. Every grotto needed a lake and this one was no exception. It filled most of the space beneath the vault. Most surreal was the gilded shell-shaped boat, glittering with crystals, complete with a shell-shaped throne. It no longer floated on the water, but instead rested on a metal pedestal that projected just above the surface.

He recalled reading that Ludwig loved to be rowed across the lake by a servant while colored lights played across the ceiling, especially in a particular shade of deep blue that had been tough to create. Another machine had even produced waves on the lake. Sometimes live opera had been sung from the stage.

Fenn stood twenty feet away, his arms outstretched. "Ludwig's dream world."

That it was.

Two more men entered from behind, neither of whom carried a weapon. He wondered how many assets Fenn and Ming had on-site. More than enough already.

The two newcomers advanced on Albert, each grabbing an arm and lifting the man off the ground. They then hopped from the stone walkway down into the lake, which was about waist-high, splashing into the water but keeping a hold on the duke. Cotton moved to intercede but was cut off by one of the two remaining armed guards who raised his rifle, ready to fire.

He stopped.

One of the men forced the duke's head under the water and held it there. The older man's arms thrashed as he tried to escape, but the assassins kept a firm hold, the head never again finding air.

Thirty seconds and all movement stopped.

Cotton stared over at Fenn, who stood thirty feet away, watching in silence. The two men in the water kept Albert's head submerged a few more seconds, then brought it up, satisfied the man was dead.

"It had to be done," Ming said in a flat voice.

"Easy to kill an overweight old man."

"It is never easy to kill," Ming noted. "But there are times when it has to be done."

The killers climbed from the lake and lifted out the Duke of Bavaria's body.

"He just had his brother, Stefan, killed," Ming said.

"Another of those times?" Cotton asked.

"Albert so wanted to be king," Ming said. "But, unfortunately for him, Germany is not interested in an independent Bavaria. They are interested in finding that deed—so as to give it to us. For you see, Mr. Malone, Germany needs China. Badly."

Albert's wet corpse lay on the rocky floor.

"The Germans worked with Stefan and Albert," Ming said. "Separately. Hoping one or both would find the deed. But we were their true benefactors. Once you and the rest of the CIA became overly involved, it was decided to eliminate certain participants."

"You have an interesting way to describe cold-blooded murder."

"And you have never killed anyone?"

"I've never murdered anyone."

Ming glared at him. Then looked over at the two wet men. "Take him back to Neuschwanstein and drop him into the Pöllat gorge with his brother. Careful no one sees you. We'll let the press muse as to how and why they both ended up there. Another Wittelsbach tragedy, perhaps."

"What do you get out of this?" Cotton asked Fenn.

"Millions of euros."

"And all that bullshit about Bavaria and Ludwig and independence?"

"It all sounds wonderful, yet impossible to achieve. Money, on the other hand, is easily obtainable. But do get the duke's body gone before my brothers arrive. I prefer they not see such a sight."

Albert was slung over the shoulder of one of the

men who killed him and, together with his partner, they left the grotto.

"Nobody cares about the Wittelsbachs," Ming said. "They are nothing but a rare mention in a German history book. They lost their kingdom, never to return. The last thing the Germans want is to lose their largest state. It was foolish of both Stefan and Albert to think otherwise. Ambition clouds judgment."

"Which is another reason," Fenn said from the other side of the grotto, "that I chose money over ideals. The Chinese required help, and I provided it. And, by the way, so have several of your ex–CIA agents."

"For money too?" he asked, curious.

"Surely. But their true motivation was far more primal. Shelley said it best. 'Revenge is the naked idol of the worship of a semi-barbarous age.' But enough about what has already occurred. Let us focus on what is about to happen. Here is what we seek."

He focused on the enormous illuminated mural that filled the wall behind a rock-framed stage.

"Isn't it marvelous," Fenn said. "Groups of roguish cupids play all around a shell-throne where Venus herself, the goddess of love, full of seductive charm, watches over a slumbering Tannhäuser, resting at her feet. Doves fly all around and about the lovers. Above them, Amourettes bear flowered garlands. The Three Graces stand off to one side." Fenn gestured with his arms like a showman. "*Tannhäuser on the Venus Mount.* Painted for Ludwig II by August von Heckel."

He studied the mural and recalled the deciphered text.

Through the Venus mount to the redoubt.

He also further noticed the ongoing construction. Scaffolding extended out of the shallow lake up to the ceiling. It appeared some extensive repair work was going on. More scaffolding rose against a far wall where the structure's iron underbelly was exposed. Tools, compressors, and a generator dotted the minimal amount of dry space that ringed the lake. The shell boat in the center was sheathed in clear plastic. The whole place was like a movie theater after the show was over and the lights came on. The magic and make-believe gone, only the reality that had been there all along remained. The air cast an oily, metallic odor.

"Where do you believe we should look?" Ming asked.

"It is quite clear," Fenn said. "Though a mural was first created in the 1870s, this is not the original. That suffered extensive damage from neglect during the First World War. So much that it was heavily repaired in 1920. By then Ludwig III was no longer king, but the restoration happened anyway. It is not widely known, nor was it advertised, but a large portion of this mural had to be quietly reproduced. My guess? Ludwig III took advantage of that restoration. I believe what we seek is on the other side of the wall behind me. 'Through the Venus mount to the redoubt.'"

He agreed. It made sense.

"Fitting he called it a redoubt," Fenn said. "A place of retreat. Where one took their last stand."

Cotton heard the distant *rat-tat-tat* of gunfire. The others noticed too. Which could mean a multitude of things. The two men with the guns stood behind him, limiting his options.

But he wondered.

Had Koger arrived?

LUKE LAY STILL ON THE FRIGID GROUND, HIS RIGHT cheek chilled from the snow. They'd all dove for the side of the path and lain flat in the instant before the shooting started, staying down as rounds whined by. Once the firing stopped they'd remained down. The idea was to draw their attackers in, casting a sense that the threat had been neutralized. So he lay motionless, only his left eye squinted open enough for him to see anything approaching.

"There's two of them," Toni whispered, lying next to him.

Yep. But he lay farthest from the paved path. Toni had dropped between him and concrete. She was closer. That meant the first move would be hers. Koger lay on the other side with Dorner beside him. He kept a close watch. Toni was right. Two forms materialized from the darkness. One came their way, the other toward Koger. Both toted rifles. One of the forms stepped close, still cradling the weapon, finger on the trigger, but not pointed their way. Almost like he was thinking, *Job done, killed them all, now let's verify and get out of here.* Was he really going to—

The guy crouched down.

Toni moved in a flash, clipping his feet out from under him with a sweep of her arm. The legs went forward, feet in the air, and the guy's butt pounded down hard. She sprang up and slammed her right elbow into his face, sending the back of his head thudding into the pavement. Luke came up, ready to react, but the guy wasn't moving.

"That's going to leave a mark," he said to her.

"I hope so."

He glanced over to see that Koger had dispatched his man just as quickly.

"How are the ribs?" he asked.

"I've felt worse."

Say what you want about him, but Koger was tough.

They disarmed both attackers, tossing the weapons deep into the foliage.

"We need to get to Malone," Koger said.

He heard the roar of an engine from behind them. Back from where they'd left the car.

More company?

"Off the path," he told everyone.

And they scampered into the woods.

Headlights appeared from around a bend.

CHAPTER 82

Cotton heard no more gunfire.

"I was just informed by text," Fenn said, "that three of my associates are here. A gate has been destroyed and there is a vehicle parked just past it. My men are driving this way and will investigate. I told them your two men are out there as well."

"Between them, they can deal with any problems," Ming said. "In the meantime, Mr. Malone, how about bringing that sledgehammer over here and let us see what's through the Venus mount."

He had to stall, hoping the commotion outside came from the side of right and might. But more operatives on the scene could not be a good thing. He still had two here with guns to deal with. So he eased over and gripped the sledgehammer. One of the smaller ones with a short handle, but a solid business end. He followed a narrow walkway that led around the lake to the stage where Fenn waited. That same narrowness existed there, too, not much room for anyone to perform.

"During the 1920 restoration I am told this plaster wall was repaired extensively for large cracks," Fenn said. "I am thinking, during that work, something more was added, behind it."

"What do you want me to do? Smash it up?" he asked.

Fenn shrugged. "Why not?"

But where? This was one big mural.

From this new vantage point Cotton noticed the ceiling above where Ming and the two guys with guns stood on the other side of the small lake. Bunches of faux stalactites, reflecting more of an overriding compulsion to build and create the illusion of a cave, hung from the ceiling.

Lots of them.

Could he do it?

Sure.

Should he?

Why not.

LUKE WATCHED FROM THE TREES AS THE CAR STOPPED right before the two men lying on the pavement. They'd left them there on purpose and the diversion worked. This new threat had to be dealt with, but preferably without any more gunfire.

The doors opened.

Three men climbed out, the driver stayed inside, keeping the engine idling. They waited for two of the men to crouch down and check the bodies, the third keeping a watch. Then he, Koger, and Toni pounced. Each zeroed in on a target. He took the lookout, throwing his hip into the guy, flipping him up and over his shoulder. The body landed hard. But a kick to the head kept him down.

He turned.

Toni's arm streaked up like a piston, the fingers of her hand curled back to expose the heel, which she smashed into one of the men's jaw. She then delivered a fist below the rib cage, knocking all the wind out of him, paralyzing breathing. She shoved the guy onto the car's hood. Two more punches to the face and down he went. She added a kick to the head for good measure.

"You've got some anger issues," he told her.

"Yeah, I do."

Koger was finishing his man off with a kick to the spine that spun the body over and down to the snow like a sack.

A shot rang out.

He whirled.

The driver's-side door hung open, the fourth man staggering back with a gun in his right hand. To his left, on the other side of the car, Trinity stood with her weapon aimed. The driver had taken one round from her and was trying to gain some semblance of control, swinging the gun back around for a shot, but Trinity fired again and dropped him to the ground.

They all three stared at her.

She stood motionless, arms extended, both hands gripping the stock.

"We appreciate that," Koger said.

No time for reflection or sentiment.

"Get the guns," Luke ordered.

DERRICK INCHED OVER TOWARD TRINITY AS LUKE AND Toni gathered up the weapons, checking the four downed men for any they'd missed. These were not Chinese operatives. These were Europeans. Most likely some of Fenn's contingent. Trinity lowered her gun and still had not uttered a sound, her eyes focused to where the dead man lay, though the body was blocked by the car.

"First time is always tough," he quietly said to her.

She stared at him with eyes that, after all the years he'd known her, showed something other than utter confidence.

But only for an instant.

Then she regained her usual control.

But he had to ask, "You okay?"

"He was going to shoot all of you."

"You did what you had to do."

She did not seem reassured.

"It's never easy," he told her.

And he meant it.

Hotshots never survived long. The best agents were the ones who killed reluctantly, only as a last resort. And who detested it. Men and women who thought more and risked less. He'd just killed two men himself. Both of whom had been trying to kill him. But he still was bothered.

As he should be.

"What now?" she asked.

Luke and Toni came over.

"They're clean," Luke said. "We tossed the guns in the woods. They should be out awhile."

Derrick stared ahead into the darkness.

"Let's go save the day."

CHAPTER 83

COTTON USED THE SLEDGEHAMMER AND GENTLY TAPPED the mural, listening for any changes in pitch. If there was a chamber behind the wall, there should be some difference in sound.

And there was.

A little past left center, just below a reclining Tannhäuser's chest.

He continued to tap downward and defined the boundaries of the hollow sound. Interesting how an artist worked for months, applying knowledge gained during a lifetime, to create something any fool with a hammer could smash in a second. Obviously, the government was spending an enormous amount of money to repair the roof and preserve everything here. Especially the mural, which seemed the primary focal point in a place loaded with focal points.

"I think you have found it," Fenn said, still holding the gun, which he motioned with. "Please, open it up."

He stood with the sledgehammer down at his right side and completed his estimates. The toss would be about twenty feet. Ming and the two men stood on the other side of the lake, directly beneath a cluster of the fake stalactites. His guess? They were fashioned from some kind of webbed wiring, coated with plaster and concrete, shaped to appear like natural formations. Each was big and meaty. Should make quite a mess.

He pivoted and, like a shot-putter, launched the sledgehammer into the air. The handle rotated around the head and whooped upward, its mass smashing into the hanging decorations, ripping through them like a bowling ball into pins.

Fenn's attention drifted.

As expected.

He used that moment to snatch the weapon away and shoved the older man over a short wall of scattered rock into the lake. Fenn hit with a splash just as the sledgehammer finished its carnage and chunks of concrete and plaster rained down. Ming and the two men with guns raised their arms to shield their heads from the incoming storm of dust and debris. The sledgehammer completed its journey and pounded to the ground, not hitting anyone. He watched from the safety of the other side of the grotto.

Fenn stood in the waist-high water, no longer a threat.

Cotton marched around the lake on the narrow walkway. Pieces and particles continued to fall. Behind the three Chinese, through the dust cloud, he caught movement.

More threats had returned.

He stopped, took cover, and leveled his weapon, ready for a fight with whomever.

Luke appeared. Followed by Koger, one woman he did not know, the other woman the same one who'd been at Herrenchiemsee. All of them armed.

He lowered the gun and stepped out.

"Looks like you didn't need much help," Koger said.

He shrugged. "Good to see you too."

But something required immediate attention. He walked straight to Ming, who was down on one knee, coughing out dust. Luke and the others disarmed the other two. He yanked Ming up. The walking stick dropped aside. He jammed the gun into Ming's throat.

"Get your phone out and make the call. Tell them to stand down."

Ming hesitated.

He clicked the hammer into place. "I have no problem blowing your head off. And, by the way, nobody would give a damn, since I'm not even supposed to be here."

"I know I wouldn't care," Koger said. "Anybody else?"

"I'm good," Luke noted.

Ming fished the phone from his coat pocket, punched in a number, then spoke in Chinese.

"English," Cotton ordered.

"They do not speak it."

"He just told them to kill her," the older of the two women said. "Whoever 'her' is."

He rapped the gun across the side of Ming's face, sending the older man down. "You need to decide if this is worth dying for. One more time. Screw it up and you're dead." He aimed the gun at Ming. "Five seconds."

Ming did nothing.

Blood trickled from the side of his mouth.

"Four."

"Three."

Ming raised the phone to his ear.

"Two."

He tightened his arm, ready to fire.

The others stared in silence.

"One."

"Stand down," Ming said into the phone. In English. "Return to the consulate."

Cotton snatched the phone away.

And ended the call.

KOGER HEAVED A SIGH OF RELIEF.

He would have had a hard time explaining to Langley why a Chinese intelligence operative had been killed by a man he was not even supposed to be doing business with. That would have strained things even for him. And when one side killed someone from the other, there was usually retaliation. It may take time, but a tit for tat always came.

Across the grotto Fenn was hauling himself from the lake, soaking wet.

He assumed command. "Toni, make sure we don't have any more company from outside. Luke, keep these three here and out of the way." He pointed at Trinity and they walked over to Malone. "Why are you here?"

"It could be the end of the trail."

"The deed?" the older woman asked.

Malone asked, "Who are you?"

"Trinity Dorner. Deputy National Security Adviser."

"What's the damn White House doing here?"

She said nothing.

Malone pointed at Koger. "You knew?"

He nodded. "Not my doin'."

"Fox is involved?"

"The White House is involved," he made clear. "Which happened before I was involved. I got stuck with 'em. Don't shoot the messenger."

"What did he promise you?"

Leave it to Maloney to cut right to the quick.

"Excuse me, Mr. Malone," Dorner said. "But I'm the ranking official here."

"Really, now? Do you know what I think about that?"

Derrick held up a hand. "Slow down, cowboy. Trinity has been right there for us, all the way. We got here thanks in part to her. She's not the problem."

Malone did not seem impressed and pointed. "What were *you* promised?"

"Not a damn thing."

Malone glared at TOO.

"It's true," she said. "Nothing at all. But we still have a job to do."

Malone stepped over and lifted a sledgehammer from the mess on the floor.

"What's that for?" Trinity asked.

"Follow me and you'll find out."

CHAPTER 84

COTTON HEADED BACK FOR THE MURAL.

Fenn waited, water dripping from his clothes. "That was uncalled for."

He was not in the mood. "If you can't take the heat, you know where you shouldn't be."

He returned to the area on the mural he'd already identified and found the center of the hollow space. He stepped back and cocked his arm, slamming the business end of the sledgehammer into the wall.

With little effect.

But what had he expected?

He pounded again.

And again.

Cracks developed across Tannhäuser's chest. He expanded them with more blows. Finally, the wall gave way and a section broke off, crumbling to the floor. It seemed the wall was more plaster than thick concrete. Which should help.

"Did that cipher lead here?" Koger asked.

"Right to it."

And he kept hammering the wall, opening up a small doorway about two feet wide and five feet tall.

He stepped back and allowed the dust to clear. Across the lake he saw the others watching intently, Luke keeping guard over them.

He turned back.

Koger was a step ahead of him, already heading for one of the light bars workers had set up to illuminate the ceiling, which he carried over, setting the tripod just inside the doorway and switching on the array.

Cotton led the way inside.

Beyond was a chamber about twenty feet deep and at least that wide. The ceiling reached up to the heights of the grotto, which made sense, as the hidden chamber was just another part of the overall enclosed space. But nothing fancy here. The walls were plain gray concrete, none of them artistically fashioned in any way. Which also made sense. Hiding something away was tough enough. Hiding it away inside some fantastical space that would require a score of craftsmen months to design and create? That was next to impossible. Not to mention costs. Instead, you just commandeer a hole in the wall.

Around the outer perimeter were three caskets, each atop a stone plinth. Again, nothing elaborate. Simple unadorned wood and stone. The only decorations were chiseled names.

Otto, Luitpold, and a third.

Ludovicus II Rex. Bavar. Com. Palat.

Ludwig II, King of Bavaria, Count Palatine.

A round table, sheathed by a richly embroidered cloth thick with dust, filled the center. The top was littered with papers and books. He stepped over and studied them without touching.

"Careful," he said. "A lot of this is really fragile. It would not take much to turn things to dust."

Fenn was carefully examining the books and papers.

He'd allowed him to come inside since they might need his expertise. He was hoping the guy's fanaticism would get the best of him. "Many of these bound volumes are personal journals. The loose papers are various family documents. Birth certificates. Investitures. Financial accountings. Inventories."

He heard what was not said.

But no deed.

Koger and Dorner had stayed quiet, but both were studying the surroundings with trained eyes. Two wooden trunks sat on the gritty floor. He bent down and lifted one of the lids. Inside were more smaller wooden boxes that, when opened, contained jewelry, crystal, glassware, silver and gold objects. All varieties of things.

"The family's wealth," Fenn said. "Or what was left of it after everyone had their choice of taking after Ludwig II died."

"We have to go through all of this," Dorner said. "And make sure there is no deed. I assume everyone thinks it has to be here."

"It has to be," Fenn said. "There is no place else."

"Unless it doesn't exist," Koger stated. "It was signed a long time ago and has never been seen since. This could all be a wild-goose chase."

Maybe. Maybe not. A solution seemed there, though tantalizing in its incompleteness. A lot of thought had gone into creating this repository. He had to assume that everything in it had been carefully selected based on value and importance. In the overall hierarchy of things, that deed had to be right at the top.

"What would Ludwig have thought of that deed?" he asked.

"Von Löher, the man who visited Hawaii," Fenn said, "wrote in his journal that Ludwig made the comment, after the deed was signed in 1881. *At least permit me this final joy. I adore the mysterious and wish to remain an eternal enigma.* So it is safe to say that the deed was vitally important to him."

"Which means," Fenn said, "it was also important to the regent, Luitpold, and his son Ludwig III. But more for sentimentality than anything else. Those two could not even manage to hold on to Bavaria, much less lay claim to an American territory."

"No," Dorner said. "That endeavor had to wait until the twenty-first century."

If all that were true, then there was but one explanation.

He stepped over to Ludwig II's casket. Its mahogany exterior had definitely deteriorated over time, but it was still reasonably intact. He released the brass latches and steeled himself.

Not every day you opened a king's grave.

He hinged the lid upward.

Ludwig lay prone, most of the skin and tissue gone, just bones and tattered pieces of clothing. He'd been buried in black silk breeches, a black velvet cloak, and a white shirt with ruffles. Remnants of those remained, along with a heavy gold chain collar and medal that had been left around the neck.

The others came close.

"The king was buried in the robes of the Knights of the Order of St. George," Fenn said. "The collar and medal are from the order too."

Lying on the chest, atop the decayed clothing and collapsed rib cage, was an oilskin pouch. It appeared to be of some sort of sailcloth with a thin layer of tar for added protection. He freed the pouch, which had survived in reasonably good condition. It measured about eighteen inches square. The top was sealed with more tar.

Cotton closed the casket. "Let's allow the man to rest in peace."

He walked back to the table and carefully felt the pouch. Something was inside. Stiff. With enough thickness that he could feel its edges.

"We have to know what's in there," Dorner said to him.

"I realize that."

Koger produced a pocketknife. He accepted the blade and punctured the oilskin, keeping the blade between the outer layer and whatever was inside. He cut a slit in the material. Beneath he saw that it contained a piece of stiff, yellowed parchment. Now that he knew what was there, he worked the knife and opened the oilskin up, exposing one side of the parchment, which was blank. He carefully removed the page and turned it over. At the top, in a large Edwardian script.

This Indenture, made this eighth day of August in the year of our Lord one thousand eight hundred and eighty-one between His Royal Highness, King David Kalakaua, of the first part, and His Royal Highness, King Ludwig Friedrich Wilhelm von Wittelsbach II, of the second part.

The deed went on and proclaimed

Witnesseth. That the said party of the first part does hereby present, grant, and convey to the said party of the second part, his heirs and assigns, all that part or parcel of islands located within the

Pacific Ocean and known to the world as the
sovereign kingdom of Hawaii.

Then it verified and asserted that

the said party of the first for himself, along with his
heirs and assigns, does hereby covenant and agree to
with the said party of the second part, along with
his heirs and assigns, that he shall have quiet and
peaceable possession of the said islands and all of
the land and lawful territory associated therewith
and that he will forever warrant and defend it
against any person whomsoever lawfully claiming
the same or any part thereof.

The deed was signed by both kings in a stark, heavy, masculine script and was properly witnessed by four individuals, their names and addresses noted.

"Is it valid?" Koger asked.

"That doesn't matter," Dorner said. "It's a legal document that the Germans can use to assert a legal claim in the courts. And when they assign it to the Chinese, that will double the problem." She paused. "It's a battle we don't want, or need, to fight in front of the world."

He knew that was true. But he was holding something important and history mattered. Yet there was still reality.

And now he realized why the White House was involved.

He looked at Trinity Dorner. "You or me?"

She nodded toward him.

He lifted the parchment and stepped from the chamber back into the grotto.

The others followed.

Ming stood on the far side watching.

"Here it is," he said to him. "The deed you wanted."

He tore it into pieces, the parchment yielding easily, ripping in clean strips, which he mutilated into smaller pieces. Then he allowed them all to rain down onto the surface of the lake, where the water claimed them, eradicating all evidence of what might have been there.

"It's over," he said.

CHAPTER 85

LUKE WALKED THE CHRISTMAS MARKET AND ADMIRED all the crafts and food for sale. Toni was with him. They'd spent yesterday being debriefed by Koger. Today, they were off the clock. Enjoying themselves.

The bodies of Prince Stefan and his brother, the Duke of Bavaria, had been located in the cold waters of the Pöllat gorge. Both had drowned and suffered severe injuries after obviously falling from great heights. The press and public were baffled as to their sudden deaths, the speculation running rampant. The truth would never be revealed since everything that happened would surely be stamped top secret, a felony for him, or anyone else associated with the mission, to ever speak of it. No danger of him talking. He might be young, brash, and too eager for his own good, but he knew how to keep his mouth shut. And, like Malone told him years ago, that was half the fight to becoming a good agent.

They'd left the grotto violated for others to find. Ming and his men were released and quickly retreated back to the safety of their consulate.

Mission failed for them.

Fenn and his band of merry men also retreated, taking the body of the one man Trinity Dorner had plugged with them. His respect level for Dorner had increased tenfold. He'd actually not thought she had it in her, but she'd handled herself well. Killing people wasn't easy. But you did what you had to do. And she'd done just that. And the fact that he'd escaped the situation without any holes in his skin was much appreciated.

"Check this out," Toni said.

And they stopped at one of the booths, this one selling an assortment of miniature sheep, hay, tools, shepherds, angels, and other things found in a manger.

"They go to nativity scenes," she said.

He noticed an assortment of small stables and grottoes fashioned from wood.

Toni lifted one of the carved angels. "My parents have one. You buy the various pieces and set up a model, at Christmas, of the birth of Christ in the manger."

Luke recited, "'And on the third day, after the birth of our Lord Jesus Christ, Mary went out of the cave, and, entering a stable, placed the child in a manger, and an ox and an ass adored him.'"

"Look at you. A biblical scholar."

"My mother demanded that we Daniels all know the Holy Book."

She replaced the angel among the others for sale. They'd spent last night together, enjoying each other. He liked her. A lot. But his job did not bode well for emotional attachments. She'd seemed to abide by the same rule.

"Where do you go now?" he asked her as they kept walking through the cold and the evening crowd.

"I'm not sure," she said. "There's talk of sending me to England, or perhaps South Africa."

He knew better than to ask why.

That was, as the Germans would say, "verboten."

"And you?" she asked.

"Back to the Magellan Billet."

He had a sense she was leading him. So he decided to not resist or question, but simply to follow. They passed through the Marienplatz, following a route similar to the one they'd taken two nights ago when the police were after them. Thankfully, all of that nonsense had been straightened out by people much higher up than him. Christophe had died in the police assault, and that fatality had seemed enough to satisfy the powers that be.

They left the main market route and headed down one of the side streets. People were still everywhere. The evening's weather was cold with no snow, a clear sky overhead with a half-full moon. Christmas was two weeks away and he'd already decided to spend it in Tennessee with his mother and brothers, provided of course he was not on assignment.

He noticed a car parked ahead along the curb, taillights on, condensation seeping from the tailpipe signaling an idling engine.

"Here's my ride," she said.

He'd actually hoped they'd have at least one more night together.

But, alas, not to be.

She stopped. "I enjoyed it."

"Me too."

He'd never been one for goodbyes, especially with women. Most he never saw again anyway. But this one twitched his gut ever so slightly.

Enough that he noticed.

She came close and kissed him on the cheek.

Then she turned for the car and opened the rear door. Before climbing inside she glanced back. "Hey, soldier. See you around the world somewhere."

He smiled. "I certainly hope so."

CHAPTER 86

DERRICK FINISHED PACKING HIS BAG AND READYING himself for the flight to Brussels. He was hitching a ride back with Trinity aboard a military Learjet. She'd drop him off, then continue on to Washington, DC. All in all, things had worked out fine. It was unfortunate that the duke and his brother were killed, but that's what happened when you played with fire.

And the Chinese were definitely fire.

His cell phone buzzed.

The screen showed Private.

What the hell?

He answered.

"Derrick, it's Warner Fox."

He went to high alert.

Which was what happened when the president of the United States called you.

"Good job. And I mean it. Well done. I just spoke with the Germans and told them we did not appreciate what they tried. They, of course, denied everything. But I could tell they were glad there'd be no secession vote. I hate it when they lie to my face. I meant what I said. I owe you, Derrick. Use that chip wisely. It's all yours, when you're ready." Fox paused. "But don't wait too long. There is an expiration date, after which it goes stale."

"Roger that."

"You clipped the Scythe really good. Intel says they are in disarray. Rife was the ringleader. With him dead, a message was sent and apparently received."

"Paul Bryie needs to be arrested."

"They're looking for him. He's vanished for the moment. But we'll get him. We're also going to finish cleaning house at Langley. I'm going to fire the agency's inspector general."

The IG handled independent oversight of the CIA. He or she was nominated by the president, confirmed by the Senate, and could be fired only by the president. That office reported to not only the CIA director, but directly to Congress as an oversight to deter fraud, waste, and abuse.

"I may need a new one soon," Fox said. "You interested?"

"It requires confirmation by the Senate. I have a past."

"I know. But I control the Senate."

He realized that Fox was sending a message. He wanted him on board, but he did not have to call in his chip to get it.

"I'll think on it," he said.

"You do that."

***

COTTON SAT INSIDE A BUSY RESTAURANT NOT FAR FROM the Marienplatz, a place that specialized in roasted pork knuckles. In fact, according to the server, they'd been roasting pigs here for the last four hundred years. The time was a little after 6:00 P.M. The olden-style dining room was packed with a lively dinner crowd. Outside, beyond the plate glass windows, the sidewalks were thick with people enjoying the nightly Christmas market.

He was headed back to Copenhagen after spending yesterday with Luke, Koger, Trinity Dorner, and Toni Sims, debriefing the American ambassador to Germany so he could deal with Berlin. The BND had flexed its muscle after the discovery of the two dead senior members of the House of Wittelsbach. But Dorner had handled them expertly. Koger had told him about what she'd done before they appeared in the grotto.

And he could sympathize.

The first time pulling the trigger was tough.

Marc Fenn had disappeared back to his castle, sworn to secrecy about all that happened on pain of prosecution. Fenn had committed a litany of crimes and seemed to understand his precarious legal position. Dorner had likewise secured from Fenn a nondisclosure agreement that contained a waiver as to any statute of limitations.

So the threat of his prosecution would continue indefinitely.

He'd given his order to the server and was enjoying a little solitude among the crowd. He ate a lot of his meals alone, so dining solo was nothing unusual.

"May I intrude?"

He returned from his thoughts and saw Trinity Dorner standing before him.

He smiled and motioned. "Of course. Have a seat."

He wondered how she'd found him, but realized this was a person of resources. She handed him a cell phone. His had been destroyed a couple of days ago.

"It's Magellan Billet–issued," she said. "I had it sent yesterday." She provided him the new number. "I don't have to ask if you'll remember that, right?"

He grinned and nodded. "Thank you."

"The least we could do."

The phone buzzed on the tabletop.

He stared at Dorner, whose face remained like granite. Then he glanced down at the screen and saw Answer it as the caller ID. He debated whether to ignore the call but decided not to be that arrogant. He lifted the phone and answered, using the noise and commotion around him as a privacy shield.

"No need to speak," Warner Fox said. "Just listen."

He stared at Dorner, who offered nothing back.

"I was wrong, Malone. I made a big mistake in Poland and lost a friend. You were right. I was wrong."

He said nothing.

"I was wrong on Stephanie Nell too. I've ordered everything stopped regarding her termination and the Magellan Billet reinstated. And that's not because of any deals. I was wrong and I'm willing to admit that to you."

His mother once told him to "forgive and forget, not revenge and gloat." The president of the United States was admitting he'd been wrong.

Let it go.

"We're good," he said.

"That's all I ask. I've also lifted the order on not using you by our agencies."

"I appreciate that."

"You did good here. We were headed for a vise that would have been difficult to get out of. How about you and I forget the past and move forward. Who knows? I might need you."

"Fair enough."

"Goodbye, Cotton."

The call ended.

He laid the phone down.

Trinity slid an envelope across the table, then stood from the booth. "That's a token of his appreciation. He realizes you're a bookseller, with a business to run, so this is some compensation for your time."

He wanted to say no, but knew that he shouldn't.

Forgive and forget.

"Thank you. Would you like to eat with me?"

"I have a plane to catch. But not to worry, Mr. Malone. Something tells me you and I are going to see each other again."

He watched as she threaded her way through the crowded tables and left.

She was right.

Something told him the same thing.

WRITER'S NOTE

This novel is one I've been wanting to write for a long time, ever since first visiting Bavaria in 1987. Since then, I've returned many times. Elizabeth and I spent ten days there specifically researching this story, studying Neuschwanstein, Linderhof, and Herrenchiemsee. And though we were there in spring, we have visited at Christmas (like Cotton does here) and enjoyed the holiday markets.

Time now to separate fact from fiction.

As to locales: The Chiemsee is a majestic body of water—the German sea as it is known. The ferryboat upon it exists (chapters 1, 3, 5, 7, 35, and 36) and the islands of Herreninsel (chapters 1, 3, 5, 7, 15, and 21) and Fraueninsel (chapters 5 and 7) dot its surface. The palace of Herrenchiemsee occupies the former, while a town and ancient convent dominate the latter. Only the church and tunnel on Fraueninsel (chapters 7 and 8) are my invention. The Starnberger See lies south of Munich (chapters 11, 12, 17, 18, 20, 21, and 54) and is loaded with lore. The Berg Castle, once the haunt of Ludwig II, is gone, replaced by an unremarkable house owned by the Wittelsbach family.

Munich is accurately described throughout (chapters 6 and 18), including its storied past, busy Marienplatz, and famous beer halls (chapters 14, 16, and 19). Other notable spots within the city that make an appearance are: the Charles Hotel (chapter 6), which is a wonderful place to stay; St. Ludwig's Church (chapters 52 and 53) near the Bavarian State Library (chapters 14 and 48); the Jesuit Church of St. Michael (chapter 6), along with the crypt beneath (chapters 11 and 12) where a number of Wittelsbachs are buried, including Ludwig II; the former royal Residenz (chapters 10 and 24), along with its magnificent Hall of Antiquities; and the storied Frauenkirche (chapters 6, 23, 48, and 57) where Ludwig III is buried (though his real tomb is not empty).

The annual Christmas markets, which dot Germany each year, make several appearances in the story. The one in Munich is huge and well attended. The medieval version noted in chapter 44 is likewise worth a visit.

A few miscellaneous items: prostitution has long been legal in Germany (chapter 6); the Appalachian superstitions noted in chapter 19 are accurate; the quote from Teddy Roosevelt noted in chapter 57 is quite famous; the language used in the OSS memos quoted in chapters 47 and 55 is taken from actual ones from the war, though any reference to the last kingdom is my addition; Lehmanns is a fictitious law firm (chapters 34 and 45), though there are many such megafirms located all over the world; and the South China Sea dispute, referenced in chapter 33, is still ongoing.

The three castles of Ludwig II all make an appearance. The palace of Herrenchiemsee is accurately portrayed, including the king's study and ornate desk (chapters 1, 2, and 15), which was delivered after Ludwig II's death. Its two secret compartments were my creation. Neuschwanstein Castle is truly a place of fairy tales and is faithfully re-created (chapters 59, 61, 62, 63, 66, and 71), which includes the third-floor layout, king's study, and Singers' Hall (chapters 62 and 76). But there are no secret compartments that I know of in the cabinet located in the study (chapter 65). The Marienbrücke is there, named for Ludwig II's mother, and the view from its towering span above the Pöllat gorge is spectacular (chapters 59 and 66). There is no helicopter pad (chapter 63). Linderhof is the smallest of Ludwig's creations and the only one he completed (chapters 11 and 79). The Venus Grotto is there and is quite fantastical (chapters 66 and 81). During the writing of this book the grotto was undergoing a multiyear renovation (just like in the story). The mural, *Tannhäuser on the Venus Mount* (chapter 81), is inside the grotto but no secret room is located behind it. Ludwig had intended to build a fourth castle at Falkenstein (chapter 21), but died before that could happen. All that stands there now is an ancient ruin.

The cipher wheel from chapters 70, 72, and 73 was used by the Confederacy during the Civil War and proved quite effective. There are only five originals left in the world, though copies are plentiful. All of the references to Angus Adams, Cotton's ancestor and namesake (chapters 70 and 72), are more fully fleshed out in another Cotton Malone adventure, *The Lost Order*. It's true that Ludwig II loved codes, and he would have surely been fascinated with the cipher wheel.

The puzzling lines of text quoted in chapter 15 are from another mystery that deals with World War II, Martin Bormann, and a sheet of music. It's called the March Impromptu Code and supposedly leads to a secret stash of diamonds and Nazi gold. Of course, no one has ever deciphered the code and no gold or diamonds have ever been found. But the words worked here. The solutions to each line of text are the invention of others, the anagram beneath was my creation.

The Nostradamus prophecy quoted in chapter 51, "When Good Friday falls on St. George's Day, Easter on St. Mark's Day, and Corpus Christi on St. John's Day, all the world will weep," is real and was long associated with the Wittelsbachs and Ludwig II. Interestingly, the three dates aligned in 1886, the year Ludwig II died. The rest of the clues noted in chapter 51 are my invention.

Bavaria is of vital political importance to Germany (chapter 9). An independent streak, though, has long existed. Bavaria did not sign the Bamberg Constitution in 1919, the founding treaty for the Federal Republic of Germany in 1948, or the Basic Law of Germany (chapter 9). But no revolutionary movement like that depicted in the story exists in reality. Germany's deep political and financial connections to China, though, are a matter of fact (chapter 37). China has been, and remains, Germany's number one trading and political partner.

Hawaii's history (chapter 25) is accurately related, including the coup that occurred in 1893. American planters, with American military assistance, stole the islands and ended the monarchy (chapters 25 and 27). President Grover Cleveland was appalled, and his admonition from 1893, quoted in chapter 27, is real. A congressional inquiry at the time exposed all of the wrongdoing. But nothing was ever done to right that wrong and Hawaii became an American territory in 1898 and a state in 1959. The Apology Resolution of 1993, issued by Congress on the hundredth anniversary of the coup, is real (chapter 27), but I added Section 1, Paragraph 6.

David Kalākaua was king of Hawaii in 1881 (chapter 21). His flamboyant personal history, and that of the Hawaiian monarchy in general, is accurately revealed. He was, in fact, quite similar to Ludwig II (chapter 26). He also made a world tour in 1881(the first monarch to ever do so), which included Austria and Germany, but I added the meeting with the king of Bavaria (prologue and chapter 26). Amazingly, Ludwig II was awarded (in 1865) the Knight's Grand Cross and the badge of the Royal Order of Kamehameha I. He was one of the first non-Hawaiians to ever receive it.

Why was that done?

No one knows.

Rare earths are vitally important to the world (chapter 31). Nearly every electric device on the planet uses some form of them. All of the information noted in chapter 31 is correct. China has long dominated the world market on rare earths (with control of eighty to ninety percent), which remains a matter of national security for not only the United States but all other nations too. An enormous concentration of rare earths, enough to change China's near monopoly, does in fact lie off the coast of Hawaii (chapters 31 and 33), waiting to be harvested.

The Guglmänner exists (chapter 19). They wear black robes and hoods and engage in all sorts of stunts and public relations ploys designed to bring attention to (in their words) "the murder of Ludwig II and an independent Bavaria" (chapters 20 and 23). The initiation ceremony depicted in chapter 32 was taken from another organization. Surely the black hoods have a similar ritual, but the particulars of that are not public record.

The Wittelsbachs were once a powerful royal family. They ruled Bavaria for over eight hundred years. All that ended on November 12, 1918, with the signing of the Anif Declaration. Prince Stefan and Duke Albert herein are my creations, but their ancestors noted throughout the story are accurately described. Prince Regent Luitpold (chapter 18) governed wisely in place of his deranged nephew, King Otto, who succeeded his brother, Ludwig II. Luitpold was so popular that when he died in 1912, his son, Ludwig III, was made king. Ludwig III (chapters 49 and 58) was another tragic figure who had the misfortune to rule during a world war and among violent revolutionary feelings that were spawned from that conflict. He lost his kingdom in 1919. Of course, his secreting away of bodies and documents for posterity is wholly my creation.

Franz von Löher is a historical figure and Ludwig II did engage him to search out and find a new kingdom (chapter 10). Von Löher made two trips abroad (1873 and 1875) and reported back on some promising locations, many of which are detailed in chapter 21. Nothing suitable was found and the whole endeavor remained secret, revealed only after Ludwig II's death. I added Hawaii to the list of places visited. Von Löher wrote the books listed in chapter 10, and ultimately wrote a final book about his work for Ludwig. The last kingdom of this novel is wholly my concoction. But the language in the deed that is found in chapter 84 is from nineteenth-century legal instruments.

This story focuses on Ludwig Friedrich Wilhelm von Wittelsbach, otherwise known as King Ludwig II of Bavaria. History has offered him a mixed bag of reviews. From visionary, to genius, to spendthrift, to insane. He certainly possessed his share of mental instability. Today he might be labeled bipolar or chronically depressed and treated with medication. But no such treatments existed in the second half of the nineteenth century.

Clearly, Ludwig was a complex man, but contrary to what many have said and written, he did not bankrupt Bavaria. Instead, he utilized the money allocated to him annually for his personal upkeep to finance his construction projects, then borrowed to supplement those funds. He essentially bankrupted himself, overspending and overborrowing. But all of those debts were satisfied by the Bavarian government after his death.

Ludwig was a vain, stubborn man, afflicted with a fair share of narcissism and megalomania. He eventually placed the Bavarian government in an untenable situation, refusing to perform his duties, leaving them no choice. He was involuntarily removed (chapter 11) with little supporting evidence through a curious provision in the Bavarian constitution. His comment to the official commission that came to take him into custody is interesting (chapter 11). *You have come to tell an insane man that he is insane? Does that not imply that I be sane?* Quite an insightful inquiry from someone supposedly mentally impaired.

Ludwig's connections to the composer Richard Wagner were deep and emotional (chapter 14), amounting to an unhealthy obsession. He loved opera to the point of irrationality and became Wagner's sole financial patron. His castles, especially Neuschwanstein, were sheathed in images from Wagner's work. That made it easy for me to title the book uncovered at Herrenchiemsee (chapter 14) *Tannhäuser and the Minnesinger's Contest at Wartburg*, after a Wagner opera. I also utilized more Wagner references with the *Sängerkrieg* and *Rätselspiel* (chapter

58). When Wagner died in 1883, Ludwig ordered all of the palace pianos draped in black and never to be played again (chapter 14).

How Ludwig II himself died (chapter 11), so conveniently one day after being deposed, will forever be a mystery. The explanation in chapter 17 is the most logical one, absent any conspiracy theory. It is not mine. Instead, it came from a wonderful biography, *The Mad King*, by Greg King. Speculation about Ludwig's death still abounds. His state funeral (chapters 11, 13, and 23) was elaborate and his tomb beneath the Jesuit Church of St. Michael has remained sealed since 1886. Which means that no modern scientific techniques have been applied in an effort to determine the cause of death.

Perhaps a comment Ludwig once made about another matter could likewise be applied to his death:

AT LEAST PERMIT ME THIS FINAL JOY.
I ADORE THE MYSTERIOUS AND WISH TO REMAIN
AN ETERNAL ENIGMA.

ABOUT THE AUTHOR

STEVE BERRY is the *New York Times* and #1 internationally bestselling author of seventeen Cotton Malone novels, five stand-alone thrillers, and several works of short fiction. He has twenty-six million books in print, translated into forty-one languages. With his wife, Elizabeth, he is the founder of History Matters, an organization dedicated to historical preservation. He serves as an emeritus member of the Smithsonian Libraries Advisory Board and was a founding member of International Thriller Writers, formerly serving as its copresident.

SteveBerry.org

Facebook.com/SteveBerryWriter

Cotton Malone returns in *New York Times*
bestselling author Steve Berry's next
page-turning adventure, in which Malone must
unravel a mystery from World War II involving
a legendary lost treasure
worth billions.

THE ATLAS
MANEUVER

Available February 2024
Please turn the page for a preview.

PROLOGUE

General Tomoyuki Yamashita toasted the group for the final time. A hundred and seventy-five men stood before him in the dimly lit underground chamber. All engineers. Specially selected. Each having accomplished his task to perfection. One hiding place created per man. They'd performed so well and so fast that he'd ordered a celebration. Fried brown rice, boiled eggs, grilled sweet potatoes, and dried cow's meat. All washed down with copious amounts of sake. For the past two hours they'd sung patriotic songs and shouted *banzai*, long life, until they were hoarse. All the harshness of war had been set aside for a few precious hours.

He'd been reassigned to the islands last October, charged with stopping the rapidly advancing American forces. Prior to that he'd led the Imperial Army during the invasion of Malaya and the Battle of Singapore. Both resounding victories. He took pride in how Churchill had described the fall of Singapore. *The worst disaster and largest capitulation in British military history.*

But everything here had gone wrong.

Now he was doing nothing more than delaying the inevitable. The war was lost. MacArthur had returned. Japan was isolated. And he was trapped in the mountains north of Manila, low on supplies, with the Americans rapidly closing in. For the past few months he'd been less a military commander and more a miner. And banker. Taking deposits. Building vaults. Securing their presence for future withdrawals.

"For you," he said to the engineers, his metal cup held high. "And a job well done. *Banzai.*"

They echoed his good wishes.

The underground chamber around him was the largest they'd constructed, perhaps as big as twenty meters square, illuminated by battery-powered bulbs. Rectangular bronze boxes, filled with gold bars, were stacked eight high against the walls, each bar around seventy-five kilograms and individually marked by weight and purity. A little under thirty-seven million total kilograms.

An enormous amount of wealth.

With this being just one of a 175 buried vaults, each of the others containing a similar hoard of treasure. All plundered from Asian countries, starting with China in 1937. More came from Korea, Thailand, Myanmar, Vietnam, Cambodia, Malaysia, Hong Kong, Timor, Indonesia, and New Guinea. National treasuries, banks, religious shrines, private estates, museums, factories, homes, galleries. Anything and everything had been looted. A grand larceny of wealth that had been accumulated by its owners for thousands of years. A lot of it had already made it toward Japan, over land, through Korea. The rest was to go by sea, through the Philippines. But the Americans had stopped that redistribution with a submarine blockade. No way now to ship anything, much less something as heavy and bulky as gold.

So another way had been conceived.

Hide it all in the mountains of Luzon and come back for it after the war.

The plan had been formulated at the highest level, all the way to Emperor Hirohito himself. Several of the lesser royal princes had headed teams of thieves that had fanned out across the conquered territories, but the emperor's charming and cultivated brother, Prince Chichibu, had supervised the overall plunder, along with its secreting away, naming the entire scheme *kin no yuri*, Golden Lily, after a poem the emperor had written.

"To each of you," Prince Chichibu said, his metal cup raised. "The emperor extends his thanks for your dedicated work. He wishes great blessings to you all."

The engineers returned the toast and offered long life and blessings to the emperor. Many of their eyes were watering with emotion. None of them had ever been this close to someone of the royal house. Nearly all Japanese, Yamashita included, spent their whole lives in awe of the imperial family. The emperor controlled the entire sovereign state, commanded the armed forces, headed the national religion, and was believed to be a living god.

Chichibu stepped close to Yamashita and whispered, "Is all ready?"

He nodded.

Months ago, Prince Chichibu had moved his headquarters from Singapore to Manila and ordered all plunder still on the Asian mainland to be brought to the islands. Thousands of slave laborers and prisoners of war had spent the past few months digging tunnels and fortifying caves with concrete. Each site had to withstand earthquakes, aerial bombing, flooding, and, most of all, time. So the vaults had been constructed like military bunkers. As each was completed the prince had come to personally inspect, like tonight, so there was nothing unusual about his presence.

The men continued to enjoy the revelry, their job completed. The last of the 175 vaults—this one, Tunnel 8—had been finished three days ago. All of the architectural drawings, inventories, instruments, and tools had been crated and removed. With each vault's completion the prisoners-of-war laborers had been shot, their bodies sealed inside. Also, Japanese soldiers had been included with the doomed so that their spirits would help guard the treasure in the years ahead. Which sounded good, but it only masked the real purpose, which was to limit the number of eyewitnesses.

"Is the map secure?" the prince asked him.

"In your car, awaiting your departure."

Everything had been sped up after MacArthur landed at Leyte. Two hundred thousand enemy troops were gaining ground every day, the Japanese forces slowly retreating ever higher into the mountains. A submarine awaited Prince Chichibu to take him back to Japan, along with the map that led to each of the vaults. Natural markers that worked as pointers had been left across the lush landscape. Subtle. Hard to decipher. Part of the jungle. All of it in an ancient code called Chako. The map would be returned to the emperor, who would hold it until the time for retrieval arrived. They might lose the war militarily, but Japan had no intention of losing financially. The idea was to hold the Philippines through a negotiated peace so they could return and retrieve the gold. How much wealth had they hidden? More than anyone could have ever imagined. Somewhere around fifty million kilograms of precious metals.

For the glory of the emperor.

"Time for us to leave," he whispered to the prince. Then he turned his attention back to the engineers. "Enjoy the food and the drink. You have earned it. It is private, quiet, and safe here. We shall see you in the morning when we evacuate."

The group offered him a collective *banzai*, which he returned, noticing the smiles all around from the men. Then he and the prince left the chamber and made their way to a crude elevator that led back up seventy meters to ground level. Along the way he noticed the dynamite that had been set in the shaft while the celebration had been ongoing. A separate access tunnel had also been rigged to explode, the charges spaced far enough apart to seal the passage, but not close enough to totally destroy the path.

He and the prince left the elevator and emerged out into the steamy tropical night. Three demolition experts waited for them. Once the shaft and tunnel were blown the last remnants of human consciousness, the one hundred and seventy-five engineers, who knew the precise location of the caches, would be dead. Most would suffocate, but some would surely commit ritual suicide in service to their emperor.

He turned to one of the soldiers and nodded.

The charges were ignited.

Explosions rumbled and the ground shook, the charges detonating in a predetermined sequence, each one bringing down a portion of the excavation. The final charge obliterated the main entrance in a cascade of dirt and rock. Before dawn it would be smoothed and dressed, and within a few weeks, the jungle would replace the lost foliage, completing the camouflage.

They walked toward a waiting vehicle.

"What of these soldiers?" Chichibu asked of the demolition team.

"They will be dead by morning."

Which should end the killing. And with 7,107 islands in the Philippines, even if the enemy knew what had been done, searching for those 175 caches would take decades.

But he had to wonder?

"What of me?" he asked the prince. "Am I to die as well?"

"You are a high-ranking general in the Imperial Army," the prince said. "Sworn by oath to allegiance with the emperor."

They reached the car.

The prince opened the rear door and retrieved a leather satchel. From inside he withdrew a Japanese battle flag. A red disc atop a white background, with sixteen rays emanating from it, symbolizing the rising sun.

Chichibu laid it out flat across the hood. "I thought you might be apprehensive. Let us be frank. The war is over. All is lost. It is time now to prepare for the future. I have to return to Japan and work with my brother to secure that future. You have to stay here and hold the Americans at bay for as long as possible."

Which made sense.

The younger man withdrew a small ceremonial blade from the satchel and pricked the tip of his little finger. Yamashita knew what was expected. He took the knife and punctured his own little finger. Together, they dripped blood onto the flag in a ritual that dated back centuries, one that supposedly bound the participants together in a blood oath.

"We are one," Chichibu said.

He suddenly felt the same pride that those engineers had experienced. "I will do honor to the trust you have shown in me."

"You will be needed," the prince said, "once this war ends and we return to retrieve what is ours. And we will, Tomoyuki. We will be back. Japan will survive. The emperor will survive. In the meantime stay safe, and I will see you then."

Chichibu climbed into the vehicle. The driver was already behind the wheel. The engine coughed to life and the transport drove off down the narrow, rutted road. One of the demolition experts approached, stood at attention, and saluted. He knew what the man wanted to hear. "Set the traps. Secure the site."

Every one of the caches had been rigged with explosives and a variety of other lethal, defensive measures. If anyone dared to breach the vaults they would pay a heavy price.

In the distance he heard gunfire and mortars.

It would not be long before the enemy controlled the islands.

Thankfully, though, Golden Lily was finished.

PRESENT DAY

CHAPTER 1

COTTON MALONE COULD NOT DECIDE IF THE THREAT was real or imaginary. He'd been sent to assess the situation, keep an eye on the target, and intervene. But only if necessary.

Did this qualify?

The streets of Basel were busy. Not surprising given this city of two hundred thousand had been a commercial hub and cultural center since the Renaissance. Six hundred years ago it was one of Europe's great cities. Location helped, strategically placed where Switzerland, France, and Germany converged, the Rhine River divided downtown into two distinct sections. One from the past, the other rooted in today. Its old town filled two hills that rose against the river's southern bank. A place full of ivy-clad half-timber houses, which cast the last traces of a long-ago medieval town, the cobbled paths a mix of pedestrian-only and light-traffic streets.

He stood, bathed in sunshine, beside one of the more congested traffic routes and enjoyed a bag of roasted chestnuts purchased from a nearby vendor. His target was inside a small boutique on the other side of the street, about two hundred feet away, where she'd been for the past thirty minutes. Windows of fashionable stores and shops drew a continuous stream of patrons. Lots of cafés, shops, jewelers, designer clothing, and, his personal favorite, antique bookstores. Plenty of them too. Each reminiscent of his own bookshop back in Copenhagen. He'd owned it now for several years, the store modest in size, tastefully appointed, and well stocked. He catered not only to bibliophiles, but also to the countless tourists who visited Copenhagen. He'd netted a profit every year, though he spent more time away from the shop than he liked. He was also the current secretary of the Danish Antiquarian Booksellers Association, a first for him as he was not much of a joiner.

But what the hell?

He loved books. They loved books.

People moved steadily in every direction, his brain attentive to the slightest detail that had always signaled trouble in his former profession. No one stared or lingered too long. Nothing at all out of sync, except for one car. A dark-colored Saab. Parked thirty yards away among other vehicles nestled to the curb. All of the others were empty. But not the Saab. It contained two people whose forms he could make out through the lightly tinted windshield. The driver and another in the backseat. None of which, in and of itself, should spark any suspicions to most people.

But he wasn't most people.

He was a trained intelligence officer who'd worked a dozen years for the Magellan Billet, a covert investigative unit of the United States Justice Department. He'd been one of the first people recruited by his old friend Stephanie Nelle, who both created and continued to run the unit. She'd recently found some trouble with the new American president, Warner Fox, but all that had been resolved and now she was back in command. And though he'd been retired from the Billet for a while now, he continued to work freelance for Stephanie whenever she managed to entice him away from his bookshop. He liked that he was still needed, so he rarely refused her. Sure, there'd come a day when she would ask less frequently and he would become only a bookseller. But thankfully, for now, he still had his uses, though he wasn't here for Stephanie. This favor was for another friend, whom he'd encountered a few months back in Germany.

Derrick Koger.

Recently promoted European station chief for the Central Intelligence Agency. Who'd piqued his curiosity with an amazing tale.

Toward the end of World War II billions of dollars in plundered gold, silver, and platinum had been systematically hidden underground by the Japanese across the Philippine Islands, mainly in the mountains north of Manila. General Tomoyuki Yamashita, who'd commanded the final defense of the islands, supervised its secretion. Yamashita surrendered to the Allies in September 1945, then was quickly tried and convicted of war crimes in December 1945. Two months later Yamashita was hanged.

Why so fast?

Simple.

The Office of Strategic Services, precursor to the CIA, had learned about 175 buried vaults. Yamashita flatly refused to cooperate with locating them and the last thing the Americans wanted was him still alive, able to tell the world about the gold.

So they hanged him.

Once that loose end had been eliminated, and the

island of Luzon militarily secured, the OSS moved in and managed to retrieve several of the larger caches, tons of unaccounted-for gold, which was shipped off to repositories in forty-two countries across the world. All done with the full knowledge and blessing of both General Douglas MacArthur and President Harry Truman.

Why was it taken?

Three reasons.

First, if the recovery of such a huge mass of stolen gold had become known, thousands of people would have come forward to claim it, many of them fraudulently, and governments would have been bogged down for decades resolving ownership.

Second, the sheer volume of the gold, if dumped back on the open market, would have devalued the price. At the time most countries linked their currencies to the US dollar, and the dollar was tied to gold, so an unexpected plummet in price would have caused a worldwide financial disaster.

And finally, once Hitler and Japan had been defeated, the greatest threat to world security now came from the Soviet Union. Communism had to be stopped. At all costs. And hundreds of millions of dollars in unaccounted for wealth could certainly be channeled into that purpose.

So, slowly, over time, the retrieved gold was consolidated to one location under the control of what came to be known as the Black Eagle Trust. Where was it centralized? The Bank of St. George in Luxembourg. And there that wealth had sat since 1949, safe behind a wall of secrecy that had only, according to Koger, in the past few months fallen.

The whole thing was fascinating.

The car with the two occupants cranked to life.

Cotton's attention shifted from the vehicle to the boutique.

His target had appeared, stepping from the front doorway and turning onto the busy sidewalk. Had the car cranking been just coincidence?

Doubtful.

He'd only seen one photo of Kelly Austin, who was employed by the Bank of St. George. Her job? He had no idea. All he'd been told was to look after her and intervene only if absolutely required. Koger had been emphatic on that last detail. Which was why he'd positioned himself across the street, among people walking here and there, oblivious to anything around them outside of their own concerns.

Kelly Austin walked away from the Saab, which swung from its parking place and crept forward in the street. No cars were behind it, but one was ahead. The one in front accelerated and headed off past Cotton. The Saab though never changed speed.

No question. This was a threat.

Austin kept walking his way, on the other side of the street. No head turns. No looking around. No hesitation. Just one step after another with a shopping bag dangling from one hand, a purse slung over the other shoulder.

Oblivious.

He tossed the chestnuts into the waste can beside him and stepped from the curb, zigzagging against the lanes of traffic to the pedestrian bay at the center. There, at the first break in the cars, he crossed, fifty feet ahead of Austin. People passed by, heading in the opposite direction. The Saab kept coming, moving a little faster, now nearly parallel with Austin.

The rear window descended.

A gun barrel came into view.

No time existed to get closer to Austin. Too far away. So he reached back beneath his jacket and found the Beretta. Magellan Billet issued. Which he'd been allowed to keep after retiring out early. The appearance of the weapon sent a panic through some of the pedestrians. No way to keep the gun out of view.

He told himself to focus.

In his mind the all-pervasive background noise common to cities around the world ground to a halt. Silence dominated his thoughts and his eyes assumed command of the rest of his senses. He leveled the gun and fired two shots into the open rear window. The Saab immediately accelerated, tires grabbing the pavement as the car squealed past. The danger from return fire seemed great. So he sent another bullet into the open window.

People scattered. Many hit the ground.

The Saab raced away.

He focused on the license plate and etched the letters and numbers into his eidetic memory. The car came to the next intersection, then disappeared around the corner. He quickly stuffed the gun back under his jacket and looked around.

His lungs inflated in short, quick breaths.

Kelly Austin was nowhere to be seen.